Talk

They were two women who thought they'd
blown their only chance at love! But now
fate had thrown each another lifeline.
Were they woman enough to grab it?

In *Stay...* by Allison Leigh,
a girl who had always been seen
by the man she loved as a tagalong pest
gets another chance to show him
how grown-up she really is....

And in *Here Comes the Groom* by Patricia Kay,
she'd left him at the altar four years before.
So why was he still the only man
she wanted as her husband?

ALLISON LEIGH

has been a finalist in the Rita® Award and the Holt Medallion contests. But the true highlights of her day as a writer are when she receives word from a reader that they laughed, cried or lost a night of sleep while reading one of her books.

Born in Southern California, Allison has lived in several different cities in four different states. She has been, at one time or another, a cosmetologist, a computer programmer and a secretary. She has recently begun writing full-time after spending nearly a decade as an administrative assistant for a busy neighborhood church, and currently makes her home in Arizona with her family. She loves to hear from her readers, who can write to her at P.O. Box 40772, Mesa, AZ 85274-0772.

PATRICIA KAY,

formerly writing as Trisha Alexander, is the *USA TODAY* bestselling author of more than thirty contemporary romances. She has three grown children, three adored grandchildren and lives in Houston, Texas, with her husband and their cats. To learn more about her, check out her Web site at www.patriciakay.com.

A Long Road Home

ALLISON LEIGH
PATRICIA KAY

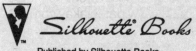

Published by Silhouette Books
America's Publisher of Contemporary Romance

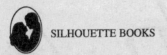 SILHOUETTE BOOKS

ISBN 0-373-23014-1

by Request

A LONG ROAD HOME

Copyright © 2003 by Harlequin Books S.A.

The publisher acknowledges the copyright holders of the individual works as follows:

STAY...
Copyright © 1998 by Allison Lee Kinnaird

HERE COMES THE GROOM
Originally published under the name Trisha Alexander
Copyright © 1993 by Patricia A. Kay

CONTENTS

Dear Reader,

As an author, I've been asked countless times, of all my heroes, who is my favorite? Over the years, my answer, honestly, is that my favorite is the hero of the book I'm currently writing. But when I received the lovely news that *Stay...* was to be included in *A Long Road Home,* that particular question popped into my mind all on its own.

Did I actually have a favorite hero? One who was more meaningful to me than all the rest? Perhaps. Perhaps not. (I am, after all, currently writing a book and the hero is...well, my current favorite!) What I do know is that Jefferson Clay was the hero of my first published romance. And there is always something particularly memorable about an author's "first." After all, there can be only one.

So, welcome to my "first." The world of the Clay family and the love story of Jefferson and Emily. I hope you enjoy it as much as I did.

Allison

STAY...
Allison Leigh

Prologue

"Don't let him send me away." Her young voice was muffled against the saddle blanket hugged against her chest. "*Please*, Jefferson, don't let him. I'll die in that school. I know I will."

His eyebrows lowered and he gently pried her fingers from the soft blue-gray plaid. "Don't say that."

Bereft of the blanket that he'd tossed over the stall door, she crossed her arms protectively across her chest. "If you'd just talk to him. I don't need some school to teach me how to be a girl—"

His eyes flickered over her short, dark brown hair and down her sweat-stained shirt to her torn jeans. Her rough 'n tumble appearance couldn't hide the developing curves. She wasn't the little seven-year-old anymore who'd been his constant shadow. Who'd followed his every step, asking a million questions, or just chattering away in her sweet little-girl voice.

She was fourteen now. And rapidly developing into a hellion that easily rivaled any one of his brothers. The problem was, she wasn't a *boy*. And something needed to be done. His father was at his wit's end. "It's not up to me," he said softly.

"But he'd listen to you—"

"It's not up to me," he repeated gently. Inflexibly.

Hot tears flooded her eyes and she turned away. "If I was a boy, he wouldn't send me away."

He cursed softly, but didn't disagree. He wouldn't lie to her. He couldn't change the situation. Hell, he had to catch a flight to Turkey first thing in the morning, and his mind was humming with the hoard of details involved. This brief stopover hadn't been in his plans at all.

He studied the young female. A sister. Yet not his sister. His cousin. Yet not. But family, nevertheless. "That boarding school might not be so bad, you know," he murmured, reaching past her hunched form for the bridle she'd thrown to the concrete floor a few minutes earlier in a fit of temper. "You'll meet kids your own age. Make some new friends."

"Tris's my own age," she replied, exaggerating only slightly. "And I have all the friends I need." She swiped her sleeve beneath her nose. "Matthew and Daniel—"

He sighed. "Girls. You'll meet *girls* your age."

The snort she gave was decidedly unfeminine. As was the explicit word she spat in opinion of his words. He raised one eyebrow. "*That's* one of the reasons you're going."

She swore again, and whirled around like a dervish, kicking her dusty boot against a wooden post. The metal bucket hanging from a nail in the post rocked loose and clattered to the floor, narrowly missing the dog who'd been sleeping in the corner near the tack room. The dog shot to his feet, barking furiously.

Frustrated...angry...but most of all scared, she kicked the fallen bucket and it crashed against the stone wall opposite them, toppling a pitchfork onto its side where it missed crowning the dog by mere inches. Yelping, the dog skittered for shelter. Every curse word she'd ever heard poured from her. And being raised among five boys, she knew more than a few.

Long arms wrapped around her waist, and Jefferson lifted her right off her feet. Twisting, she pushed at him. "I won't go," she gritted.

She was held firmly, high against his hard chest. His breath was warm against her ear as he whispered softly. Soothing. Calming her in the same way he'd often done whenever she'd awakened from a bad dream when she was little. She wasn't so little now, though, and the wide chest pressed against her cheek set off all sorts of new feelings.

"You'll go."

Her head reared back, ready for another round. But his dark blue eyes met hers steadily and the words died. Her head collapsed against his chest and she sobbed brokenly.

In the end she went.

Chapter One

Twelve years later

Emily Nichols downshifted the car's gears and nudged her sunglasses a speck up her nose. She checked her mirrors, but the traffic on the freeway's four lanes was solid. And stopped, dead cold. So much for getting home in time to make a trip out to the stable before dark.

She shifted into neutral, and rolled her head slowly from side to side, working out the kinks from sitting at a computer all day long. Grimacing at the traffic report coming from the car radio, she flipped open the case containing an assortment of cassette tapes.

Tristan kept telling her to switch to CDs. But she'd been collecting these cassettes since she'd been fourteen when she'd received the first two as a Christmas gift.

More than a decade later, and she was still cherishing each and every tape. She sighed at that thought and popped a Zeppelin tape in and turned up the volume.

Since the sun was still high in the cloudless blue sky, she thought about putting up the top of her convertible and turning on the air-conditioning. The cars in front of her began inching forward before she could put the idea into action, and she shifted into gear to follow suit. With one hand she twisted her long hair off her neck and held it up, hoping for a whiff of cool air. But she let go after a moment. Sitting in the middle of a gridlocked freeway in downtown San Diego during rush hour wasn't the likeliest place to catch a fresh ocean breeze.

The traffic continued inching forward, and though she was still miles away from the exit ramp closest to the house she shared with Tristan, she flipped her turn signal on and worked her way off the freeway. Driving surface streets, even with all the congestion and stoplights, was better than sitting like a lump on the freeway.

Maybe she'd also stop and pick up a pizza for supper. Tristan wasn't likely to be there, anyway. And even if he was, he wouldn't be likely to turn up his nose at pizza. Even frozen pizza. It was food, after all. Cardboardlikeness notwithstanding. And he could pack it away like nobody she'd ever seen.

A few miles away from home, she pulled into a grocery store and put the top up on her precious Mustang. She shrugged out of the off-white jacket she'd worn over a matching vest and slacks and tossed it over the seat before heading into the store. When she emerged again, she carried more than a mere box of pizza, and by the time she had arranged the half dozen grocery bags in the trunk, the sun was lowering toward the horizon. And the air had begun to cool. Thankfully.

The weather in San Diego was usually pleasant year-round. But the middle of August was generally miserable. No matter what part of the country you lived in. Even Matt, who was running the Double-C Ranch up in Wyoming, had been complaining recently about the sweltering temperatures.

Emily stood beside the trunk, looking over the sea of cars parked in the huge parking lot of the supermarket complex. Deep, bone-thumping vibrations suddenly accosted her, and she looked over her shoulder at the old sedan slowly driving past. The car's stereo was so loud it made her chest hurt. The driver sneered at her, pitching his cigarette out his window and right at her feet.

Staring right back at the driver, who probably wasn't more than seventeen years old despite the world-wise look in his dark eyes, she slowly ground her foot over the burning cigarette. Her keys were locked between her fingers, jutting out in four jagged weapons. Sighing faintly, she turned away from the car, aware of it continuing on its way. She climbed into her own car, switched the cassette to a soothing Mozart and drove home.

An unfamiliar black car sat in the driveway, blocking the garage. "Girlfriend number 310," she muttered, and whipped the car into a U-turn to park on the street along the curb. Tristan must be home after all. And since he couldn't get his girlfriends to park in the street, as Emily was forever asking, he could carry in the darn groceries himself.

She shoved open the car door, reaching back for her slender gray briefcase and the jacket. The massive black front door opened as she headed up the terraced steps. A dark blond male head appeared as she stooped to pick up that morning's newspaper. "I don't know how that kid always manages to nail the flowers,'' she complained as she extracted the half-buried paper from a glorious display of white petunias. She straightened and picked a velvety bloom out of the rubber band. ''Groceries are in the car,'' she called out. ''You can have the honors, since it's your fault I'm parked on the street.''

''You've developed a bossy streak,'' the man said, stepping outside and into the fading, golden twilight.

Emily's fingers loosened spasmodically at the man's voice, and she nearly dropped the newspaper right back into the flowers. Her heart clenched and she was grateful for the sunglasses shading her eyes as they flew to him, shocked.

Jefferson Clay was back.

Her fingers dug into the newspaper, tearing jagged little holes in the outermost page. She didn't notice. It was all she could do to contain the urge to turn tail and race back to her car. Instead, she stood rooted right where she was, her greedy eyes not willing to look away from him.

His hair was longer than it had been the last time she'd seen him, more than two years ago. It now hung past his shoulders in wild disarray. On most men, it would have looked feminine. But not on him. Not with his face. Hard. Masculine. And thinner than it had been the last time she'd seen him. In fact, he was probably fifteen pounds thinner. It made him look even more carved. More unapproachable than he'd seemed before.

''Aren't you even going to say hello, Em?''

She drew in a steadying breath, gathering her composure, then climbed the last few steps leading into the house. ''Hello, Jefferson,'' she said, managing to present a slight smile. Even in her high-heeled pumps, she

had to reach up to drop a light kiss on his cheek. Her
lips tingled from the impact of his five-o'clock shadow,
and she slipped past him into the house, telling herself
she wasn't breathless from just that little peck. "What
are you doing here? Is Squire okay?"

She set the paper, her jacket and the briefcase on the
narrow hall table and pretended to study the pile of mail
that Tristan had left lying there.

"He's fine. As far as I know."

Her eyebrows rose and she looked over her shoulder
at him.

"I haven't talked to him in a while," he said.

She nodded, unsurprised, and turned her attention
back to the mail. But it was Jefferson's image imprinted
on her mind that she saw. Not the collection of bills and
circulars she was paging through.

No man had a right to look that good. It simply
wasn't fair to the women of the world.

"Your hair's grown." His voice was low. Husky.

She closed her eyes for a moment. "So has yours."
She gave up on the mail and tossed it beside her jacket.
"Is Tristan here?"

"He's on the phone."

She nodded. Finally she simply gave in again and let
her eyes rove over him. From the tailored fit of his
pleated black trousers to his narrow waist to the single
unfastened button of his white shirt at his brown throat.
She wanted to ask him where he'd been all this time.
Why he hadn't called. Written. "When will you be leaving?"

The corner of his mouth tilted, causing the slashing
dimple in his cheek to appear briefly. "Here's your hat,
what's your hurry," he murmured.

Emily felt the flush rise in her cheeks. Considering

that Jefferson's presence in her life for more than ten years had been a brief series of arrivals *always* followed by an indecently hasty departure, she wasn't, however, feeling inclined to apologize. Her lips twisted. Facts were facts.

"Ah, Em…"

His soft voice seemed filled with regret. She wondered if he'd known she was living here before he'd come. A fanciful, wishful thought on her part, no doubt. Annoyed with herself, she pulled off her sunglasses and dropped them alongside the mail before turning toward the kitchen. What was she going to fix for supper? Jefferson was a meat-and-potatoes kind of guy and she wasn't sure they had anything—

"Darn it," she grumbled, swiveling about on her heel. The groceries.

Jefferson stood right behind her, and he warded her off with a raised hand, keeping her from plowing into him. "Whoa."

Then she noticed it. The carved, wooden cane. She stared at it. At his long brown fingers, curved over the rounded handle. How she'd ever missed it in the first place was a testament to how stunned she was to see him at all. "Oh, my God," she fell back a step. "What's happened?"

His lashes hid his expression, and his lips compressed. "Little accident."

Swallowing an abrupt wave of nausea, Emily strode across the foyer into the great room and flipped on a lamp. In the light, she studied him more closely. He'd been collecting little scars on his face ever since she could remember. But he'd added a few new ones since she'd seen him last. The thin line slicing along his angular jaw was still faintly pink. As was the crescent outlining the corner of his right eye. "How little?"

She watched his expression deliberately lighten. And the grin that flirted with his lips almost convinced her. But she'd known him too long. "Jefferson?"

He shrugged and moved across the room to lower himself onto the long caramel-colored couch. "Cracked some ribs." He lifted his left leg onto the coffee table and propped the cane on the couch beside him. "Broke a few bones. All healed up now."

He was making light of his injuries. She knew it. And he knew she knew it. "What did you do? Fall off some bridge you were building or something?"

He was quiet for a moment. "Or something."

Shaking her head, she crossed over to him and grabbed a throw pillow. She bent over him and tucked it beneath his knee, scooting the table closer to the couch to provide more support. Her long hair fell over her shoulder and drifted across his pant leg and he tucked it behind her ear. She froze, half-bent over him.

"It's good to see you, Emily." His finger skipped from her ear to her bare arm, then away.

Irrational tears burned behind her lids, and she straightened abruptly, moving away. Far away. "I've got groceries in the car," she muttered, and left the room.

Jefferson watched her practically run from the room. He'd have offered to help, but in his shape, he'd be more of a hindrance. He closed his eyes wearily and dropped his head back against the butter-soft couch. He didn't like second-guessing his decisions, but maybe it had been a mistake for him to come here. Even after all this time. Wasn't there a saying somewhere that you could never go home?

"You look like someone rode you too hard then put you up wet."

Jefferson opened one eye and stared at his brother. Tristan was the youngest of the Clay brothers. And the biggest. At six foot five, his blond head practically brushed the top of the wide doorway leading from the foyer into the great room. "You sound like Squire."

Tristan grinned. "Flattery'll get you nowhere." He dropped his hulking length into an oversize leather wing chair and draped one leg over the arm.

"Wasn't flattery."

Tristan chuckled soundlessly. "No kidding." He swung his leg. "Speaking of our father, have you talked to him lately?"

"No."

"Plan to?"

"No."

Tristan snorted softly. "I guess that's clear then. How about Matt? Daniel? Sawyer?"

Jefferson shook his head at each mention of their other three brothers. When he could feel his baby brother's eyes drilling into him, he lifted his head and cocked one eyebrow. "They're all okay."

"How would you know?" Tristan asked mildly. "We haven't heard from you in more than two years."

Jefferson closed his eyes and leaned his head back again. "I've kept track of them." Except for those nine months, anyway. Then, before Tristan could poke his nose in, he said, "I've kept track of you, too." Jefferson rolled his head to one side and looked at his brother. "You've done well for yourself." He lifted his chin, indicating the comfortably spacious house that his baby brother called home. "I saw an article in *Time* a few months ago. 'Bout that hacker you tracked to Sweden."

Tristan shrugged. "It sounded more exciting than it was. How'd you get all busted up?"

"Emily's bringing in some groceries," Jefferson pointed out abruptly. "Why don't you get off your butt and go help her."

"And butt out of your business." Tristan concluded accurately. He tugged on his earlobe, then straightened from the chair. "You'll spill it eventually." His good nature was still evident.

"Don't count on it," Jefferson warned.

His brother's mouth curved in silent laughter and he went out to help Emily, leaving Jefferson to wonder when the hell his baby brother had gotten all grown up. His leg was aching, and his toes were numb, but he pushed himself slowly to his feet and crossed the room to the wide bay window overlooking the front of the house. The sun still hadn't fallen below the horizon, and through the delicate, off-white lace, he watched his brother lope down the shallow brick steps to the street level where Emily was pulling grocery sacks from the trunk.

As he watched, she set a bag down on the first step and leaned against the cherry red car. A picture of weariness. She was shaking her head to something Tristan was saying, then she raked her long hair back from her face and stared off down the street. Even from a distance, Jefferson could see the fine arch of her cheekbone. The sculpted curve of her lower lip. Her upraised arms tightened the loose-fitted white vest across her chest, and Jefferson knew that his little Emily was grown up, too.

The last time he'd allowed himself to really look at Emily had been when she was nineteen. His gut still tightened, thinking of that time. She'd been incredibly lovely then. Sweet. Fresh as a spring flower. And way too innocent. His jaw tightened.

She was still incredibly lovely. But she was seven years older. And he should be shot for the dog he was for wondering if she was still the innocent she'd been back then.

Her arms lowered, and her hair, heavy glistening strands of dark brown silk, settled about her shoulders. She shook her head again, her hand slicing through the air. But Tristan caught the hand and pulled her to him. Tristan's size engulfed her slender form and, mouth tight, Jefferson turned away from the sight.

Emily pushed out of Tristan's arms. "I'm okay," she insisted.

Tristan stopped her from reaching for the grocery bags sitting on the step. "He probably won't stay long."

"He never stays anywhere for long." She avoided Tristan's eyes. They were shades lighter than Jefferson's dark blue, but they could be every bit as piercing. She stepped away from his reach and hefted up the grocery bags. "I'll be fine," she insisted. "I'm not going to fall apart simply because Jefferson has returned." She could read Tristan's thoughts almost as well as he could read hers. "And I won't fall apart when he leaves."

"Something is wrong this time." Tristan removed one of the bags from her arms and started up the steps. "Deep down. He's changed."

Emily didn't question how Tristan was so sure about that. Tristan just *knew* things. Always had. And she'd given up, years ago, asking him how, since her curiosity always met with glib non-answers. And now, regardless of Tristan's uncanny insight, Emily didn't want to think about whether Jefferson had changed. She didn't want to worry about how he'd gotten himself into such a bad condition. She didn't want to think about him at all. She wanted to drive to the stable where she boarded her horse, Bird, saddle up and ride for hours until she could manage to tuck away the ultimately futile feelings that Jefferson's presence always roused within her.

"He'll tell you about it if he wants," she said, stooping at the top of the steps to thread her fingers through the handles of the plastic bags she'd already carried that far. "Jefferson will tell you things he never tells any of the rest of us."

"He didn't tell me about what happened between the two of you," Tristan said as he grabbed up the rest of the sacks. "Not that I couldn't figure it out for myself."

Emily stopped in her tracks. "There's nothing to tell."

"Right."

"Tris—"

"All right," his big shoulders lifted innocently. "Don't get your shorts in a knot."

"Charming," she remarked, shouldering her way through the door and heading down the hall toward the kitchen. "It's no wonder you can't get a decent woman to go out with you."

He laughed. "Honey pie, when I'm on a date, I'm not looking for *decency.*"

Rolling her eyes, Emily felt her mood lighten a fraction. Tristan was good at that. He dumped the grocery bags on the pristine white-tiled counters and she waved him off. "Go bug your brother," she ordered, pulling out the rectangular boxes of frozen pizza and turning toward the wide freezer. "Supper will take a while."

Tristan stepped between her and the refrigerator and pulled out two apples from the crisper. "Whenever."

what he paid for,'' she assured Jefferson dryly. It had been a long time since she'd gotten over her anger at Jefferson's father for sending her to boarding school when she was a teenager. She nodded toward the enchilada dish. ''I took a Southwest cooking class a year ago at the community college to learn how to do that.''

''Thank God, too,'' Tristan inserted. ''I was getting sick of watercress and—'' The telephone rang, and he leaned back in his chair to grab the cordless unit with a long arm. ''Yup,'' he answered lazily. His eyebrows rose as he listened. ''Well, sweetheart, I can't think of a single thing I'd rather do than have supper with you this evening.'' Tristan grinned wolfishly at whatever ''sweetheart'' had to say, and he rose, ignoring the fact that he'd just packed away a good portion of supper already.

''You want me to wear *what?* Why you naughty girl....'' Ignoring Jefferson and Emily, he wandered out of the kitchen, the phone tucked at his ear.

Emily rolled her eyes at Tristan's back. ''Girlfriend 372.'' She smiled faintly and reached for her own beer.

Without the easygoing presence of his overgrown baby brother to provide a buffer, Jefferson silently concentrated on his meal. ''I was surprised to discover you're living out here,'' he said finally.

Emily sipped her beer. Well, now she knew for certain that he hadn't come to San Diego to see her. ''Here, as in San Diego? Or here, as in Tristan's house?''

''Either. Both.''

''I'm an accountant,'' she reminded.

''I know. I'd have thought you'd return to the Double-C. Help Matthew with the books or something like that. Start your own business, even.''

She shrugged, pleased with her nonchalance. ''Pay's

better here. Besides, Matt handles the books just fine on his own. I'd have been bored stiff.'' She studied her beer.

He frowned. ''Liar.''

Emily glanced at him, then lowered her gaze. She wasn't about to tell him that he was the reason she hadn't returned to live at the ranch that had been her home since she'd been seven years old. She lifted one shoulder and sipped at her beer. ''Think what you want. But the fact is, once I passed the CPA exam, I was offered too good a job to turn it down. The corporate office just happened to be in San Diego. Tristan was already out here. Living with him is...convenient.''

His jaw ached. ''Convenient.''

Emily smiled mockingly, and Jefferson caught a glimpse of the spirited teenager she'd been. ''Yes. Convenient.''

''What does Squire think of this?''

Her delicately arched eyebrow rose. ''Do you think he wouldn't approve?'' Her lips twisted as the past suddenly twined between them. A bittersweet, tangible thing. ''He figures that by living with Tristan, my... virtue...is well protected.''

''Does he?''

''What?''

''Does Tristan protect your virtue?''

Emily's dark eyes narrowed until only a slit of pansy brown remained. ''I don't need any one of the infamous Clay brothers to protect my virtue. I can do that just fine, *when I choose to,* on my own, thank you very much.'' She rose and began clearing the dishes.

Jefferson wiped his mouth with the napkin and crumpled it in his fist. ''I hope you're being smart about it,'' he warned softly.

She looked over her shoulder. "Excuse me?"

"When you're *choosing*."

Her lips curved. "Good Lord, Jefferson. Are you try-ing to tell me to practice safe sex?" She laughed abruptly. Harshly. "That's just *too* sweet."

"You never used to be such a brat."

Emily flipped on the water and began rinsing plates. "Yes, I was. You just weren't around to notice." She shot him a flippant smile and bent to stack the dishes in the dishwasher.

"I wasn't always gone."

Emily paused, then straightened and reached for an-other plate. "That was a long time ago," she said brusquely.

He held out his empty mug and she reached for it. "Feels like yesterday." He held on to the mug as she tugged at it. "Sometimes."

Her short-lived bravado died a quiet death. "I'm not going to talk about this with you."

"I didn't plan on talking about it, either."

Her eyes, when they rose to his, were pained. "Then why are you? We've managed to see each other a few times since—" She could count on half the fingers of one hand the few times they'd seen each other since the week of her nineteenth birthday. And she could count on the other hand the number of words they'd ex-changed.

"You can't even say it, can you."

Emily let go of the mug. She reached for the green-and-white dish towel hanging from the oven door and slowly dried her hands. Staring blindly at the smoked-glass oven door, she felt him moving around the island counter to stand behind her. "What do you want from me, Jefferson? Do you want me to tell you that Tristan and I aren't involved?'' She folded the towel in a neat rectangle. "Is that what's bugging you? Well, we're not. He's my best friend. My brother.''

"He's no more your brother than I am.''

"Well.'' She refolded the towel. "I guess that puts me in my place, doesn't it. My last name is, after all, Nichols. Not Clay. I'm just the kid your father took in when my parents died in the crash. Because of some absurdly remote familial relationship we have. What was it? His great-grandfather's second wife was my mother's second cousin's aunt's mother-in-law's uncle?''

"Dammit, Em. That's not what I meant.''

She flipped the towel over the oven door handle. She knew that wasn't what he meant. But this was far safer than touching on *that*. Waving her hand, she stepped away and went back to the table to continue clearing the dishes. "Just forget it, would you, please?''

He leaned back against the refrigerator and crossed his arms. Emily stifled a sigh as she couldn't help noticing the way he'd rolled up the sleeves of his shirt. The way his sinewy forearms tapered into long, narrow wrists. They were golden brown. Just like the rest of him. She'd never known a man with such intrinsically strong wrists. Just looking at them made her want all sort of indecent—

She blinked and began gathering up the used napkins.

"The men in California can't be blind,'' Jefferson finally said. "There must be someone you're involved with.''

Flattening her palms on the table, Emily bowed her head. "For God's sake, Jefferson. Your nosiness exceeds even Tristan's.''

"It's not being nosy to want to know what's going on in my sister's life."

She shook her head. "We've established already that you're not my brother."

"I'll just find out from Tris."

She moistened her lips and dropped into a chair. "Let me just get this straight. Are you asking me if I'm dating anyone? Do you want their names, addresses and phone numbers so you can personally check them out to find out if they are suitable for your nonsister? Or are you asking me if I'm sleeping with anyone?"

His eyes were dark. Inscrutable. "Are you?"

"Are you?" She fired back.

"No."

"My condolences."

His eyes never wavered. "Save 'em. I answered. Now it's your turn."

"I'm not sleeping with anyone," she announced slowly, deliberately. If it had been anyone but Jefferson questioning her this way, she'd have told them to take a flying leap. "Are you satisfied? Is the inquisition over? May I be excused now like a good little girl? Though, first perhaps I should ask a few questions, too." She turned her face away. "Like where have you been for the past two and a half years? Building bridges, still? Or working on an oil rig? Not that you've ever told us *exactly* what you do.

"How did you injure yourself? Why didn't you even call Squire to let him know you were okay? Alive." She hesitated. "Or have you lost that sense of *family responsibility* that used to be so all-fired important to you?" She looked at him.

He silently looked back, a shadow coming and going

in his deep blue eyes. After a moment, he turned and slowly limped out of the kitchen.

"Dammit," Emily buried her head in her arms on the table. This is what happened when she and Jefferson talked too much. If they'd just keep their exchanges in the realm of "nice weather we're having" and "what team do you think will make the Super Bowl" everyone would be happier. She couldn't put all the blame on Jefferson, either. She shared the responsibility.

"Hey, squirt, where's Jefferson?"

Emily lifted her head and shrugged. "I expect he's not far, considering the way he's favoring that leg." She was accustomed to seeing Tristan in various attires, but this time she was surprised. "Since when do you wear a tie?"

His hand ran down the sedate magenta paisley. "Is it straight?"

Emily shook her head and rose to help him pull it neatly to center. "Where're you going?" He stood still long enough to let her finish. Barely.

"Coronado."

"So, I, uh, shouldn't wait up for you?"

He grinned, and slipped his arms into a finely tailored black suit coat. "Like you've ever bothered to do that."

Emily smiled faintly and leaned back against the island, her arms crossed.

"Hey." Tristan chucked her chin up with a long finger. "You and Jefferson could come with us."

Her eyebrows shot up. "I bet that's not what 'sweetheart' had in mind."

He shrugged. "So, come anyway. It'd do you good to get out and have some fun for once."

"I don't think so."

"Why not?"

Faintly exasperated, she shook her head. "We don't all work in our own homes, at our own leisure, you know. I do have to go to work in the morning."

"Consider it a celebration that Jefferson's back."

Emily heaved a sigh. "Tristan—"

"Okay, okay." He dropped a kiss on the top of her head and pulled her hair. "Behave while I'm gone."

"That's a laugh," she murmured. "Why don't *you* behave for once?"

Tristan just smiled and with a wave he left. He must have found Jefferson easily, because she heard their deep voices, if not their words, soon followed by the slam of the heavy front door.

After a deep, cleansing breath, she went in search of Jefferson. The huge great room was empty, and she peeked in Tristan's office and the den. She finally found him in the rear of the house where Tristan had glassed in a high-ceilinged atrium.

She watched from a distance as he seemingly examined the leaf of a fern. He slowly moved along the brick-paved floor, disappearing behind a ficus, then reappearing on the other side. He'd folded up the long sleeves of the loose white shirt another couple of turns, and a second button was loose at his throat, hinting at the strength of his chest. She watched him silently, filling up an empty place inside her with just the sight of him. Longing, sweet and bitter, flooded through her.

Why did she have to feel this way about Jefferson, of all people? Why couldn't she have picked an easier man. Like Stuart Hansen, a manager from her office whom she occasionally dated. Or Luke, the man who owned the stable where she kept Bird. Or even Tristan, for that matter. Why Jefferson? It was a question that had plagued her for years.

Unfortunately, she was no closer to an answer than she'd ever been.

Sighing, she pushed open the French door leading into the atrium. "I'm going to put fresh sheets on the bed in the guest room," she told him, attracting his attention. "There's a bathroom attached. With a whirlpool tub. It might feel good on your leg."

Jefferson gently snapped a tiny white flower from its stem. "Fine."

"Well." Emily flipped over her wrist to look at her watch. It wasn't the least bit late. Maybe she should have taken up Tristan's offer. Then at least she wouldn't be *alone* with Jefferson. "It's the first room to the left at the top of the stairs."

"Tris showed me when I arrived."

"Oh." She fiddled with her watch again.

He crushed the bloom between his fingers. "If you've got somewhere you need to go, don't let me keep you."

"Hmm? Oh, no. No. I'll just go take care of those sheets." She spun around and headed for the stairs.

At the top, she snatched a set of clean sheets from the linen closet and went into the guest room. A single duffel bag sat at the foot of the bed. The bag had probably once been black leather, but now was worn nearly colorless in most places. She reached out to move it, pausing over the collection of airline stubs hanging from the handle. There must have been a dozen or more, and with merely a glance knew she didn't recognize any of the abbreviations.

Closing her fingers over the handle, she moved it to the top of the dresser, out of her way. It hardly weighed enough to warrant the size of the bag. Jefferson obviously had perfected the art of traveling light.

She flipped back the dark blue down comforter and

smoothed the fresh white sheets in place. She had the edge of a plump bed pillow caught between her teeth when Jefferson silently appeared in the doorway. Ignoring him, or at least pretending to, she finished pulling on the pillowcase and dropped the pillow next to its twin at the head of the full-size bed. With a flick, she pulled up the comforter once more and, reaching across the bed, smoothed a wrinkle.

"I remember when you used to refuse to make your own bed."

Emily tossed several decorative pillows back onto the bed and straightened.

"You insisted that it was a waste of time, when you were only going to mess it up again when you had to go to bed."

"It was good logic," she answered lightly. "Squire never climbed on you boys when any of you didn't clean your room. Or didn't make your bed each morning. Apparently that was something he reserved for *girls.*"

Jefferson crossed to the opposite side of the bed and stooped to pick up a small square pillow that had fallen to the floor. His fingers hovered over the deep blue and maroon needlepoint pattern. "Was it so bad, then? Being raised by Squire?"

Emily shook her head. This, at least, was something she could be perfectly honest about. "No. It wasn't bad." She smiled faintly. "What could be bad about being raised on a ranch? There were dogs and cats. Horses. The swimming hole. And several big 'brothers' to tag after. It wasn't bad." She headed back into the hall and the linen closet. It had been heaven on earth to a lonely little girl. It would be heaven on earth to a lonely woman, too.

He followed her to the doorway and leaned against the doorjamb. "How often do you get back to the ranch?"

She pulled a couple of oversize towels from the closet and turned back to the bedroom. "Two or three times a year, I guess. I've tried to get back each Christmas, but with work and all..." She passed by him and hung the towels over the brass rods in the bathroom. "When you're the low man on the totem pole, other people usually get first crack at holiday vacations."

"Squire doesn't celebrate much at Christmas, anyway."

"Considering that your mother died on Christmas Eve, who can blame him?" She halted and squared the edge of his duffel bag against the corner of the dresser. She glanced at him. "You were never around on Christmas, either. Even when you still lived at home, you went to the cabin rather than stay in the big house. Sawyer was in Europe by then. Dan was—"

"Off raising hell," Jefferson finished. "And Matthew was either closed up in the office or out on the range somewhere. Just one big happy family." Jefferson watched her, his eyes brooding. "And Tristan—"

"What?" She prompted when he broke off.

He shrugged. "Nothing."

Emily leaned her hip against the dresser and absently caught her hair back to weave it into a loose braid. She could take a stab at what Jefferson was thinking.

"Your mother died giving birth to him. Naturally that left a mark on him." She dropped the braid and headed for the door. "If you want to watch a video or read, you'll probably find something to your taste in Tristan's room. He's got everything under the sun."

"What are you going to do?"

Escape. She cupped the side of the doorjamb with one palm. "I brought home some work from the office." It wasn't strictly a lie. "You, um… Let me know if you need anything." Her lips sketched a smile and she fled.

Jefferson pinched the bridge of his nose and collapsed on the side of the bed. Arms outstretched, he gingerly lifted his leg until he sprawled across the bed diagonally. His toes tingled as sensation returned. His head was pounding and his hip ached worse now than it had six months ago when he'd first been discharged from the hospital in Germany. Even his shoulder was kicking up a protest. Due, no doubt, from the horrendously long flight from Amsterdam. He had some pain medication in his duffel bag, but just then he didn't have the energy to retrieve it from across the room.

Restlessly he shifted, and his hand brushed against the pillows. He nudged aside the assortment of ruffled and tucked shapes until he reached the plain white bed pillow. Slowly his fingers closed over the edge and he pulled it to him. When it was near his face, and he could almost smell Emily's clean, pure scent on the pillowcase, he closed his eyes with a sigh.

And slept.

Chapter Two

When her head jerked upright just before hitting the edge of her laptop, Emily blinked, owlishly. She stared at the garbled spreadsheet displayed on the screen. Her fingers must have been pressing on the keyboard. Blinking, she erased the gobbledygook, closed the file and shut down the computer system.

A huge yawn made her eyes water, and she rubbed her eyes. Another yawn.

Still functioning, barely, she remembered to put the computer disk in her briefcase so she wouldn't forget it in the morning. Standing up from the leather chair she'd been perched in, she set the computer on the coffee table and arched her back, wiggling her bare toes. The antique clock sitting on the mantel chimed softly, and she realized it was after three in the morning. Yawning yet again, she padded out to the kitchen and retrieved a cold bottle of water from the refrigerator.

Before shutting off the light and heading upstairs, she peeked into the garage. Jefferson's rental was parked neatly beside her Mustang. His work? Or Tristan's?

She twisted off the cap to the bottle and shut off the few remaining lights, checking the front door and the back French doors that overlooked the swimming pool beyond the atrium. In darkness she moved back through the great room and up the stairs. The door to Jefferson's room was open and the light was still on.

Pausing at the head of the stairs, she sipped on the water, studying the rectangle of light cast upon the dark green and maroon carpet runner that ran the length of the upstairs hallway. The house was quiet in the way that houses were. She could hear the quiet tick of the clock on the downstairs mantel. The gentle sighing of wood as it settled for the night.

She set the bottle on the square newel post and moved over to the doorway, peering around the edge. Jefferson was stretched across the bed at an awkward angle. One leg, obviously the one he'd injured, was flat on the bed, but his other leg was bent at the knee and hung over the edge of the bed, the worn slanted heel of his leather cowboy boot flat on the floor. His face was turned away from her, tucked in the edge of the pillow that sat beside, rather than under, his head.

She bit the inside of her lip and leaned against the door frame. Who was she kidding? To pretend that life would just continue on as normal, now that Jefferson had returned. However temporary his return might be. "Oh, Jefferson," she murmured, watching him sleep for a long moment.

Without a sound, she went to her own bedroom, turned on the light, retrieved the softly nubby afghan that usually sat folded at the foot of her bed and returned to his room. She snapped off the lamp and decided against trying to remove his boots for fear that he'd waken. She leaned across him, lightly spreading the blanket across his chest.

He didn't stir. She began to straighten and her fingers grazed the thick ends of his hair. She froze, her fingers tingling. Swallowing, she curled her fingers into a fist and snatched her hand away before she could succumb to the temptation of running her fingers through its heavy softness.

She didn't know what happened then. One minute she was tucking her hair behind her ears and backing away from the bed. The next, Jefferson sprang at her with a feral growl, his large hands gripping her upper arms like manacles. He swiveled and pushed her onto the bed hard enough to jar the breath from her chest.

Speechless, she stared up at him.

His breath was harsh, and his hands tightened painfully as his weight pressed across her midriff. "You're dead," he growled.

Shock held her immobile as surely as his hands around her arms. "Jeff...er...son," she gasped faintly.

Even in the pale light coming from her room down the hall she could see his teeth bared. Her heart was pounding painfully, and her head ached with the adrenaline shooting through her veins. "Jefferson. It's me."

His eyes, blackish pools, looked down at her, unblinking. In another time. Another place. A terrible, dark, painful place.

"It's me. Emily," her soft voice shook, but he held himself still for a long moment. "Shh," she whispered faintly. "It's okay, Jefferson."

His arms seemed to sway, and he loosened his iron grip.

"It's all right now," she breathed, and closed her eyes on a faint sob when he lowered his head to the curve of her breast. As gentle as they'd been painful, his hands slid up her arms to her shoulders. Wide-eyed, she lay stiffly beneath him, looking down at the crown of his head as he seemed to just collapse. As abruptly as he'd charged.

Biting down on her lip, she closed her eyes tightly. Tears burned their way from beneath her lids anyway. Oh, Jefferson, what's happened to you?

She hauled in a shaky breath, half-afraid that he'd rouse again, in Lord-only-knew what kind of state. But he was still.

After long minutes she lifted her hand and smoothed his heavy hair away from his forehead. Letting the tears come, she lay there, still trapped beneath his weight. Her hand gently stroking through the silky blond strands.

"It will be okay, Jefferson," she whispered. "Everything will be okay."

A few hours later, her eyes were gritty with the snatches of sporadic sleep, and the gray light of dawn was slipping through the slats of the cherry shutters hanging at the windows. The arm trapped beneath Jefferson's shoulder was completely numb. But he seemed to be sleeping easier now. More naturally, if the deep breathing that wasn't quite a snore was any indication.

Grimacing against the pins that immediately began stabbing her fingers when she gradually worked her arm from beneath him, she edged away from his weight until she was free to slip from the end of the bed.

He sighed deeply and turned back into the pillow, one hand eclipsing an entire corner of it.

Hunched against the furious feeling returning to her arm, she found herself reaching for the afghan that had fallen to the floor at some point. Far too disturbed to wonder at her daring, she slipped the covering over his shoulders before leaving the room and closing the door softly behind her.

The bottle of water was right where she'd left it on the newel post, and she swayed, fresh tears clogging her throat. Gritting her teeth, she grabbed the bottle and closed herself in her own bedroom. She poured the water among the various plants growing in her room, and the empty bottle she dropped on the pristine white eyelet bedspread. Her clothes landed haphazardly where her hands dropped them, and she stood there, numb. Unthinking. Sleep would be impossible. Goose bumps danced across her skin, and she automatically pulled on softly warm sweatpants. She covered the T-shirt she pulled on with an oversize sweatshirt that Tristan had cast aside.

Her cold fingers nimbly pulled her hair into a braid and she fastened a Velcro wrist wallet containing a house key and five dollars around her wrist. In minutes, she was quietly letting herself out the front door, into the chilly dawn. The afternoons in mid-August might be sweltering. But the crack of dawn in San Diego was bound to be cool. And, that morning, foggy as well.

Emily eyed the house as she methodically warmed up her cold muscles, and then stretched gently. When she set off up the block in a slow jog, all she could see in her mind were Jefferson's eyes. Wounded. Black with pain.

Her jogging shoes thumped steadily as she rounded a curve in the street and began the ascent that would eventually, after exactly 2.4 miles, lead to the stable. And Bird. But she didn't hear the slap of her shoes against the pavement. Nor did she hear the gradual awakening of the neighborhood. Car engines starting. Front doors slamming as morning newspapers were retrieved. She heard nothing. Only the memory of Jefferson's deadened voice.

"You're dead."

It was afternoon when Jefferson finally woke. And he probably wouldn't have even then if it weren't for his baby brother standing over him, shaking the toe of his boot hard enough to rattle his teeth.

Jefferson peeled open his eyes, squinting at the bright California sunshine blasting through the windows. "What?"

"Rise and shine, bro. The day is awastin'."

Wearily, Jefferson closed his eyes again. He bunched the pillow beneath his head and scratched his chest. "Says who."

"Me. Come on, Jeff. You keep sleeping the way you are and we're gonna have to call in the paramedics just to see if you're still alive."

"Go surf the 'net. Or whatever the hell you do on those computers of yours."

"No work today," Tristan said cheerfully. "We're going out." He yanked the pillow from beneath Jefferson's head.

"Speak for yourself."

"Or we can stay here and you can tell me what the hell's been going on with you the past few years."

Jefferson pushed himself up until he was sitting. A blue knitted thing drifted across his lap. A stray thought hovered at the edge of his mind as he looked at it. Frowning, he shoved it aside and held out his hand. "Help me up."

"Damn, buddy," Tristan said as he pulled Jefferson to his feet. "You're really gettin' decrepit, aren't you."

Jefferson planted a hand on Tristan's chest and shoved him out of the way. "I can still whip your butt," he warned. Pulling his shirt free, he balled it up and dropped it on the foot of the bed.

"Holy sh—"

Jefferson ignored Tristan's muffled curse as his brother obviously saw the scar on his back and continued into the bathroom. He sat on the closed lid of the commode and studied his boots. He wiggled his toes. At least, he *thought* he wiggled them. They'd gone numb again. Grimacing, he bent his knee and began tugging.

"Maybe you should just get it over with," Tristan said as he appeared quietly in the doorway. "Ain't nothing you can say that's going to outdo what my imagination is coming up with."

"Don't be too sure." Jefferson's teeth clenched as he managed to pull his foot free from the high boot.

"You ought to stick to bedroom slippers at that rate," Tristan advised. "They're a whole lot easier to get on and off."

Jefferson politely told his brother what he could do with the advice.

Tristan watched Jefferson struggle with the other boot for a long minute. "Oh, for crying—" He bent down and pulled the boot off himself, dropping it to the marble-tiled floor with a heavy thud. Then he turned and flipped on all four faucets full blast. The Jacuzzi tub began to fill. He watched the water rise. "How long you been out?"

Jefferson went still for a moment. "Out of where?"

He slid open drawers until he found a disposable razor and a toothbrush still in the plastic package.

"The hospital."

Relax. He ripped off the plastic wrapping and tossed it aside. "Long enough."

Tristan grunted and left the bathroom. He returned moments later, bearing a tube of toothpaste. "Here."

"Hope you give Em more privacy than you're giving me," Jefferson commented blackly as he squeezed toothpaste onto the new toothbrush.

"I'm not likely to be overcome with lust at the sight of your bod, if that's what's bugging you," Tristan assured dryly.

"At least California hasn't warped you completely." Closing his eyes, Jefferson enjoyed the simple act of brushing his teeth. For too long he'd not had access to such simple things. And then when he did have access, he'd been unable to do it himself.

Tristan flipped off the water as it neared the top of the tub. "What kind of gun makes a hole like that," he wondered after a moment.

Jefferson spat and rinsed his mouth. Slowly, he set the toothbrush on the side of the sink. He cupped cold water in his hands and doused his face with it, running his fingers through his hair and away from his face. He looked into the mirror and saw his brother watching him silently.

"The same kind that I'm never gonna carry again," Jefferson finally said.

Tristan's eyes narrowed, but he didn't comment on that. After a moment he nodded. "I'm glad you made it back," he said simply.

Jefferson eyed himself in the mirror. He looked every day of his thirty-six years. And then some. For the first

time in more than a year, though, he could honestly say
the words. "I'm glad, too."

The two brothers shared a look. Then abruptly Tristan
nodded. "Well, holler if you need help crawling out of
that swimming hole when you're done." He cupped the
back of Jefferson's neck in his big palm for a brief moment. "Then we're gonna go have a beer. Maybe admire a few lovelies along the way," he said gruffly. He
dropped his hand. Nodded once. And left.

Jefferson slowly shucked his pants and lowered himself into the tub, thinking how much Tristan had grown
to be like their father. It was both a curse and a blessing.

He groaned aloud when he flipped on the Jacuzzi jets
and the water began churning. In that moment, the five-
by-eight dirt-floored room in Lebanon, the hospital in
Germany and the doctors in D.C. all seemed very far
away.

Eventually Jefferson, clean and muscles and joints
loosened somewhat from the soothing water, climbed
out unaided from the tub and dried himself. He ran a
comb through his tangled hair, thinking it was high time
he got a haircut. He rummaged through the drawers
again, but gave up when he couldn't find any rubber
bands. Back in the bedroom he unzipped his bag and
pulled out some clean clothes. His eyes were on the blue
blanket as he tucked the long tails of his shirt into his
jeans and buttoned up the fly. He leaned over and picked
it up by the edge, his thumb and forefinger absently
smoothing the fluffy softness.

"You ready yet?" Tristan yelled from somewhere in
the house. Jefferson took a last look at the blanket and
dropped it back on the bed. He shoved his wallet in his
pocket and grabbed a clean pair of socks before retrieving his boots from the bathroom.

Tristan's heavy feet pounded up the stairs. "Come on, Jeff. It'll be dark at the rate you're going—"

Jefferson stepped into the hallway, ignoring his cane where it was propped next to the dresser. "I'm ready." He waved his boots at his brother who thundered back down the stairs. He followed more quietly, then sank down on the last step to pull on his socks.

"Want to borrow some shoes?"

Jefferson tucked his tongue in his cheek as he glanced over at the huge white high-tops Tristan wore. "I'll wear my boots. Thanks." Lips tight, he shoved his foot into the worn-soft leather and tugged. Thank God they were easier to put on than take off.

He pulled himself up by the banister and stomped once. Once a pair of boots were broken in, they were more comfortable than any other kind of footwear. He'd believed it since he'd been eleven years old.

The corner of Tristan's lips curled slightly and he turned for the door. "Gonna die with them things on, aren't you."

"Yup."

Jefferson waited while Tristan set the security system and securely locked the door. In minutes, they were hurtling down the freeway in Tristan's battered half-ton pickup. Jefferson edged a stack of books out from beneath his boot. They started to slide and he bent over to shove them away so his feet had somewhere to go. He sat up again, and hunched his shoulder so as not to knock over the computer that occupied the middle portion of the seat. Atop the computer was a beaten-up leather deck shoe with half the sole missing. "You know," he pointed out as he pulled the leather lacing from the shoe. "We could've driven the rental." He reached up and pulled the annoying hair away from his face and tied it into a ponytail with the lace.

Tristan looked at the conglomeration of stuff as if for the first time. "Push it behind the seat if it's bugging you."

Jefferson's chuckle was rusty. Then he watched in amazement as a tiny little compact car sped around them and pulled right in front of them, slowing down abruptly. He caught the computer just as it began to slide when Tristan hit the brakes, swearing. In seconds everything was back to normal, and Jefferson shook his head. The traffic heading the opposite direction was already heavy. "Driving in this would do me in," he muttered.

Tristan grunted, switched lanes, slowed down and switched lanes again. "You get used to it. I couldn't do what Em does though." He maneuvered around a lumbering panel truck and headed for the exit. "She drives about forty miles round-trip every day."

"Does she like her job?"

Tristan pulled up at a stoplight. He checked the traffic, then turned right and right again, coming to a halt in a nearly deserted parking lot. The beach was merely yards away, a jumble of umbrellas and kids and kites. "She's as happy there as she's going to be anywhere, I'd guess." He climbed out of the truck.

Jefferson got out too, eyeing Tristan over the dusty roof of the cab. "Meaning?"

Tristan turned, his eyes squinting in the late afternoon sun. After a brief moment, he shrugged. "Meaning nothing." He rounded the truck and headed for the weather-beaten wooden building. "Come on. Beer's getting warm while we're sitting here yakking."

Jefferson tucked his fingers in his pockets and followed his brother into the dimly lit bar. He'd been in a hundred similar establishments in a hundred different cities.

Tristan held up two fingers as he passed the bartender. "Hey, Joe. How's it hanging?"

The bartender slid two foaming glasses of beer toward Tristan. "Can't complain."

Tristan tossed a couple of bills on the bar. "Say hi to my big brother," he told the other man.

Joe nodded and held out his beefy hand. Jefferson reached over and shook it. "Joe Pastorini," he introduced himself. "Your brother here's a good man. Helped my daughter out of a jam a while back." He pushed the money back toward Tristan. "That's no good here, boy."

Silently, Jefferson watched Tristan grab up a few peanuts from a brown bowl and pop them into his mouth. He noticed that Tristan didn't take back the money.

"How's little Emily doing? Haven't seen her in here for a while."

Tristan picked up one of the glasses and handed it to Jefferson. "She's fine." He grinned. "I think that CPA she's dating from the firm frequents the finer establishments."

Jefferson zeroed in on that. CPA?

"No finer place than this," Joe was defending.

"That's why I come here, Joe," Tristan assured dryly. He waved and headed toward the back of the room where a pool table sat. He placed his glass on the wide edge of the table. "Rack 'em up, Jeff."

Jefferson hadn't played pool in years. But he easily recognized the good-natured challenge in Tristan's eyes. Pushing aside thoughts of Emily and her CPA, he racked them.

Four games and two beers later, Jefferson placed the cue on the wall rack. "Enough."

Tristan sipped at his diet cola. He'd switched after the first beer. "Can't take the heat?"

"What heat," Jefferson asked lazily. He perched against the high stool he'd dragged over to the table from the bar after the first game and stretched his long legs. "I've won the last two."

Tristan seemed to consider that. He walked over to the wall rack and placed his cue there, also. "You know," he said, absently watching a young blond woman enter the bar, "Squire was the only one who could ever beat us hands down."

"Except for Daniel."

Tristan chuckled soundlessly. "Dan spends all his free time in the pool halls. He's practically a pro." He waved his nearly empty glass. "So he doesn't count."

Jefferson drained his glass and plunked it on the side of the pool table. It felt good. Not the beers, necessarily. But the easygoing company of his brother. Talking about their other brothers. His head was buzzing ever so slightly. "Who's the CPA?"

"Huh?"

"Emily's CPA."

Tristan stood up. "Come on. Let's go home."

Jefferson waited.

Tristan's lips compressed. He noticed the curvy blonde was staring at them. He lifted his chin in her direction. "Why don't you go say hello. She's interested."

Jefferson couldn't care less. The woman could have paraded around the pool table naked, and he wouldn't have cared. "Is it serious?"

long look "—are more experienced." She moistened her lips and cocked her hip, bending forward just enough that he could have looked straight down her loose shirt, had he been interested.

He wasn't. "This boy doesn't want to...play. Either," he assured her politely.

She straightened. Flipping her hair over one shoulder, she shrugged and wandered over to a man sitting alone in one of the booths.

Tristan pretended to shiver. "Scary," he muttered, and headed for the door, sketching a wave toward Joe as they left.

This time Jefferson shoved some of the books behind the seat before climbing into the truck. "Why'd you throw her off the scent?"

His brother coaxed the engine to life and headed them home. "You kidding? Even if I ever touched her, she'd be crying palimony, or abuse or some kind of garbage like that inside of two weeks. Just until she got a nice fat check." His lips twisted. "Amazing how money brings 'em out. Like worms after a rain."

Jefferson shook his head. He thought about telling his brother that he was too young to sound so jaded. But he saved his breath. "So who is the CPA?"

Tristan just shook his head.

When they let themselves into the house a while later, Tristan still wasn't answering. And Jefferson had quit asking. For now.

The house was quiet, and Jefferson knew instinctively that Emily wasn't home. Tristan headed for his office almost immediately, and Jefferson went to the kitchen. He drank down a narrow bottle of fancy water from the fridge and tossed the empty container into the sink.

Frowning, he paused next to the counter, his palm flat on the white tile. He closed his eyes and imagined her.

Emily.

Moving around the kitchen. Cooking. Loading the dishwasher.

Laughing with Tristan over one of his stupid jokes.

His fingers pressed into the cold tile.

When the phone rang right beside his hand, he nearly jumped out of his skin. He bit back a violent curse. He hadn't quite been able to lick it yet. The unexpected attack of nerves. The jumps.

Maybe he'd never be able to.

The thought of which was almost more than he could bear. Swearing again, he flipped on the water and bent over the sink, throwing water over his face with hands that weren't quite steady.

"Jefferson?"

He froze, still hunched over the sink. He lowered his forehead in his hands. He hadn't even heard her come in, much less walk up behind him. Damn.

Emily slowly reached around him and shut off the gushing water. She settled her weight against the counter and leaned to the side until she was at his level. "What is it, Jefferson? What's wrong?"

Her scent. So cool. So clean. It matched her voice. Gentle. Soft.

Without looking, he knew her long brown hair would be pooling on the stark white tile. That her large eyes would be velvety brown and filled with emotion. He straightened abruptly, raking back the hair that had fallen loose from the shoelace tie.

He watched her straighten, also. The severely tailored dress that covered her from neck to knee shouldn't have been flattering on her slender figure. But it was. The black color suited her. As did the narrow lines that followed each curve and valley. His fingers curled.

"I shouldn't have come here."

She flinched. As if he'd physically struck her. It took her a moment before her expression smoothed out. "Then why did you?" Her voice was steady. "Never mind. I know why," she continued when he said nothing. "You came to see Tristan. So go ahead and tell him what it is that's eating you up inside." She blinked her long lashes and aimed her glance somewhere around his shoulder. "Then maybe you'll get some peace."

"There's no peace left anymore," he said, the words dredged up. "Not for me."

He could hear her breath hissing between her teeth when she drew it in. Suddenly her palm, cool and smooth, cupped his cheek. Her brown eyes captured his gaze in their liquid depths. "Yes, there is," she promised him. Her thumb gently stroked his jaw. "It's just hiding from you right now," she spoke softly. "But it's there, Jefferson. You'll find peace again."

Her hand started to slide away, and he caught it with his own. "Where?" His gut hurt. "Where is it hiding, Emily?" He shook his head once. "Nowhere. That's where."

"You're wrong." She paused. "You know you're wrong. That's why you came here in the first place. To get rid of this—" she shook her head, unable to put a word to whatever *this* was. "Because you and...and Tristan are connected."

He released her fingers and put his hand to her shoulder to nudge her away. But his palm closed over the curve instead. "You're a dreamer, Emily," he didn't mean the words unkindly. It was just that he didn't have any dreams left. Only nightmares.

His hand slid down, cupping the upper curve of her arm through the black fabric of her dress. She bit her lip. "Maybe I am," she agreed sadly. She shifted and his hand dropped away. She caught it between her own and looked down. "You'll find peace," she assured him again. "It's hiding underneath the pain. The tears."

He gently touched her head. Silky. "I don't have any tears left, Emily."

She lifted her chin and looked him full in the face. A tiny droplet slipped from her eye, leaving a silvery trail in its wake. "I have tears," her words were barely audible. "I'll give you my tears." Her gaze skittered away from his, then returned. Another drop slid past her long lashes.

His jaw ached. With his thumb, he caught the next tear before it fell to her cheek. Then his hand slid behind her neck and he hauled her into his arms. Her hands slipped behind his shoulders, holding him tightly. Securely.

Her face turned into his neck and he could feel her tears. Groaning, he lowered his head to her shoulder and held her as she wept.

For him.

When the phone rang this time, Jefferson didn't flinch.

But Emily stiffened at the sound and pulled away a few inches. After that first, single ring, the phone was once again silent. She backed away a few more inches. She carefully removed her fingers from their clutch on his wide shoulders and tried to wipe her face. But Jefferson stopped her. His hands cradled her head and she felt tears clogging her throat anew at the tortured expression darkening his blue eyes until they were nearly black.

She closed her eyes, swallowing. "I'm sorry," she whispered. Why did she think *she* would be able to help him?

He shushed her so quietly she wasn't sure he'd actually made a sound. But his hands were lifting her chin, and, helpless, she looked up into his hard face. Her eyes fluttered closed when he dropped the lightest of kisses across her lids. She trembled when he softly kissed away the traces of tears still on her cheeks.

His breath whispered over her brow. Her temples.

"Sweet Emily," he murmured.

The floor seemed to sway beneath her feet and she clutched his arms for support. That deep, aching longing that had been her heart's constant companion for years nearly overwhelmed her. To be in his arms again.

A soundless sob rose in her throat and she pulled away from his hands. A strand of her hair caught on the rough bristles blurring his carved jaw and she froze. A single strand of hair. Binding them together, for however brief a moment.

He slid a finger into her hair, slipping it behind her ear, then pausing to circle the small pearl stud earring. "Sweet, sweet Emily," he whispered again. His jaw clenched and he closed his eyes. Then he opened them. Watched her. Lowered his head.

Emily couldn't move. His lips grazed hers. Lifted. Lowered to sample once more.

His face blurred in her vision, and she instinctively closed her eyes, lifting toward him when he seemed to retreat.

"Jefferson," she whispered his name against his lips. "Let me help you."

He pressed his forehead against hers, struggling with the need that thundered in his blood. It wasn't just a sexual thing. He'd long grown accustomed to the fact that Emily aroused him, like no other being on the face of the planet could arouse him. For just as long he'd been beating down that flame. Knowing that it should never be allowed to freely burn.

She lifted her cheek, pressing it against his. He felt her tremble against him. Yet he knew she wasn't weak. She was strong. So strong he could let her take his pain, if only for a little while. That was the need that nearly overwhelmed him. But he didn't deserve the respite that only she could provide. He didn't deserve the freedom.

And he wouldn't sully her with the filth. It was, perhaps, the only thing in this damned world that he could do for her.

He clasped her arms gently and set her away. "No."

Her mouth opened soundlessly. Shut again. "It's always the same, isn't it, Jefferson," she managed eventually. Her arms crossed protectively across her chest, and he was abruptly reminded of the sweetly defiant teenager she'd once been.

"What's the same?"

She shook her wispy bangs away from her eyes, sending her hair rippling over her shoulders. "You don't want anybody getting too close. You don't…want… *me*…getting too close." She blinked her eyes away from his, rocking slightly on her heels, cupping her elbows in her palms. Regret curved her soft lips.

"Em—"

She looked back at him. There was simply too much emotion between them. The things she'd wanted from him. That he couldn't…wouldn't give. She blindly focused on the way his loose cotton shirt draped across his wide chest. "I used to think," she mused softly, "that you always—" Her lips trembled and she sniffed, dredging the depths for some control. "That you always left because you didn't care enough about the things you left behind. The people. The ranch." *Her.* "Because you cared more about the adventures waiting for you in some godforsaken country."

"Em—"

"Sooner or later you'll have to stop running, Jefferson." She blinked rapidly. Enough tears had been shed today. "That's really what you've been doing all along, isn't it? But one day you're going to have to stop running. And come home again."

His jaw tightened. He could have disagreed with her. Could have denied it. He heard her quick, harsh breath, her delicate features drawn tight with pain.

"Coward," she accused softly. Swallowing, she bit her lip and looked away. Another tear slipped down her cheek and crept along her jaw. Spinning on her heel, she walked away.

Jefferson reeled. Swearing, he slammed his flat palm against a cupboard door. It bounced open violently and jounced shut. He dug his fingers into his temples, reining in the impulse to hit something again. "Dammit," he whispered. "Dammit!" He wrapped his fingers around the edge of the tile, his head bowed. Still, he couldn't contain a low growl. He shoved away from the counter and rounded it, his leg tight and most of his foot numb, as he stalked unevenly out of the kitchen. He headed through the great room and ended up slumped on the brick bench in the middle of the soaring atrium.

The violence drained away, leaving him tired. Weary beyond words. And what did he have to be so angry about, anyway? Emily spoke only the truth.

He heard a soft footfall. He stopped wiggling his foot.

He picked up a leaf that had fallen to the ground and twirled it in his fingers.

"I'm sorry, Jefferson." She halted a few feet away. "I had no right to say what I did."

"Forget it."

Emily watched his fingers outline the delicate edges of the drying leaf. "I can't forget it." As soon as she said the words, he dropped the leaf. It landed near the toe of her shoe.

"Yes." He looked up at her, his expression closed. "You can."

Moth to a flame. That's what she was. Drawn to his light, no matter how deadly. Over and over again. In a single motion, she crouched at his feet, her hands lightly resting on his knees. "We used to be friends, Jefferson," she reminded him.

She bit back a protest when he carefully lifted her hands from his knees. He didn't even hold her hands, but circled her wrists with his fingers. As if he didn't even want to touch her. He shook his head, and her heart, already beaten and battered, received a fresh bruise. It was one thing to sense that their friendship was gone. It was another to have him confirm it. "Not family. Not friends." She was hardly aware that she spoke the thought aloud. "Not even old…"

"Lovers," he supplied the word when she couldn't.

"No. Not even that."

"I don't mean to hurt you, Emily." His fingers tightened gently on her wrists. "That's the last thing I've ever wanted."

She forced the corners of her mouth upward. "Forget it."

"Touché."

Somewhere in the depths of the house, the telephone

rang again. Jefferson let go of her wrists, and Emily straightened. She smoothed down her dress. Without a backward glance she left him alone.

Through the open door to his office, Emily saw Tristan hunched at his desk, the phone at his ear. She passed by, retrieving her briefcase and her laptop, which she carried upstairs to her bedroom. She couldn't allow herself to think. For thought brought a fresh stab of pain. And with each stab of pain, she wanted to turn to the only one who could bring comfort.

But how could she do that when the source of her greatest comfort was also the source of her greatest pain?

Chapter Three

That night found Emily, once again, prowling around downstairs. Her eyes were beginning to sting from this second night of disturbed rest. But each time she'd tried to lay her head down in her own bed, her eyes had refused to shut. Her mind had refused to relax. Eventually, she'd simply given up and headed downstairs. Her restless wandering finally easing when she ended up in the kitchen.

Nothing like baking in the middle of the night. Opening up the refrigerator, she took out the carton of eggs and set it on the counter. She added the eggs to the mixture she'd started. Her toe absently tapped the base of the cabinets in time to the music playing softly on the radio. In her present state of mind, she'd be lucky not to eat the whole darn pan of brownies.

Sighing, she reached for the pan of melted chocolate, which she'd left to cool, and poured it in a slender stream into the batter. Her thoughts drifting, she scraped the edges of the pan with a spatula and began mixing once more.

She remembered the first time she'd tried her hand at cooking. She'd been nine years old, and she'd misread the recipe. The results had been practically inedible. Squire had turned nearly green when he'd taken his first bite. Tristan had comically started to make gagging motions. Matthew, bless his loving heart, had stoically eaten a small portion, as had Daniel.

But it was Jefferson who'd taken her aside the next day to help her read the recipe. It was Jefferson who'd stood by in the kitchen when she'd been determined to make that stupid casserole. He'd stood there, answering her questions as best he could. But never interfering. For he had known how important it had been to her to do it on her own. And when she'd presented the casserole again the next night, Squire and the boys had eaten every last bite.

Emily reached for the flour-dusted pan and filled it with batter, then slid it neatly into the oven. Returning to the counter, she perched her hip on the edge of the bar stool and slid her finger around the edge of the bowl. The dark chocolate was sticky and sweet and she savored the taste as she licked her finger clean. Then, before she could polish off the rest of the batter clinging to the inside of the glass bowl, she stuck the whole thing in the sink and rinsed it with hot water before shoving it into the dishwasher.

She absently set the timer on the oven and finished cleaning up the kitchen. There wasn't much to do. Tristan had been called out on some computer thing before supper and Jefferson had never reappeared. Emily had been torn between relief and despair when she'd sat down alone to the salad she'd prepared for herself.

In minutes the kitchen was completely restored to its usual pristine state. The dishwasher was humming softly below the low music from the radio, and the first warming scent of baking brownies filled the room. She returned to the bar stool and leaned her elbows on the counter, cupping her chin in her hands. The smoked-glass door of the wall oven threw her reflection back at her.

She stared. Hard. But in her mind she wasn't seeing herself. She was seeing the tall, broad shape of a man. His heavy hair was a streaky golden mass that fell, shaggy, past his shoulders. His brows were darker than his hair and straight over his deep blue eyes. His jaw angled sharply to his chin where a long-ago adventure had left a tiny scar marring its otherwise perfection.

Emily rubbed her eyes wearily. But the sight of Jefferson was engraved in her mind. His broad shoulders. His wide chest, all bronzed and smooth. The corrugated muscles narrowing to—

She caught herself and blinked. Reaching out, she snatched up an apple-shaped pot holder and went to the oven, needlessly checking on the baking brownies. As soon as she cracked the oven door, a waft of heated chocolate escaped and she carefully shut the oven, tossing the pot holder aside as she turned.

Seeing him standing in the door, Emily wasn't sure she hadn't conjured him up from her imaginings. But her imaginings, no matter how detailed, didn't speak.

"Can't sleep?"

Emily shrugged, abruptly—painfully—aware of the brevity of the ruffled white nightshirt she wore. Aware of how thin it was.

Jefferson grimaced and leaning heavily on the cane, crossed to the bar stool. He lowered himself onto the round seat and propped the cane against the counter. "Neither can I," he admitted. He folded his arms on the bar, much as Emily had done earlier, and his unbuttoned shirt separated several inches.

She sank her teeth into the inner softness of her lip. "Do you, uh, want something to eat?" Her bare toes curled. "You didn't come down for supper."

She couldn't read a thing in the dark gaze he ran over her. She managed not to tug on the hem of the shirt, and he looked away, shaking his head. "No, thanks."

The low throb of music filled the kitchen. Swallowing, Emily stepped over to the wide pantry and, opening it, reached to the upper shelf for the powdered sugar. A strangled sound startled her, and clutching the package to her chest, she swiveled. "What?"

Jefferson had risen and, moving faster than she'd thought him capable, now stood beside her. His eyes burned as he lifted her arm above her head. The loose ruffles serving as a sleeve fell back to her shoulder.

Emily, confused, tried to pull away, but his hand gently detained her.

Jefferson took the package of sugar and placed it on the counter. He let her lower her arm, only to shove up the fabric at her other arm. "How?"

"What?"

His lips tightened, his teeth baring for a moment. White. Clenched. His hand flashed out and suddenly the button holding the loose shirt at the neck was unfastened and the fabric slid off her shoulders.

She gasped and grabbed at the fabric before it fell away. Color stained her cheeks. "What are you doing!"

He tugged on the fabric, pulling it well below her

shoulders and she backed away, only to be brought up short by the cool surface of the refrigerator door. Soundlessly he smoothed her hair back from her face and, looking down, she realized what disturbed him so.

Angry blackish bruises circled her upper arms. Bruises in the perfect shape of a hand. A hand that he was even now carefully fitting around her arm, matching up exactly the dark marks marring her pale skin.

He drew back, as if the contact burned. "I did this." He backed away, his hands raking through his hair.

The lingering soreness of her upper arms was nothing compared to the stark expression in his eyes. She reached for him and he seemed to scramble backward, warding her off with an outstretched hand.

"Don't," he growled. Begged. He turned away, as if he couldn't bear the sight. But his eyes kept swiveling back to her, his long lashes not quite guarding his horror.

"It was my fault," Emily told him softly. "I shouldn't have disturbed your sleep last night." She took a step toward him. "I only meant to cover you." Another step. "You were having a bad dream."

"Nightmare," he corrected dully. "One huge, long, unending, goddamned nightmare."

She stepped forward an inch more and caught his hand in hers.

"Why, Jefferson? Why the nightmares?" She couldn't help the question. She wanted to know why he'd muttered "You're dead" in his sleep. Even though she knew he wouldn't say.

"I frightened you," he said, grimacing. "Marked you."

"You would not have hurt me." She clasped his hand

close and dropped a kiss on his whitened knuckles. "No matter what your nightmare."

"You're foolish," he ground out.

"No." It was imperative that she get through to him. On this, if nothing else. Her heart beat unsteadily. "You listen to me, Jefferson Clay. I know that you would not have hurt me. And *yes*," she said, keeping a grip on his hand when he would have turned away. "I was frightened last night. But frightened for you. For whatever hell that you've been through. I was not frightened *of* you."

"Then you truly are a fool," he pronounced, bending over her. "If you had two ounces of sense in that beautiful head of yours, you'd be heading for the hills, instead of sticking around me."

"I won't run away from you, Jefferson," she said deliberately. "Running isn't my style."

Twin embers seemed to burn deep in his eyes. "It should be," he warned her.

The fine hairs on the back of her neck prickled. The hand clasped in hers suddenly wasn't tugging away. It was nudging forward. Her mouth ran dry.

"You should be running fast and furious, Em."

She swallowed and shook her head. His palm had flattened against her collarbone, his fingertips resting on the mad pulse beating in her neck. "I'm not a child, Jefferson," she whispered. "I can take whatever you dish out."

"Can you?" His fingers grazed across her skin to her shoulder. With the flick of a finger, the loosened collar fell off her shoulder. "I wonder."

Emily shook her bangs out of her eyes then stood, unmoving as his heavy-lidded eyes studied her bare shoulder. The ruffled fabric was halted by her bent elbow, preventing it from completely baring her breast to his eyes.

His hand moved to her other shoulder, to nudge away the fabric there also, she thought. But instead, he adjusted the collar upward, securely over her shoulder. His fingers drifted across the wide ruffle running down the neckline to the valley between her breasts. Up again his hand went, this time pulling the fabric taut. The heel of his palm brushed against the dark shadow of her nipple clearly outlined against the thin white cotton.

Emily's breath stopped. Her eyelids flickered, but she didn't lower her gaze when he pinned her with his.

"Ready to run yet, Emily?" His hand brushed over that tight peak once again.

"No." Her voice was steady, though her heart was not.

He bent his head suddenly and his lips burned her neck where it curved into her shoulder.

Her legs weren't steady when he ran his lips up her neck to her ear. His breath wasn't quite steady, either. "Now?"

She swallowed. Moistened her lips. "No."

His head hovered next to hers, and his breath was warm across her skin. She jumped a little when his teeth scraped gently over her collarbone, and her head fell back, weak, as his head passed beneath her chin. She didn't sway, however. Not until he captured her pebbled nipple in his mouth, wetting the light fabric.

And then her knees did buckle. He was there, though, one long arm sliding around her waist, holding her up, her back arched. An offering to him.

"Now?"

If it had begun as a game to him, then he was surely caught. Just as she was. He held her so closely she could feel the unsteady beat of his heart. Could feel his arousal pressed against her.

The knowledge gave her strength. She willed her heart not to give way on her and she let go of her grip on the shirt. It slipped from her shoulder. Drifted down her back, held in place by his arm and their bodies pressed together at her waist.

"No," she said clearly. "I'm not running, Jefferson." She placed her hands flat on his chest, nudging beneath the edges of his shirt. "I'm not running until we finish what we started when I was nineteen years old." Her fingers slipped up his chest to his throat. Curved behind his neck. Grasped a handful of silky, thick hair. Tugged. Pulling his head down to hers.

It wasn't easy. He resisted. He wasn't going to kiss her. She knew it. Rising on tiptoe, she pressed her mouth to his. She tasted. She nibbled. She let out all her pent-up feelings for him as she delicately plundered his lips. But he didn't kiss her back.

Maddened, frustrated, she lowered her heels. Her hands raced to his shirt and jerked it wide. Then she nearly reeled, and bit down on her tongue to keep from crying at the sight of that gilded chest. The sleek muscle. The narrow strip of white briefs visible where the top buttons of his jeans hung loose. Mindless, she pulled her arms out of the nightshirt and she pressed herself, bare, to his chest.

"God!" His hands closed convulsively over her shoulders and he thrust her away. Without his arm wrapped around her, the last barrier was gone and her nightshirt drifted to her feet, leaving her clad only in a minuscule scrap of lace that hid nothing from his eyes. His lips parted as if he couldn't get enough air.

She'd been lovely at nineteen. All sweet, young, innocence. Now she was older. Still young. Still sweet. But ripe now. A woman. A woman who was still too young for the likes of him.

Jefferson told himself to turn away. Knowing that the pain he'd cause her by turning away would be far less than if he didn't. He knew all that. He'd been living with that for years now. His hand reached out, and he ran his fingertips down her shoulder, past the bruises on her arms. He felt the shivers dance to the surface of her silky skin. He placed both his hands on her waist and she didn't shrink away. She just continued watching him. Her large brown eyes luminous. Unblinking.

He could hear her breath tumble past her slightly parted lips. The tip of her tongue peeped out and left a glisten of moisture on that sweet, sexy curve.

Who was teaching who a lesson, he wondered with that minute portion still capable of coherent thought.

Her mouth formed his name, though she said not a word.

His jaw tight, he lifted her slight weight. Lifted her right out of the nightshirt pooling about her feet to set her on the counter. Her knees were smooth. Her thighs smoother. His hands, damn them, anyway, lingered without his permission and somehow he found his fingers had slipped down. Nudged apart her legs, so he could stand between them. So he could slip his palms around to the firm curves barely covered with lace.

He'd misjudged. Badly. He knew it right down in his bones just moments before she placed her warm hands on his chest and lifted those long, sleek legs to his waist. Wrapped around him. Pulled him against that intimate spot where he wanted, so badly, to be. Where he could never allow himself to go.

Her breath was a little sob that hitched in her throat,

and he knew she could feel him through the barriers of denim and lace. For he could feel her. He dragged his hands from the curve of her bottom and reached for the wooden cupboard above her head. He closed his eyes tightly and tried to summon a vision of his father. But Squire's disapproving expression wouldn't appear.

All he could see, eyes open or closed, was Emily. Her long, silky dark lashes casting shadows on her cheeks where a flush of color rode high. Her heart beating so rapidly that he could see it shimmering through her creamy skin.

His eyes opened at the touch of her hand on his face. Her palm lay gently, soothingly, against his cheek. A diamond-bright tear hovered on the tips of her eyelashes. "Please," she whispered, stroking his stubbled cheek. The tear glided downward.

She trembled against him. The hand left his cheek, and her knuckles glided down his chest and brushed against his stomach when her fingers closed over the top unfastened button. He sucked in his breath harshly, looking down and wishing he hadn't. The memory of her lithe fingers tugging apart his half-loose jeans was one which wouldn't soon leave him.

Her fingertip scalded him as it traced the edge of elastic. "Please," she whispered again. This time leaning forward, obscuring his downward vision with the silky crown of her head as she pressed her lips to his chest.

Her hand, unseen now, but felt to his very soul, moved. Lightly covered him. Shaped his length through the worn denim. The pain was more than physical. His eyes burned. But he had to do it. He closed his hands over her silky shoulders and gently, inexorably, pushed her away.

He took a step backward, and her legs loosened, seeming to fall away from his waist in slow motion.

Her eyes had the expression of a doe he'd once had in his sights. Soft. Sadly accepting. He found himself wondering if Emily's eyes ever smiled anymore. The way they had years ago. Before.

And knew himself damned for all eternity that he was the cause of all this.

But she wasn't so accepting after all, it seemed. "Why?" Her head was bent, her expression hidden. "Why do you pull back, Jefferson?" Her hands clasped the counter on either side of her hips. "Do you really not…want…me?" With a little shake, her hair rippled out of her eyes and she looked up at him. Her lips stretched in a macabre imitation of a smile. "Is the notion so distasteful?"

Jefferson swore. "Dammit, Emily—"

"No, really. I, uh, I want to know. Obviously you're not, um—" she staved him off with a raised hand "—unaffected by me," she enunciated carefully, even while her eyes grew red rimmed. "I might be stupid, but I'm not *that* stupid."

"You're not stupid."

She chuckled humorlessly at that. She blinked rapidly and stared off to the side, sniffed and abruptly dropped from the counter.

Jefferson felt like he'd been gut kicked. Her rose-tipped breasts swayed gently with the impact. He couldn't have moved if his life had depended on it.

She leaned over and picked up the nightshirt. He supposed she felt more secure by presenting him with the long curve of her back as she pulled it over her head. He could have told her that the vision of her smooth, taut skin, narrowing into a tiny waist then flaring out gently was as disturbing to him as the front side. The white fabric settled about her thighs, hiding that glorious expanse of creamy skin as she turned back.

"What do I do that makes you turn away from me?" Her fingers toyed with the pot holder sitting on the counter, and she shot him a defiant glance. "If you'd just tell me, then maybe I won't make the same mistake with someone else."

His teeth clenched. "The CPA, you mean?"

Her eyebrows contracted. "Who? Oh." Her expression smoothed out. "Perhaps."

"Don't even *think* about it."

"Why not, Jefferson?" She seemed to be as pained with the words that she spoke as he was by hearing them. "Why shouldn't I think about it? You all but made love to me before. That time when you visited me at school. You had an excuse then when you stopped. That I was barely nineteen. And that claptrap about us being family and all. Well, I'm twenty-six now. We still don't have a drop of common blood running in our veins, and you still turn me away. Why shouldn't I find a man who won't turn me away?" The pot holder crumpled in her fist. "Why should I go through my life waiting for something you'll never share?"

The oven timer went off. For a long moment she stared at him while the annoying buzz went on. And on.

She went over to the oven. Shut off the buzzer. Pulled out the pan and set it on the square wooden chopping block.

Finally, she carefully hung the pot holder on a hook beside the oven and turned back to him. When she looked at him this time, there were no tears in her eyes. "You want to know the ultimate irony, Jefferson? I want somebody in my life. I want my own home. My own family." She touched her temple. "I have a picture in my head, you know?" She dropped her hand. "Me, sitting at the breakfast table. One child working on his homework at the last minute. One trying to stuff cereal in her little face, but managing to spread more of it on the floor."

Her expression was soft. Dreamy. Jefferson found himself picturing exactly what her words conjured. A boy with her brown hair. The baby girl with blon—

"And at the other end of the table," her voice went on, "should be my husband. My lover. My…my…soul mate. But he's not there. I can't picture him." She frowned faintly. "I wish I could picture him, Jefferson. I wish I could find a man who wouldn't turn me away. Who would share his life with me. Who'd be the father of my children." She seemed to rouse herself then and abruptly turned off the oven. "You've never even taken *me*, Jefferson. But you've taken away all the rest. Because I can't bear to share myself with any other man but you. And the one person you refuse to share yourself with…is me."

She pressed her lips together, and he knew the effort it took her to maintain her control. He knew the effort it took him. To not reach for her. To not take her to him and make her his. To let her turn and walk away. From him.

Emily was shaking so badly that her legs wouldn't even carry her up all the stairs. Several steps shy of the top, she sank down, her forehead pressed against the carved wooden rail. She had no idea how long she sat there. All she knew was that she never saw Jefferson come out of the kitchen. And eventually, when her feet had grown cold and her legs gone stiff, she heard the front door open and close. Then Tristan was there, trudging up the stairs.

Midway up, he stopped, peering at her in the dark. He seemed to sigh and then he was carefully stepping past her, lifting his briefcase and the padded holder containing his notebook computer over her head. In minutes he returned and stood a few steps lower than the one where she still sat.

"Come on," he said softly.

"Why does it have to be him, Tristan?"

He lifted his shoulders. Understanding everything without needing the words. "Just is."

He stood over her silently, then sighed again and reached down. "Come on," he said, and lifted her into his arms.

Emily's head lolled against Tristan's shoulder as he carried her up the rest of the stairs. "I wish it was you instead," she murmured.

He seemed to find that amusing. "No, you don't."

"It'd be so much easier."

"No." He shouldered his way into her bedroom. Holding her in one arm, he straightened her blankets slightly and then lowered her to the mattress.

Emily clutched at him when he would have straightened and moved away. "What is it with us, Tristan? You go through women like there's no tomorrow and—"

"I don't 'go through women,'" he objected. He tucked the covers beneath her chin. "And you'll find what you're looking for."

"I don't think so."

"Don't give up on him just yet, squirt."

"I don't know that I have a choice. He won't give an inch, Tristan. Not where I'm concerned."

"It'll be different this time."

"How do you know?" Emily pushed up on her elbow. "If I could just believe there was a possibility…oh, who am I kidding?" She sighed. "It doesn't matter what I believe. Jefferson isn't about to let me into his life. Not that way. And even if he remotely considered it, he'd be haring off on some adventure before we'd even have a chance."

"I have a feeling he's tiring of his traveling days," Tristan murmured. "Just hang in there."

Emily brushed the hair out of her eyes. "He didn't even know I was living here, Tris. I have to be realistic."

"Since when is love realistic?" He flicked the tip of her nose with a light finger. "Get some sleep."

Emily lay back on the pillows and watched Tristan leave the room, closing the door softly behind him. "Realistic," she murmured, staring into the dark. It was a lofty goal. And one she could never hope to attain. Rolling onto her side, she punched the pillow into shape and closed her eyes.

Jefferson lifted his head, hearing a door close along the hall. He dropped the corner of the soft blue blanket he'd been holding onto the seat of the chair. Silently, he lifted his duffel from the dresser and placed it on the bed. The zipper sounded loud when he opened the bag. He eyed the single pair of jeans sitting in the bottom of the bag. The weight of the footfalls heading closer warned him of Tristan's approach.

"Are you unpacking? Or packing?" Tristan said quietly from the doorway.

"Wish I knew," Jefferson muttered to himself. He reached for the clothing that he'd worn the day before and rolled them into a ball. "Packing," he said, and stuffed the bundle into the duffel.

"Why?"

Jefferson snorted. "Why not?"

Tristan sighed and moved over to the bed. He dropped down onto it and circled his head wearily. "Don't be an ass, Jefferson. Cutting out now isn't going to make it go away."

Jefferson hesitated, but continued gathering his meager possessions to place in the duffel. "Stay out of this."

"You brought me into it when you came here," Tristan countered.

"I came to see you."

"She thinks you didn't even know she lived here."

"So?"

"So." Tristan's lips tightened. "We both know that's not true. You knew, and you came, anyway. So don't try to tell me to butt out. Jesus, Jefferson...she'd die for you!"

Jefferson viciously shoved another shirt into the bag. "Do you think I don't know that?"

"Then what the hell are you doing? Why can't you two just get your act together and be happy for the rest of your lives?"

"There's too many reasons to list them all."

"That's a cop-out."

Jefferson glared at his younger brother. "She's off-limits. Okay?"

"Why?"

"Have you lost your mind? Why do you think?"

"So, she was raised with us. Big deal."

"It is a big deal." He ran his hand behind his neck. "A very big deal. And even if it weren't..."

"What?"

"I'm too old for her." And way too beaten up.

Tristan just shook his head. "You're a fool."

"Yeah, well, I may be a fool." Jefferson zipped his bag shut. "But my coming here has only hurt her."

"What's hurting her is knowing that you're going to leave again."

He shook his head, remembering the bruises he'd inflicted. "It's better this way."

Tristan obviously thought differently. He fingered the ragged airline tags hanging from the strap of the duffel. "So, where will you go?"

Jefferson shrugged. It didn't matter where he went, and Lord knew the ranch wasn't an option. His nightmares would follow wherever he went. But at least he couldn't hurt Emily anymore.

"What about money?"

That amused him as much as anything could, just then. "What about it?"

Tristan shrugged and let the matter drop. "You going to tell her goodbye? Or just let her wake up in the morning to find you've left."

"You can tell her." He lifted the bag and slung the strap over his shoulder. "Don't pretend that she'll be shocked I left, Tris. It's exactly what she expects."

His brother nodded. "Don't worry about the CPA," he said abruptly.

Jefferson stopped shy of the door.

"She's not seriously interested in him," Tristan added.

He didn't feel relieved. It just added to his mountains of guilt. "Take care of her."

Tristan sighed again. Jefferson heard it all the way by the door. "You're sure about this?"

"I'd say so, considering the way she's licking her chops over there." Tristan smiled faintly.

Jefferson waited.

Tristan returned Jefferson's stare with one just as silent. Just as long.

It was the blonde who finally interrupted. "Excuse me—" she glided to a stop next to Tristan, her green eyes sharp and her painted mouth smiling "—aren't you that cyberspy guy?"

Tristan raised his eyebrows. "Cyberspy?" He shot Jefferson a confused look, the picture of a befuddled male. "What's that? Some new kind of deodorant?"

The woman's eyes narrowed faintly. "You are," she insisted. "Your picture was in the *New York Times* a few weeks ago."

Tristan hooted. "New York? Geez, baby," he leered down at her, giving a good impression of a rather sunbaked beachboy. "I stick to the Pacific side of the states. Better babes. Too uptight over there, I'd bet."

The avaricious interest in the woman's eyes waned slightly. But she wasn't ready to give up just yet. She turned to Jefferson. "I bet you're brothers," she said. "Am I right?"

Jefferson shrugged, amused at the way his brother was sidling away from the blonde.

"So, tell me," she ran a long red fingernail along the arm of the bar stool where Jefferson leaned. "Are you into computers, too?"

"Not lately."

She looked over her shoulder at Tristan. "He is that guy," she insisted. "I hear he's loaded. Pity he doesn't want to…play." She turned back to Jefferson and leaned forward, encasing him in a cloud of her spicy perfume. "But I can see that you—" she flashed him a stood at attention. If it had been anyone but his brother standing before him, he'd have reduced the man to a pulp. "She'd never share her bed with you, much less marry you," he drawled. "And we both know it. So drop the act."

Tristan smiled humorlessly. "You want her to spend her life as alone and miserable as you are? That's one hell of a love you've got for her."

Jefferson bent and picked up his duffel to stop himself from weakening and planting his fist in Tristan's face, brother or not. His head knew that his brother was trying to manipulate him, but his gut churned at the very notion of Emily with someone else. Even Tristan. Or, perhaps *particularly* Tristan.

"She deserves some happiness," Tristan said.

"Do you think I don't know that?" Jefferson growled. "I *want* her to be happy. I want her to be safe, too. And if I stay, she won't be safe." His head pounded and his breathing grew harsh. "She won't be safe from me."

Tristan frowned. "You'd never—"

"Take a look at her arms, Tris." Jefferson kept his eyes open, knowing as soon as he closed them he'd be seeing those black bruises. Bruises that *he'd* inflicted. "You'll see for yourself why I have to go."

"She could help you through this, if you'd let her."

"No."

"She's a strong piece of work," Tristan continued. "Just tell her what happened."

"Nothing happened," Jefferson ground out the blatant lie.

Tristan sighed. "Until you can admit that something *did*, I guess there's nothing more to say, is there."

"Exactly."

Tristan picked up the cane beside the dresser and held it toward his brother. "Except that while you're off denying what's gone on in your life, Emily might just decide to move on with her own."

Chapter Four

Emily rose the next morning and mechanically moved through her morning jog to the stable. She had to force her mind to stay on her riding, however, lest Bird toss her onto her backside in the bushes lining the dirt trail. By the time she turned back for the stable, she was fully awake and Bird had worked out his jitters. If only the rest of her life were so easily controlled.

Jefferson was gone.

She hadn't needed to peek into the guest room to see if his duffel was still sitting on the dresser. Nor had she needed to look into the garage to see if the black rental car was still there.

She'd instinctively known.

Her steps dragged as she walked back to the house. He'd only been there two days, but she knew the house would feel empty without him. As empty as she felt herself.

She'd survive. Just as she'd told Tristan she would. She'd had plenty of practice. She'd been surviving for years now.

So she prepared for the day and drove off to work, telling herself that she was going to get on with her life. She would, once again, hide away her hopeless feelings for Jefferson. Maybe this time she'd even be able to move past them.

It was with that thought in mind that the next day she accepted Stuart Hansen's invitation to join him and a few of his friends for the weekend. They were driving down to Mexico, he told her. They'd leave Friday after work and return Sunday evening. Just some guys and girls getting together for some sunshine and seafood. No pressure, he assured. She could bunk with the other two women who were going.

Tristan frowned at her when she told him that night over supper that she'd be gone for the weekend. "I thought you weren't serious about the bean-counter."

"I'm a bean-counter," Emily responded smoothly. "And who says I have to be serious about Stuart? We're just going to Rosarita Beach for the weekend with some other people."

"Why now?"

"Because he invited me now, that's why."

"Where will you be staying?"

Emily shrugged. She wouldn't be surprised if they ended up camping on the beach. "We'll wing it, I'm sure. Don't worry," she smiled tightly, "I'm not going to do anything foolish. Like elope on the rebound or something."

"Not with that dope, at least," Tristan shuddered.

"You're awful. I thought you liked Stuart."

Tristan shrugged and leaned his chair back on two legs. "He's okay. He's just not…"

Emily's lips tightened. "Not Jefferson," she finished. She rose and took her plate to the sink. Her appetite was nil, anyway. She meticulously rinsed off the uneaten casserole and placed the dishes in the dishwasher. "Look, Tristan, Jefferson is gone. I knew he'd leave. So, I'd just as soon we not talk about him."

"You're the one talking, sweet pea. I was just going to say that Stuart isn't real exciting."

Emily flushed. "Maybe I don't want exciting," she said. "Maybe I want someone nice and steady. Reliable."

"Jefferson's reliable."

She laughed abruptly. "Right. You can always rely on Jefferson to leave." Tristan just watched her and her eyes began burning. "I'm going to Mexico tomorrow night," she said flatly. "We're leaving from the office, so I won't see you until we get back, I guess."

"I'd feel better if I at least knew where you'd be staying."

"Perhaps you'd like to come along and play chaperone," Emily suggested tartly. "But somehow I don't think you'd qualify for the part."

"At least take the mobile."

Emily didn't want to take the mobile phone. But she would. Only because Tristan seemed to think it was important. "Fine," she agreed tiredly. "It's your turn to clean up," she reminded Tristan. "I'm going to pack." She turned and left before he could find another concern to latch on to.

At the top of the stairs, she looked at the open doorway to the guest room. Closing her eyes, she wished with all her heart that she'd never heard of Jefferson

Clay. And then promptly retracted the wish. Mentally squaring her shoulders, she strode into the room and yanked back the comforter, causing pillows to tumble every which way. She pulled off the sheets and bunched them in a heap, then remade the bed with fresh linens. With the ones she'd removed balled up in her arms, she clumped down the stairs and through the kitchen, straight to the laundry room.

"Don't pussyfoot around," Jefferson warned, his temper short. He'd been sitting in this bloody office for an hour, waiting for the surgeon to return. "The fragment's moving. Right?"

The doctor, who looked young enough to still be in high school, moved past Jefferson and rounded his desk to sit down. He opened a thick file and seemed to study it for a while. He nodded. "We knew it was a possibility that the shrapnel would eventually begin to shift. That's what's been causing the numbness in your toes and foot." He folded his hands across the file and watched Jefferson across the paper-strewn desk. "You're going to have to decide, soon, Jeff. The surgery to remove the fragment is risky enough right now. The closer it moves to your spinal column—"

Jefferson waved his hand, cutting off the surgeon's words. He'd heard the spiel so many times he knew it by heart. "You know how many surgeries I've had since I..."

The surgeon nodded. He knew full well what Jefferson had been through. The thickness of the medical file his arms rested upon testified to that fact. "Nevertheless," he continued steadily, "you're going to have to go through one more."

"One more that could leave me paralyzed." Or dead.

"You may become paralyzed without it," the surgeon countered. He sighed and leaned back in his chair. "The possibility that the fragment wouldn't move did exist. That's why I didn't push the issue of the surgery when I met with you in Amsterdam. But it's obviously not the scenario we're looking at now. It is moving. And it will get worse. You could die, Jeff."

Either way, the odds weren't in his favor. Unable to sit in the high-backed leather chair another minute, Jefferson rose, and moved over to the wide window. He looked out on the expanse of neatly groomed grounds. No one looking at the sprawling building located in upper Connecticut would take it for anything other than what it appeared. A commonplace industrial complex.

Except the trucks that periodically entered and left the grounds weren't carrying your everyday goods. Jefferson himself had arrived at the center thirty-six hours ago safely hidden away in the trailer of a semi that for all the world appeared to be carrying paper products. Toilet paper, to be exact.

Considering his life seemed to be in the toilet, it was a fitting touch. "I don't want to get cut on again," he said. Never mind the weeks and weeks of therapy he'd have to undergo once, *if,* the surgery was a success.

"Your foot's numb right now, isn't it?"

Jefferson didn't answer.

"Pretty soon, your calf will feel the same way. Then the rest of your leg. You won't be able to move your knee. Already the reflexes in your other leg are diminishing." The surgeon tapped his finger against the file.

Jefferson pressed his fist against the windowpane.

"You'll never be able to return to the field, unless you do something soon."

"I don't give a good goddamn about getting back in

the field,'' Jefferson said, gritting his teeth. He'd given enough of his life to the agency. Whatever time he had left would be his own.

The other man closed the medical file. ''What about the nightmares?''

Damn that psychiatrist bitch. Nothing was private in this place. ''What about 'em?''

''The therapy sessions would help, Jeff. If you weren't so damn stubborn.''

''You know what kept me alive in that hellhole?'' Jefferson queried. ''Stubbornness.'' It was also what had kept him going in the months since.

''Okay. You've no plans to return to the field. What do you plan to do? Transfer to a different sector? Sit at a desk? Teach? Assuming that you even last more than a year or two. What? Regardless of what you choose to do with your future, Jeff, the surgery is still a necessity.'' The surgeon swiveled his chair around so he could face Jefferson directly. ''What about marriage? Children? Why cut off the possibility of those things if you don't have to?''

Every muscle in Jefferson's body tensed. He couldn't let himself think about that. Not when those thoughts were irrevocably twined with thoughts of Emily. It was a road he simply couldn't travel down. ''How long before I can get out of here?''

''You know the routine. Seventy-two hours.''

Leaving him a day and a half before he'd be transported back to the city by, in all probability, another toilet paper truck. He raked his fingers through his hair and pressed the heels of his palms to his eyes. Thirty-six more hours of people probing his mind and his body. Invading his dreams and his thoughts.

The other man sighed. He might look like a kid, but

he was one of the top men in his field. And he'd known Jefferson Clay for years. Pretty much knew what made the man tick. Jefferson Clay had been the best in the business. He'd had a golden touch for so long, that it had gotten pretty darn spooky. People stood in line to be on one of his missions, because despite the danger, everyone knew that when Jefferson Clay was the lead man, bloodshed on his team was nonexistent.

The man had pulled off more successful missions than any other agent, and he'd only once failed. And it was that very single failure that even now continued torturing the tense man standing across the room. "Jeff, it wasn't your fault that Kim died. You have to accept that. He knew the risks."

"Cold comfort for his wife." Jefferson wheeled around and began pacing the length of the office. "Or for his little son." His partner…*his friend*…had had every reason to live. Yet he'd died in that little square of a room that he'd been held in. The whole mission had been a fiasco from start to finish. But they'd waited and planned. And endured. Until the day had arrived when they made their break. The day their plans got shot to hell once again.

It hadn't gone the way they'd planned at all. Kim wasn't supposed to have died. He'd been just a kid, practically. Hardly old enough to be married with a son of his own.

"Are we finished here?" Jefferson asked abruptly. He knew the futility of just walking out. They'd find some way to drag him back.

The surgeon sighed again and scribbled out a note. "Here," he said as he shoved it into Jefferson's hand. "Have it filled at the dispensary before you leave. It'll help with the pain."

Jefferson stuffed the prescription in his pocket. He still had a nearly full bottle of pills from his last exam. He could handle the physical pain. It was that damned numbness that unnerved him.

"I hope you change your mind about the surgery," the man said as Jefferson prepared to leave the office. "Your chances are better with it than without."

Jefferson didn't respond. He left the office and headed downstairs. If he didn't show up in the cafeteria and eat something, he'd just be visited by that nurse-from-hell upstairs who had myriad ways of wearing a man down.

The cafeteria more closely resembled a quiet, elegant restaurant than a person's idea of a hospital cafeteria. He found himself a table that wasn't occupied and dragged a second chair around so he could prop his leg on it. Then whittled away the next hour by nursing a bottomless cup of strong coffee and pushing a ridiculously mild enchilada around his plate. The chef could have used a few tips from Emily.

"You should have ordered the roast beef," a deep voice said next to him. "It's overcooked and dry, but it's a lot better than that crud."

Jefferson's head swiveled. He looked up at the dark-haired man who'd seemingly appeared out of nowhere. Shock held him still for a long moment. "Well," he finally mused. "Fancy seeing you here."

Sawyer Clay, eldest brother of the Clay crew, grinned wryly and clapped his brother on the shoulder. "Good to see you, too." He turned away briefly to signal the waitress for a cup of coffee. Then he took over the chair that Jefferson's boot had kindly vacated. He shook his head. "Damn, Jefferson, you look like something the cat dragged in."

"Another bit of Clay wisdom," Jefferson grimaced.

He knew he looked beat. He *felt* beat. "I have a feeling your presence here is no coincidence. So cut to the chase. Why are you here?"

Sawyer's dark head turned as he leisurely studied the room. "It's been a while since I was here," he said. "But I see nothing's changed. Do they still have that nurse upstairs…what was her name? Bertha?"

Jefferson noticed the gold insignia on his brother's dark blue uniform. Yet another notch up the ladder. He also noticed the way Sawyer hadn't answered his question. "Beulah," he supplied grimly.

"Beulah," Sawyer repeated. He grinned wickedly. "I've never seen a nurse who filled out her uniform like that."

"You're crazy. She might look like something out of a teenage boy's fantasy, but she's got the temperament of a…geez, I can't think of anything bad enough to describe that devil-in-nurse's-white."

"You just don't know how to handle her."

"Who wants to handle her? I see her coming and head the opposite direction."

Sawyer chuckled softly. He removed his coffee cup from the saucer and poured about half the cup's steaming contents into the saucer.

Jefferson watched his brother drink his coffee from the nearly flat saucer. "I haven't seen anybody do that in a while," he commented, putting away for the moment the questions he had for his brother. Questions like why his big brother, Mr. Navy-All-the-Way, was here at this private medical complex. Like why Sawyer even knew of its existence, much less Beulah's existence.

Sawyer set the saucer down, managing not to spill a single drop. "Proving that you haven't been home in *a while,*" he said. "Squire never drinks coffee from the cup. It's the only way to inhale hot coffee the way he does.''

''Well, I've known other Swedes who don't insist it's the only way to properly drink coffee. Despite what Squire maintains,'' Jefferson said. He'd never gotten the hang of drinking out of saucers. Oh, he'd tried it often enough when he was a kid, trying to be like his older brother and his father. But he'd always managed to spill it or burn his fingers or something. He liked his coffee in a mug, thank you. Not in his lap.

Sawyer finished the coffee and nudged the empty saucer to one side. The time for chitchat was over. ''What did the doc say about your back?''

Jefferson squared the end of the knife with the end of the spoon. He wondered exactly how much Sawyer knew about his activities. About the events that had brought him here to this medical facility in the first place.

His lips twisted. Knowing Sawyer, he probably knew it all. His brother had the ability to find out anything he wanted about anybody. Apparently, even a brother who'd been so far underground that rumors had had him dead and buried. ''I'm surprised you haven't read the medical report yourself.'' He leaned back in his chair, crossing his arms over his chest. Despite his casual pose, his eyes were sharp on his brother's face. ''Or have you?''

Sawyer shrugged. ''I know the gist of it,'' he admitted. ''What are you going to do?''

''I've just been this route with the good Doctor Beauman. I really don't feel like getting into it again.''

''So you're still refusing to have the surgery. Well—'' Sawyer waved off the waitress before she could approach the table ''—I can't say I'm surprised.

You always were stubborn. Nobody ever could tell you what to do. Have you talked to Tris about it? No. I'd guess not. You obviously know where Emily's been living, too. That must have been interesting.'' He continued speaking, clearly not expecting an answer from Jefferson. "Do you have plans? No? Well, good. Because I came to take you home."

Jefferson's eyebrows shot up.

"Not my home," Sawyer elaborated. "My apartment isn't big enough for two Clays. I'm taking you to the ranch. Tonight."

Jefferson straightened abruptly. "The hell you are. I don't want to see Squire just now. Thanks all the same." Even if it did mean an early escape from the white-coats.

Sawyer studied him. And Jefferson felt his stomach clench.

"It's time to go home, Jefferson. Not just for your sake, either." Sawyer's lips tightened. "Squire's in the hospital. He had a heart attack a few days ago."

Emily's hand shook as she held the note up to the light, reading it through once again. "Oh, my God," she whispered. Her legs gave way and she sank onto the kitchen chair. The note fell from her fingers and drifted to the floor.

Squire was in the hospital, Tristan had written in his messy scrawl. He'd had a heart attack, and Emily should get to Wyoming as soon as she could. He'd tried calling her on the mobile but hadn't been able to get through. Eventually he'd gone ahead and flown home.

Of course he'd not been able to reach her on the mobile. Emily looked over at the bag she'd dropped just inside the door. The mobile was safely inside the bag.

She *had* taken it, as Tristan had insisted. Even if she'd been within range, with a dead battery, the phone had been useless.

Brushing her hair out of her face, she tried to think. She had to pack a few things to take with her. She had to let her office know that she'd be away for a while. She had to—

Please, oh please, oh please, let Squire be okay.

She reached for the phone and punched out the main number at the ranch. It would be nearly midnight there. She let it ring and ring, but no one picked up. Which probably meant that no one was at the big house. They were all at the hospital.

Her fingers trembled, but she managed to hang up and dial the airline. She booked herself on the last flight out that night. Which left her about twenty-five minutes to clean up and leave for the airport.

The shortage of time was a blessing. It didn't leave her any time to worry. But once she was on the plane...

The plane was only about a third full, and most of those people had tucked pillows under their heads, preparing to sleep all the way to Dallas. Emily studied the phone that was tucked in the back of the middle seat in front of her. Warily, she removed the phone from the seat and read the instructions. In minutes, it was ringing. After about thirty rings, however, she gave up. Twice more, before the plane landed in Dallas, she tried phoning the house, to no avail. Then, while sitting in the airport she thought of calling the hospital itself.

Stupid, stupid. She hurried over to the bank of pay phones and got out her calling card. It took two different calls, but she finally connected with the hospital's information desk and was informed that Squire was in ICU. His condition wasn't available.

Emily closed her eyes and leaned her forehead against her bent forearm lying across the top of the two-sided enclosure. Nausea clawed at her stomach. "Could I speak with the nurse's station in ICU, at least?"

"One moment," the disembodied voice told her, then the line clicked several times. She was treated, ever so briefly, to a moment of piped-in music. The line clicked once again. And the phone went dead. Rather, the connection went dead, since the dial tone told her very neatly that the phone itself was still operating.

Emily huffed, and glanced over her shoulder at the clock on the wall. She had about twenty minutes before her plane should be boarding. She began punching in the numbers once more that would connect her to the hospital.

"ICU, please." No more wasting time with information desks.

After just a few rings, the phone was picked up at the nurses' station. "This is Emily Nichols. You have a patient there, Squire Clay. Could you tell me what his condition is please?"

"Just a moment." On hold again. "Are you immediate family?"

Emily thought she might throw up right there. She swallowed. "Yes." It was close enough to the truth.

"Just a moment." Hold, once more. "Ma'am? Mr. Clay's condition is critical—"

Oh, God, please—

"—but stable. He has some family in the waiting room. Would you like me to connect you?"

Emily barely had time to answer before the nurse had transferred her call and it was ringing again. And ringing. And ringing.

Finally it was picked up. But the woman who an-

Jefferson looked over his shoulder. "Yes."

He watched Tristan nod again and stand. His younger brother ran his long fingers through his blond hair and stretched. Tristan rubbed his chin and looked back at Jefferson through narrowed eyes. "Then I guess the way is finally clear for me."

"I'm not in the mood for games, Tris."

"Neither am I, Jeff," Tristan said steadily.

There was a sick feeling swelling in the pit of Jefferson's stomach. "You're not interested in her that way."

Tristan cocked his head slightly. "Says who?" His eyebrows rose. "You? You're not even going to be around by tomorrow. Emily and I *do* live together."

Jefferson's knuckles whitened. "She's not interested in you, either, Tris, so just forget it. It's not working."

Tristan's jaw tightened, and he stepped closer to Jefferson. His voice was very low. "Listen up, Jefferson, and listen good. Em and I aren't kids anymore. We've been sharing this place for a good while now. We'll be sharing this place after you leave again. She wants a life you're not going to give her, and I'm tired of watching her wait. When I take her into my bed you can take it to the bank that she won't be thinking about you. She'll be thinking about me." He leaned closer and his voice dropped another notch. "She'll be thinking about the babies I'm planting in her flat little belly."

Jefferson's duffel hit the floor. "You so much as lay a hand on her and I'll—"

"You'll what?" Tristan straightened and his lips twisted. "You're not going to be around to witness anything. But if you leave some sort of address, I'll be sure you get a wedding invitation."

His palms itched. The hair on the back of his neck

swered told Emily that there was no one in the waiting room beside herself. Though she`did say that there had been a few men in and out earlier. Emily thanked the woman and hung up. She glanced at the clock again and tried dialing the house once more. But her efforts were futile.

Swallowing a wad of tears, Emily gathered her tote bag up and returned to the gate just in time to board.

The morning sun was steadily rising when Emily finally neared the main gate of the Clay ranch. Her tired eyes absently noticed the new iron sign proclaiming the boundary of the Double-C, and it was second nature for her to drive up next to the big metal mailbox alongside the road. She reached through the window and pulled out a large stack of envelopes, packages and circulars, which she dumped on the seat beside her. The newspaper box was on a sturdy post next to the mailbox, and she inched forward in the car and with her fingers snagged the bound-up paper. Tossing it onto the mail, she turned sharply and drove through the open gate.

Dust billowed and rolled behind her car as she left the pavement for the hard-packed dirt road, and she rolled up the windows and turned on the air-conditioning. She still had a few miles to go.

When the buildings came into sight, the car was covered with a film of tan dust. Emily coasted to a stop and for just a moment she didn't worry about Squire. Didn't worry about Jefferson. She didn't worry about anything. She just sat, her arms folded across the steering wheel, as she looked through the slick sheen of threatening tears.

Directly ahead stood the big house. Its sturdy stone and wood lines meandered from the central two-story structure to the right and the left with the additions that had been added here and there over the years. A porch ran the entire width of the front, and geraniums bloomed from the window boxes. Lilac bushes clustered at the south corner of the house. A grouping of aspens stood off to the side in the circular lawn situated in front of the house. Even from her distance, she could see the golden retriever sleeping in the soft green grass beneath the trees.

She was home.

She blinked and took a long, deep breath. She drove up around the circle drive, parking between the lawn and the house. The car door squeaked faintly as she pushed it open, and she climbed out, arching her back. She looked around, but all was silent. It wasn't a usual sight for the Double-C. Even the dog didn't raise her head.

The worry was back, and she grabbed the mail and paper, shut the car door and headed for the house, automatically bypassing the wide double-doored front entry. Her tennis shoes crunched over the gravel drive then sank into the soft green grass surrounding the house as she headed past the lilac bushes to the rear.

She entered through the mudroom, where the wooden screen door slapped closed behind her with an achingly familiar sound. Cowboy hats hung from the rack on the wall, and there were several sets of cowboy boots lying in the mudroom all in varying states, from dusty to muddy, to— Her nose wrinkled and she pushed open the door to the kitchen.

"Well, there she is." Matthew Clay rose from the oblong oak table that had held center stage of the spacious kitchen for as long as Emily could remember. He swung his long leg over his chair and reached Emily in just two steps before engulfing her in his big hug. "Tris said you'd make your way here one way or the other." He dropped a kiss on her cheek and lifted his head to study her with his nearly translucent blue eyes. "How ya doing, peanut?"

She shrugged, sharing his feeling smile. "About the same as you, I suppose." He let her go, and she tossed the mail onto the table before heading for the commercial-size steel refrigerator across the room. "How's Squire?" She pulled out a cold bottle of apple juice and drank nearly half of it in one swallow.

Matthew ran his hand over his closely cropped blond hair. "He's alive," he said bluntly.

Emily's teeth chattered before she clenched her jaw. She looked away from Matthew's piercing eyes and stared blindly out the wide uncurtained windows looking over the recently mown backyard. She swallowed the lump blocking her throat. "Is he going to stay that way?"

"Damn straight he is," another voice said.

Emily looked over her shoulder to the doorway leading into the dining room. "Hi, Daniel." She set her apple juice on the counter and went over to receive another Clay hug.

"Hey, babycakes," the fourth Clay son said as he swung her into his arms. He planted a kiss on her lips before letting her feet once more find the floor. "Don't you worry about Squire, hear? He's a stubborn mule and not about to leave this earth before someone starts giving him grandkids to spoil."

Matthew snorted and Daniel shrugged. "It's true, isn't it? 'Cept it'll probably be up to Em here to have the babies. Since none of us seem inclined to procreate."

Emily's smile faded at the corners. She tilted her head, and her hair slid forward as she retrieved her apple juice. She swallowed the rest of the juice and cradled the squat round bottle in the palm of her hand. "Does Sawyer know about Squire?" Does Jefferson?

Daniel nodded and plucked the coffeepot from the stove. He filled his mug and topped off Matthew's before returning the blackened enamel pot to the stove. He seemed about to say something, but he just nodded again and sank down into one of the sturdy chairs at the table. Matthew joined him at the table.

"Where's Tristan?"

"Right here." He appeared through the same doorway as Daniel had. He bussed her cheek and poured himself a mug of coffee. "How was Mexico?"

"Fine, I guess."

"I tried to get hold of you."

"I know." Emily grimaced. "The battery was dead," she admitted. "If only I'd checked it…I could have…"

"Could have been here a day earlier, is all," Tristan finished. "And Squire's been unconscious the whole time. Don't sweat it, Em. Sawyer's plane didn't get in until last night, and then—"

"We all spent most of the night at the hospital, cooling our heels in the damn waiting room," Daniel put in.

"I tried calling both places." Emily told them of her efforts to get hold of somebody. "Once I landed, I couldn't decide whether to go to the hospital or come here first." It was sheer cowardice that kept her from going straight to the hospital.

"We'll drive down to the hospital a little later this morning," Matthew told her. "It'll give you a chance to rest up while we finish off a few chores."

"Where is everybody?" Emily asked. "I expected you all to be in the middle of combining."

"We've got a crew coming in day after tomorrow. Between trips to the hospital and the work around here, we're keeping busy. Joe's a big help."

Emily knew Matthew was referring to Joe Greene, the foreman he'd hired a couple years ago. Joe and his wife, Maggie, who served as housekeeper and cook, lived in the tidy brick house situated on the far side of the ranch buildings.

"Speaking of chores..." Matthew lifted his coffee mug again for a long drink, then plunked it onto the table. It seemed to be a signal for his brothers to also rise as there was a general exodus.

Even Tristan, computer hacker extraordinaire, followed.

"Tristan?" Emily called him just before he disappeared after his older brothers. "Squire...you said he's been unconscious? Is he—" she broke off.

"He had a triple bypass, sweet pea. He's in tough shape. But he's a tough old man. And the tests they've run are promising." He smiled encouragingly, even though his eyes couldn't quite match the smile. "The best thing for him is the rest he's getting. And knowing we're all here for him." He smiled again and went after his brothers.

With the absence of the men, the kitchen loomed large, empty and silent. Emily hugged her arms to her and rubbed her elbows as she looked around her. The room hadn't changed much since the day Squire had brought her home. She'd been terrified. Feeling like her world had ended.

Squire had brought her into the kitchen, and the boys had all been sitting around that big oak table. All except

Sawyer, anyway. He'd already gone off on his own by then. But the rest of them had been sitting there. Shoveling down their supper with a small semblance of manners, even while they boisterously tried to top each other's accounting of their day. They'd eyed her curiously for a few moments. Then Jefferson had pushed out the empty seat between him and Tristan, and Emily had climbed onto the chair. She'd been a part of their family ever since.

Swallowing, Emily ran her fingertips over the chair at the head of the table. Squire's.

"Seems strange for the old man not to be sitting there telling us how to live our lives, doesn't it?"

Emily whirled. She smiled faintly at Sawyer, nodding. "Very strange." She glanced at the eldest Clay son. His hair was going silver at the temples, and he very much resembled the father they spoke of. The Clay men were nothing if not striking. "It seems we've all been called back to the ranch," she murmured. Where was Jefferson?

Sawyer passed by for the coffeepot, dropping a kiss on the top of her head. "Where is everybody?"

"Chores. Sawyer..."

He turned, raising his eyebrows as she hesitated.

Emily bit her lip, flushing. "Never mind."

He turned back to pouring a mug of coffee and grabbed a saucer from the cupboard. "Spit it out, Emily."

"You sound like Squire."

His wide shoulders rose and fell. "So I've been told." He laughed shortly. With his usual economy of movements, he sat at the table and poured the coffee into the saucer.

Emily closed her fingers over the top of one of the chairs. "You know everything about everybody..."

Sawyer's lips twitched. "Well, not quite."

"But, you uh, well...oh, hell. Do you know where Jefferson is? He left San Diego just last week, and he was in terrible shape, Sawyer. He wouldn't tell me...not that I expected him to, of course, I mean, he never does...but he didn't even talk to Tristan...and I'm just really—"

"Whoa!" Sawyer lifted his hand and she fell silent. "Take a breath before you pass out. And yes, I do know where Jefferson is. He's here."

Emily caught her breath. "Then he *did* come here when he left California."

"No. He didn't get here until last night. He flew in with me."

"Then where—"

"You'll have to ask him that." He sipped his coffee, watching her over the rim of the saucer.

Emily looked away from Sawyer. "Is he, uh, in his room?"

He shrugged. "Have no idea."

The screen door to the kitchen squeaked and Daniel appeared. "Hey, Em...oh, great, Sawyer, come out here for a minute, will ya? That damned horny horse of Matt's kicked out half his stall trying to get to the mares and we need your help for a sec."

Emily followed the men out. But she turned toward her rental car to retrieve her suitcase when they headed for the horse barn. She'd have time to grab a shower and freshen up before they went to the hospital. She also needed to call her office, knowing that the hasty message she'd left on Stuart's voice mail had barely been coherent. She tried focusing her thoughts on the simple tasks. But her tangled thoughts were on Squire. And Jefferson. Lord, how was she going to face Jefferson?

As she headed back to the house, a breeze kicked up. She paused for a moment, squinting against the dust swirling through the air, and grabbed her hair with her free hand. In a moment the breeze had passed and she let go of her hair, shaking the bangs out of her eyes. She supposed it was the faint squeak of the screen door that caught her attention. Or maybe it was just instinct.

When she looked up, Jefferson was slouched in the doorway. He wore jeans faded white, and a raggedy beige cotton-knit shirt clung softly to his shoulders, which despite his thinness, were as wide as ever. His wet hair was dark and combed starkly away from the sharp angles of his face.

He was beautiful.

Emily's fingers tightened on the suitcase handle. Part of her wanted to throw the luggage back in the car and hightail it out of there. The other part, the stronger part, wanted to run into his arms and never let him go.

Hardly breathing, she climbed the two steps into the mudroom and was silently relieved when he shifted, giving her room to pass. There would be no ''Clay hug'' from Jefferson, brotherly or otherwise. She couldn't think of a single thing to say. Not without embarrassing herself, anyway. She stepped across the mudroom and into the kitchen.

''Emily.''

She swallowed, schooled her expression and glanced back at him over her shoulder. ''Yes?''

His own expression was inscrutable. ''Are you all right?''

"Fine," she said evenly. "You?" She watched a muscle tick in his jaw.

"Fine," he returned.

He didn't add anything, and Emily turned once more to head upstairs to the room she'd used since childhood.

"Emily—"

Her shoulders tightened, and like a coward she pretended not to hear as she hurried up the stairs, the suitcases bumping her legs.

Jefferson watched her hair swish against her back as she raced up the stairs. Her denim jeans were well washed and lovingly fit her curves. He stood at the foot of the stairs until long after she'd disappeared. Until he heard the sound of water rushing through the pipes, and he knew she was taking a shower.

The knowledge brought all sorts of visions to his mind. None of them decent. And none of them wise, particularly when he was under Squire's roof. Biting off a curse, he went back to the kitchen and limped his way outside.

Two hours later, Emily propped her hands on her hips and glared at Tristan. "Why on earth shouldn't I drive myself to the hospital? I've been driving these roads for half of my life! I'm no more distraught over Squire than you are. And I'm not likely to drive myself into a ditch because I'm worried. Good Lord, Tristan, I managed to get myself to Wyoming without your overbearing assistance—"

"Stop arguing," Matthew ordered abruptly, walking up behind them. "You've been sniping at each other for ten minutes. Tris, you know darn well there isn't room for all of us to go in one vehicle, so quit bugging Emily. She can go to the hospital however she wants, and she's already said she doesn't want to be cooped up in the Blazer with the rest of us. She could drive one of the pickups if she wanted.''

The screen door squeaked open and slammed shut and Tristan suddenly capitulated. He shrugged, tugged a lock of Emily's hair and opened the passenger door to the rental. ''I'll ride with you, then,'' he announced.

''What a nut,'' Emily grumbled as she went around to the driver's side of her rental. Then she noticed what she hadn't before, because Tristan had been acting so impossible. Jefferson stood several feet away, his legs braced and his weight obviously leaning on the cane. The sunlight struck him full in the face and his eyes were narrowed as he watched Emily.

Her throat went dry. He looked so...*alone*. Even standing mere feet away from his passel of brothers. She moistened her lips. His name was a whisper on her lips.

''Yo, Jeff!'' Daniel called as he climbed into the rear seat of Matthew's Blazer. ''Load it up, man.''

Jefferson's head slowly swiveled to the other vehicle. Emily could see the muscle ticking in his jaw, and he finally moved over to the truck, climbing into the front passenger seat. His door slammed shut and Emily lowered herself into the rental.

Tristan's knees were practically buckled up beneath his chin. ''You just gonna sit here, or are we going to follow Matt to the hospital?''

She started the engine and placed her hands on the sun-heated steering wheel, flexing her fingers. ''I don't know if I can handle this,'' she muttered.

''Seeing Squire in the hospital?'' Tristan reached around under the seat and managed to scoot it back a few more precious inches. ''You'll manage just fine.'' He reached over and flipped on the air-conditioning.

"I don't mean just Squire," Emily admitted as she followed the Blazer away from the ranch.

"You'll manage Jefferson, too, sweet pea."

She choked on a miserable laugh. "That'll be a first."

Chapter Five

The visitation policy in the Intensive Care Unit would allow only two family members in at a time. Emily was shaking so badly that she thought she might be sick, and she was glad when Matthew and Sawyer went first. She, Jefferson, Daniel and Tristan remained in the waiting room located around the corner from ICU. The room was nearly full of people, and they had to split up in order to find a seat.

It took Daniel all of two minutes before he rose again, obviously restless. He murmured something to Jefferson and strode out of the room. Minutes later, she saw him outside through the windows that overlooked a small grassy area behind the hospital.

He stood with his back to the building, his dark gold hair ruffling in the faint breeze. He lit a cigarette, then moved abruptly and strode out of sight.

Emily looked down at her hands, twisted together in

her lap. She smoothed the cuff of her off-white linen shorts. A teenager turned on the television situated in the corner of the room. The phone rang. The two people sitting to her left continued discussing an article they'd read in that morning's newspaper.

She looked up, her gaze colliding with Jefferson's. His expression inscrutable, he didn't bother hiding the fact that he'd been studying her. She wished that she'd worn something with sleeves. The sleeveless vest that matched her shorts was cool and comfortable. But it also revealed the fading yellow outline of the bruises he'd left on her arms. A movement in the doorway caught his attention, and he looked away briefly. Long enough for her to see that muscle in his jaw. Still ticking.

Matthew and Sawyer returned. Emily looked closely at them, her stomach clenching anew at their expressions. She rose nervously, and Sawyer closed his palm over her shoulder.

"Daniel went in a minute ago," Sawyer told them. Tristan rose instantly and headed to ICU. Sawyer squeezed her shoulder once more, then left, saying he needed some coffee.

A middle-aged couple departed, emptying the two seats next to Jefferson. Matthew nudged her toward them, taking the seat in the middle between her and Jefferson.

"What's he like this morning?" Jefferson asked.

"The nurse said he had a good night," Matthew answered. "And his color's quite a bit better."

Jefferson twirled his cane between his palms. "Still unconscious?"

Matthew nodded. His chest rose and fell in a deep sigh, and he leaned his head back against the wall behind the chairs.

Emily twisted the narrow leather strap of her small purse into a knot. "How did it happen? I mean, has Squire been having heart problems all along? He never said anything. Did he?"

"Not a word." Matthew stretched his legs out before him and crossed his ankles. He clasped his hands together across his flat stomach and looked down at his thumbs. "But we all know Squire. He never gives anything away. Turns out he's been seeing a cardiologist here in Casper for the past couple years. Anyway, he'd ridden Carbon out to do some fishing."

Jefferson's head lifted at the horse's name. He himself had bought the ornery young colt many years ago. Back when he'd still been in Squire's good graces. Before he'd made the mistake of sharing his conflicting feelings toward Emily with Squire.

"Near as we can tell," Matthew continued, "he found some downed fence. Stock was probably straying." He pressed his thumbs together. "Instead of riding back and sending someone else out to round 'em up and fix the fence, he stayed and did it himself." He pinched the bridge of his nose. "Carbon came back alone. When we found Squire, he was unconscious. Lying next to the fence he'd repaired. The wire cutters were still in his hand." He shook his head. "Damned stubborn old man."

Suddenly his legs jackknifed and he stood. "I need some fresh air."

Emily glanced across the empty seat at Jefferson. His chin was propped on his fist, his thumb moving across his tight lips. His bad leg was stretched out straight, the tip of his boot rhythmically ticking an inch or so back and forth. His attention was focused ahead.

She wished he'd say something. Anything. And

called herself a coward for not being able to say anything herself. Tears threatened again and she blinked
rapidly. Crying was not going to do anybody a bit of
good. She pulled a tissue from her purse and surreptitiously wiped her eyes and nose.

Jefferson's arm reached across the empty space between them and he took her hand in his, threading her
fingers through his own. She shot him a startled glance.
His attention was still focused forward. But his palm
was warm and dry against hers.

For now, it was enough.

Before long, Daniel returned. "Tristan went to talk
to the cardiologist himself," he told them. "You guys
can go in now."

Jefferson let go of her hand, and Emily tried not to
feel bereft. She drew in a steadying breath and rose. She
placed the strap of her purse over her shoulder. Without
waiting for Jefferson, Emily walked over to the swinging doors leading into ICU. She paused, then straightened her shoulders and pushed through the doors. She
hadn't been raised like a Clay for nothing. She knew
Jefferson was right behind her but didn't let herself focus on that. If she did, she knew she'd fall apart.

The nurses' station was situated in the center of the
unit, with the beds radiating out like spokes of a wheel.
Glass walls separated the beds from each other, but only
heavy white curtains separated the beds from the nursing station. Squire was in the very first "room." She
saw him as soon as she cleared the double doors, and
stopped short.

Jefferson nearly bumped into her, and he closed his
hand over the back of her neck.

Emily swallowed and moved out from his touch, entering Squire's cubicle. Tubes snaked out of his nose

and his arms, and machines surrounded his bed. If it weren't for all that, she'd have suspected that he was merely sleeping. His thick silvered hair sprang back from his chiseled forehead, and he was slightly pale beneath his permanently tanned skin. A stark white bandage covered most of his bare chest and a pale blue sheet covered him to his waist.

"Do you think he knows we're here?"

Jefferson nodded and moved around to the opposite side of the bed. He was leaning hard on the cane.

Now that she'd seen Squire, Emily didn't feel quite so terrified. Her instincts told her that everything would be all right. Hoping that those instincts weren't leading her astray, she sank into the chair situated next to the bed and gently touched Squire's hand.

She leaned over to kiss his weathered cheek. "Squire, it's Emily. You didn't have to go to all this trouble just to get us home for a visit, you know." She looked up at Jefferson. His lips were pursed and his eyes narrowed as he looked down at his father. She positively ached with his buried pain. Squire wasn't the only Clay man who found it hard to "give anything away" as Matthew had put it earlier.

All too quickly, their allotted five minutes were up, yet Jefferson hadn't said a word to his father. Emily felt like crying. Or hitting him. Either one would have made her feel better. She squelched both urges and pressed a gentle kiss to Squire's cool cheek, promising him that she'd return soon to see him.

The rest of the men were back in the waiting room. Emily took one look at Tristan, and the tears started squeezing out of her eyes again. He enclosed her in his gentle bear hug, and she only cried harder. As much as she loved Tristan, it was Jefferson's arms she wanted around her. But he was standing over by the window, his expression brooding as he watched the rest of them.

"Why don't we head across the street to that restaurant and grab some lunch. Then you all could go on back to the ranch," Sawyer suggested, his eyes playing over his brothers and Emily. "I can stick around here, and somebody can come and get me tonight when visiting hours end."

Daniel needed no second urging. He was nodding and heading outside almost before Sawyer finished speaking. Matthew was obviously torn, wanting to stay. Needing to go. He had work to take care of.

"Emily?" Tristan nudged her for her opinion.

She swiped her cheeks and nodded tiredly.

Sawyer caught Jefferson's glance, who shrugged. "Okay then."

They all trooped out and headed for the restaurant. It took several minutes for them to set up a table to accommodate all six of them. Despite Emily's best efforts, she ended up seated next to Jefferson. That's what she got for stopping first at the rest room to freshen her face.

Tristan sat directly across the table from Jefferson, and he smiled blandly. She could have kicked him, knowing that he was responsible for the seating arrangement.

The young waitress took one look at the men sitting around the table and brightened. Emily had to bite back a chuckle when, after returning with their orders of iced tea all around, the girl, "I'll be your server—call me Candy," had freshened her pale lipstick and loosened the top few buttons of her fitted pink uniform.

She opened the laminated menu and automatically glanced over the selections, even though she wasn't sure her stomach really wanted food. She closed the menu and laid it on the table alongside her tea.

"Decided already?" Daniel's menu was lying on the table also and he nudged the container of artificial sweetener toward her. "Let me guess. French dip. Right?"

She took a little packet and ripped it open, pouring it into her tea. "Call me consistent."

"Consistent!" Tristan chuckled. "She's ordered that for lunch or supper in damn near every restaurant we've ever been in since she was ten years old."

"So?" Emily wasn't fazed in the least. "I can't help it if I know what I like."

She felt Jefferson shift beside her. When she glanced at him, he was leaning over to retrieve his napkin from the floor.

"Well," she pulled her attention back from the way his navy blue shirt stretched taut across his long back, "you'd better decide yourself what you want mighty quick. Before Candy, there, comes back to get the order."

Daniel sipped his tea and looked across the room to where the waitress was taking an order from a young family. "Whatcha want to bet she's gonna have another button undone when she comes back?" He set his glass down and leaned slightly forward. "She'll lean over your shoulder again, Tris, and give you a real view."

Matthew shook his head. Sawyer looked bored. Tristan laughed. Jefferson shifted again, and his knee brushed against hers.

When Candy returned, Daniel won the bet.

That day set the pattern for the ones that followed. They'd all go to the hospital in the same two vehicles. They had lunch at the same restaurant each day. Then they'd all return to the ranch, with one of the brothers staying behind. The second day, Daniel volunteered to stay. On the third, Matthew. And so it went. For the next several days.

Five days passed since she'd first seen Squire in the hospital before she found herself back in Squire's cubicle with Jefferson. Somehow, between the two of them avoiding each other, they'd managed to not say three words to each other since that first day at the hospital. She'd been sure not to sit next to him at the restaurant. Only, she'd found it nearly as heartbreaking to watch him over lunch as it had been to sit beside him.

She'd nearly fallen off her waiting room chair when Jefferson said he'd accompany her to ICU that morning.

Tristan shot her a brows-raised look, but nobody else seemed to think anything of Jefferson's quiet comment.

So that's how she came to be sitting once again in Squire's room, with Jefferson holding up the wall on the opposite side of the bed. It no longer surprised her that he didn't seem inclined to say anything.

But she was determined not to brood over Jefferson. At least not in Squire's ICU cubicle. "Squire, we really want you to wake up," she said in a clear voice, after kissing him hello. "Matt needs to know about an invoice he got for some equipment it looks like you ordered. And I'm sure I saw Daniel trying to sneak a smoke earlier. You know how hard it was for him to quit last year." She pushed out her lip and glanced toward Jefferson. He wasn't looking at the man in the bed. He was staring at Emily, his eyes dark and unreadable.

She swallowed and moistened her lips. "I'm going to run out of leave time from work next week and I expect you to be up by then," she continued. "Joe

Greene's got a crew in now. Combining should be done this week."

She picked up his cool hand and smoothed her thumb over the back. "There's a pretty nurse just a few feet away," she wheedled. "If you'd just wake up, I'll bet you'd have her swept off her feet in no time at all with just one look from those blue eyes of yours."

She slid a glance over her shoulder at the two nurses manning the desk just a few feet away. One was very definitely a man. The other nurse's gray hair was so tightly curled next to her head that it almost looked like wool, and she looked about two days away from retirement. "She's got long auburn hair, Squire."

She ignored Jefferson's raised eyebrows. "And beautiful green eyes," she added for good measure. "But you should wake up and see for yourself."

She fell silent for a few moments. Jefferson still said not a word. "Bird's looking real good," she said. "You were right about his temperament when we picked him out at that auction. But I'm still glad we didn't have him gelded. His bloodline would be good to breed. You're gonna have to get well quick, though, or by the time I get back, he won't be fit to ride for a month of Sundays."

She fell silent as the male nurse entered the room. He smiled cheerfully and after looking at the machines, made a few notations on the chart at the foot of Squire's bed, then left again.

Emily lifted Squire's hand and held it to her cheek. She closed her eyes. "Jefferson's here too, Squire," she finally said. "He's right here on the other side of your bed. Actually, he looks almost worse than you do." She opened her eyes, defiantly ignoring the glint that had appeared in Jefferson's. "He's added a couple of new

scars to his ugly mug. Maybe if you'd wake up, he'll
tell you what he's been doing the past few years.''

Jefferson snorted. "Not likely."

"Ah, he speaks," Emily quipped. Squire's fingers
flexed against hers, as if in agreement. Startled, she
looked at the man in the bed. "Squire?"

"What is it?"

"He moved his hand, Jefferson." She leaned closer
to Squire. "Squire, can you hear me? Squeeze my fingers again. Oh, please Squire, just squeeze my fingers
again."

She nearly shot out of the chair when she felt the
faint pressure against her fingers. She leaned forward
and kissed Squire's cheek again. "I'm going to get the
nurse," she said and gently laid Squire's hand back on
the mattress.

Jefferson readjusted his grip on the cane. He could
see Emily talking urgently to the older nurse. "Come
on, old man," he said softly. "I didn't come all the way
here to keep watching you lie in that bed like a sack of
feed."

Emily stuck her head back in. "Has he moved again?
Oh, for God's sake, Jefferson, sit down and hold his
hand!" She went back to the nurse's station.

"I guess she told me, didn't she." Jefferson couldn't
help the slight grin on his face as he did as she'd ordered. Well, he sat down, at least. He didn't hold his
father's hand. He knew it wouldn't be what Squire
wanted.

"She can be pretty bossy, you know. Emily. Must be
the Clay influence." He looked for a long time at his
father, then propped his elbows on the edge of the bed.
"I know you can hear me, Squire. Maybe hearing me

talk to you will be annoying enough that you'll get your old carcass up and out of this place.''

He raked his fingers through his hair, his eyes skipping over the monitors. God, he hated hospitals. Hated the antiseptic smell. The quiet noises. ''I know I heard every damned word they whispered around me when I was in the hospital a while back.'' It was amazing how easily the words came when Squire was helpless to respond. ''Blasted medical people,'' he continued. ''Talking about you like you're dead, when all along you know exactly what's going on. Even if the old bod doesn't let you get it across to them.''

Emily stepped up behind him, her clean scent enveloping him. She laid her hand across his shoulder as she leaned forward. ''Squire, your doctor's going to be here soon. Promise me that you'll prove to him that I didn't imagine you squeezing my hand.''

Jefferson's jaw clenched. Her hair drifted across his shoulder. Touched his cheek. If he turned his head a few inches, his lips would touch her shoulder, left bare by the sleeveless white sweater she wore. She'd been torturing him all week wearing an assortment of skimpy, sleeveless things.

Squire's lashes moved. Once. Twice. Then lifted infinitesimally until a pale blue narrowly gleamed from between his thick, spiky lashes. His lips parted, and, still leaning across Jefferson, Emily held the plastic cup with the bendable straw to Squire's lips. His eyes closed again as he gathered the energy to sip water through the straw.

Squire sighed and relaxed, and Emily put the cup back on the table beside the bed. Her fingers dug into Jefferson's shoulder, and she pressed her head against the top of Jefferson's. He knew she was trying not to cry. Just as he knew, as Squire's eyes opened once again, the picture his father saw looking at the two of them beside his bed.

Jefferson's fingers were already closing over the handle of his cane, when Squire's lips moved.

"Get…away…" he mouthed.

Emily's head shot up, and Jefferson rose, his lips twisted. "Welcome back, old man." The chair scraped back with a sharp screech, and Jefferson limped out of the room.

Dismayed, Emily's eyes went back and forth between Jefferson's departing back and Squire's squinting eyes. "What—"

"Emily," Squire's voice could barely be heard. She stepped next to the bed, looking over her shoulder. Jefferson stopped only to say a brief word to the male nurse, who rounded the counter immediately and headed toward them.

"I'm here, Squire." She lifted his hand again and turned her attention back to him. His eyes were closed once more.

The nurse checked the monitors, flashed a light in Squire's eyes. "Looking good," he pronounced. "I'll notify his doctor that he's conscious. He needs some rest," he told Emily. "Why don't you come back this afternoon."

Emily jerked out a nod. She kissed Squire's hand, saying a silent prayer of thanks when he squeezed hers in return. She laid his hand on the bed. "I'll see you later, Squire."

She practically raced back to the waiting room. They were all there, except for Jefferson. She knew that he'd been there, however briefly. Obviously Jefferson had told his brothers that Squire was conscious. She knew that, just by looking at the collected relief on their faces.

"Where'd Jefferson go?"

"Back to the ranch," Tristan said.

"The Blazer?" She didn't understand why he'd leave the lot of them stranded at the hospital.

"He said he was going to find a cab or walk."

"Oh, for Pete's sake," Emily scraped her hair out of her eyes. "You can't be serious." Clearly, he was. "Why didn't he just wait until the rest of us went or have one of you drive him back?"

"If you'd hurry, you'll probably catch him down in the lobby," Daniel murmured close to her ear as he headed to the door.

"Stupid, stubborn Clays," Emily muttered. "I'll see you guys later." She decided not to wait on the elevator and raced down the stairwell instead. Her heart was pounding when she burst into the lobby, and she made herself take a huge, calming breath when she saw him leaning against the wall outside the hospital's main entrance.

One way or another she was going to find out what was going on between Jefferson and Squire. She might as well start with the son.

She straightened her purse strap and took another cleansing breath. When she walked through the automatic sliding glass doors, she knew her expression was calm. Jefferson didn't even glance at her when she took up a similar position right next to him.

Silently she stood beside him and watched a small bird hop around the grass growing beneath a young tree. It pecked at something unseen in the grass. A car slowly drove by, looking for a parking space, and the bird flew off. Emily took a faint breath. "You want to tell me what that was all about up there?"

"No."

"Come on, Jefferson. I know you weren't even surprised at what he said in there. It was like you expected it. Good grief, you were already half out of your seat when he…when he, um—"

Jefferson looked at her, his expression bland. "When he told me to get out."

"You don't know that's what he meant."

His eyebrows rose slightly. As if he couldn't believe she'd even suggest such a notion. He shook his head. "I know."

Emily moved around to face him. "Okay, so then why did he say it? Why on earth wouldn't he want you to be there?" There was no point in suggesting that Squire hadn't directed his comment straight at Jefferson.

"Leave it alone, Emily."

She crossed her arms. "I won't leave it alone." If he insisted he was simply a brother figure to her, then she'd treat him the way she would any of the rest of the Clays. At least she'd try. "Did the two of you argue? I know it can't have been recently, since until you showed up at Tristan's, you'd pretty well dropped off the face of the planet for more than two years. Is *that* why you were gone so long? Did you and Squire have some major falling out or something?"

"I said to drop it." Each word was bitten off between his teeth.

"Jefferson." Unable to contain herself, she reached up to touch his cheek. "Whatever it is, it can be fixed. I know it can."

"There is nothing to be fixed."

"You're just like him, you know." Emily folded her

arms once more. "Completely inflexible." She shook her head, disgusted. She opened her purse and rooted through its narrow confines for the single key to the rental. "Here," she held it out to him when she found it. "You can drive the rental back to the ranch. I'll ride with Matthew and the others when they leave."

He didn't take the key from her hand.

"You'd rather spend a fortune on a cab than use *my* rental? Assuming that a cab would even make the trip." She rocked back on her heels. She should have known she couldn't come out of a conversation with him unscathed.

"Don't do that." He bit off a curse. "Don't look at me like I just shot your puppy."

"I can't help it," she snapped. "Some of us haven't stomped out all semblance of emotion from our lives." She flipped open her purse and dropped the key back inside. "Get yourself back to the ranch however you want to." She spun on her heel.

He swore again and grabbed her arm before she'd gotten two feet. Angrily, she shrugged off his touch.

"I can't drive."

She stopped in the entryway to the hospital. Surely she'd misheard. His voice had been so low, she'd barely heard him. "What?"

Jefferson's jaw clenched. The glass doors slid shut. Opened. Shut. Opened. Emily finally stepped off the entryway, and the doors slid closed. She moved closer to him. "What did you say?"

His jaw set. "I said…I can't…drive."

She blinked. Talk about male pride. "Well, good grief, Jefferson, why didn't you just say so?" She extracted the key once again and headed toward the parking lot, still speaking. "Come on, then. I'll drive you back. Is it because the rental's a manual? The car you had in California was an automatic. Your knee won't let you work a clutch yet, I'll bet. How long is your knee going to take to heal, anyway?''

Jefferson closed his eyes briefly. ''A while,'' he said grimly, earning himself a quick look from Emily. But she didn't comment or question further, and he stepped away from the wall, following her slowly. She was cutting diagonally across the parking lot, slipping between two cars.

He followed, then nearly fell flat on his face when his boot caught on a cement parking stop. Swearing a blue streak, he shot his arm out and latched on to the side of the truck bed of the pickup backed into the parking space beside him. His hip banged painfully against the side of the truck, but he kept himself from landing on the ground. His cane rolled under the car on the other side.

Emily whirled around, gasping when she saw what had happened. She rushed back and went to grab him, but stopped cold at the expression in his eyes. Vulnerability wasn't something he'd chosen to share lately.

Giving him a moment, she dropped to her hands and knees and fished around for his cane from beneath the car. With it tucked under her arm, she stood and brushed the dust from her hands.

Fearing that he'd bite her head off if she tried to assist him, she silently handed him the cane and made herself turn around and continue to her car. She managed not to look back to see how he was progressing. But she did suck in a relieved breath when she went around to the passenger side to unlock the door and casually glanced across the top of the car to see that he was heading her way.

How on earth was she supposed to stick to her decision to move on with her life? How could she when every fiber of her soul was telling her that Jefferson needed her? Whether he admitted it or not.

Worrying the inside of her lower lip, she unlocked her side and climbed behind the wheel, starting the engine. She kept silent when Jefferson awkwardly maneuvered himself into the passenger seat. She turned up the radio when he stifled a groan. And she didn't offer to help him out of the car hours later when she pulled to a stop in front of the big house.

The back door was unlocked, as usual. She went into the kitchen, her ears perked to Jefferson's uneven gait. But the path around the house from the front was grass, and she heard nothing. She quickly raced into the dining room and peeped through the lace curtains hanging at the tall windows just in time to see him round the corner toward the back of the house. When the wooden screen door squeaked open and banged shut, she was standing in the kitchen, one arm propped on the counter near the sink.

She glanced up casually, her heart beating unevenly, then turned her attention to the leather sandal she was sliding from her foot. The piece of gravel that she'd picked up from the drive fell out, and she slid the shoe back on and tossed the little pebble in the trash.

Watching him from the corner of her eye, she headed for the refrigerator and pulled out an apple juice. ''Want one?'' She held up the bottle for him to see.

He shook his head, appearing as if he would just pass through the kitchen. Then he seemed to change his mind and abruptly pulled out a chair and sat down.

Emily closed the refrigerator door and joined him at the table. It was then that she noticed the blood streaking the palm of his right hand. She caught his wrist in her hand and turned his palm upward. "You've cut yourself."

He curled his fingers shut. "It's nothing."

"Don't be a mule," she muttered, pushing at his closed fist with her fingertips. "Let me see."

"I snagged it on the truck. No big deal."

Her eyebrows lowered and she let go. With a shrug, she picked up her juice and left.

Jefferson grimaced. He opened his hand and poked at the cut with his other. Fresh blood spurted through the shallow cut. He reached for the basket of paper napkins sitting in the center of the table and pressed a few to his palm. He'd get up and wash it off in a minute.

He lifted the wad of napkin, to see if the bleeding had stopped. It had. Pushing his left hand flat on the table, he began levering himself up off the chair, abruptly changed his mind and sank down.

Maybe he'd wash it off in five minutes.

He crumpled the napkin and left it on the table. It wasn't the cut on his palm that had him concerned. It was the unexpectedly sharp pain arrowing from his hip down toward his thigh. Hopefully he'd just bruised himself knocking into the truck and hadn't done any damage to the artificial hip he'd received in Germany.

He glared at his boots. As if they were to blame for catching on that parking stop. When he knew full well why his foot had dragged. His brain had told him he'd cleared that damned block of cement. The message just hadn't extended to his foot. Something that was happening more often than he liked.

Which was why he hadn't put himself behind the wheel of a car since he left San Diego. He'd probably end up killing someone if he did.

Emily came back into the room. Her bare feet padded softly across the wood-planked floor and she set a rectangular white box on the table. She opened the first aid kit, her attention on its contents. She'd pulled her hair back into a loose braid, and he could tell by the way her smooth jaw was drawn up all tight that she wasn't as calm as her expression indicated. She ripped open an antiseptic wipe and waited.

"This wasn't necessary." But he held up his hand, anyway. "I was going to clean it."

"Shut up."

For some reason his humor kicked in. He squelched the grin wanting to spring free. "Mule, huh?"

Her head tilted slightly to one side, and she firmly pressed the wipe to the cut.

"Ow!" He jerked his hand away, but she grabbed hold. "That stuff stings."

She spared him no mercy. "You're Mr. Macho," she said. "Surely you can stand a little antiseptic."

When the cut was clean, she dried it with a gauze pad and covered it with a plastic bandage. His palm still stung when she let go of his hand. "Brat. Squire should have spanked you more often."

"Huh! Squire never laid a hand on me, and you know it."

"Obviously."

Emily gathered up the trash and dropped it into the trash can beneath the sink. "The only one who ever dared to spank me was you, mister. That time when—"

"—you filched one of Squire's cigarettes and tried smoking it out in the barn. You nearly set fire to the loft trying to light that stupid thing."

"I did not nearly set fire to anything," she defended lightly. She remained at the sink, looking out the window. "You would never have even known I was up there if you hadn't taken that...that...*girl* in there to, um, make out."

"You were pretty pissed off. Such a dinky thing, too. Damned if you didn't punch me right in the stomach after I took away that cigarette and swatted your butt."

Emily's lips twisted. She rinsed out the dishrag and needlessly wiped down the sink rim. "I was fourteen," she said. And she had been angry with Jefferson for daring to bring that girl with him on his brief stay. So angry that she'd have done almost anything to get his attention away from that tall, blond, *curvy* female. She'd succeeded, all right. Just not in the way she'd planned. Jefferson had been disgusted with her, calling her careless and immature. He'd left the next day, taking Miss Curves with him.

"Fourteen or not, you were still dinky. That was the summer you went off to school, wasn't it?"

"Mmm." She began wiping off the counter. "I thought my bacon was saved when you came back unexpectedly." She rinsed the cloth again and squeezed the water out of it, watching the water drip into the white sink. "It seemed like fate to me. I was so sure you'd change Squire's mind about sending me." It had broken her heart that Jefferson hadn't even tried.

He'd breezed in and breezed right back out again within less than twenty-four hours. And though she received a tattered postcard from him now and then over the years, and the cassette tapes each and every Christmas, she'd seen him only once in person from the time she'd left for boarding school and the time she'd been in college.

She closed her palms over the edge of the sink, curving her fingers down. For a long minute they were both silent. "Jefferson?"

"Yeah?"

She closed her eyes, willing her heart not to jump out of her chest. "Why did you come to see me at school that time?" She heard the creak of his chair as he shifted his weight. "When I was nineteen," she added unnecessarily.

"You'd just had a birthday. You hadn't made it back home yet that year. Squire wanted to give you—"

"Yes," she said, interrupting his bland explanation. "I know all that. Squire wanted to make sure I received that pearl necklace of your mother's safely, and he didn't trust the mail. But he could have brought it himself when he came to visit me, or just waited until I came home for vacation." She looked over her shoulder. "Why *you*?"

He was fiddling with the scissors from the first aid kit. "Just turned out that way. I'd been by here. Saw Squire. When he found out I was on my way to Washington, he asked me to stop off and give you your birthday gift."

She'd heard the story before. Yet she kept hoping... "You stayed in New Hampshire nearly a week."

"I had some time on my hands." He turned the scissors point down and balanced his hand atop them.

"So you were just...passing the time, then." She didn't know why she kept at this. It was like picking at an old wound. Painful. Yet morbidly fascinating.

"What do you want me to say?" He sighed and flipped the scissors into the box. "Well, Emily? Are we talking about the fact that I visited you at school, or are we talking about the fact that I practically stole your innocence while I was there?"

Emily's breath dissipated, leaving her light-headed. She moistened her lips and slipped into a chair across the table. "It wasn't *stealing*," she managed. They'd spent five solid days together. Walking together. Talking. Laughing. Falling in love, or so she'd thought. Each night when he'd left her to return to his motel room, it had been harder and harder to let him leave. And then that night, when his chaste kiss on her forehead had turned into something more...

"Why do you insist on rehashing this?"

"You never answer!"

He stifled a curse. "You were barely nineteen."

"Is that why you stopped? Because I didn't have any experience and wasn't any good at it? Did you get bored? You wanted to find some other way to kill some time? What?"

He made an exasperated sound. "For Pete's sake—"

"Wait!" She scrambled out of her chair, kneeling before him before he could get up and leave. "I have to know, Jefferson. Can't you understand that?" Her hands closed urgently over his legs, her fingers pressing into him. "I have to know!"

"You want to know?" His eyes darkened and the muscle in his jaw twitched. "Then know this." He moved suddenly and Emily found her face captured between his hard hands. He covered her mouth with his, forcing open her lips and sweeping inside.

One hand went to her nape and held her still while he ravaged her mouth. By the time he lifted his head, Emily was trembling. She could taste the faint coppery tang of blood from her lip yet refused to cry. Though she wanted to throw herself on the floor and weep. Weep for all the pain she sensed in him. Pain that he kept hidden behind his rough actions.

"I wanted to do that," he said baldly. "When you were nineteen." His hand was like iron about her neck. "Just looking at you made me hard." He watched her cheeks pinken. Watched the tip of her tongue sneak out and touch her upper lip.

"I wanted to tear off your shirt," he growled. "I wanted to do this." He dropped his hand to her breast and molded the fullness with a less-than-gentle touch. He leaned over, and his breath was harsh against her ear. "I wanted to tear off your panties," he said, running his hand from her breast to the flat of her stomach. "I wanted to touch you." He rotated his palm and his fingers arrowed lower. "*There.* I wanted to taste you. *There.*" His hard hand slipped between her thighs. "You were dreaming of roses and candlelight and all I wanted was to find a bed and bury myself in you. Right there. Hell, a bed wasn't even necessary."

Emily swayed. His touch branded her. Then, just as suddenly as he'd swooped over her, he sat back, withdrawing his hands. His warmth.

"You damn sure weren't prepared for that when you were nineteen." He picked up the scissors once again, not looking at her. "You still aren't."

Shivers danced across her shoulders. They weren't shivers of fear. "You're not frightening me, Jefferson. You didn't frighten me when I was nineteen. You didn't frighten me in San Diego. *And you're not frightening me now.*" She rose smoothly and walked away, dignity gathered around her like a cloak.

The room was empty. Lifeless without her presence. Jefferson stared at his hands.

"I frighten myself," he murmured.

But there was no one there to hear him.

Chapter Six

"What do you mean you're not going to the hospital today?"

Frowning, Emily finished securing her ponytail with a scrunchy and hurried out into the hall. Tristan had just stepped out of his room, looking curious.

"Did you hear that yelling?" she asked.

"Who didn't?" he answered. "Sounds like someone got up on the wrong side of the bed. Betcha I know who's planning to stick to the ranch today, though." He dropped his arm across her shoulders and herded her downstairs. "You look very nice today," he said as they entered the kitchen. He dropped a kiss on the top of her head and headed for the coffee.

Emily glanced down at her well-worn blue jeans and thin, cropped white shirt. The clothes were clean, but hardly on the cutting edge of fashion. Just about to ask

Tristan what had gotten into him, raised voices sounded just outside the mudroom.

The screen door banged shut as Jefferson stalked in, Matthew charging after him. "I don't care what Squire said," Matthew yelled.

Jefferson swiveled on his heel, stopping his brother short. His fingers were white over the handle of his cane. "Back off!"

Emily hastily filled a mug of coffee and stuck it into Matthew's raised hand. "Have some coffee," she muttered.

He looked at her. At the mug of coffee. Some of his anger drained away. Despite its scalding temperature, he drank half of it down and set the mug on the table. "Look, Jeff, we've all got stuff we need to be doing. I've got fifty things that I've let slide since Squire went into the hospital. This place doesn't run itself, even with Joe Greene's help. But I'm going to the hospital this morning. Just like usual. We're all going. *And so are you.*"

Jefferson looked terrible. Emily could tell just by looking at the lines bracketing his eyes that he hadn't slept much the night before. Tristan caught her glance and shook his head slightly, as if he knew she was ready to move between the two men. To take Jefferson's arm and—

"Not today," Jefferson stated softly. He turned around, his eyes colliding with Emily's. Lips tight, he looked away and went back outside.

Matthew swore, but Tristan caught his shoulder before Matthew could take off after Jefferson. "Let him be." His eyes sent the same message to Emily.

It wouldn't have mattered if Tristan had pinned her to the floor; if she'd wanted to follow Jefferson, she would have. Unfortunately, she didn't have a clue what she'd say to him, so in the kitchen she stayed. Well, the mudroom, at least. Where she watched him walk toward the bunkhouse.

Matthew shrugged off Tristan's hand. "Does he think this is easy for any of us?" His fingers raked through his hair. The phone jangled and he yanked up the receiver. "Yeah? Oh, sorry, Maggie. What's up?" Matthew's expression tightened as he listened. "No, sure, that's fine. Yeah…fine…okay…yeah. Bye." He waited until he'd hung up before losing his temper. "First Squire. Then Jefferson, and now this?" He slammed his palm flat against the door frame. "How much is a person supposed to stand?" Without looking back, he headed outside.

"Well, that was enlightening," Tristan commented, tongue firmly in cheek. The phone rang again and he picked it up. He spoke briefly, then hung up just as Daniel came in. "Hey, Dan, isn't Jaimie Greene Joe's little sister?"

"Yeah." Daniel flipped on the faucet and stuck his head beneath the cool water. Emily pushed a dish towel into his groping hand. "Ahh," he sighed thankfully, catching the dripping water with the towel. "Damn but it's already hot out there. What's this about Jaimie?"

Tristan nodded toward the telephone. "That was Maggie just now on the phone. She said she forgot to give Matthew Jaimie's flight number."

Daniel lowered the towel from his face. "Jaimie's coming? Here?" His lips pursed and his eyes lit with an unholy gleam. "And Matt knows?"

"Apparently. He's picking her up at the airport this afternoon."

Daniel started laughing. ''Man, oh, man, this ought to be good.''

''*Who* is Jaimie Greene?'' Emily asked.

''She's Joe's little sister,'' Dan said. ''Oh, that's right. You guys haven't met her. Well, anyway, she worked here for a while last summer. I'll bet Matt's shorts are in a knot but good.'' He laughed again, shaking his head. ''Never thought she'd come back here,'' he said, once he'd gotten control of himself. ''I guess you could say that she and Matt rubbed each other all wrong.''

''I didn't know there was anybody that Matthew didn't get along with,'' Emily said.

''Normally I'd agree,'' Dan answered. ''But, I swear, those two took one look at each other—'' He broke off when a horn blasted through the air. He tossed the towel on the table and looked out the window to see Matthew leaning on the horn. ''He acted like a wet hen all summer long, and it looks like we're in for more of the same this year.'' He grinned again and headed for the door. ''Didn't help his mood any that he couldn't look at her without slobbering all over himself. Tris, you coming?''

''Yup,'' Tristan quickly drank down his coffee and left the mug in the sink. ''Don't know why though,'' he grumbled, following in Daniel's wake. ''I *hate* haying.''

Truck doors slammed and they drove off, leaving an unnatural silence behind. Emily peered out the window for a long moment. She knew that they wouldn't have turned down an offer of help from her, if she'd expressed one. She also knew that they didn't need her help, and if the truth were known, she hated the hot chore worse than Tristan did.

Turning her attention to the kitchen, she busied herself washing and putting away the few dishes the men had left in the sink.

It was still early in the morning, and they wouldn't be driving out to see Squire for a few hours yet. Retrieving her organizer from her bedroom, she returned to the kitchen and opened it to her calendar. Settling at the big table, she called her office in San Diego. It wasn't a particularly satisfying call. She made a few notes on the calendar, and called Luke Hawkins where she stabled Bird. He assured her he was exercising Bird regularly and that the horse was doing just fine.

She hung up, tapping her pen against the open calendar. You'd think that her horse, at least, would have the decency to miss her. Tossing down the pen, she slammed the organizer shut, grabbed an apple from the bowl on the counter and went outside. The ever-present breeze drifted over her and she breathed in the distinctive scent of open fields. Of cattle and horses.

Her mood lifted somewhat. Who needed offices and computers and spreadsheets when a person had all this? The horse barn was the closest building to the big house and that's where her boots took her. More than half the horses were out, but she found a nice gray mare. Crooning to the sleek animal, she fed her the remainder of her apple and slipped into the stall.

Within minutes, she'd made a fast friend and the horse willingly let Emily slide a halter on and they went out into the sunshine. The mare was the picture of good health, but Emily wasn't about to just take her pick of a horse without checking with Matthew or Dan first. Unfortunately they were nowhere in sight, obviously out on the tractors somewhere.

She led the horse past all the buildings. She found

Maggie in the huge, commercial-type kitchen attached to the bunkhouse.

They visited for a while and then Maggie asked about San Diego and her job.

Emily shrugged. She didn't want to talk about work. If her employers had their way, she'd be returning to it all too soon. "Do you know where the guys are working this morning?"

Maggie dragged a large stockpot off a high shelf. "I think Matt and the boys were headed out toward Dawson's Bend." Puffing a lock of pale blond hair out of her eyes, Maggie maneuvered the big pot into the extra deep stainless steel sink. She pressed her palms to the small of her back and straightened again, seeming to sway for just a moment. "They'll probably be back in an hour or so. You all are heading out to the hospital, then, aren't you?"

"Mmm-hmm." Emily reached out and touched Maggie's elbow. "Are you feeling all right?"

A wan smile spread across the other woman's face. "Yes. Just a bit of morning sickness."

"You're pregnant?" Emily stared at the gargantuan pot the woman had just wrestled all by herself. "What on earth are you doing moving things like that around? Does Matt know?"

"I'm doing my job," Maggie said dryly. "As for Matt, I have no idea. Joe and I just found out a couple weeks ago. Don't worry. I'm fine."

Emily wasn't so sure, but she held her tongue. For now. But she'd make darn sure Matthew knew what kind of strenuous tasks Maggie was completing. Lord, there were enough men around the place that she shouldn't have to be pulling pots and pans off ten-foot-high shelves.

She reminded herself of the reason she'd come into the bunkhouse in the first place and looked out the long side window overlooking the corrals situated across the gravel road. "Do you know anything about that gray? I thought I'd take her out for a ride."

Maggie followed Emily's pointing finger. "Oh, sure. Daisy's the mare Jaimie used last summer. I ride her pretty regularly, myself, now." Her hand touched her still-flat abdomen. "Well..." She smiled faintly. "Take her out," she encouraged. "She's a real sweetie."

Emily watched Maggie turn toward the double-wide freezer and pull out a large package. She plunked the butcher-paper-wrapped bundle on the wide butcher block. "I'm fixing roast beef for dinner tonight," she said. "I'll bring it up to the house before six, if that's all right."

Emily tugged at her earlobe. "You know, Maggie, I could cook for us...." The other woman's expression fell slightly, and it occurred to Emily that Maggie Greene was probably only a few years older than herself. "Not that your cooking isn't wonderful," she added hastily. "But, you know, if you're not feeling well, or...or something. I'd be happy to, uh, help out."

Level blue-green eyes looked out from Maggie's pale face. She seemed to relax slightly and a smile flitted across her mouth. "Thanks. I'm sure I'll be fine. But... thanks."

Nodding, and still feeling like she'd just taken a huge bite of her own foot, Emily left Maggie to her duties. Using a rung on the fence for a boost, she slipped onto Daisy's bare back. Emily didn't really have a destination in mind. But she gave Daisy her head and after a meandering romp, ended up at the swimming hole that lay about two miles east of the big house.

She dismounted and let the reins fall. Daisy didn't wander. Obviously familiar with the spot, she bent her graceful head and nibbled at the lush grass surrounding the tiny lake, affectionately termed the hole. To please his wife, Squire had fenced it off from the stock, and as far as Emily knew, he'd only had to bring cattle down for the water once or twice.

It had been Sarah Clay who'd planted the lilac bushes that still grew in such profusion around the spring-fed swimming hole. She'd nurtured the clover and wildflowers that still came back each spring, almost before the snow was gone. It was a place that Squire's wife had obviously loved. It was fitting that her headstone lay on the far side.

Not for the first time, Emily wondered about the woman who had borne Squire's five sons. Her portrait hung in the living room above the fireplace. She'd been a lovely woman with golden blond hair and deep blue eyes. With a gently rounded chin and a dimple in one cheek. It was Jefferson and Tristan who resembled her the most, at least coloringwise. All the Clay sons, as anyone with a speck of vision could see, had acquired their strong facial features from Squire.

Emily kicked off her boots and socks and stepped up on the flat boulder that stuck out over the water, serving as a rough-hewn diving board. She sat on the end, letting her toes dip into the cool water. Her eyes were on the opposite bank, and even though she couldn't see the small granite headstone because of the bushes and trees, she still felt the aura of love and happiness left behind by Mrs. Squire Clay.

"How did you handle all these males, Sarah?"

The only answer she received was the ripple of water as she lifted her feet up to rest on the rock. Sighing, she

lowered her cheek to her knees. She had no idea how
long she sat there before the sound of a twig breaking
brought her head up. She looked over to Daisy, but the
horse was contentedly munching her way closer to the
water's edge.

"You always did like it out here."

Her breath caught and held. She swallowed and
turned around to see Jefferson leaning against a tree.
"Yes. I did."

His hand wrapped around the thick rope hanging from
one of the high branches, and he swung it out over the
water. "You used to swing on this rope and drop off
right in the middle of the water. You and Tristan. You
were like two little monkeys playing in the trees."

"I remember." Through her lashes, she watched him
step over a fallen branch. If he could behave like their
encounter in the kitchen the day before had never happened, then so could she. "You did your share of swimming here, too."

"That I did." Ducking beneath a branch, he walked
over to the boulder.

"How'd you get out here?"

"Walked." He grimaced. "Limped."

"Where's your cane?"

The corner of his mouth twisted. "Somewhere in the
middle of a field, where I pitched it."

Her eyebrows rose. "You threw it into the middle of
a field."

"Yup." He lowered himself onto the rock and lay
near the edge projecting farthest over the water. A solid
foot of space separated them. "Course I'll be regretting
it come this afternoon when I get all stiffened up
again."

Emily found herself responding to his faint, dry smile.

''Perhaps you should have taught Matt's dog to play fetch-the-cane before you went off and did it.''

They both smiled, then fell silent. Emily's teeth worried the inside of her lip, and she looked at him over her arms, folded across the tops of her knees. Before she knew what she was doing, she'd reached out to run her finger along his angled jaw. ''What's this scar from?''

Jefferson caught her finger in his. ''My stupidity,'' he answered. Which was no answer at all.

She tucked her hand back over her knee. ''Jefferson—''

''Shh,'' he said, his eyes dark pools. ''Don't.''

''You don't even know what I was going to say.''

''Yeah, I probably do. And it's a bad idea.''

''Your ego is monstrous.'' She turned her head to look out at the water. She'd only been toying with the idea of trying to persuade him to go to the hospital.

''Don't.'' He tugged lightly on her ponytail. ''Let's just enjoy the morning.''

''Oh, so you *can* enjoy something, can you? How refreshing.''

''Snot.''

''Yup.''

Jefferson sighed. He shifted on the boulder until he was lying on his back. Just to see if he could, he wiggled his toes. And was relieved when he felt the inside of his boot. The numbness seemed to be gone. For now. ''Tell me about your job,'' he said.

''My job.''

''Your job.''

''Ohhh-kay,'' she murmured. She stretched out her leg and dipped her toe in the water. ''Well, let's see. I've been there a few years now. I guess you know that already.'' She went on to tell him a little of her daily routine.

"And who's the CPA you're dating?"

"Stuart? I'd hardly call it dating. Well, of course we did go to Mexico just before I flew up here, but that hardly—"

"You went to Mexico with him?"

Emily chastised herself for the twinge of satisfaction she felt at Jefferson's obvious displeasure. "Just for the weekend,'' she elaborated.

"Just you and this *Stuart* guy? What the hell was Tristan doing, letting—"

"Hey,'' she shot him a glare. "Tristan doesn't *let* me do anything. I make my own decisions."

"And smart ones, too. Haring off to Mexico with some joker. What if he—"

"What? What if he what? Put the *moves* on me? What if he did? What if I wanted him to? What if I *liked* it?"

Jefferson's jaw ticked. Then abruptly he smiled. So broadly that the dimple in his cheek broke free. He folded his arms behind his head and lay back. "Nothing happened."

She wasn't sure who she was more disgusted with. Jefferson for his ridiculous attitude. Or herself for almost falling off the boulder after one glance at his little-used megawatt smile. She clambered to her feet. "How do you know? There are some men on the face of this earth who do find me attractive, you know."

"Oh, I don't doubt that,'' he agreed, his low voice whiskey smooth. His lashes shaded his eyes partially as he ran his glance up and down her slender figure. "You grew up real nice, Emily."

"Gee," she replied as she propped her fists on her hips, "thanks. I'm so touched."

"Anytime."

Huffing, Emily shook her head and looked to the sky, then back down at Jefferson's sprawling body. She stepped back onto the rock and crouched down beside him. "You know what occurs to me, Jefferson?"

His eyes were closed, a half smile still hovering about his lips. "What?"

"It occurs to me, that you probably *haven't* had a good swim in a while." With that, she pushed at his waist. Off balance, he rolled right off the boulder into the swimming hole.

Water splashed over her feet and calves. Satisfied, she looked down at him as he slowly rose. Standing on the bottom, the water lapped at his shoulders. He shook his head, and his drenched hair flipped away from his face. He wiped the water from his eyes.

She was several feet above him. Yet, even from that safe distance, her feet edged backward, away from the water. "Wait, no, wait, Jefferson," she shook her head as his hands closed over the edge of the boulder. "You deserved that," she insisted, backing up another step.

Water sluiced from his shoulders as he heaved himself up onto the boulder. He looked down at his feet. "My boots are wet," he observed.

"Well, yes, I guess they are." She bit her lip and backed up another step, eyeing the short distance between her and Daisy out of the corner of her eye. Her bare heel felt grass beneath it. "They'll dry. Or—" she replied, backing up another step "—or, I'll buy you another pair."

"Do you know," he asked as he slicked dripping water away from his forehead, "how long it takes to break in a pair of boots? Years." Jefferson started to sit down and groaned.

Instantly Emily decided against escape and went to him. And found herself flying through the air. She barely had time to close her eyes when she splashed into the water. Her toes skimmed the gravelly bottom and she surfaced. "Hey!" She treaded water, wishing for a few more inches in height. She shoved her palm across the surface, sending a cascade of water flying in his face. "Faker."

Jefferson laughed.

Stunned, she forgot to tread and went under again. When she came up sputtering, he was still laughing.

It was a glorious sound. Bemused, she smiled up at him. But eventually, the goose bumps could no longer be ignored and she swam over to the boulder. "Much as I'd like to listen to you laugh yourself silly, it's getting a tad cold in here." She reached her hand up.

He linked his fingers with hers and hauled her out of the water. She shook her hands, and droplets of water splattered everywhere. Not that it mattered, what with the puddles surrounding their feet. "I can't believe we used to swim in that sometimes until the middle of September." She grinned and looked up. "Then we only had to wait a few weeks, it seemed like, and we'd put away the swimming suits and break out the ice skates."

His laughter had faded, though the smile still lingered in his eyes. The leaves in the trees rustled and the breeze set off a fresh crop of goose bumps. Autumn was definitely coming. She plucked at the hem of her shirt and wrung out the water as best she could.

Jefferson swore softly.

"What is it?"

He shook his head and began unbuttoning his shirt. Shrugging out of it, he handed it to her. "Here."

"I hate to tell you this, Jefferson, but I'm not going to warm up any by putting your wet shirt on over my own wet shirt."

"No, but at least I can't see right through the fabric of mine." He dangled his shirt in front of her. "And I'm not missing any little pieces of underwear this morning, either."

Her eyes flew down and she realized how transparent the cropped top had become. The wet shirt clearly displayed the bare curves beneath. "Oh."

"Yeah. *Oh.* Give me a break, would you?"

Emily eyed the bare expanse of chest right in front of her. She wanted more than anything to press herself right up against that hard plane. She wanted to explore each ridge of muscle. Kiss each nick. Each scar. "Give *me* a break," she returned, trying to sound unaffected. But she took the shirt and slid her arms into it. Even though he'd folded the sleeves up to just below his elbows, they hung nearly to her wrists. Wrinkling her nose at yet another layer of wet fabric, she wrung out the shirttails as best she could, then tied them at her waist and shoved the sleeves up her arms.

Jefferson was busy pulling off his boots. "These used to be my favorite boots," he informed her as he upended them. A thin stream of water poured out.

"They're still your favorites," Emily assured him, trying desperately not to gawk at his golden chest.

"They're ruined."

"They're wet."

"Ruined."

She finally turned and looked toward the middle of the lake. "You've worn them in the rain, haven't you?

And in the snow, probably. You'd walk through puddles in the middle of the street, rather than walking around them. What's the difference?''

Jefferson pulled the boots back on. ''The difference, angelface, is that on those occasions, the wet was on the outside.'' He grimaced as his socks squished when he stood. ''Now it's on the inside.'' A quick sharp whistle from between his teeth brought Daisy ambling over. He caught the reins and with one swing of his long leg, mounted up. He reached his hand down for her. ''Come on, let's get you back for some dry clothes.''

He pulled her onto the horse, sitting her in front of him. Though still soaking, his body heat blasted through her sodden layers. She felt, rather than heard, the groan that rumbled through his chest. His arm slipped around her waist, and he turned Daisy through the trees back toward the big house.

There was simply no way for two people to ride one horse bareback and keep any distance between their bodies. Emily didn't even bother trying. She smoothed her palm across the hard arm holding her firmly against him. She leaned back and enjoyed.

''So why aren't you out haying with the rest of them?'' She asked as Daisy meandered through the long grass toward the gravel road.

''They didn't need me.''

''Me, either.'' Her fingertips feathered through the hair lightly sprinkled across his wrist. It seemed perfectly natural to tilt her head and kiss the biceps curving past her shoulder. She barely stopped herself from pressing her lips to his warm skin.

He snorted softly. ''Angelface, the last time you went haying, Squire ended up hauling you to the doctor's for six stitches in your leg. But if you want to think that

Matt wants your assistance, you go on ahead and keep dreaming.''

"I could do it," she insisted halfheartedly. "If I put my mind to it. *If* I wanted to."

He clicked his tongue, and Daisy picked up her pace. "If you put your mind to it, you can do anything. But perhaps you'd best keep your interests trained toward the horses rather than the tractors, hmm?"

"I like horses better, anyway. I do miss Bird." She leaned forward and patted Daisy's strong neck. "Although this pretty lady is a nice one, isn't she? Remember how you used to talk about having your own spread? Do you still want that?"

His palm pressed her backward until she nestled, once more, against his chest. "I talked about a lot of things. I was young then."

Emily choked on a laugh. "You're not exactly decrepit, you know. You talk as if you have one foot in the grave."

He stiffened slightly against her back. "You need some dry clothes," he said abruptly, urging Daisy into an easy lope that rapidly ate up the last several yards. He halted near the rear entrance of the big house. "Go in. I'll take care of Daisy."

The bright, happy morning they'd spent together ended. Just like that. Silently she slid to the ground. He waited just long enough for her to move away before wheeling Daisy around and heading for the horse barn.

For about the millionth time, she wished she knew what thoughts whirled in Jefferson's head. What caused his silent torment. She wiped a drip of water from her forehead and turned to the house.

Since there was no one about, in the mudroom she shucked off all the wet clothes except her panties. After wrapping herself in a big blue towel that had been folded atop a stack of clean laundry, she dumped her clothing into the washing machine.

The few items were hardly worth running a load, but she started one, anyway. It was purely habit that took her upstairs to the bedrooms where she found empty hampers in Matthew's and Daniel's rooms. She nearly tripped over the faded black duffel bag laying on the floor of Sawyer's room.

She frowned, wondering why Jefferson's duffel was in Sawyer's room. Then she noticed the luggage tag clearly printed with Sawyer's name and address. She picked it up and tossed it onto the bed, watching the tangle of airport tags bounce. Sawyer had almost as many tags hanging off the bag as Jefferson had hanging on his. Sawyer's duties with the navy were obviously keeping him as busy as ever.

She headed to Tristan's room after finding Sawyer's hamper empty. She gathered up the meager collection in Tristan's hamper. Then, since she'd already checked the other rooms, she made herself walk into Jefferson's room.

Like Sawyer, his duffel was lying in the middle of the floor. Brothers. She shook her head and, balancing Tristan's bundle on one hip, leaned down and plucked the items out of the wicker hamper. Quickly, she nipped down to the mudroom and started tossing Tristan's clothing in, her fingers automatically searching through his pockets. The man was notorious for leaving pens and pencils stuck in his pockets. She'd ruined more than one load of clothing before she'd learned her lesson.

Sure enough, she found two ballpoint pens. Shaking her head, she set them on the shelf above the washer and dumped the jeans into the agitating tub. Tucking the edge of the towel more securely between her breasts, she bent down and picked up Jefferson's jeans. Paper crinkled from inside one of the pockets, and she fished it out, then added the jeans to the load. She absently noticed the small square of paper was a prescription. She'd have to ask him if he needed it filled, then realized he'd had ample opportunities to do so at the hospital when they visited Squire.

She reached for the shirt lying on the floor, turning when the door squeaked open. Jefferson stepped in. He'd found a faded denim shirt somewhere, though it hung unbuttoned over his chest.

"Here," she handed him the prescription. "It was in your pants pocket."

Jefferson automatically pocketed the slip. "What are you doing?"

"Oh, a load of wash. Might as well make a full load. Want to throw your wet stuff in, too?"

"You're wearing a towel."

"No kidding." She rolled her eyes. Turning back to the washing machine, she dropped in his shirt and closed the lid. "I wasn't going to track water all through the house."

"You're parading around a house full of men, wearing nothing but a towel."

Good Lord, the man was furious. "You can't be serious. For Pete's sake, Jefferson, I'm more covered now than if I were wearing a bathing suit. Besides, nobody is even around. Except you."

"Is this the way you behave in San Diego?"

"Behave?" She echoed. "Behave?" Her voice rose as she repeated the word. Tires crunched over gravel and through the window she saw Daniel, Matthew and

Tristan pile out of the truck. *Great. Just great. So much for being alone.*

Matthew and Daniel passed through, hardly giving her a second glance, though Daniel seemed ready to make some remark about Jefferson's wet jeans. But he took one look at his brother and reconsidered, choosing instead to follow Matthew back to the office. Tristan, of course, wasn't nearly so cooperative.

He took one look at Jefferson's wet pants, and Emily's lack of them and whistled. "Well, lookee here. While the cat's away..."

"Can it," Emily snapped without even glancing Tristan's way. With her hands on her hips, she continued glaring up at Jefferson. "What exactly are you implying? Does it bother you to think that I might," she clapped dramatic palms to her cheeks, "oh, my, dare I say it, actually *wear* a towel in my own home?" Oblivious of Tristan's interested observance, she lifted furious hands to the knot holding the towel in place. "Lord, Jefferson, you'd probably have a coronary if you thought I might actually find myself nude once in a while. I hate to shock you, of course, but it's easier to bathe that way."

Tristan choked on his snicker and at the twin glares he received, turned around and went right back outside. Emily transferred her attention back to Jefferson. Turmoil bubbled within her. "All my life, *all* my life, I've been surrounded by men who find it perfectly acceptable to walk around in their underwear. But *Heaven forbid* if I should present myself in anything less than a nun's habit." She flipped loose the knot in the towel and shoved it into Jefferson's chest. "Well, there. This is about as bad as it gets." She waved her arms. "But wait, the roof isn't caving in. Oh, dear."

Jefferson whipped the towel back around her shoulders faster than a ladies' maid. "That's it," he muttered. Bending down, he grabbed her up, flinging her over his shoulder. A hard arm clamped over her thighs, holding her, and the towel, in place as she struggled. "Cut it out."

Emily pounded on his back. "Put me down! I'm not a child."

"Then stop acting like one." He shouldered his way through the door, striding through the empty kitchen and not stopping until he reached her bedroom. He let her go, unceremoniously dumping her onto the bed. The towel that had been wrapped about her shoulders flew free. The pillows at the head of the mattress bounced madly. "You're asking for it, Em."

"Promises, promises," she taunted.

He leaned forward suddenly, his arms braced on the mattress to either side of her. "Acting the tart doesn't impress me, Emily."

He caught her palm before it could connect with his cheek. She struggled, and he settled the matter by pinning her arms above her head.

"Let...me...go." She twisted against his hold but he easily subdued her efforts. His eyes closed, as if in pain, and she suddenly stilled. "What's the matter?"

He grunted. "You've got to be kidding. Even *you* are not that naive."

Insulted, she renewed her efforts to wriggle out of his hold.

"Dammit," he cursed, quickly evading her knee aimed at emasculating him. She was slicker than a greased doorknob. But he managed to subdue her legs with one of his. And then had to look away at the planks in the wood floor, the beam of sunlight shining through the opened curtains. Anything rather than her taut, creamy skin. Her slender waist. Her rose-tipped breasts.

He bit off another curse and abruptly released her, moving so fast that the mattress bounced all over again. "Cover yourself." He tossed the towel at her.

She caught it and threw it at his head, scrambling off the bed. "If you don't like the sights, then take your chauvinistic carcass out of here."

The towel hit the wall behind him. Ignoring it, he pulled open a dresser drawer. Then another until he found what he wanted. Turning back to her, he held out a long-sleeved T-shirt. "Put it on." He felt a peculiar satisfaction as her hackles bristled all over again at his shamelessly autocratic order.

She arched a flippant "make-me" eyebrow and crossed her arms. Her nipples peeked out over her arms. And she knew it, the little witch. He yanked the shirt over her head, pulling it down over her shoulders. Her arms were caught inside. "You're trying my patience," he warned.

"Too damn bad."

He tugged on a bunched fold of shirt, jerking her off balance, but she set to wriggling again, earning himself a painful elbow in the ribs. "Dammit, Em. Be still."

"Don't order me around." She twisted, trying to make sense of the shirt tangled about her neck and shoulders. "Just because you say *jump,* doesn't mean I'm going to ask how high." She made a frustrated face then yanked off the shirt rather than try to make sense out of the twisted mess.

His jaw locked. She shook out the shirt, seeming to take an inordinate amount of time with it. "I warned you," he gritted, anchoring his hand in her hair. Then he kissed her.

She bit his lip.

He slowly lifted his head and touched a finger to the tiny bead of blood. "Like it rough, do you?"

Her cheeks flamed. No other person in existence had the ability to drive her beyond the borders of reasonable behavior. She looked everywhere but at him. For the truth of it was, she liked *it* any way it came as long as *it* was from him. She fumbled with the shirt trying to pull it down, but his hands blocked hers.

Going still, she looked up at him. Her breasts swelled from the heat blazing in his eyes. Without conscious thought, she swayed toward him and groaned low in her throat when his fingers brushed across her flesh. Thumb and finger circled a peak and she lost her breath. His fingers lightly pinched the taut nipple, and desire arrowed sharply to her core. Then his mouth replaced his hand, his teeth scraping over her hypersensitive skin.

Her hands knotted in his hair. Her breath hissed between her teeth. Before she knew what she was doing, her hands had dropped her shirt and were sliding into the neck of *his*.

Just that fast, he shoved himself away from her, raking his fingers through his hair.

Reeling, she spied the alarm clock on the bedside table. "Get out. I want to get ready to see Squire," she said, hating the way her voice shook.

At the mention of his father, Jefferson's eyes darkened. His face went curiously blank, and he inclined his head. "By all means."

Then he was gone.

Emily sank onto the edge of the bed, absently aware of the way the quilt was all bunched and wrinkled beneath her. Her heart was thudding so unevenly she felt dizzy. She pulled on the stupid shirt and, tilting to her side, pulled her legs up onto the mattress and waited for the room to stop spinning. And then she cried.

Tristan, walking past the open door several minutes later, glanced in. He silently took in the tumbled bed and the soft snuffles from the hunched figure facing away from the doorway. As silently as he'd approached, he retreated.

He strode down to the kitchen. Clapped his hand over Jefferson's shoulder and pulled him around from where he stood at the sink. Water spewed across the floor from the glass in Jefferson's hand.

"Dammit, Tris. What the hell's wrong with you?" Jefferson growled. He dropped the glass in the sink.

Tristan straightened to his full height, topping Jefferson by a few solid inches. His fists curled. "You *stupid* son of a bitch."

The screen door slammed, and Matthew trotted in, his eyes taking in the scene. In a flash he went between the two angry brothers, lifting a steadying hand, even as he grabbed for one of the chairs he'd bumped. Ignoring Matthew, Jefferson scooted out of the way to avoid the wooden chair skittering crazily toward him.

Matthew planted his palm on Tristan's chest, keeping him from moving toward Jefferson. "Come on, guys."

Tristan shook off Matthew. "Get out of my way," he warned.

Daniel barely paused in the doorway, taking in the tumult. "For God's sake," he muttered. "Somebody not have their prunes this morning?" Starting forward, his boot slipped in the water pooled on the floor. Arms waving, his momentum carried him against a tipped chair and he went down with a racket and a curse. Bright blood spurted onto his shirt. Matthew muttered under his breath and tossed his brother a dish towel.

Jefferson looked at Tristan. "Look what you started, you idiot."

Tristan, shoving past Matthew's not inconsiderable barrier, went nose to nose with Jefferson. "*I* started? You're the one breaking Emily's heart. I never thought you'd be the type to tumble her in bed and leave her crying. You're my brother, but I swear to God, Jefferson, you'd better do right by her. Or, I'll—"

Jefferson's eyebrow lifted.

"What do you mean *tumble* her in bed?" Daniel's voice was muffled through the cloth held to his dripping nose.

"What do you think?" Tristan said sarcastically.

Suddenly, Jefferson found himself the object of not just one angry brother, but three. All he needed was for Sawyer to join the fray. "I didn't *tumble* Emily," he said stiffly, aware that he'd wanted to do just that. He bit back a stream of vicious words and shouldered his way past Matthew and Tristan, stepped over Daniel, and stomped outside.

Matthew wearily righted a chair and plunked down on it. "Well, this was fun," he said to no one in particular.

"Jefferson's sleeping with Emily?" Still sprawled on the floor, Daniel shook his head in disbelief. "She's practically our baby sister!"

Emily stepped into the room. She'd heard most of the fracas from the staircase, but it had begun and ended so abruptly she'd not had a chance to step in. "Jefferson is *not* sleeping with Emily," she said bluntly, garnering several startled looks. "But not for lack of trying on her part," she added for good measure. "So, if you're going to be horrified at someone's behavior, aim it at me. Not Jefferson. He deserves better from you."

With her hands propped on her hips, she studied the motley collection of Clays. They were, at the moment, a pathetic bunch. And she loved them all. "Now, I'm going to the hospital to see Squire. So if you're coming, get a move on."

Matthew slid back his chair and rose. Daniel retrieved a fresh towel and shirt from the stack in the mudroom and Tristan righted the rest of the chairs. Silently they followed Emily out to the Blazer. Sawyer came out from the horse barn, his steps faltering as he saw his brothers' expressions. But he held his tongue. They piled into the truck, with Emily taking the driver's seat.

There was no more talk of Jefferson accompanying them.

Chapter Seven

Squire was awake when they arrived. The nurse on duty even said they could all go in together to see him. Propped back against a stack of pillows, his vivid blue eyes tracked their entrance.

Emily dropped a kiss on his cheek. "You're looking much better."

He grunted. "Can't say the same for Daniel there. You been picking on my boys again, missy?" He folded his arms across his chest, studying his sons. His eyes narrowed when no explanation was forthcoming. "Where's Jefferson?"

Emily sat in the single chair and scooted closer to the bed. "He's feeling under the weather," she murmured, sliding a warning look toward Tristan.

"How are you feeling today?" Sawyer asked, smoothly taking Squire's attention.

The older man harrumphed. "Like a damn pincushion. Ever' time I'm ready to snooze, that battle-ax out there comes in disturbin' me. The least they could do for a dyin' man would be to provide some pretty nurses."

"You're not dying," Sawyer countered.

"Although you certainly seemed to try," Emily commented. She slid her hand into Squire's. "You gave us quite a scare, you know."

He just harrumphed grumpily. But his fingers gently squeezed hers, and she smiled and fell silent as he ordered Matthew and Dan to bring him up to speed on affairs at the Double-C.

"And when're you coming home to stay?" Squire said, seeming satisfied with the ranch report and turning his startlingly translucent blue eyes on Emily.

"Squire, you know I have a job in San Diego."

"So? Don't tell me you're happy with it. I can look in your eyes, girl, and tell that something's pluckin' at you. If it ain't that damn boring job you got, then what is it?"

"My job isn't boring," she defended lightly. "In fact, there's been some indications that I might get to do more consulting, and that will mean I get to travel. How bad can that be?"

"Airports and more airports. Pretty soon it'll seem like all you see is the inside of airports," Sawyer answered quietly.

"Airports, oh, geez," Matthew shoveled his fingers through his hair, making the short strands stand on end. "What time is it?" He grabbed Daniel's arm and turned it around to see the watch. "Great. That's just great. I forgot all about Jaimie. I knew there was a reason we were supposed to drive separately. Now I'll have to make an extra trip back home to take her up to the ranch from the airport.''

"What's this about Jaimie? You talking about Joe's sis?'' Squire pushed himself up against the pillows, grimacing against the pull of the adhesive tape covering his chest.

"One and the same,'' Daniel answered, a faint grin playing with his lips.

"Just come back here with her before driving to the ranch,'' Emily suggested to Matthew. "Then you guys can go on, and I'll stay here until later. Somebody can come back and get me.''

"That boy's sure got his shorts in a twist,'' Squire commented after Matthew had left, grumbling something about a stupid waste of driving time. "All 'cause that girl's coming back. Never did see what the beef was between them. She seemed kinda sweet, if ya' ask me.''

The question of Jaimie Greene's sweetness had to go unanswered when the nurse on duty came in and shooed them out. "This is ICU, you know,'' she reminded them needlessly. "Besides, we're moving Mr. Clay to a regular room this afternoon.''

Sawyer suggested they hit the café for lunch, and they left after Emily promised Squire she'd track him down, regardless of where they stuck him in the hospital.

As usual, Candy was on duty and her young face perked up markedly as they trooped into the café. She hastily splashed coffee into her present customer's cup, then plunked the pot right onto the table in front of the woman. She snatched up several menus and rushed over. "Hi,'' she greeted them breathlessly, her eyes wide on Tristan's face.

He smiled slowly, and color rushed into Candy's face.

Blinking, she turned, nearly bumping into another waitress, and led them back to their usual table.

"You're mean," Emily pinched Tristan's arm.

"What did I do?"

"You know."

"What? I smiled at the girl. What's so bad about
that?"

"You're twenty miles out of her league," Emily said
under her breath as she slid into the chair Tristan held
out for her.

"Relax, would ya? There's nothing wrong with—"

"She sees you smile at her, and she's going to think
something's going to come of it. And we both know
that nothing will."

"Hey," he said as he tapped her nose with his fingers, "don't take out your problems with Jefferson on
me. All I did was smile at the girl. She's pretty. She's
worth smiling at. So relax." He turned just as Candy
reappeared. "Bring a pitcher of beer," he told her.
"We're celebrating. Our father is getting out of ICU
today."

"How wonderful," she gushed, then fumbled with
the apron tied tightly about her hips for the pad to write
down their orders.

They were more than halfway through the meal when
Matthew arrived. A tall, slender redhead followed him,
her dark green eyes shooting daggers into Matthew's
back. But when he stopped beside their table and introduced her around, her expression lightened and she
greeted everyone with a musical voice.

Emily scooted over so there was room to pull up a
chair beside her, and Jaimie slid into it, dumping her
huge shoulder bag over the chair back. She turned down

the offer of food and declined a mug of beer, softly asking Candy to bring her a glass of iced tea instead.

The table fairly rattled when Matthew plunked himself down onto the chair between Sawyer and Daniel. He reached for the pitcher and poured the last of it into an empty water glass. He lifted the glass to his lips and steadily drank it down, his eyes watching Jaimie as he did so. "Ahh," he said when finished, and thumped the glass onto the table. "Nothin' like a cold beer."

Jaimie sniffed and turned toward Emily. "How is Mr. Clay doing? My brother told me what happened."

Emily instinctively liked the other woman. And despite the sullen looks they received from Matthew, the two women visited their way through the meal that Candy hurriedly brought for Matthew and the dessert that Tristan indulged in. Sawyer had excused himself quite a while earlier to use the phone, and Daniel was reading the newspaper he'd purchased from the machine in front of the café.

"I can't wait to see Maggie," Jaimie was saying. "What with her pregnancy and all, I'm hoping to stay until the baby comes—"

Daniel's and Matthew's heads came up simultaneously. "What?"

Jaimie jumped faintly at the twin demands. Eyes rounded, Jaimie looked toward the brothers. "What?"

"What did you say about Maggie?" Daniel asked.

"Well, I thought you'd all know. But I suppose what with your father and all…"

"What about her," Matthew interrupted.

Jaimie's eyes narrowed at Matthew's arrogant tone. "She is preg…nant," she announced slowly, as if to a dim-witted child.

But Matthew waved off that point. "About staying."

"And I hope to stay until the baby is born," she obliged, her tone dulcet.

Clearly, this did not thrill Matthew Clay. But he contained himself. Emily figured it was only because they were in a public place. Matthew was the least flappable of all the Clay men. Yet the news that this lovely redhead planned to be around awhile obviously jangled him.

"Pregnant?" Daniel touched Jaimie's hand, taking the woman's attention from his older, disgruntled, brother. "Maggie's pregnant?"

Matthew grunted and shoved back his chair. "That's what she said, Dan. More than once. Can we get a move on here? Where'd Sawyer go, anyway?" He snatched up the check and his wallet in one motion and headed toward the front of the restaurant.

Tristan pointed toward the windows at the rear of the restaurant through which Sawyer could be seen leaning against the glass-enclosed public phone. He scooped up the last of his gargantuan slice of apple pie.

"Why don't you just lick the plate," Emily suggested on a laugh.

Tristan shrugged, unrepentant, and waved her off. "You going across to the hospital now?"

Emily nodded. "I'll see you guys later. Don't forget to come back and get me, or else I'll have to take a room at the motel next door." She turned to Jaimie. "We'll have to go riding soon. Tomorrow," she suggested, having learned the other woman also loved horses.

"I'd like that," Jaimie's smile wavered as she looked past Emily's shoulder. "As long as I have time," she finished.

"We'll make time," Emily insisted, fully aware that

Matthew was standing just a few feet away. "It's long past time there were more women around the place, and I intend to enjoy every minute of it." She smiled again, waved goodbye and sailed past Matthew, just daring him to make some comment.

She looked over her shoulder as she pushed through the café door. A person could practically see the sparks arcing between Matthew and Jaimie. Biting back a laugh, she returned to the hospital.

Squire had been moved to a room on the third floor. He was sleeping when she peeked in, so she backed out quietly and wandered down to the gift shop. But a person could only kill so much time looking at infant gifts, get-well cards and magazines. She ended up purchasing a paperback and a can of soda and slowly made her way back to Squire's room. She'd plowed through four chapters of the book before Squire's eyes opened.

She closed her book and looked at him.

"What? I been drooling in my sleep?"

"No," she chuckled. "It's just good to see you." She helped him situate his pillows and adjust the head of the bed up. "Want some water or something?"

"What I want," Squire said as he caught her hand, dropping his good ol' boy routine, "is for you to tell me what's bothering you."

His expression could have been Jefferson's. Or Tristan's. Or any one of his other sons. And though she might be able to hold her own with each one of her nonbrothers, it was a different matter with Squire. This was the man who'd been the only father she'd known since she was seven years old.

Her natural parents were such a hazy image in her memory that she had to look at her old photo albums now and then to remind herself what they had looked like. And though there was a touch of sadness in that reality, Emily had been raised by the gruff man propped up in the hospital bed, and he'd done it with love.

"Well?"

Emily perched on the edge of the hard chair. She tucked her hands between her knees and pondered the wisdom of bringing up the subject. Finally she gave up and took the bull by the horns. "I want to know what's wrong between you and Jefferson."

Squire's expression went stony. "Who said any-thing's wrong?"

Emily tucked her tongue between her teeth and counted to ten. "The first thing you said to your son," she said eventually, "after you woke up in ICU was *get away*." She sighed slightly and had to fight with herself to maintain eye contact with the stubborn, intimidating man. "A son you hadn't seen in over two years," she added softly. "I'd like to know why."

"Ever think it might be none of your concern, little lady?"

"I'm concerned about Jefferson. And you," she said steadily.

"I'm gonna be as good as new."

She nodded. "I believe that. I do. But that's not what I meant." And he knew it. She could tell. "Squire, I lo— I can help him." Her fingers twisted together. "I know I can. But not while I'm floundering around in the dark."

"Who says he needs help?" Squire barked. "What's he gone and done?"

Emily caught his shoulders as he leaned forward. "Relax," she nudged him back against the pillows. "He's not in any trouble," she assured him soothingly. And hoped like fury that it wasn't a lie.

"Then what the hell you going on about?"

Smothering her frustration, she sat back. "It hurt him terribly, Squire, when you told him to leave."

"I didn't tell him to leave," he said abruptly.

"Oh, Squire, for Pete's sake! I was there."

His expression was set. And Emily knew she would get no further with Squire than she had with Jefferson. She wanted to howl with frustration. But a hospital room occupied by a newly recovering Squire was no place to vent it. "Okay," she said in a tight voice. "You win."

He seemed to soften slightly. "There's no winning or losing here, girl."

"We're all losing," she murmured sadly, unaware of the sharp look Squire shot her way. Standing up, she loosened her neck and shoulder muscles. "I'm going to walk a bit. Can I bring you back anything? Some magazines? A book?"

"How 'bout that red-haired nurse I vaguely remember someone telling me about?"

"No one could ever question where your sons inherited their stamina from." Emily shook her head, a reluctant smile tilting her lips. "You're incorrigible."

"Go," he said, waving her off. "Don't want you watching me drooling while I sleep."

Squire had eaten dinner and was soundly beating Emily at checkers when the hospital room door swung inward with a telltale whoosh. "I told you not to move that one," Squire was saying. "Now I'm gonna have to capture this one. And this one." He set aside her two pieces. "I told you."

"Yeah," Emily snorted. "Like you've left me a whole lot of choices on where to move." She looked over, expecting Tristan. Or Sawyer, perhaps. She'd *never* imagined that Jefferson would be the one standing just inside the door. Her fingers accidentally scattered several checker pieces across the board. ''Hi.''

He nodded, but didn't move from the doorway.

''Did you drive?''

His lip curled mockingly. ''Tristan's waiting in the parking lot.''

''Oh.''

Squire tapped Emily's arm with the box that had held the checkers. ''Wake up, girl.''

She tore her eyes from Jefferson. ''Hmm? Oh, right.'' Heat engulfed her, and she scooted the pieces into the box, the game obviously over, and set it on the stand beside Squire's bed. ''Next time I'm gonna stomp you.''

''Sure you are,'' he agreed dryly. ''Go on with you. Let an old man get some sleep.''

''Old man my foot,'' Emily muttered. She glanced at him briefly, wondering again what was between the two men. Then she leaned over and kissed his bristly cheek. ''See you tomorrow evening.''

He grunted, tugged on a lock of her hair and settled back against his pillows.

Emily tried to draw up some of her anger with Jefferson from that morning. But it wouldn't come. It was always that way. She gathered up the nearly finished paperback and her purse and went over to Jefferson. Her eyes clung to his, but he merely moved a few inches out of her way, holding the door open.

''Son.''

Jefferson stiffened and nudged Emily through the door. ''I'll be right down.''

''I'll w—''

''Go.'' He didn't want her around to hear whatever

it was his father would sermonize about this time. "Go on." He cut off the protest forming on her soft lips.

She went silent and wheeled about, hurrying down the corridor, leaving Jefferson feeling as if he'd just kicked a puppy. "Dammit," he muttered.

"Close the bloody door, son."

Jefferson pulled his attention from Emily, who was now pacing in a tight square as she waited for the elevator. He looked over at his father. Except for the darkening shadow of whiskers and the wrinkled hospital gown covering the man's shoulders, Squire looked almost like his old self. Right down to the autocratic expression in his icy blue eyes.

Jefferson folded his arms across his chest and leaned against the wall. "What do you want?"

Squire looked from the still-open door to his middle son.

"Get to the point, old man. I'm no more thrilled with hanging around hospital rooms than you are to have me here."

Squire looked pained. "That's not true, son."

Jefferson's eyebrow climbed. A movement in his peripheral vision alerted him to the fact that Emily's elevator had finally arrived. He watched her until she disappeared from view.

"You still can't keep your eyes off her, can you?"

His eyes turned back to his father. "If that's all you wanted to keep me up here for, you're wasting your time and mine." Jefferson straightened and took a step for the door.

"Just hold on there," Squire said testily.

"I'm not going to listen to your lectures about Emily," Jefferson warned.

"I never lectured—"

"Bull."

Squire glared. Then coughed. And coughed. His color went pale.

In two quick steps Jefferson pushed his father's water within easy reach, and after a few sips, Squire quieted. When he leaned back against the pillow, he looked as though he'd aged a few years. Jefferson pinched the bridge of his nose. "Hell, Squire, I don't want to fight with you."

Squire sighed heavily. "'Cause you figure I'm too old now to take it?"

"You're out of your tree, you know that?" Jefferson shook his head. "What did you want? Spit it out, or I'm going home."

"Home. Well now there's an interesting choice of words." Squire's long fingers tapped the mattress. "Does it mean you've finally come home? Quit wandering?"

"Why? You worried that I might decide to hang around here for a while? Afraid you're gonna have to kick me off the ranch again? I'd think you'd be glad I might stay here in Wyoming, considering Em lives all the way out in California."

"Stop twisting my words, boy," Squire's voice rose.

Jefferson's voice lowered. "Then stop wasting my time. If you just want to rehash your disapproval of me, I'm not interested."

"Dammit, boy, I never said I disapproved of you!"

"Gentlemen!" The stern voice interrupted them and Jefferson turned to see a nurse standing in the doorway, her hands propped on shapely hips. "Would you kindly keep it down? We can hear you down the hall!"

She strode into the room, rounding Squire's bed. She

flipped the bedclothes smooth with a brisk hand. "Visiting hours *are* over, you know."

"You should've closed the door like I told you to," Squire groused.

"I'm not the one yelling," Jefferson pointed out.

"You shouldn't be exciting yourself," the nurse chided. And before Squire could utter another word, she popped a thermometer into his mouth. Looking across the bed, she smiled brightly. "I'm assuming my patient here is your father, yes? Well, you can visit your father tomorrow."

Squire took out the thermometer. "I'm not finished—"

"Yes," she plucked the thermometer out of his fingers and tucked it into his mouth again. "You are finished. For tonight, anyway. Ah-ah-ah," she lightly slapped his hand down when he lifted it again. "Be a darling and let me do my job."

Jefferson felt an unwilling smile tug at his lips. "Good night then. Miss...?"

"Mrs. Day," she provided.

Squire looked up at the white-clad curves standing over him. His eyes met Jefferson's and despite the dissension between them, they shared a simple moment of purely male appreciation. "Pity," Squire murmured around the thermometer.

There wasn't a thing wrong with Mrs. Day's hearing, and a cloud of pink suffused her high cheekbones. She merely arched an eyebrow and shook her head, making a few notes on Squire's chart. With a nod toward his father, Jefferson left the nurse and patient to their business.

The minutes ticked by while he waited for the elevator. He eyed the entrance to the stairwell and stifled a curse. He should've been able to manage three measly flights. He even began to step toward the door, but his knee chose that moment to begin throbbing. Almost like a taunt.

Biting back a curse, he leaned his weight against the wall and tried to be patient. Each passing minute seemed to take longer and longer, until finally the elevator doors ground open and he stepped in. Something in his expression must have startled the couple already inside, for they both scooted right back against the wall.

Well, that suited him fine, too.

Tristan was behind the wheel when Jefferson made his way out to the truck. And he remembered why he'd suddenly told his brother he'd ride back to the hospital with him. Because he didn't want Emily and Tristan cooped up, all alone, in the pickup cab.

And he'd accused his father of being out of his tree. Hell, Jefferson was already sprawled at the base of the tree, figuratively speaking. He jerked open the door. "Scoot over," he ordered.

Emily, who'd been leaning back against the door, nearly fell out. "For crying out loud," she said as she righted herself and slid to the middle of the seat. "Got a burr under your saddle?"

Jefferson pulled himself up into the cab and slammed the door shut. The yellow gleam of the parking-lot light glinted through the windshield, and he looked down into her face, surrounded by a silky cloud of dark hair. Desire slammed into his gut. It was all he could do not to kiss her right then and there. His fingers dug into his thigh, but he hardly noticed. "What're you waiting for?" He looked over Emily's head toward Tristan. "The first snow?"

His little brother grinned. ''Snow might cool things off a bit,'' he said as he started the engine.

The parking lot was riddled with speed bumps and Tristan jerked and rocked over each and every one. Emily tried not to slide on the seat, but it was nearly impossible, and more than once she found herself bumping over against Jefferson's increasingly stiff form. Her legs angled toward Jefferson's side, leaving room for Tristan to get at the gearshift sticking up from the floor. She tried holding on to the dashboard, but it did no good. Tristan jounced over the next bump, and her hips nudged against Jefferson's. She felt, more than heard, him swear under his breath.

''I'm sorry, all right?'' She snapped at him. ''There's no seat belt. Maybe you'd be more comfortable if I sat in the truck bed.''

The truck rocked again. ''Pothole,'' Tristan announced. Gleefully, Emily decided. She shot him a look, but he was oblivious.

They bumped over yet another bump and Jefferson's arm darted in front of her, holding her against the back of the cab seat. ''Cut it out, Tris,'' he said.

''Hey, I can't help it if the parking lot needs paving again,'' Tristan said in defense. He turned out onto the smoother street and headed for the highway. ''Is that better?''

''Much,'' Emily ground out. Jefferson took his arm away, and she held herself still, trying to keep her knees from touching him.

After several miles Jefferson muttered beneath his breath and lifted his arm behind Emily's shoulder. He shifted her until she was leaning gently against him. His firm hand on her shoulder told her not to budge. By the time Emily dared look up at him, his head was leaning back against the rear window, his eyes closed.

She tried swallowing the lump in her throat and tried to breathe more slowly. Hoped that her racing heart would slow. But his slackened fingers hung past her shoulder, grazing the upper curve of her breast, and her heart continued tripping along a path bumpier than the hospital's parking lot.

Tristan caught her eye, and his teeth flashed as he grinned. Turning up the radio a notch, he shifted slightly, seeming to take up even more than his share of the bench seat and pushing her farther against Jefferson.

"Stop it," Emily jabbed him in the ribs viciously. She hastily looked up, but Jefferson slept on.

Tristan made a face, covering his ribs with his other hand. "Brat," he accused fondly. "So tell me about that consulting garbage you were talking about this afternoon."

"It wasn't *garbage*," Emily muttered. "Well, it wasn't," she added, when he shot her a disbelieving look. "Stuart told me that the 'suits' are going ahead with the reorganization."

"I thought that was dropped."

"So did I. But apparently the board of directors was more serious than anyone expected. You know they booted John Cornell out of the presidency not too long ago."

"Have they replaced him yet?"

"Not permanently. Anyway, the board wanted to downsize and they're doing it. Once John was out of the way, they were able to push their plan forward."

"Which means...what?"

Emily felt a pain take root in her temple. "Bottom

line? It means that unless I agree to travel, I'm going to effectively be out of a job.'' She grimaced. ''So much for job security, huh?''

''So, tell them to take a hike. You haven't been happy there, anyway.''

''I've been perfectly content there,'' Emily argued.

''Right.''

Jefferson listened to their soft conversation. What was it like to have someone to share your day with? To talk the simple and not-so-simple things over with? Envy curled through him, closely followed by disgust for being envious of his very own brother. Who was he to wish now for things he'd never wanted in the first place? Lord knew he didn't deserve them. He certainly didn't deserve Emily. He'd bring her nothing but pain. Just like he'd been doing for the better part of ten years now.

Beneath his arm, Emily shifted, and her cool fingers slipped through his, throwing his thinking offtrack for a long moment. He drew in a slow breath, feeling the faint scent of her hair fill his lungs, and recalling that it was the memory of that very same freshly innocent scent that had kept him sane when he'd been locked in a room the size of a closet.

His throat closed, and he cut off that line of thinking. But it didn't matter whether he was thinking about it or not. The fact was that he didn't deserve Emily. One way or the other, he'd end up hurting her.

But he absolutely could not stomach the thought of Emily with someone else. Not even his own brother. Particularly his own brother.

At long last the tires left the paved highway, crossed a series of cattle guards and crunched along the gravel drive. Emily slumped against him, genuine in her sleep, while he was not. Tristan parked and turned off the engine. Jefferson opened his eyes to meet his brother's steady gaze. Jefferson might have fooled Emily, but not Tristan.

The brothers eyed each other, while the cooling engine ticked softly. Finally Tristan palmed the truck keys and reached for the door. "See you in the morning," was all he said before he pushed the door closed with a quiet click and walked around to the back of the house.

Jefferson's head fell back wearily against the seat. Emily was a sweet, warm weight against his side, and he could have happily stayed there for hours while she slept so trustingly against him. Sighing, he pushed open his door, gently dislodging Emily from his shoulder. "Come on, sweetheart, it's time to wake up."

She murmured unintelligibly and scrunched up her face when the interior light came on.

"Emily, honey, come on." He started to take his hand from hers but her fingers convulsed over his.

"Don't," she murmured sleepily.

He lowered his boots to the ground and jiggled her hand. "Em, we're home."

"Mmm-hmm." Still more asleep than awake, she scooted toward him, looping her free hand over his shoulder. Her nose found its niche in the curve of his neck and shoulder, and she sighed deeply.

Jefferson stifled a curse even as his palm slid around her slender hip. Somehow or other he ended up standing outside the truck with Emily's thighs hugging his hips as her cheek lay on his chest. It took every fiber of decency in him not to nudge her down onto the seat. Not to grind his aching hardness against her.

"Emily," his voice was sharper than he intended, and her eyes flew open, staring blankly at him. She blinked a few times and cleared her throat. Brushing a strand of hair out of her eyes, she pushed his shoulder and he moved aside while she slipped out of the truck. She weaved toward the house, then abruptly stopped, seeming to wonder for a moment where she was before correcting course for the back door.

Jefferson shut the truck door and followed her, scooping his arm around her waist as she nearly wandered into the side of the house. "Over here," he murmured, guiding her up the steps and into the mudroom. By the time they made it through the darkened kitchen and halfway up the stairs, Emily was leaning against him again, all but asleep. He gave up the fight and scooped her off her feet to carry her the rest of the way.

It wasn't smart. All this carrying her around. But what was a sharp pain in his hip or the dull throb in his back, compared to the gentle weight of her in his arms. He turned sideways and carried her into her bedroom and deposited her in the middle of the bed.

"Jefferson," she whispered sleepily, her fingers tangling in his hair.

He knew he was a weak man when he let her pull his head lower until her lips found his. Her kiss was soft and sleepy and utterly bewitching.

His forehead met hers as he took a long, shuddering breath. Finally, he pulled her hands away and pressed them gently to the pillow beside her head. "Sweet dreams," he told her softly as he allowed himself one last chaste kiss.

He straightened. Watched her sigh and turn onto her side, curling against the pillow. Turning on his heel, he went into his room, bypassed the bed and headed straight for a cold shower.

Sweet dreams, hell, he thought.

Chapter Eight

Emily woke well before dawn. She pulled off her shoes and slipped out of her clothes then climbed under the blankets again for a few more minutes of sleep.

The few minutes stretched into a few hours. When she finally pushed the pillow off her head and looked around her, she knew the house was empty. Her face split in a yawn as she swung her legs over the side of the bed and stood. Outside her window a dog barked. An engine rumbled to life.

After a hasty wash and a tug or two with the brush, she pulled on a loose pair of shorts she'd made long ago by cutting the legs off an old pair of sweatpants. She added a sport bra and a muscle-T and with socks and running shoes in hand, headed downstairs.

She was standing in the mudroom, stretching her calf muscles, when the phone rang. She went into the kitchen and picked up the phone, but someone else had already answered on another extension. Maggie, she realized and hastily, quietly, hung up before she could overhear anymore of the softly hissed, angry conversation between Maggie and the caller. Joe. Emily returned to her stretching. When she felt loosened up, she headed down the porch and jogged past the barns and the bunkhouse, slowing ever so slightly as she heard the heated voice coming from within. Seemed like everyone was arguing these days. And judging from the clearly audible one-sided phone conversation that was obviously continuing, even Maggie and Joe were.

Turning a deaf ear, Emily picked up speed and returned the way she came, heading instead in the direction of the swimming hole. She hadn't planned on going that direction. In her mind the spot was too closely linked with Jefferson. So she kept her eyes on the ground in front of her as she thumped past the trees and bushes. Eventually, winded and sweaty, she turned and headed back. But this time her eyes wouldn't stay in front of her and she found herself crunching through the fallen leaves and twigs to the edge of the water.

Stretching, she lifted her clinging hair off her neck and eyed the water. Yesterday, it had been freezing. But she hadn't been drenched in sweat, either. If she had more nerve, she would strip off and dive in. After a mental shrug, she pulled off the loose T-shirt and contented herself with dunking it in the cold water and pulling it over her head. It served the purpose of cooling her down, and she began walking back to the house.

Tristan was in the kitchen, the phone at his ear, and when he saw her, he held it toward her. "Stuart," he told her.

Emily pondered the receiver. She didn't really want to talk to Stuart. He wanted a decision from her regarding her job, and she didn't want to give it to him. Taking the receiver from Tristan, she covered it with her hand. "Too bad I wasn't a few minutes later."

"Just tell him what you want to do."

"If I only knew," she muttered. Pulling a clean dish towel out of the drawer she draped it around her neck and dabbed her face. Then she sat down at the table and lifted the phone to her ear. "Hello, Stuart," she greeted.

Ten minutes later Emily wasn't sure if she still had a job or not. She hadn't agreed to take on the consulting position. But Stuart hadn't fired her, either. She supposed it was a good sign. She set the phone on the table, then picked it up again when it suddenly rang. It was for Matthew, so Emily took a message, then went to find him to deliver it.

It was no surprise that he wasn't around, but Emily went to check the bunkhouse just in case. Through the open door she saw Maggie and called out her name.

Maggie whirled around nervously, her fingers brushing her cheeks.

Emily forgot the slip of paper tucked in her palm. "Maggie? What's wrong?" The snatch of argument she'd overheard flitted through her head.

Maggie shook her head. "Nothing." She turned away and pulled an apron around her waist, clearing her throat. "Did you need something?"

"Just looking for Matt. Um, Maggie, you're feeling all right. Aren't you?" It was so obvious the other woman didn't want to talk, that Emily felt like an intruder for even expressing her concern. But she couldn't ignore the fact that Maggie had been crying. No doubt a result of the argument Emily had inadvertently overheard.

"Matt's out with the vet," Maggie answered.

Emily could take a hint. "I'll leave this in his office, then," she wagged the slip slightly. "I sort of made arrangements to go riding with Jaimie this morning, but she's probably given up on me by now. Is she around somewhere?"

"She's with Matt, also. She did mention riding, but that it would need to wait until she finished her chores."

"She surely doesn't need to be tied up every minute with chores. She's a guest, for heaven's sake!"

Some of the tension eased from Maggie's drawn face as she shrugged. "Jaimie wants to do the work. She likes it. Of course it drives Matt up—" she broke off, seeming to realize that she was speaking to a member of Matt's family.

"Up the wall," Emily finished easily. "Good. He needs someone to shake up his world a little. Well, we'll get together later. If you can, perhaps you'll join us? That is if it's all right for you to be riding, what with the baby and all."

The smooth skin around Maggie's eyes seemed to draw up tight. "Maybe," she allowed. She turned to the large refrigerator and yanked open the door. "Let me know later when you're going," she added, her voice muffled by the door.

"Sure." Emily hesitated a moment longer, watching Maggie bend over the deep shelves of the refrigerator. What more could she say? She didn't see any reason on earth why she couldn't become friends with Maggie. They were similarly aged. They were the only women living at the Double-C. Well, add Jaimie to that, for now, Emily amended silently.

Feeling edgy, Emily made her way to Matt's office and left the message on his desk. Then, putting off her shower for a few more minutes, she headed into the horse barn. Daisy greeted her with a soft nicker, and Emily retrieved a brush and currycomb and let herself into Daisy's stall.

She missed her own horse. Missed the morning rides when Bird was frisky and full of sass and vinegar. Missed the regular, soothing ritual of grooming him. Emily ran the brush over Daisy's back. "But you're not too bad, either," she assured the horse softly. "You and Bird would make some pretty babies, too. Wouldn't you?" Daisy's tail flicked. "Of course with him in San Diego and you here, there's not much chance of that." She switched to the comb and smoothly worked on Daisy's mane. "In fact, you have about as much chance with Bird as I do with Jefferson." Daisy's head bobbed. "You agree with me, don't you?

"But," Emily continued, "if I end up with no job, maybe you'll end up meeting Bird after all." Emily hung her arm over the horse's neck and sighed. "What am I going to do, Daisy? I know you're a smart girl. I can see it in your eyes. So what do you think I should do? Hmm?"

"Stop asking horses for advice for one thing."

Emily whirled around, tangling the comb in Daisy's mane. "Dammit, Jefferson, don't sneak up on me." She turned back to the horse and worked the comb free. He was still standing there when she finished, and she shot him a look over her shoulder. "What do you want?"

"Crabby today, eh?"

"So? Did you think you had a corner on that market?" She let herself out of the stall, expecting him to move aside. But he didn't. Her brow rose. "Do you mind?"

Silently, he let her pass. She returned the comb and brush to the tack room and came out to find him still standing by Daisy's stall. His faded jeans were wearing through at the knee, and his denim shirt had been washed nearly colorless. She knew people who paid fortunes to obtain the "distressed" look. But Jefferson wasn't trying to be vogue. He simply looked mouth-watering no matter what he wore.

Next to him, Emily felt like a dirty dishrag in her baggy shorts and wet T-shirt. She probably smelled like something that needed shoveling off the floor, too. Great, just great. She shoved a limp tendril of hair away from her face, wishing like everything that she'd hit the shower instead of—

"Why didn't you tell me you were worried about your job?"

"What?" Her brain sluggishly switched tracks.

"Yesterday, when we were out at the pond."

She shrugged, studying the dusty toes of her running shoes. "It didn't come up."

He lifted her chin with a long finger. "I specifically asked you about your job," he chided. "You didn't say much of anything."

As they were wont to do, Emily's thought processes grew muddled when she looked up into his azure eyes. Her teeth worried the inner corner of her lips. "It, um, didn't seem important," she heard herself say faintly.

"It was important enough to tell Tristan."

Emily blinked away visions of those mobile lips pressed to her skin and concentrated on his words. My Lord, he'd sounded almost jealous. Her mouth went dry, and she slowly moistened her lips. "I'd have told you if I had thought you were really interested."

He went still, his shoulders stiff beneath the denim shirt.

"I'd *tell* you anything," she added softly. "I'd *listen*

to anything you said to me. If you…were—" she hesitated when his finger dropped away from her chin "—interested," she finished, feeling stranded.

She ached at the glimpse of torment in his eyes before he turned away.

His fingers whitened when he closed them over the top rail of Daisy's stall, and his back bowed as he lowered his head. "Leave."

She tentatively touched his hand. "Jefferson—"

He yanked away from even that small touch. "Dammit, Emily, *go.*"

Her mouth opened soundlessly, and she snatched her hand away, clasping it at her waist. She closed her eyes for a moment. Looking anywhere but at him, she instinctively turned toward escape, praying that she wouldn't embarrass herself further by tripping over her wooden feet.

She hurried past the stalls, flinching when she heard his soft curse. Her stomach churned, the need to somehow help him warring with the need to protect herself from more pain. She kept her focus on the sunshine beyond the yawning entry, determined not to turn back. Not even when she heard the sharp crack of something hard and unyielding strike something else equally hard and unyielding.

She heard his footsteps, yet wasn't prepared for the arm he scooped about her waist, pulling her around to him.

She pushed at his arms. "Let me go," she pleaded. Being in his arms was a double-edged sword. Easing distress. Adding tension. Making her crazy.

"I'm sorry," he breathed against her temple. His palms cradled her head as his lips covered hers. "Sorry," he murmured, "so sorry."

She could no more resist his gentle kiss than she could stop breathing. She reached for him, but he caught her hands in his, pressing them to his chest.

"I don't deserve your touch," he muttered between short, burning kisses that left her quaking for more.

She wanted to know what he meant by that. She wanted him to tell her what was in his heart. In his dreams. His nightmares. But his hands were sliding up her arms, into the oversize armholes of her wet shirt. Seeking the swelling curve of breast. The tight crests.

"I can't think," she whispered, her fingertips frantically catching over the buttons on his shirt.

"Just feel." His low growl rustled along her neck as he gently tugged on her ponytail, revealing the curve of her throat to his lips.

She swallowed a moan. He held her arched so tightly to him that she couldn't move her hands from his chest. His heat seared through their clothing, and she strained even closer. Their breath sounded harsh in the silent barn before he closed his mouth over hers.

His large palms molded her shoulders. Moved down her back. Glided over her hips and tilted her against him, rocking against her. His lips fused to hers, his kiss deep, thrusting, and Emily felt it down to her toes. Colors were swirling in her head as he slipped his fingers up the loose leg of her raggedy shorts. He swallowed her cry when he brushed his thumb across her smooth hip. Her naked hip.

He groaned her name as his hand shifted, cupping her bare bottom.

Daisy snorted, and Jefferson's head shot up.

"No," Emily cried faintly. Her knees were so weak she could only sag against him. But she heard the same thing that Jefferson did. The sound of boots crunching across the gravel. Definitely drawing closer, accompanied by the indistinct murmur of voices.

Jefferson slowly withdrew his hand and adjusted her shorts. Wordlessly he set her away from him, and moments before Daniel rounded the yawning entry to the barn Jefferson disappeared out the back.

She fruitlessly smoothed her ponytail. Her body hummed with yearning, and no doubt Daniel would know with a single glance just what was what. Sawyer appeared just moments behind Dan, but the men merely greeted her with lifted arms before veering off to the side and heading down the other row.

She sagged. Relieved. Frustrated. Her legs were none too steady when she walked toward the back side of the barn, but when she looked out, Jefferson was nowhere in sight. Damn the man, anyway. She kicked the side of the barn, but it didn't help. And she was left with a set of throbbing toes.

She stomped back to the house, not even pausing when she heard the raised voices coming from inside. She let the screen door slam nice and loud as she entered and walked in to find Jaimie and Matthew squared off on either side of the big table. "Stop arguing," she said wearily. "Can't anyone around here carry on a normal conversation? Can't any of us have normal relationships with each other?"

Matthew snorted, but his eyes were trained on Jaimie. "If people were *reasonable,*" he began.

Jaimie huffed, clearly girding herself for another skirmish. "Reasonable? Look who's talking! I was perfectly capable of handling that truck—"

"Capable! You backed it into a fence."

"Then why were you waving for me to keep going?"

"I was waving for you to stop," he gritted.

Emily raked her fingers through her hair. ''I am going upstairs,'' she announced, even though it was perfectly obvious that the other two had already forgotten her presence.

After showering, Emily changed into a deep blue sundress. Still restless and out of sorts, she dried her hair and pulled it back into a loose braid, then smoothed on some makeup. She might feel like a wreck on the inside, but at least from the outside she appeared perfectly controlled. It was some small comfort.

She tidied up the room, then headed downstairs. She heard the clang of the bell from the bunkhouse kitchen. Maggie, announcing the noon meal. Her bare feet were soundless as she entered the blessedly empty kitchen. Propping her chin on her hands, she leaned against the counter and looked through the window at the activity Maggie's summons had spurred. A pickup rolled by and a group of young men hopped out, heading straight for the bunkhouse. They looked like high school kids.

Probably were, since it was still summer vacation. Matt would've hired the kids, giving them a chance to earn some money. Within minutes, it all quieted. Everyone was probably seated at that huge long slab of a table, tucking in to the rib-sticking meal that Maggie, most capably, would have laid out for them.

Operations at the Double-C were running as always, smooth as glass.

So where did she fit in?

There was not a lick of work around this place that wasn't already being handled by someone else. And from the way things were progressing at her office, she was either going to have to agree to the type of job she'd never wanted, or look elsewhere.

Knowing that she was sinking into a depressing

mood, she sighed deeply and straightened. It wasn't as
if she weren't capable of finding a new job, she reasoned
with herself as she began opening cupboards and pulling
out ingredients.

She was well qualified and had an excellent employment history. She even enjoyed her work. Found it satisfying to make everything balance out in the end. Numbers were numbers. They could be counted on. Oh, sure,
you could manipulate them just like anything else, but
the numbers themselves? They were always constant.
Unlike some things.

She thumped a bag of flour on the counter and a little
puff of white floated into the air. *Be honest, Emily, my
girl. You are never going to be completely satisfied. Because what you really want is a family. A husband. Not
just any husband, either.*

"What on earth are you planning to make? Pickle-
flavored cookies?"

Tristan's voice startled her, and she accidentally
knocked the box of unsweetened chocolate off the
counter with her elbow. Aware that he'd bent to pick
up the box, she blinked at the conglomeration of items
she'd gathered. Sure enough, among the flour and sugar,
butter and vanilla, sat a huge jar of dill pickles. Grimacing, she returned the jar to the refrigerator.

"Okay, squirt, what's bugging you?"

"Aside from my entire life?" She answered flip-
pantly. "Not a thing." She pulled out a small saucepan
and automatically began melting butter and chocolate
squares.

"Now, come on." He poured himself a glass of water
and drank it down in a single gulp, then refilled it and
did it again. "It can't be that bad," he finally said.

"Says who," she muttered. She lowered the heat and

turned around, her arms crossed. She cocked her head and cast a considering eye his way. "You know, Tristan, you really are an attractive man."

His eyebrows shot up.

"No, I'm serious." She considered him for a few more moments. "How come you've never...you know." She flapped her hand.

"You know?" He echoed warily. "What, *you know?*"

"You know," her eyes widened meaningfully. "You. Me. It's not as if you don't like women."

"Cripes, Em! We don't feel that way and you know it. Geez..." He shook his head, and headed for the back door.

"Wait a minute," Emily stopped him with a hand on his arm. His white T-shirt was sweaty and his jeans were covered with dust. His golden tan had deepened to an even darker hue from working outside, and his familiar blue eyes looked warily down at her from his towering height. The man had a brain that was darn-near frightening, and he had looks that rivaled Jefferson's. If there was a single man on the face of the earth who could measure up to Jefferson Clay, it would be his youngest brother.

But to her, Tristan was simply her best friend. Nothing more. Nothing less.

"What? If I don't hurry up, there's not gonna be any food left."

"Forget your stomach for a minute." She frowned. "I'm serious. Tell me why."

"Em—"

"Come on. Consider it research."

"Gee, thanks."

"Tristan—"

"Oh, hell." He flipped the hair off his forehead, clearly aggrieved.

"You're impossible." She turned back to the stove. "It was just a question."

He sighed abruptly and plopped down onto a kitchen chair. "The things you ask of me," he muttered. "Never let it be said that I disappointed a woman."

"Just forget it, will you? I changed my mind. I don't *want* to know."

"Well...inquiring minds want to know and all that."

She shot him a look.

He shrugged, dropping the sarcasm as she slumped into a chair. "You know what your problem is?"

"I'm sure you'll tell me."

"Lack of sex."

She groaned and dropped her head to the table. "Tell me something I don't know," she said, her voice muffled. Her shoulders heaved with a huge sigh and she sat up. "Tell me what to do, Tris. I'm at a loss. And I'm not referring to sex," she added hastily.

"Thank God. I love ya squirt, but lessons in sex are not something I'm willing to give you. I prefer pupils who have some...personal...interest in me."

She made a disgusted sound and rose to remove the chocolate from the stove. "I live with you," she reminded him. "I've seen your *pupils*."

"Okay, this emotional quandary is either about your job, or about Jefferson. I'll pick door number two and choose my big, bad brother. And much as it pains me to say it, I don't have a clue what you should do."

"There's a first."

"Snottiness will get you nowhere, runt."

"Being a good little girl isn't getting me anywhere, either." She cracked an egg and tossed the shell into the sink, then followed it with two more. "I'm not sure I should stay here any longer," she said, voicing the unpalatable idea that had been swimming in her mind.

"Emily, this is as much your home as anyone's."

She smiled sadly, clearly showing that she had very nearly made up her mind. She heard him stifle a curse.

"It's ironic, Tristan. All these years of enduring Jefferson's departures. And this time, I'm going to be the one to leave."

"You'll go back to San Diego, then."

Her lashes kept him from seeing her expression, but she worried her lip.

"Emily?"

"Maybe it's time for a change," she whispered. "Past time."

"Dammit! I don't want to lose my best friend because my brother's too stubborn to see what is right under his nose!"

Emily turned back to the batter, stirring blindly. "Don't be angry with Jefferson. He can't help the way—"

Tristan stopped her with a blunt word. "He's in love with you, Emily. Pure and simple."

"If he loves me," she nearly choked on the words, "he'd stop pushing me away." She gave up trying to mix the batter. "I know he has feelings for me," she acknowledged. "That he's attracted to me." Color rose in her cheeks, but she made herself continue. "But I need him to share himself with me. You know? His thoughts. His dreams. His past. But even more, *he* needs someone that he can share himself with that way." Her jaw worked. "That person isn't me. It's time I faced that." She looked up at Tristan.

"So you're going to use his example and run away from the people who love you?"

It hurt Emily to hear Tristan phrase it so bluntly. "That's probably what I'm doing," she admitted. "But I can't go on this way. Maybe a complete break will help."

"It's not gonna help me," Tristan argued. "It's sure as hell not going to help Jefferson. And what about Matt and Dan? What about Squire? What are you going to tell Squire?"

"I don't know!" She cried. "But Jefferson *is* a Clay. And he needs you all so much. He just doesn't know how to say it. I can't bear for him to be so unhappy, and my presence here is only making it worse!"

"Neither of you has to leave. And you're a Clay, too," Tristan said firmly. "That fact is half of Jefferson's problem."

"What?"

"It's stupid, as far as I'm concerned," Tristan continued. "And he'll probably break my legs for me when he finds out I said something. But he's gotten some crazy idea about his feelings for you not being appropriate. What with Squire raising you and all."

"But that's ridiculous. Jefferson knows we're not related." Her lips twisted. "We've even talked about it."

Tristan shrugged. "Have you told Jefferson that you're planning to leave?"

"Not yet."

"Promise me one thing, then."

"What?"

"Promise first."

She rolled her eyes. "I promise."

"Don't tell Squire or anyone else that you're leaving until after you've told Jefferson." He yanked open the door. "I swear, Emily, you're not going to give up your home and family, even if I have to make good on my threat to Jefferson and marry you myself."

Emily blinked. After a moment's delayed confusion, she jogged out to the mudroom and swung out the screen door, looking at his departing back. "What's that supposed to mean? Tristan?" She yelled after him, but he ignored her.

"Remember your promise," he yelled back, moments before swinging up into the back of the pickup that had rolled to a stop behind him.

Through narrowed eyes she watched the crew head back out to the fields.

What had Tristan gone and said to Jefferson?

Chapter Nine

Emily had halfway planned to ask Sawyer what he thought about employment prospects back East, but her promise to Tristan kept her silent. Instead, she found herself counting the minutes of each hour of the day until after their early supper, when they'd all troop to town to visit Squire. All of them except Jefferson.

The man who'd basically kept to himself all day long, she reminded herself as she followed Daniel outside to the vehicles, a plastic-wrapped plate of brownies in her hand.

Sawyer and Jefferson were standing several yards away. Another arguing pair. Emily watched them openly, though she couldn't hear a word.

"Are you planning to stand there all day?" Tristan nudged her arm toward the car. "I'd drive that little tin can you rented, but your seat doesn't go back far enough."

"What do you suppose that's all about?" She hunched her shoulder in the direction of Sawyer and Jefferson.

Tristan dropped his arm over her shoulders. "Hard to say. Maybe wise old Sawyer is giving Jefferson some advice on his love life."

Emily elbowed Tristan in the ribs. "Very funny." She rounded the car and yanked open the door. Across the roof of the vehicle she watched Sawyer gesture. Jefferson suddenly lifted his head, and across the distance his eyes searched out Emily. She found herself holding her breath.

Jefferson said something to Sawyer who shook his head sharply. But after a moment, the two men shook hands. Jefferson stood watching as Sawyer returned to the Blazer. A faded duffel bag sat on the gravel near the truck, and Sawyer picked it up and tossed it into the rear before going around to climb in beside Matthew.

She looked at the spot where the bag had been. The pang that shot through her left her knees weak. "What's the bag for?" she asked Tristan.

"Hmm?" He noticed her expression. "What's wrong?"

"Is Jefferson leaving?"

Tristan started. "Hell no, he's not leaving! You're the one talking about that nonsense."

"But the duffel—"

Tristan squinted and looked over to the truck. "Oh, that was probably just some clothes of Squire's. He wanted us to bring him some of his own stuff. Relax, would ya?"

"So why didn't Sawyer use Squire's suitcase?" she asked as she placed the brownies on the floor in the back seat.

"What?"

"The duffel," Emily said impatiently. "Why would Sawyer take Squire's stuff in Jefferson's duffel? Or it could be Sawyer's duffel, I guess."

"Well how on earth should I know? Maybe he couldn't find Squire's suitcase. Geez, Emily. Get a grip would ya?"

"You'd tell me if Jefferson was leaving, wouldn't you?"

Tristan heaved a sigh. "I'd tell you," he promised. "And he's not leaving."

Emily bit the inside of her lip. Her eyes went from Tristan's exasperated gaze to Matt's truck. Jefferson was the only one not inside the truck. "Okay, I believe you," she mumbled and climbed into the car. She started the engine and pulled in behind the Blazer, far enough back that they weren't choked in the dust stirred up by the other vehicle.

In her rearview mirror, she caught sight of Jefferson as he lingered by the aspen trees, watching their departure. After a moment he turned away and walked out of sight behind the big house. Suddenly she took her foot off the gas and coasted to a stop.

"What are you doing?"

Emily's fingers tapped on the steering wheel and pinned Tristan with a firm look. "You didn't really tell Jefferson we were involved, did you?"

Tristan looked uncomfortable.

"You didn't." She wanted to throttle him. "Tristan, what am I going to do with you? No wonder Jefferson keeps giving us strange looks."

"He didn't believe me," Tristan assured her. "I was just trying to light a fire under him. For all the good it did," he added darkly. "Hey, what are you doing?"

Emily unsnapped the safety belt and got out. "You'll have to drive. Legroom or not. Tell Squire I'll see him tomorrow," she said. "And give his nurses the brownies, please. Don't eat them all before you get there."

"What are you planning to do?"

"Get some answers," she replied. "Or make a complete and utter fool of myself." She shrugged. "Take your pick."

Tristan got out and rounded the car. "Tell him about your crazy idea of leaving," he advised as he began folding himself into the driver's seat. He knocked his knee on the steering wheel and grunted. "Maybe I should just stay behind," he muttered.

"Don't you dare," Emily pushed his head inside and closed the door on him. "This is one evening the place isn't crawling with people, and I plan to take advantage of it." Color rose in her cheeks. "I mean—"

Tristan chuckled and started the engine. "Don't let him scare you off," he said, sobering. "You're exactly what he needs." He gave her a thumbs-up and shifted into gear.

Emily hastily backtracked so she wouldn't get an eyeful of dust. "Exactly what he needs," she repeated, wishing that she could be as confident of the notion as Tristan seemed to be.

She drew in a deep breath and brushed a strand of hair out of her eyes. With her heart in her throat, she began walking back toward the house.

It took a little longer than she'd expected. And she felt hot and sticky by the time she walked into the kitchen. She prowled through the rooms of the main floor, but Jefferson was nowhere in sight. Nor was he upstairs or in the den or in the basement. In fact, Emily finally gave up and acknowledged that the man wasn't anywhere in the house at all.

Feeling anticlimactic, she retreated to her room. When she freshened up and looked at herself in the mirror, she knew she was being cowardly. Jefferson had to be somewhere. If she wanted to find him, she could. She would.

She let herself out through the front door, narrowing her eyes against the fiery sunlight that hovered just above the horizon. Streaks of red and orange blazed across the sky in a magnificent sunset. The wooden swing that had always been on the front porch was empty, swaying gently in the warm breeze. She went down the steps and headed around the side of the house, scanning the grounds for some sign of Jefferson.

She stuck her head inside the horse barn. But the only sounds that greeted her were the soft nickers from the half dozen horses enclosed in their stalls. She walked around to the corrals, but the only one who paid attention was the golden retriever that slowly rose from her sprawl in the fading sun to join Emily. "Hey, Sandy," she softly greeted Matthew's dog and bent down to scratch behind her ears. "Where's Jefferson?"

But the dog merely cocked her head and looked back with her gentle eyes.

Emily gave the dog a final pat and stood. To her right lay the gravel road that led toward the machinery barn. Voices and music rang from the bunkhouse as the men finished up their evening meal. She headed that way and stuck her head inside the side door. Many heads turned her way, smiling and nodding and calling out greetings. But Jefferson's blond head wasn't one of them.

She returned Maggie's wave and left.

Situated farthest from the big house, was another set

of corrals used primarily during branding. The foreman's home was west of the corrals. She could just see the back side of the brick house. She propped her hands on her hips. Still no sign of Jefferson.

Pursing her lips, she began walking back the way she'd come. She passed the horse barn again and paused. In a smooth curve, the gravel road led to the swimming hole.

She set off for the trees, forgoing the gravel for the softer knee-high grass alongside the road. When she came upon the lilac bushes growing lush and thick among the trees surrounding the natural spring, the sun was casting its last efforts of daylight. Twigs crackled beneath her sandals as she slipped between two trees.

A slender shaft of sunlight arrowed through the trees, highlighting the man's shaggy golden mane. Emily stopped cold, her hand pressing flat to her stomach. Jefferson was sprawled on his back atop the flattish boulder that jutted out from the bank.

His head was toward the water, his sun-gilded hair drifting from the rock toward the still water. Almost like a dream, she watched his eyes turn directly toward her. As if he'd been expecting her.

Desire clenched inside her. Low and demanding. This was no dream.

She stepped forward.

In just the moment it took to cross the few yards to the boulder, the shaft of sunlight flickered then slid away to nothing. Twilight still hovered in the air, holding back the evening darkness, and she saw his chest slowly rise and fall.

"I thought you were going to see Squire," he said.

"I was," she toed off her sandals and stepped closer. Beneath her foot, the boulder was still warm from the day's heat. "I'm here to see you instead." She looked down at him.

He opened his eyes and looked up at her, silent. She couldn't tell what he was thinking. It was too dark now. Not that she'd be able to tell even if it were broad daylight.

"Squire'll miss you," he murmured.

"I'm sure he misses you, too. No matter what the problem is between you. But he's doing much better and his cardiologist is talking about releasing him soon."

He lifted his arm and bent it across his eyes.

"Aren't you glad he'll be home soon?" she asked.

"Of course I am." It was true. He was glad his father was improving. Glad that the man would be returning to his own home soon. It also meant, though, that Jefferson would have to be moving on soon. And the thought of leaving the ranch again brought on a curious sense of grief.

"Pardon me, but you don't look overjoyed."

He deliberately forced his hand to relax before it could curl into a fist.

"I know, I know," Emily said. "None of my business."

He heard her walking around the boulder and then felt the warmth of her against his knee when she sat down beside him. He watched her from beneath his arm. She stretched out one leg until her toe broke the glassy surface of the water. Drawing in her breath, she retracted her foot. It was one thing to go for a dunking during the middle of the day. But the evening was another matter entirely.

"I remember when Squire taught you how to swim

out here. You were like a little fish. It didn't matter how cold the water got, you still wanted to go swimming.''

Beneath the full skirt, she propped her foot on the rock and clasped her arms around her bent knees. ''You do that a lot, you know,'' she pointed out. ''Veer our conversations back to my childhood.''

She lowered her cheek to her knees and continued speaking softly, amazed that her voice was steady when her heart was thundering so unevenly. ''As if by putting my existence in that context you won't have to deal with me. You won't have to acknowledge what's going on between us. You won't have to give up any of those precious secrets you keep hoarded so close to your chest.

''There is nothing going on between me and Tristan. I don't know exactly *what* he said to you. Only that he said *something*. But he and I are just friends. Exactly like I told you in San Diego. He was just…just…'' She broke off.

''I know what he was doing.''

Emily nibbled on the inside of her lip and was grateful for the gathering darkness. She softly cleared her throat. ''Would it have mattered to you? If it had been true?''

Jefferson took the question like a blow to his midriff. He wanted to tell her. Tell her exactly how much every little thing about her mattered. He wanted to spill his bloody guts and let her sweetness wash over him. But it all came back to those damned secrets she accused him of hoarding.

Secrets. He was so sick and tired of secrets. Of partial truths. Of cover stories. But he didn't think he was up to the aversion he'd see in her pansy brown eyes if she knew the truth. He didn't even know if he knew how to get the words out anymore.

She made a frustrated sound at his continued silence and pushed up from the rock. She bent and picked up her sandals. "One of these days," she murmured bitterly as she walked back toward the trees, "I'm going to learn how to leave you alone." Her voice went slightly hoarse, but he still heard her words. "I'm going to finally get it through my head that you don't want, or need, anything from me."

Jefferson sat up and watched her pick her way back through the trees. He even called her name, but she didn't hear. Or perhaps she did. Calling himself a fool, he pushed himself up from the boulder and went after her.

She was leaning against a tree trunk, pulling on her sandals. "Emily."

She looked over her shoulder at him, and he realized she was crying. "Go away."

"That's my line." He took the other shoe from her and bent over. He brushed away the crushed leaves from the sole of her foot before sliding on the sandal. She went to step away from the tree, but he moved, blocking her from leaving. He brushed his thumb across her cheek. "I'm sorry."

"I'm sorry, too," she sniffed. "I'm sorry you're a sorry, stubborn, mangy, moth-eaten, mulish, jackass—"

He shut her up the simplest way he knew. He kissed her.

Her breath was tumbling past her lips when he raised his head. But at least she was quiet. "Moth-eaten?"

"Damn you, Jefferson Clay," she muttered, curling her palm behind his neck. She pulled his head down and kissed him back.

His breath was uneven when he raised his head. He pulled her hands from his neck, and with one hand he anchored them safely above her head, against the tree. "We can't do this."

"So you've said."

She tugged at her hands, and he adjusted his grip accordingly.

"Over and over again," she added, renewing her efforts to unleash herself.

Her squirming succeeded in arching her back away from the tree trunk, and had he been a gentleman he'd have stepped back when her curves thrust up against his chest. Of course, had he been a gentleman he wouldn't have her trapped against the tree, either.

She seemed to realize her position and suddenly ceased struggling, choosing to plaster herself back against the peeling tree bark. A good half foot out of touching range. "Let me go," she ordered.

He had to look away from the dark eyes bravely staring him down. He stifled a curse. "I wish I could," he muttered.

She let loose a stream of invectives he hadn't heard her use since she was a teenager. "Impressive," he said, dryly applauding her efforts. But he still didn't let her loose.

She sagged. Her head drooped like a broken flower. "*Please,* Jefferson. Don't toy with me."

He gently cupped her satin-smooth cheek. "Ah, Em...*oof*...dammit!"

She'd punched him in the stomach! Hard enough to get his attention. Surprise held him still for the minuscule moment it took for her to slip around him and stalk off toward the house.

He set off after her, and uneven though his gait was,

he soon overtook her. "Hold it," he muttered, scooping an arm around her waist.

She pushed at his hands, trying to move forward. "Shove it," she spat. "I hate you!"

"Oh, hell," Jefferson grumbled and simply took her to the ground. He cushioned her fall with his body, but she was scrambling about so that he twisted until she lay pinned beneath him.

His body's reaction was all too predictable.

"I hate you," she repeated, even as her hands slipped over his shoulders.

"Good. It's safer that way."

A broken laugh escaped, and her softly ragged breath struck his throat, followed by the butter-soft glide of her tongue, then her lips. It was torturous heaven. He pushed up on his arms, painfully aware of the way her thighs, beneath the flowing dress, relaxed to cradle him. Painfully aware that they were fully out of sight of the buildings. That, lying here in the darkness, hidden in the long grass, they could do exactly what they wanted, with no one to see.

Her breath hissed in sweetly when he pressed against the juncture where their two bodies collided. Her head fell back in the long grass, exposing a silken line of throat to the rising moon.

He had to taste that skin. His hunger for her was killing him. He pressed his open mouth to her throat, feeling her throat work. She was sweeter than honey. He slid his hand to her cheek, and she turned into his touch, burning his palm with her kiss.

Angling his weight to the side, he slid his leg over hers, running his palm along her hip and across the flat of her stomach. Her dark eyes were bottomless in the shadowed moonlight. His palm glided upward and cupped her breast. Gently plucked the pebbled peak.

"I watched you drive away this evening," he said, barely audible. He lowered his head and took the nipple between his teeth, fabric and all. She arched against him. "I knew I'd never seen anything so beautiful as you. And then you showed up here, by the water and it was like I'd conjured you out of my thoughts."

His name whispered from her lips.

"I knew—" he lifted his head and looked up at the stars beginning to sparkle overhead "—I knew what you were thinking."

He felt her fingers tangle in his hair, pulling it from the leather string holding it back. When he looked back down at her, she was still again.

And he knew she was bracing herself. Waiting for him to push her away again.

"You were thinking about us together. About me touching you. Filling you." He closed his eyes and prayed for forgiveness. "I was thinking it, too." He opened his eyes to see her swallow. "God help me, I can't stop this," he admitted, his voice raw and as quiet as the night.

Her heart was so full, she thought she'd burst. "Maybe God doesn't want you to stop," she whispered. She knew she was praying that Jefferson wouldn't.

His teeth flashed when he threw back his head. "You should be properly married."

It was what she'd been taught all her life. But the only one she would *ever* marry would be this man. And he'd never put his head in that particular noose. A peculiar calm spread through her. "I should be loved," she said steadily. "Truly loved."

He flinched, as if she'd punched him in the stomach again. "Don't."

"Jefferson—"

His hand left her breast and touched her lips. "Shh."

Emily took the hand in hers and kissed it. The stars twinkled dizzily above their heads. She wondered why on earth it had taken her so long to admit the truth to him. "I love you, Jefferson."

He shook his head slightly, his lips tight. "No."

"Yes." She held on to his hand when he would have pulled back. "I love you."

"You don't mean it."

She pressed his palm to her heart. "I do."

His fingers curled into the cool cotton. "You're just...caught up in the moment."

She pushed herself up until she sat, facing him. Her resolve was already shaking. How many times had she wanted to tell Jefferson what was in her heart? How many times, faced with his displeasure, had she backed down?

Not this time. Not yet. "I've loved you for as long as I can remember, Jefferson. If I'm caught up in *the moment* as you say..." She had to swallow before the words would emerge. "Then so are you." On her knees, she leaned forward and speared her fingers through his hair. She kissed his brow. His temple. The now-familiar scar at the corner of his eye.

His breath was warm on her cheek, and she moved until her lips were a hair's breadth from his. "You don't have to say it back, Jefferson," she whispered. "Just don't pretend that I'm too young, or too naive or too whatever to know what my own feelings are."

Her tongue flicked out to lightly taste the corner of his lips. "I *do* love you." She kissed his jaw, ran the tip of her tongue along the narrow ridge of scar tissue. "And I believe, if you'd let yourself, that we could be happy together. But what I want most right now is just you. And me."

She caught his earlobe between her teeth, then soothed it with her tongue. "I want you to make love to me," she murmured against his ear. "More than I've ever wanted anything in my life." She held her breath and forced herself to sit back on her heels. "But if you tell me right now that you...don't...want me," she said as she drew in a shaky breath, "then I'll leave you alone." She didn't know how she'd be able to keep the promise. But she would. She'd go away, just as she'd told Tristan she would. She'd leave. So that, if only this one time, Jefferson could stay.

Her heart stopped when he sat up, too. She was going to have to keep her word. Oh, God, please.

She looked back over her shoulder toward the buildings. The spotlight high on the corner of the horse barn threw its bright light over part of the corrals. Someone, Joe, probably back from wherever he'd been earlier, was working a big dark horse. Squire was lying in a hospital bed, and life at the ranch still moved on. Somehow or other, she would, too.

The thought did nothing to stop a hot tear from squeezing out the corner of her eye. Dammit, she wasn't going to fall apart. She just wasn't! "My love for you isn't going to go away. It hasn't even after all these years." Emily realized she'd said the thought aloud and she dashed another tear from her cheek. Sniffing, she looked down at her hands. "Seeing you, being near you and not...not—" She broke off, swallowing another wad of tears. "I know you're hurting inside and you won't let me help.'' Her hands moved helplessly. ''It's tearing me apart.''

She felt, more than heard, the rough sound he made. He raked back his hair with one hand. ''Poor Jefferson,'' she murmured. ''This is exactly the sort of thing you hate. I'm sorry,'' she managed to push herself unevenly to her feet and turned instinctively toward the buildings. She was so cold inside.

''Emily, stop.''

Hardly daring to breathe, she hesitated, then turned back. Her heart filled her throat when he rose to his feet. She searched his expression, but the night shadows made it impossible. The breeze stirred, lifting his hair across his face. The cool air danced around her bare shoulders.

He turned his face into the breeze, letting it wash over him. ''I'm too old for you, Emily. I always have been.

''Wait,'' he said as her shoulders drooped. ''I'm not finished yet. There's an eon of living. Existing.'' He took a step closer. ''My entire life separates us. But that doesn't keep me from wanting you.'' Squire's anger...his disapproval...his threat to have Jefferson drawn and quartered if he so much as laid a hand on Emily...hadn't kept him from wanting her. ''I don't want to hurt you, Emily, and I know I will.''

''So it's better to hurt me now, than later. Right?'' She hugged her arms close.

''No! Dammit, that's not what I'm saying.'' He reached for her shoulders and pulled her to him. ''I'm saying I want you so badly I ache to my back teeth with it. And right now I'm too damn tired and too selfish to push you away again.''

He'd pulled her off balance, and her arms were

trapped between them. "Be very sure, Emily," he warned. "Because once I start, I'm not going to stop."

Time slowly ticked by. A rogue cloud drifted across the moon, briefly obscuring the cool light. She moistened her dry lips. "I'm sure."

The rigidity left his shoulders. He ran his thumbs over her cheeks, drying the trail of tears. She could barely breathe, her heart thudded so slowly and painfully. He stepped back, slipping her hand into his.

"We're not going back to the house?" She looked over her shoulder toward the lights shining from the big windows. When she looked back at him, his gaze seemed trained on the house. "Jefferson?"

"No. Not there." He continued toward the swimming hole, tugging her hand gently. "This way."

Emily followed, brushing a strand of hair out of her eyes. He led them back through the trees and across to the opposite side of the swimming hole where the thick grass vied with a heavy mat of clover for supremacy. The water's edge was only a foot away, still and reflecting the faint sliver of the moon. A frog croaked. The leaves in the trees rustled. She'd never heard such sweet music.

Jefferson began unbuttoning his shirt and she swallowed, suddenly nervous. He tugged the tails loose from his jeans and shrugged out of it. He tossed it to the side, away from the water, then crouched at her feet.

"Lift," he instructed softly. She obeyed and he removed first one sandal. Then the other. The grass was cool and soft beneath her feet. His palms circled her ankles and she trembled. Her fingers found his shoulder, steadying her. His hands smoothed the full skirt about her calves, slipped beneath to glide across her bare legs, curving behind her knees. He held her there for a long moment, looking up at her, giving her time to steady. Her fingers went from his shoulder to his forehead, pushing his hair back, letting the moonlight find his features.

His eyes captured hers, holding them steady when his fingertips slipped up to her hips and slowly, so slowly, eased beneath the lacy edge of her panties. The fabric of her dress rustled as he drew them away. She knew her love for him was in her own eyes. Could he *see* the truth of the words he didn't want to believe?

Her panties slipped to her feet, and she automatically stepped out of them. Jefferson tossed the lacy scrap over by his shirt and slowly pushed himself upright. Tall and straight, he seemed to tower over her, even blocking out the cool white moonlight.

For a moment he seemed carved from stone. The long, roping muscles in his arms, the broad, hard plane of his chest, down to the lean stomach. She reached out to touch the ridge of muscle just above his waistband. He was almost too perfect to be real. But the washboard muscles flexed beneath her touch, and she knew he was real. Real, and so very, very warm.

Her fingers meandered up over his taut skin, which gleamed golden even in the moonlight. She felt the ridges of his ribs. An indentation in his skin. Another scar, she realized. Her hand skimmed up, over his chest. Felt a flat male nipple rub against her palm. Stopped directly over his heart. Rejoiced that his heartbeat was just that little bit uneven. That little bit too hard.

Her breath was tumbling past her lips, and her fingers trembled. Jefferson nudged her chin up and gently captured her lips. She swayed and grabbed hold of his belt loops, vaguely aware of his fingers guiding down the zipper at the back of her dress. His lips left hers and forged trails of heat as he worked his way to the curve of her shoulder. Her head felt heavy on her neck, and she blinked at the stars shining overhead. The zipper made a soft rasp, and her dress drifted loose, barely held in place by the narrow straps over her shoulders.

He drew a blunt finger up the ridge of her spine, setting off all manner of shivers. His name escaped her lips as his finger grazed the pulse beating at her neck, then dipped beneath the fabric barely covering her breasts. The strap slipped from her shoulder, baring one full breast to his eyes. Then he slid his finger up, finding her achingly hard nipple.

It was torture, the way he circled and taunted. With a soft cry, she covered his hand with her own, pulling until it covered her, surrounded her soft skin with his warm touch. She looked down to see his big hand molding her breast, her smaller hand resting atop his. Unbearably aroused, she could only look at him. He smiled faintly.

"Kiss me," she whispered. He did. On her temple. Her jaw. Her shoulder. She sank her hands into his hair and tugged. "Kiss me," she begged. He responded by capturing her ponytail in one hand and gently tugging her head back. He tasted the pulse beating at the base of her neck. "You're making me crazy," she accused breathlessly.

"I want you crazy," he whispered. "Crazy and as bloody desperate as I've been all these years."

His tongue explored the shell-like curves of her ear, and shivers danced down her entire body. She squirmed against him, enjoying the way his skin leaped when she ran her palms across his abdomen. His lips were traveling again. Exploring her other shoulder. Her head bent over his when he passed beneath her chin, replacing the coolness of the night air with the warmth of his breath. Then his mouth trailed over the slope of her breast and closed over the rigid peak. A soft moan filled the night, and she realized it was coming from her.

He slipped his arm behind her back, holding her steady when her knees went lax as he gently suckled her. She trembled violently as he meandered to her other breast and plucked at the aching peak through the fabric still covering her. She gasped his name when he went onto his knees before her.

Leaning back on his heels, Jefferson looked up at her. At the sheen of wetness on the jutting curve of her breast. His hands slipped beneath the dress. Her fingers were digging into his shoulders, but he barely noticed. Just as he barely noticed his hip and knee protesting at his position. "Do you have any idea how much I want you?" He leaned forward and pressed his lips to her belly. He felt her trembling. "How often I've dreamed about you?"

Her fingers went to his hair, tangling in it. And he realized why he hadn't cut it all off, just yet. He'd been waiting for her touch. Waiting for this.

He should be shot for what he was doing. There was no future for them. No future for him.

"Jefferson?" Her soft voice glided over him.

He gritted his teeth, forcing himself to keep his touch gentle. Slow. She deserved that much from him, at least.

"Jefferson, you, uh, you're not, um...oh, *please,*" she broke off on a little cry when his kiss burned through the dress to her abdomen. To her thigh. "Tell me this isn't just for me."

"Hmm?" He barely heard her, his attention was so focused on the heated vee beneath the blue fabric. How he wanted to touch her there. Kiss her. But not yet. Not yet.

She trembled beneath his hands and sank to her knees. He saw the way her hands twisted together. The way she hesitated. His jaw clenched as he managed to beat down the urge to tumble her onto her back and have her. Once and for all.

He should take advantage of the moment and stop this madness. He should. But he didn't. He lifted her chin with a finger. "Hey," he asked as he cocked his head so he could see her face. "What is it?"

It was his gentleness that undid her. If he'd been his usual taciturn self, she might have gotten the words out again, without feeling her entire being flush with embarrassment. She closed her eyes, desire twisting through her, fighting against the wave of mortification. "You're not doing this because you feel sorry for me, or something, are you?"

He went so still, that she *had* to look at him. "Jefferson?"

His mouth twisted wryly. "The only one I'm gonna feel sorry for is me, if we don't stop all this jabberin'."

"That's not exactly an answer," she pointed out, flushing anew.

He moved suddenly, catching her shoulders in his hands and pushing her back against the fragrant clover. His momentum carried him right on top of her, where he pressed himself against her. "Is this answer enough?" He slipped a hand behind her, tilting her hips toward him. "You think I get this way because I feel *sorry* for you?"

She'd annoyed him. She could tell. Her breath stuck in her throat as he moved again and her knees lifted instinctively to hug his hips. "Well, excuse me," she murmured tartly. "I just want to be clear on where we stand here. Oh, my…"

Jefferson lifted his head from her neck. He took a few slow breaths. "By all means, Emily. Let's be clear here. I want you. That *point* is glaringly obvious." He added dryly. "And you," he said, slipping a hand wickedly down her abdomen, making her breath whistle between her teeth, "want me. I think seven years of foreplay is long enough."

She could have slugged him again. Would he really reduce their relationship to just sex? Her hand even clenched into a fist. "Put this to better work," he murmured, pulling that hand to his button fly.

Her heart raced. "I'm going to have sex with you because I love you," she ground out, her fingers busily fumbling over the buttons strained beyond their normal capacity.

"I'm making love with you because I want you," he returned. His fingers curled into the folds of fabric caught between them. He gave a tug and the dress flew over her head.

She clenched her jaw and forced the last few buttons loose. With one hand on either side of his hips, she yanked down his jeans and briefs in one fell swoop.

Breathless, she fell back, looking up at him.

"Losing your nerve now?"

Her eyebrow shot up. Without stopping to think, she closed her hand over his rigid length. "What do you think?" She demanded.

"Geez—" he rolled onto his back, pulling her with him. She sprawled across him, all curving limbs and sweet skin. He pushed away the dress strap that somehow had twisted about her wrist. She wriggled out of his grasp. "What are you doing?" he asked.

"If you think I'm going to sit here," she broke off, to tug at his boot. "Buck naked all by myself, *oof,* then you're dreaming." The boot came loose and she tossed it aside.

A laugh strangled in Jefferson's throat. She was a slender nymph. Creamy skinned, bending over his feet and presenting him with a glorious view of her nude figure. "I am dreaming," he muttered. The other boot slid free, and he pulled her back into his arms, finding her lips with his. "You deserve candlelight and wine," he said finally, all toying aside.

Pressing her hand against his chest, she pushed herself up until she was straddling his waist. The seductive breeze drifted over them and she lifted her arms to pull her ponytail free. Her hair swung down over her shoulders. "We have moonlight and clover," she told him, encompassing their private moonlit haven with an outstretched arm. "Nothing could be more perfect," she added, her voice low.

Her hands flitted over the jeans that were still more on than off. She was an enchanting mixture of bravado and shyness. He knew he didn't deserve this stolen moment with her. He'd end up hurting her. No matter what emotions she spoke of, no matter what she believed, or felt, or *thought* she felt, he knew she should be saving it all for a man worthy of her. Lord knew that he wasn't that man. Sooner or later she'd learn that and it would destroy him. He wove their fingers together. "Come here."

She leaned over him, her eyes widening when her breasts pressed against his chest. Swallowing a groan, he rolled them to their sides. But for tonight, at least, she was his.

Emily didn't even notice the edge of fabric beneath

her back as Jefferson nudged her over. The dry humor had left his face. As had the tinge of annoyance, leaving his sharply etched features taut with desire.

This was Jefferson, she reminded herself. The same man she'd always loved. Her nervousness subsided, and she reached out to pull at his jeans. He helped her and then tossed them out of the way.

Leaning on his arm, he looked down at her. She knew he took pleasure in the sight. His dark eyes burned over her just as surely as his hands. As surely as the unyielding flesh brushing her thigh. This time the color that burned beneath her skin wasn't from embarrassment. She slid her palms over his biceps, feeling the muscles bunch.

''Close your eyes,'' he whispered.

She did, and drew in her breath when he laid his palm low over her flat stomach. She had to bite her tongue to keep silent the thought that whirled through her mind. What if she became pregnant? What if they created a baby that would nestle and grow right there inside here, beneath the very spot where his hand now rested? Like a flowering vine, the idea grew. Bloomed. A whimper rose in her throat.

His head lowered over her breast, and his palm slid across her thigh. Her smooth legs impatiently sought out his hair-roughened ones.

''Easy,'' he murmured, notching his thigh between hers. Then his hand moved, lingering over the patch of soft curls, and unbearable tension coiled within her as his palm gently pressed, his fingers slowly delved.

Her breath carried his name.

It took every ounce of self-control within him to keep the pace slow. Soft sounds fell from her lips and her hands clutched at him, pulling him down. She cradled him sweetly and he bit back a groan as he brushed against that wet heat. He was not a small man, and she was so little in his arms. So delicate. Bracing his weight on his arms, he paused at her entrance, seducing them both with the tantalizing contact.

"Now, look at me," he whispered. He wanted to see her eyes when they joined. His heart in his throat, he watched her heavy lids slowly lift. Bottomless pools looked up at him, so trusting. So filled with love that his throat tightened. Slowly, so slowly, he pressed forward into that heavenly heat.

Her teeth closed over the tip of her tongue and her eyes widened. Her fingertips dug into his arms. He felt the barrier guarding her virginity. He sucked in his breath. "Why didn't you say…"

"I told you there was no one. Don't stop," she pleaded. "Oh, Jefferson, please don't stop."

He folded his arms next to her head and leaned his forehead against hers. His chest heaved under his restraint. "Honey, I couldn't stop even if a bomb exploded next to us." He flexed his hips infinitesimally, and her breath became a hiss.

"Please." Her hands slid over his hips. "I need you inside," she cried.

Jefferson needed it, too. More than his next breath. He slipped his hand behind her knee, pulling it up.

Instinctively, she bent her other knee, opening herself to him. Her hands scrabbled at his hips, slipping over the hard curve of buttocks. She lifted herself to him, gasping against his chest as if she'd impaled herself on his flesh. But the pain was a minor companion to the thunderous pleasure.

In his head Jefferson began counting backward. By

sevens. When he thought he could speak coherently, he asked if she was okay.

Wordlessly, she nodded. And moved in such a way that rockets went off behind his eyeballs. Sweat broke out on his brow. He'd never last. And she deserved far more from him. He shifted his weight, pulling her over him. Once again, she straddled him. With one obviously major difference this time.

"You like?" His hands settled on her hips as he gently guided her movements until her instincts soon took over.

She nodded, jerkily. She felt like a cork in a champagne bottle, wrapped way too firmly. Far too tightly. She rocked against him, feeling his strength deep inside, reaching right up to her heart. She cried out his name. Her arms and legs trembled.

"I...can't... Help me..."

"It's okay," he soothed, even though his voice was rough. On her hips, his hands were strong. Safe.

She bit her lip. She couldn't breathe. She moaned his name, nearly incoherent.

"Ah, honey," he growled, sitting up, keeping her firmly in his lap. Her inner muscles gloved him, and he guided her, ruthlessly controlling himself. It was her. Always her. He worked his hand between them and slid his finger over that sweet spot.

His name was a keening cry from her that he swallowed with his lips as she convulsed over him. Lights exploded in his head as her pleasure ignited his. "Emily—"

She trembled against him, her mouth open against his chest. His control flew out the window and he rolled her over, burying himself within her.

She was everything he wanted in this world.

It was his last coherent thought before he spilled himself deep inside her.

Chapter Ten

They'd slept. The knowledge hovered in the back of Emily's mind as she slowly drifted awake. There was no sense of unfamiliarity. No moments, however brief, of wondering where she was. Or why a long, masculine arm was lying heavily across her waist, its wide palm cupping her breast. At some point he must have covered them with their discarded clothing. Her lips tilted into a soft smile, and she turned to face him, huddling against his warmth as the sky slowly lightened with the approaching dawn.

Jefferson breathed deeply and pushed her head down onto his shoulder. "Quit squirming," he mumbled sleepily.

"I thought you were sleeping." She pressed a kiss to his collarbone.

"I was."

She smiled again and curled closer to him. She loved

the way he held her. Loved the way he'd rinsed her
panties in the swimming hole to gently wipe her thighs
after the first time. Loved the way he'd tenderly woken
her later with a slow, easy loving as different and fulfilling as the first time had been. She slipped her hand
behind his neck and ran her fingers through his hair.

"Ow," he complained a moment later when her finger caught in a tangle.

"Sorry," she whispered.

He opened one eye. "I'm cutting it all off," he informed her balefully.

"I'll still love you," she warned him lightly. "I'd
love you even if you were bald."

"Empty promises," he grunted. "Squire's still got a
full head of hair, and if heredity has anything to do with
it..."

At the mention of his father, the teasing glint in Emily's eye died. "Jefferson—"

"No," he warned abruptly, knowing what was coming.

She frowned at him and sat up, pulling the skirt of
her dress over her shoulders like a shawl.

Jefferson saw that she had sprigs of grass and pieces
of crushed leaves stuck in her tangled hair. And even
though they'd already made love twice, he found himself wanting her all over again. Worse than ever.

"Why won't you tell me what's going on between
you two?"

Jefferson just shook his head and reached for her. But
she eluded his grasp, falling to her back and rolling
away. He caught the strap of her dress and pulled. She
abruptly let loose and he tossed the dress aside. "Come
here."

"No," she laughed, dodging his hands. "I'll make a deal," she offered.

His eyes narrowed. "I don't do deals."

Her lips pursed. "Ooh, don't you sound the tough man."

"Don't you sound the brave woman, sitting safely five feet away."

She grinned. "I'm no fool." She scrambled back another foot, avoiding his quick reach. "Ah-ah-ah."

Jefferson shrugged and lay back. He folded his arms beneath his head and relaxed, for all the world like a man sunning himself on a beach instead of sprawling alongside a small swimming hole in the early Wyoming dawn.

"Here's my deal," she said, her dark eyes studying him.

Beneath his lashes, he watched her watch him. Saw the way her eyes glided, stopped, held, then glided again. It was the most amazing thing. The way he got turned on by seeing her get turned on.

"I'll come over there," she pointed to the crumpled grass where she'd lain next to him. "And you'll tell me why there's such a rift between you and your father." She picked a leaf out of her hair and slowly tore it into little pieces.

"Okay," she tossed the leaf aside when he didn't respond, and crawled a foot closer. "I'll come over there, and you'll tell me what you've been doing for the past few years. Why you're having nightmares."

The ground was getting hard. He rolled onto his side and propped his head on his hand. Her nipples were the color of delicate strawberries. Now he knew they tasted even sweeter.

"Okay," she offered again, her cheeks coloring as

she realized the direction of his avid stare. "I'll come over there, and you'll tell me where you went when you left San Diego."

He smiled faintly.

She huffed and crawled closer yet. "Okay. I'll come over there, and you'll tell me why you have that scar there on your hip."

He glanced down, absently noting the surgical scar.

Her lips pursed. "*Okay,* I'll come over there, and—"

His hands closed over her waist and he pulled her down beside him. "You're already here."

"*And,* you'll tell me that last night was the absolute-best, most-fantastic, most-incredible experience you've ever had."

"Ah, well that's easy, then," he smiled. Then chuckled. And realized it was an unfamiliar sensation. "Last night was the absolute-best, most-fantastic, most-incredible experience you've ever had. Both times," he added.

She punched him in the shoulder. And dragged his head down to hers. "You should smile more often," she murmured against his lips.

He kissed her until she clung to him like a wet blanket. "Last night," he told her, tumbling her onto her back, "was the most incredible experience I've ever had in my life."

"And you want to do it again and again and again," she grinned even while her cheeks flushed pink.

"And I want to do it again and again and again," he repeated obediently. Truthfully. "But you," he said as he touched her intimately, "are probably sore."

She blushed even brighter. "Geez Louise, Jefferson—"

"Don't be embarrassed." He kissed the curve of her neck. "There're other ways, you know."

"Oh?" Her voice was faint, and he liked to think it had something to do with the delicate marauding down below. "I, uh, suppose," she broke off, her throat working as she swallowed. "You're going to show me?"

"Mmm-hmm."

She moistened her lips, her eyes glittering between her narrowed lashes. "You're decadent," she murmured.

"You're beautiful," he returned, kissing the curve of her breast.

Delightful moments later, she dug her fingertips into his unyielding back. "Inside," she begged softly. But he held himself back, filling her gently with a long finger instead.

"It's not the same," she protested faintly, arching into his palm and closing her fingers over him in return.

He groaned on a half laugh. "No. But it's not bad."

Long, exquisite minutes passed. And eventually, Emily collapsed breathlessly onto the grass. Just before she slipped back into sleep, she had to admit that he'd been right.

"Hey. Time to wake up, sleepyhead."

Emily opened her eyes, squinting against the sunlight. Jefferson was standing above her buttoning up his jeans.

She yawned and stretched.

Jefferson groaned and glanced aside. "Don't tempt me," he said and tossed her dress onto her belly.

She pointed her toes, then flexed them. Lord, she was stiff. "This camping-out stuff has some drawbacks," she grumbled. She pulled the dress over her head and stood up. "Where's the rest of my, uh…clothes?"

Jefferson looked around. "Back there," he pointed to

the splash of lace hanging haphazardly from a small lilac branch. He left them hanging there though, and picked up her sandals instead. "Here," he said, turning back to her, grinning slightly.

She was staring at him, aghast. Ignoring the sandals in his hand, she pushed at him, scooting behind him. "What the *hell* is that?"

Jefferson mentally kicked himself. He glanced at his denim shirt, lying uselessly beneath a tree. He'd been so wrapped up in her that he'd stupidly forgotten the vicious scar on his back that he'd kept her from seeing so far.

She slipped underneath his arm, her fingers running frantically over his ribs. "Emily, don't—"

But she'd already found it again. The small circle of scar tissue riding just beneath a rib. "That was a bullet wound," she realized aloud.

She went behind him again and traced the ragged edge of scar tissue below his shoulder blade. He flinched, as if burned. He turned to see her hands lifted in bewilderment. "How...what?" She asked.

Just a little while longer. He wanted more time before the rich, shining trust that filled her eyes each time she looked at him would disappear forever.

"Don't you *dare* tell me it's nothing," she warned, her tight voice shaking. "Or that you got that...that *thing* in some little accident. People don't usually shoot at bridge builders, do they?"

Had it been too much to ask for just a little more time?

"Of course they don't!" She answered her own question. "And if you've spent so much as a minute helping to build a bridge, I'll eat my hat. I'll bet you weren't really on that oil tanker, either."

"Find a hat and start nibbling," he said.

She shot him a look tight with disbelief. And hurt. "Who pays your salary?"

"Whoever I happen to be working for."

"Do you ever give a straight answer to anyone?"

"Ah, Em—"

"Don't 'Ah, Em' me," she snapped. "I want to know whether the man I'm in love with really exists. Or whether *this* Jefferson," she waved her hand at him, "is just another persona you've assumed. *Who are you?*"

"I exist, all right. I warned you, but you wouldn't listen. What you see is what you get, sweetheart. And if you don't like it, then that's too damn bad. Did it ever occur to you that it might not be any of your business?"

She jerked as if he'd slapped her. Suddenly all the barriers that were between them, all the distance *he'd* created over the past several years, all came crashing to place between them. As if they hadn't just shared the most momentous night of their lives together. He cursed himself for ten kinds of a bastard.

Her hair slid over her face as she snatched the shoes from him. But whether she hid it from him or not, he knew the expression of pain that would be in her eyes.

Emily ached to ask him the million questions flying in her mind. She pushed her feet into the shoes. Jefferson had been shot. She wasn't particularly knowledgeable about wounds of that nature, but having been raised on a ranch, she wasn't entirely naive about firearms, either. Judging by the angle of the scar on his chest and the exit wound on his back, it was a wonder he hadn't died.

Just the idea was enough to send nausea careening through her. She reached out and leaned her head against a tree. Only by slowly breathing in through her nose and out through her mouth was she slowly able to conquer the nausea. When she could raise her head without it spinning, she turned around to see him standing in the same spot, watching her. "When...how long ago, did you," she whispered, "get shot?"

His beautiful, deeply blue orbs were flat. Expressionless.

"How long?" Her voice rose and she strode over to him, shoving his chest. "You can at least answer that!"

The corner of his lips tightened. "Two years ago."

Two years. "And this?" She touched the crescent scar near his eye. "And this?" Her fingertip traced the narrow ridge on his jaw. "Are these from two years ago, also? How about the scar on your hip? That one was a surgical incision. Wasn't it? What happened to you? Oh," she said, waving her arms in frustration. "Don't bother. I know you're not going to answer me."

Pleading filled her dark eyes, despite her caustic words. He wished he could tell her. He wished he were a better man. A braver man.

"Tell me this, Jefferson," she said as she turned away abruptly, but not before he'd seen the sheen of tears in her eyes.

"What?"

"If that bullet had killed you two years ago, would we have ever known about it? Or would we have just gone on believing that you were still going around the globe, working yourself from one adventure to the next?"

Kim's wife had received a telegram, hand delivered by a chaplain appointed for such tasks. A man who'd been unable to divulge much more information than had been in the too-brief, too-horrifying message. "They'd have notified you," Jefferson said quietly.

He watched her slender shoulders tremble. *"They."* Her shoulders firmed and she turned to face him. Her arms twined about her waist and she looked anywhere but at him. "Whoever *they* are."

"Em, we need to talk."

Emily couldn't believe her ears. What did the man think she'd been trying to do with him since he came back into their lives? "That's rich coming from you," she said, her lips twisting.

"About last night."

She shifted. From a distance she heard an engine crank to life. A dog barked. The Double-C gearing up for another day. "What about it?"

"We...*I*...didn't use anything. To protect you."

Squelching every shred of emotion from her face, she looked up at him. "From what?"

Something flickered in his eyes. Just for a moment. "Pregnancy."

"Oh. That."

"What did you think I meant?"

"How should I know? HIV?"

His teeth bared for a bare second. "You think I'd take a chance with you like that?"

"How should I know?" She sighed and recanted. "No, I don't believe you would."

"I've been tested," he said stiffly.

"Fine."

"You shouldn't be so casual about it."

"Fine."

"You need to check these things out beforehand, not afterward when it's way too late."

"Like you did with this pregnancy idea?"

His eyes flashed and were carefully banked. "Seeing that you were—"

"Incredibly stupid," she supplied.

"—a virgin," he continued as if she hadn't spoken, "I suppose you're not on the pill or anything."

She studied him. Anything was preferable to his unyielding, unsmiling, unflinching control. She knew he had feelings. Emotions. Lord, the man was a seething *cauldron* of emotion. If he'd only just let out some of it. As he had when there'd been nothing between them but the layers of skin on their bodies. She'd gambled everything in her heart on breaking through to him, once and for all. Had it all been for nothing?

"Emily?"

"Don't worry about it," she finally dismissed.

His eyebrow twitched. "When's your period due?"

A tide of color burned its way up her neck to her cheeks to the tips of her ears. "That," she snapped angrily, "is none of *your* blasted business." Spinning on her heel, she took off, twigs snapping under the stomp of her sandals.

"The hell it's none of my business," he grated, starting to take after her. But their night on the ground had taken its toll and a sharp pain seared its way down his spine. Swearing, he stood stock-still, waiting for the pain to abate. And watching her slender figure moving farther and farther away.

By the time the pain eventually subsided, he was drenched with sweat. Emily was nowhere in sight. Moving slowly, he went back to get his shirt. Using a tree for support, he bent at the knees and snagged the denim between two fingers. He started to straighten and noticed the panties that still hung from the lilac bush.

He slowly reached out and untangled the bit of lace, unaccountably sad when the lace snagged and a tiny tear formed. Carefully, he worked them free. They were still slightly damp from when he'd rinsed them in the spring water. He laid them over his thigh, fingering the torn lace. Ruined. Just like so many things he touched lately.

He started to rise again. The pain that shot through him this time told him that the first one had merely been a mild warning. Nausea clawed at him and his back ached too badly to even swear. Eventually, when the stabbing pain had mutated into a stiff, throbbing pain, he slowly began walking back toward the house.

Naturally, the first person Emily saw when she slipped in through the front door of the house was Tristan. He'd set up his computer in the little-used front room. Why couldn't he still have been sleeping? Then she could have made it up to her bedroom in privacy.

He looked up when the door opened and he leaned back against the couch. "What's this? Emily, I do believe those were the very clothes you were wearing last night." He fanned himself. "Mercy me. Have you been out all night? How scandalous."

"Shut up."

His wicked grin lost some wattage. "I'm not exactly hearing the lilt of morning-after euphoria in your voice."

"Aren't you the genius," she marveled sarcastically, stepping over the electrical and phone cords stretching from the wall to where his equipment was laid out upon the gleaming cherry wood coffee table.

"Whoa," Tristan leaped off the couch and headed her off before she reached the staircase. He took her shoulders in his hands and marched her back into the living room. "Give."

She twisted out of his hold. "Not now, Tristan. I'm not in the mood."

"We've got enough people in this family who don't talk about what's bugging them. We don't need to add you to the ranks." Pulling her by the wrist, he nudged her onto the couch and set his printer on the floor to make room for himself on the coffee table facing her. "What happened?"

"Your brother happened." Her elbows propped on her knees, she buried her face in her hands. "I'm such a fool."

"No."

"*Yes.*"

He gently pried her hands away from her face. "Tell me."

Long-used to Tristan's brand of nosiness, she sighed. "It's none of your business."

"I'm wounded. This is you and my brother we're talking about here."

"Yes, well, it still doesn't concern you."

"Emily," he tsked.

She groaned and raked her hands through her hair. "Oh, all right. All right!" Her hands flopped down onto the couch. "For crying out loud, between the two of you…" She shook her head, then again plopped her face in her hands. Her voice was a muffled mumble. "Some things are just too private, you know?"

"So, tell me the parts that aren't so private." He sighed, patting her knee. "I'll start. Will that help?" In typical Tristan fashion, he plowed right on, despite the very plain shaking of her head. "Rather than visit the esteemed Squire Clay in the hospital last evening, we know you chose to seek out my stubborn brother. You found him. Knowing Jefferson, you talked while he probably sat there doing his imitation of a hunk of granite.

"Then, at some point, you probably got irritated with one another. There's no surprise there. It's what usually happens between you two. Then, one way or another, you guys ended up, shall we say, bunking down together? I know you didn't come back to the house."

"What did you do? Sit at the foot of my bed, waiting up for me?"

"No, I've been working all night. Right in this spot, squirt. I'd have heard you come in. So, how am I doing so far? Then, in the cold light of day, you or Jefferson...probably Jeff in his usual fashion...screwed it all up."

"He doesn't screw up." Emily's head lifted. "How can you say such a thing!"

Tristan smiled faintly. "Just seeing if you were listening."

"You...are...a...pig."

He smiled happily. "Yup. A Clay Pig." His big hands rubbed together. "So, what went wrong?"

Emily absently plucked a crushed leaf from the ends of her hair. "Has Jefferson told you what he's been doing the past several years?"

Tristan's eyes strayed for a moment to his computer. "Not exactly."

The leaf came free and she studiously placed it in the crystal ashtray sitting on the little round table next to the couch. "He's, um, got a scar. On his back."

"I've seen it."

"Did he tell you where he got it?"

"Nope."

"Did he tell you why he got it?"

Tristan shook his head.

"At least he's consistent," Emily pushed to her feet, stepped around Tristan's big feet and paced to the wide picture window. ''He's had surgery, too. Did he tell you about that? He certainly wouldn't tell me.''

She touched the spot on her hip where Jefferson's scar was located. Tristan's computer suddenly beeped softly, and paper began spewing from the printer. She bit her lip, staring sightlessly through the lace curtains. ''I thought it would make a difference to him. After we—'' She swallowed past the lump in her throat. ''Well, it doesn't matter anymore.''

''Of course it matters.''

''We scratched an itch, Tristan,'' Emily said deliberately. So deliberately that perhaps she would actually believe that was all she and Jefferson had shared.

''Is that what he said?'' Tristan slowly rose.

''No. But that's what it all amounts to, anyway.'' She twitched a lace panel into place. ''What is it with you guys, anyway?''

''Are we talking guys in general?'' he asked warily. ''Or the Clay species?''

Her lips twisted. ''I dunno. Clay, I suppose. You all hide so much of yourselves. You only give a little bit away.''

Tristan only grunted in reply.

Emily swiveled on her heel and waved at the array of equipment spread about the room. At the paper silently sliding into the printer tray. ''What do you do with all that stuff?''

He frowned, looking down at his equipment. ''Consulting. Stuff like that. You know.''

''No, actually I don't know. You've never really answered me whenever I've asked. And I just finally quit asking. Almost everything that I know about what you do, I've read in some magazine or newspaper article. You design software. You consult. You work for yourself, but you still work for someone else at times, or so it appears. I don't know who. You hardly take two steps out of the house without one of your little toys there at your side.

"You get calls in the middle of the night, and you'll take off for days at a time. You rack up more frequent flyer mileage than anyone I know. But I still don't really know what you do. And I *live* with you. You're almost as secretive as Sawyer, only I know he's with the navy. He, at least, wears a uniform. And then there's Jefferson. He's worse than all of you put together." She hugged her arms to her.

"We're not all operating in some cloak of secrecy, you know. Matthew and Dan are about as upfront as it gets. And you know confidentiality is an important part of my job. But a job is all it is."

"So what kind of job is it that gets Jefferson shot up with something that blows a hole through his back the size of my fist? He'd never be involved in anything illegal, I just know he wouldn't. Why does it all have to be such a big mystery?"

The window rattled under the force of Emily's open palm. "I just want him to open up to me! I thought if we…well, you know…I thought it would be a start. It's not like I expected him to propose or anything. I just need him to share himself with me. Instead, he gives me some song and dance about safe sex and getting pregnant."

Tristan's eyebrows rose slightly. "Uh, is that a possibility here?"

She gave him a stony glare.

"Sorry."

Emily sighed tiredly. Her emotions were heaving

back and forth, riding a crazy roller coaster. "I love him, Tristan. I'd do anything for him."

"I know, squirt."

"I'd walk away from him if it was what he wanted."

"It's not."

"I'm not so sure." She didn't need to close her eyes to picture the way Jefferson had looked at her earlier. As if they were two strangers passing on the street. Discussing the weather, rather than the baby he might have created with her. So effectively denying her the right or privilege of sharing the trauma he'd experienced. He'd done it as easily as turning off a light switch. "I want to believe that last night wasn't a mistake."

"Loving someone the way you love Jefferson is never a mistake," Tristan said quietly. "And you also need to remember that Jefferson doesn't do anything he doesn't choose to do."

Emily nodded sadly as she headed for the stairs. "Exactly."

Emily was sitting on the window seat in her bedroom, looking out, when Tristan came up to her room a few minutes later, carrying a stack of papers.

"Here." He held out the papers. "Maybe this'll give you some answers."

Puzzled, Emily automatically took the stack in her hands. "What is this?"

"The story of Jefferson Clay." Tristan scrubbed his hands over his face, raking his fingers through his hair. "Don't read it at bedtime, though. It'll give you nightmares."

Unwillingly her eyes scanned the first few lines of the top page. She didn't recognize the name of the company, but she certainly could identify the type of information printed. "Tristan, this is a personnel file. How'd you get it?"

"I just did. Don't question it."

"You've been hacking?" She shot to her feet. "No way! Tristan, that's illegal! You're supposed to *catch* hackers! Not *be* one!"

"I wasn't hacking," he said quietly.

"Then how—"

"It's just one of the jobs I do, okay? Don't worry about it. I didn't do a single illegal thing to get that information."

"No." Shaking her head, she shoved the papers back at him. "I'm not going to read any of this. How'd you know where to look anyway?"

He heaved a sigh. "Look, it's not important how or why I came by the info. Let's just say that Jefferson wanted to keep his business private, and I saw no reason to disabuse him of that idea. It's only been since he returned that I've been nosing around."

"I thought Sawyer was the eyes and ears in this family. Are you secretly with the navy?" She eyed him sarcastically.

"No. Look, we're straying from the point here. Which is," he said as he pushed the papers back into her hand. "This."

"You're out of your mind if you think I'm going to read this."

"Why not?

"It would be wrong, that's why not!"

"Wrong or not, it'll explain pretty much everything to you."

"I want that sort of thing to come from Jefferson's lips. Not some stack of papers you've managed to obtain! Here, take them back."

"No. Keep them. You might change your mind."

"I won't," she assured him, even though her curiosity was practically choking the life out of her. She firmly placed the stack of papers on the dresser. "You've wasted your time."

"We'll see," Tristan said. "We'll just wait and see."

"You'll just wait," Emily corrected. "Now get out of here. I want to take a shower."

He headed for the door.

"Tris, wait—"

Tristan turned. "I knew you'd change your mind. It didn't even take five minutes."

"I have not changed my mind. I was only going to ask how Squire was last night."

"Fine. They plan to release him tomorrow."

"So soon?"

"He'll have to take it easy here, for a while, of course. And his cardiologist has assigned a nurse to stay with him for the first week. Since we're so far from immediate care. But they really don't expect any problems."

"That's so wonderful." Emily blinked back relieved tears. But along with the relief came another dart of worry.

How long would Jefferson be able to stay under the same roof as his father?

Chapter Eleven

That night Emily cooked a celebratory dinner. She'd managed not to think, too often at least, about the stack of paper sitting upstairs on the dresser in her bedroom. She hadn't seen Jefferson in person since she'd left him that morning by the swimming hole, though she'd surreptitiously watched him from an upstairs window when he'd been working with a huge black horse. Carbon, she'd realized. For long minutes she'd watched him, drinking in the sight, even though she hadn't been able to see his face because of the battered cowboy hat tilted over his eyes.

It was the Jefferson she remembered. The man with an affinity for stubborn horses like no one she'd seen before or since. The man she'd fallen in love with before she'd been old enough to understand how that love would forever affect her life. She'd sat at the window, long after Jefferson had taken Carbon back to the barn, remembering every moment of the night they'd shared.

She'd sought out Maggie before noon and had shared her plans for the dinner, taking care not to step on any toes. As it turned out, Maggie had been feeling particularly nauseous. Jaimie had been helping with the huge noon meal, and it worked out perfectly that Emily would cook for the Clays that evening. It also gave Emily something productive to do.

She'd even managed to convince Maggie that she and Joe and Jaimie should join them. Emily dumped a tray of ice into the freshly steeped tea and glanced at the clock. In fact, the Greenes should be arriving any minute. Wiping her palms on the apron covering her sleeveless peach sweater and loose pants, she carried the crystal pitcher into the dining room.

"Hi, Matt. Could you get those glasses down from the top shelf of the hutch? I can't reach them without getting on a chair."

He opened the glass-fronted antique and began removing the delicate, fluted crystal. "They need rinsing," he commented.

"I know. Oh, you need three more," she mentioned.

Matthew didn't need to count the plates she'd placed around the linen-covered table to know there were too many. "Three?"

"Yeah," she took two of the champagne flutes in hand and headed for the kitchen. "Maggie, Joe and Jaimie are joining us." She stopped and looked over her shoulder. "That's okay with you isn't it?" She waggled one of the glasses. "We are celebrating, after all. I'd have invited the hands, too, except Maggie talked me out of it."

"Wouldn't have mattered," Matthew murmured.

"The work's all done and everybody cut out this afternoon. Until spring, it's just us and the Greenes."

"And Jaimie, too, don't forget." Emily stifled a chuckle when Matthew's expression grew dark. "Bring the rest of the glasses, would you?"

He did. But when the sound of voices floated into the kitchen from the mudroom, he grumbled something and stomped out.

Joe walked into the kitchen first, followed by Maggie, then Jaimie. Maggie held out a basket filled with summer flowers. "Here. I'm growing these out behind the house and thought you'd enjoy some, too."

"Oh, Maggie, they're beautiful. What a wonderful green thumb you must have." Emily set down the last of the champagne flutes and took the basket, burying her nose in the fragrant blooms. "Joe, I think there's a pool game going on in the basement, if you want to check it out."

Typically quiet, Joe plunked his dusty cowboy hat on an empty peg by the door and with a nod, clumped out of the kitchen.

Maggie watched him go, her expression hidden behind veiled lashes. Jaimie broke the vaguely awkward silence by asking Emily if she had a vase for the flowers.

Quickly Emily went back into the dining room and retrieved a vase. She set it on the kitchen table, and Jaimie began arranging the flowers. "You don't mind, do you?" she asked.

"Lord, no," Emily waved her on. "Have at it." She headed for the refrigerator, pulling a chair out from the table as she did so. "Maggie, sit down and relax. I take it you're feeling better?"

Maggie smiled faintly and sat down. She picked a

daisy out of the basket and pinched off a browning leaf on the otherwise perfect specimen. "A bit," she said, handing the flower to Jaimie. "Fill in between the dahlias," she suggested. "Today has been my worst day yet. Just yesterday I visited my obstetrician. And that man had the nerve to tell me that morning sickness was all in the head. I'd have liked to have heard him tell me that while I was lying on the bathroom floor all morning. I'd have happily vomited on his wing tips."

Emily's eyebrows shot up. "That bad, huh?"

Jaimie nodded. "Made me wonder about wanting to get pregnant, I can tell you." She shuddered delicately and after a moment's consideration, added another flower to the arrangement.

Maggie laughed softly. She laid her palm on her as-yet-flat abdomen. "When you want a baby so badly you can't think straight, you'll endure anything. Even worshipping the porcelain goddess ten times a day."

Jaimie arched her eyebrows. "If you say so," she said.

"I can't imagine anything more wonderful than carrying the child of the man you love," Emily murmured, then felt her cheeks fire. It wouldn't solve a thing if she'd conceived last night. But it would be a blessing all the same.

"Spoken like a woman in love," Jaimie teased gently. "Who's the lucky guy?"

Emily's flush crept toward the roots of her hair. "It was just an observation," she said hurriedly. "Jaimie, you really have an eye for floral arranging. Have you taken classes or something?"

Maggie giggled. Jaimie looked at the lopsided bouquet and chuckled.

"Oh." Emily bit her lip as she really looked at the

arrangement. "Perhaps a few flowers on the other side," she suggested.

In moments, all three women were giggling.

Daniel poked his head into the room. "You cooking supper in here? Or goofing off?"

Emily picked up the now-balanced vase and added water. "Put yourself to use and put this on the sideboard." She pushed the vase into his hands.

"Bossy little snot," he complained.

"Just put it on the table," she waved him toward the dining room. "We'll eat in about twenty minutes."

"Good. That'll give me enough time to win back my twenty bucks from Jefferson."

"You mean you actually lost money in a pool game?"

"Disgraceful, ain't it?" He leaned in the doorway, devil-may-care good looks stamped over his smiling face. "Jaimie, you're looking particularly lovely tonight."

Jaimie returned his grin, full measure. "And you're sounding particularly full of it tonight, Daniel."

His smile widened. "It's always a pleasure to have three beautiful women gracing our humble kitchen. What more could we ask for? We have a petite brunette. A leggy redhead—" he cocked his head Jaimie's direction "—and an angelic blonde," he added, turning his attention to Maggie. "How's our little mama doing?" he asked lightly.

Maggie's slender fingers scattered the little pile of discarded leaves they'd just been collecting. "Fine," she answered abruptly.

Jaimie glided over to slip her arm through Daniel's and guide him out of the kitchen. "Get rid of that vase,

Daniel Clay, and give me a five-minute lesson on how to become a pool shark.''

They could hear her musical laughter as Daniel led her to the basement.

''I'm so glad that Squire is coming home tomorrow,'' Maggie said. ''We've all been concerned for him. I imagine he'll be happy to get home. He doesn't strike me as the type of man to take kindly to hospital life.''

Emily smiled and nodded, but her mind was on the look in Daniel's eyes when he'd been looking at Maggie. The buzzer on the oven timer sounded and she shook off her vague disquiet as she checked the bubbling lasagna. ''This has a few more minutes,'' she decided. ''Why don't we go down and see if Daniel has any luck winning his money back.''

''Sure.''

They headed through the dining room to the stairs leading down to the basement. ''How long have you and Joe been married?''

''Ten years.''

Surprised, Emily looked at Maggie. ''You're kidding! You must have been a teenager when you got married.''

The other woman shrugged, smiling faintly. ''Seventeen and fresh out of high school. Joe came along and swept me right off my feet.''

A raucous cheer floated up the stairwell. ''Sounds like they're taking sides,'' Emily said. ''When I was seventeen, I was attending boarding school in New Hampshire.'' She looked up toward Maggie, who was following her down the stairs. ''I hated it,'' she confided lightly. ''I wanted to be home with Squire and the boys. Calving and haying and all that was much more to my liking than learning how to waltz and speak French.''

Tristan heard the last of her comment and hooked his

arm around her waist to swing her into the room. "You can't speak French."

"And you can't waltz," she tossed back as he stepped on her toe. "Let me go, you nutball."

George Strait was singing from the sound system and Tristan handed Emily off to Matthew, who took over. "I can waltz," Matthew assured her. "Mom taught me."

"You mean she *gave up* trying to teach you," Daniel corrected, taking Emily into his arms.

"I thought you were trying to win back your money," Emily protested, getting dizzy with all the whirling about.

"Darlin', I already did," he said with a grin. "Plus another twenty from old Sawyer, there."

"Who're you calling old." Sawyer adeptly took Emily into his arms. He swept her into a graceful waltz.

Emily breathed a sigh of relief and smiled up at Sawyer. "Now here's a man who can truly waltz," she pronounced.

Jefferson propped the end of his pool cue on the floor and watched Emily gracefully revolve around the huge wood-paneled room. A tiny smile tugged at the corner of his lips. Tristan reached past Jefferson to pull a cue from the rack hanging on the wall. "Looks like it's your turn to dance with Emily," he said.

Jefferson reached for the little cube of chalk. "Shut up."

Daniel changed the CD and Jimmy Buffett started singing about Margaritaville.

"Hey," Emily protested. "You can't waltz properly to this."

Sawyer simply picked up his pace, until Emily begged off, laughing. "Give someone else a chance."

His eyes smiling, Sawyer turned to Jaimie and swung her into a lively round.

Emily plopped down onto one of the long leather couches dotting the perimeter of the big square room. She watched Jefferson use the tip of his cue to gesture to a corner pocket. Tristan shook his head and Jefferson shrugged. Tristan drew out his wallet and plunked a bill down on the side of the pool table. Joe laughed and added his own bill to the pile.

Jefferson took aim and sank the ball, grinning as he pocketed the money.

The soft leather whooshed when Maggie settled her lithe body beside Emily. "You have a nice family," she said.

"I think so, too," Emily agreed, dragging her eyes from watching Jefferson too avidly. She noticed Matthew was following the progress of Jaimie and Sawyer around the floor. "Matthew seems to have eyes for your sister-in-law."

"They do nothing but argue. They started arguing the day they met last year, and they haven't stopped since." She watched the pair dancing. "I haven't danced in ages," she murmured absently.

As if he'd heard, Sawyer stopped before the couch, depositing Jaimie on the arm. "Maggie?" He held out his hand.

Rolling her eyes, Maggie brushed off the offer. "Don't be silly."

"Go on, Mags," Jaimie nudged her shoulder.

Half laughing, Maggie let Sawyer pull her from the depths of the overstuffed couch. Daniel was messing with the CD again, switching song to song after just a few measures. Sawyer ordered him to stop messing with it. Tristan hooted over another shot Jefferson managed to sink. And Emily leaned her head back, absorbing the sound of it all.

"Don't you miss this when you're in California?" Jaimie asked.

Emily nodded. "More than I can say."

"Why leave then? Surely they could use your help here."

Emily shook her head. "Not really." She pushed herself more upright. "I'm an accountant," she said. "And Matt doesn't need an accountant. He handles the books very capably. He sends everything to me to handle the taxes, and that's it."

"Isn't there anything else around here you'd be able to do, though? It seems a shame to me that you're not living in the home you obviously love."

"I do love the Double-C," Emily said, nodding. "But it's the people on it that make it what it is." She lifted her hand, indicating the crew of men. "The Clay men. We're just missing Squire to complete the picture, and you're looking at the people that mean the most to me." Emily dropped her arm. "This is the first time in years they've all been in one place."

"They came because of Mr. Clay. How wonderful for support like that." Jaimie looked at her brother, who was taking his turn sinking a ball.

"What about your family? Do you have any other brothers? Sisters?"

"No. Just me and Joe. Our folks…well, my dad had a heart attack when I was twenty. He didn't make it. Mom followed almost two years to the day later." Her eyes were still on Joe. "I think she just lost the will after Dad was gone."

She blinked and looked back at Emily, the smile back on her face. "Before that, though, they lived in Florida.'' She leaned over. ''They'd bought a condo at one of those retirement places. You know? Golf carts parked in the streets, no kids allowed. That type of place. It was fine for them. It was exactly what they wanted, but personally, the place would have bored me to tears.'' Her toe was tapping to the beat of the song, and Jaimie finally gave in and stood up. ''Come on, Joe, dance with me.''

He made a face, but he took her on a lively romp. After a few moments the song changed and he and Sawyer switched partners. Emily noticed the way Matthew was still watching Jaimie dancing with Sawyer, and she got up. ''Mind if I cut in?'' Emily asked.

''Sure.'' Jaimie handed over her partner and looked around. Matthew was the only one not occupied with a pool cue. ''Well,'' Emily heard her say as she wandered over to him. ''Are you up to the challenge?''

Matthew snorted. But, Emily was pleased to see he didn't turn Jaimie down. Now there were three couples dancing.

''My turn, I believe.''

The lilting tune dancing in her head ground to a discordant halt, even though the CD played on smoothly. She suddenly found herself standing in front of Jefferson rather than Sawyer.

''Chicken?'' He murmured for her ears alone.

Her eyebrow arched. ''Hardly.'' To prove it, she slid her hand into his. ''Are you?'' she returned.

''I'm over here, aren't I?'' He placed his hand on her waist and easily found the beat of the music. ''Just dance.'' he said softly. ''We've never done this before.''

Emily, ordinarily confident on her feet, found herself awkwardly bumping his boots.

"Relax." He pulled her closer until her cheek rested on his chest and his breath stirred the hair at her temple.

Emily's bones dissolved as she followed his lead. She closed her eyes and savored the first dance of her life with the man she loved. But when he folded their joined hands close to his chest and pressed a kiss to her knuckles, the utterly bittersweet gesture made her want to cry. "I'd better check the lasagna," she said breathlessly and pulled away.

Jefferson watched her race up the stairs. He felt chilled where she'd been pressed so warmly against him. Without thinking, he went after her.

She was standing just inside the kitchen door, her shoulders bowed.

"Emily?"

Her shoulders jerked like a marionette on a string. She grabbed up an oven mitt and opened the oven door.

"It'll be ready in just a few minutes," she said. Without looking at him, she slipped the heavy dish onto a trivet. "I just need to finish up the garlic bread."

"What's wrong?"

She flung the mitt onto the counter. "What's not wrong?" She brushed a strand of hair away from her cheek. "I can't pretend that last night didn't happen, Jefferson. Maybe you can, but I can't. So if you don't like the way I'm acting, then stay away from me."

"I can't forget last night, either," he admitted roughly.

She snapped a piece of foil from the roll and wrapped the bread to toss it into the oven. "Look, Squire's coming home tomorrow, and I'll be leaving soon. Everything will get back to normal. But for now, I'd just like to get through tonight."

"You're going to agree to that stupid job, then."

"What else am I supposed to do? I have bills to pay, for crying out loud."

"Move back here."

"And do what? I wouldn't have to pay for board for Bird, but my car still needs paying off. I'm not going to live off Squire, you know. I do share expenses with Tristan. I have bills, for Pete's sake!"

"Coming home isn't living *off* Squire. He wants you back here."

Emily took a lemon from the bowl of them on the counter and savagely cut it into wedges. "Squire wants all of us back here."

"Not all of us."

She looked at him. "What's that supposed to mean?"

A muscle ticked in Jefferson's jaw. "Squire kicked me off the ranch seven years ago," he said after a long moment.

"What?" She carefully wiped the knife and stuck it back into its slot in the wooden block. "You're not serious. You've been here since—"

"Twice. Two days out of seven years. Both times Squire made it abundantly clear that I wasn't welcome."

"No. Squire would never—" Disbelief clouded her eyes. "Why?"

"It doesn't matter."

"Of course it matters! I was here both times you were—" Her mind whirled. "Oh, my God, it's because of me?" She sank into a chair. "I know the times you've been here, because I was here when you arrived. Why would he do that to you?"

"He was protecting you."

"From what? His own son?" She felt nauseous. "I can't believe this."

"He was right."

"He was wrong," Emily wrapped her arms around her middle. "You're his *son!* How can he treat his own flesh and blood that way?"

"You're the little girl he adored. He knew, sooner or later, that I wouldn't be able to keep my hands off you, and he wanted to make sure it never happened."

"That's why you didn't want to come back to the house last night," she realized aloud. "But I was still in school seven years ago. You hadn't even lived here for years yourself! What good did he think barring you from your home would do?"

"I don't know that Squire was thinking logically at the time," Jefferson murmured with severe understatement. Squire had been beside himself with anger when Jefferson had confided in his father that his feelings for Emily had been more than brotherly. He'd needed his father's advice. But had received his father's wrath. "It really doesn't matter, anymore. This is Squire's house. He has the right to run it how he sees fit."

She bounced to her feet. "That's ludicrous. He had no right. No right, you hear me? And I'm going to tell him so the minute I see him!"

"No."

"*No?* Listen up, bub, if I want to tell Squire, I'll tell him! And you ordering me around isn't going to work."

"I'm not trying to order you around. And I also don't need you to fight my fights."

"Your fight? Seems to me I'm the subject of this fi—"

"Shh," he whispered as he dropped a hard kiss on her lips. "You can't bring this up with Squire. He's not supposed to have any undue stress right now."

Emily raked her fingers through her hair. Jefferson was right, as usual. "It just makes no sense."

"Hey, are we going to eat or not?" Tristan skidded into the room. "Whoops. 'Scuse me." He left just as abruptly.

Emily looked at the steaming pan of lasagna. She grabbed the oven mitt and removed the bread from the oven. "We need to eat before it gets cold," she said. "We're celebrating, after all." Her lips twisted. "Isn't that right?"

Jefferson took the bread from her hands before she smashed it in her shaking fingers. "Don't hate him, Emily. It would break the old man's heart."

"What heart?" She swallowed the growing lump in her throat. "A man who tells his own son he's not welcome in his home has no heart."

Jefferson set the bread on the table and closed his hands over her shoulders. "He's the same man who read you bedtime stories and taught you how to hunt and fish. He's the same man who sent you to boarding school, knowing that the education was the best thing for you, even while it broke his heart to send you away, crying. He's got a heart all right."

"How can you defend him?"

"I don't always agree with Squire," Jefferson said. "But I do understand him." With his finger he touched the tear hovering at the corner of her eye. "His kicking me off the ranch was just a gesture, Emily. He knew I'd never allow us to get involved."

That stung. "Really? Then what's he going to say when he learns about last night? What's he going to say if it turns out that what we shared results in a child?"

"We'll deal with that if and when we have to."

"How utterly logical of you, Jefferson," Emily replied caustically. She pushed herself away from him and grabbed up the pan of lasagna, hardly noticing the uncomfortable heat burning her palms. "Get the champagne, would you? After all, we're *celebrating*."

Emily managed to keep herself in hand through dinner. She smiled and laughed and cleared the dishes and prepared coffee. Inwardly, however, she alternated between seething and wanting to bawl her eyes out.

Maggie and Jaimie insisted on helping with the cleaning up, and Emily even enjoyed their company. But when the Greenes departed for the evening and Matthew had retreated to his office, when Sawyer and Daniel had headed for bed and Tristan was back at his computer, she dropped the front.

She fixed herself a mug of hot chocolate and added a healthy dollop of whipped cream. She'd jog an extra mile, she promised herself. Then she went out the front of the house and sat down on the porch swing. Sandy wandered over and propped her golden head on Emily's knee. "Hey, girl," Emily scratched the dog's silky head. "Why aren't you somewhere dreaming about chasing rabbits, hmm?"

The dog sighed and tilted her head.

Emily took the hint and rubbed behind Sandy's ears. When the dog was finally sated, she turned a few circles and settled herself at Emily's feet. The swing chains gently creaked with a rhythmic, soothing sound.

Emily thought about Tristan's papers sitting in her bedroom.

She thought about Jefferson defending his father, despite what Squire had done.

And she thought about the fact that Jefferson had chosen to share *that* truth with her at all.

Later, her hot chocolate long gone, she stopped the swing's motion and went inside. Except for the thin line of light showing beneath Matthew's office door, the house was still. Apparently even Tristan had called it a night.

She made her way through the shadows to the kitchen and rinsed out her cup. Just about to turn to go upstairs, she noticed a movement outside. Peering out the window, she thought she saw a flash of something near the horse barn.

Leaving the cup to drain dry, she quietly went back outside, carefully preventing the screen door from slamming shut. A single bulb burned in the horse barn, right over the door of the tack room. She looked inside. Jefferson was sitting on a stool, his attention bent over something. A tin of saddle soap was open beside him. "It's a little late to be cleaning saddles, isn't it?"

He jerked in surprise and looked over his shoulder at her. In answer, he held up his boot, which he'd been rubbing the soap over.

"Oh." She recognized the boots he'd worn when she'd pushed him into the swimming hole. "Well, then isn't it a little late to be cleaning boots?"

"Couldn't sleep."

"I know the feeling," she murmured. "So, can you save 'em, doc?" She scooted beside him and saw the other boot, sitting on the floor. She bent over to pick it up. It felt unnaturally stiff.

"Gonna try."

Emily picked up one of the clean rags folded on the shelf beside him. She dabbed it into the tin and started rubbing it into the boot.

"Leave it. I'll get to it," he said, flicking a brooding glance over her.

"Seems only fair," Emily answered softly. "Since I'm the one that pushed you in the water."

His lips quirked. "True." He started to hand her the boot he'd been working on. "Do them both."

Emily tried not to laugh. She loved his unexpected spurts of humor. "Dream on," she said, her tone tart.

He shrugged, casting her another look. "You shouldn't be out here. You'll get cold."

At that, Emily did smile. "Jefferson, we slept outside last night, and I was wearing far less than what I'm wearing now."

Jefferson didn't need the reminder. He'd been having enough problems putting away thoughts of their night together. It was the reason he'd not found any sleep waiting for him in his bed and had sent him, ultimately, out here to try and resurrect these boots.

"It can't ever happen again, you know."

She didn't pretend to misunderstand. "Why?"

"Because I have nothing to offer you," he answered, as if she were dim-witted. "Because nothing good will come of it."

"I disagree," Emily said, staring blindly at the long boot in her hand. "Particularly with the nothing good part."

"I hope you're not referring to a pregnancy."

"I'm going to ignore that," she replied. Her fingernail traced the detailed stitching in the brown leather. "Besides, who said you had to offer me anything?"

"Angelface, you were made for till death do us part."

"I didn't ask you for that, so what're you worried about?" Cranky all of a sudden, she globbed more saddle soap on the rag and rubbed it into the boot with a vengeance.

"Leave some leather," he reached for her hand to slow her movements.

Emily froze when his fingers covered hers.

"Don't look at me like that," he said gruffly.

Her tongue slipped out to moisten her lower lip. "Like what?"

"With your eyes all wide." He took back his hand and picked up his rag once more. "Filled with want."

Cheeks pink, she looked down at her own work. Swallowing, she folded over the rag and continued rubbing the leather. "Then stop looking at me as if you want me," she retorted, her voice husky.

He made a strangled sound.

"What?"

He swore softly and tossed the boot onto the floor. "It'd be easier to ask me to stop breathing," he growled, and reached for her.

She willingly abandoned the boot. His arms circled her waist and pulled her between his thighs. She lowered her head and molded her lips to his. "I love you," she said when the need for air finally broke their kiss.

"Em—"

"I can't keep the words inside, Jefferson. It's no use asking me to try." She ran her fingertips over his forehead, smoothing the frown between his brows. "It'd be easier to ask *me* to stop breathing."

He gently tunneled his fingers through her long hair. "Smart mouth," he murmured.

"I've learned from the best." Her lids felt heavy as she fingered a button on his loose white shirt. It looked like the same shirt he'd worn that first day in San Diego. "Oops, look at that." She looked at the button that was no longer safely through its matching hole. "Somehow your button came loose."

"Imagine that."

"Mmm. Look at that. The problem is spreading. All your buttons are jumping out of their holes."

"Must be a button revolt."

"Must be," she agreed faintly. Her fingers slid be- neath the collar of his shirt. His throat was warm and brown. And she felt his pulse throbbing beneath her fingertip. Her lips parted slightly.

His fingers tangled in her hair. His jaw locked and he closed his eyes, calling on a hidden reserve of control.

A tiny sound emerged from deep in Emily's throat. Her palms slid over the hard angle of his shoulders, and the shirt slipped down his back. "I love your chest," she murmured the thought aloud.

He pulled her head toward his. "Not as much as I love yours," he muttered darkly before kissing her senseless.

He set her from him long minutes later and stood.

Emily bit her lip, wanting back in his arms. His arms flexed, muscles moving with coiled strength. But all he did was turn away and pull his shirt back up over his shoulders. "Get yourself to bed," he suggested, his at- tention fixed on the array of riding gear hanging on the wall.

"Come with me."

He breathed deeply, hands fisted on his hips. "Don't tempt me."

"Are you tempted?"

He snorted. "Beyond reason."

The knowledge brought a curious kind of ease to her. She moved over behind him and set her hands lightly on his clenched hands. She kissed his back through the shirt, right over the spot of that horrible scar. "Does it hurt?"

"It's killing me," he groused.

"The *scar*."

He shook his head. "Not anymore."

Pressing her forehead against his spine, she felt his fists loosen and her fingers slipped between his. "It hurts me," she told him. "It hurts to think of you injured. Away from your family, God knows where. Away from the people who love you."

She slipped her hands around his waist and hugged herself to his back. Closing her eyes, she rested against him, feeling every breath he took. Feeling the muscles he held so tightly in check gradually relax beneath her touch.

Her arms tightened around him for a moment, then slipped away.

Sensing her presence by the door, he looked over his shoulder.

"Come with me, Jefferson. Come to bed."

"Not in his house."

She seemed very small in her peach-colored clothes. It occurred to him that she looked thinner than she had when he'd arrived in San Diego. Another sin on his conscience.

"Walk me in, at least?" She couldn't bear to think of him sitting out here. Alone.

What harm could that do? He covered the saddle soap and left the boots on the shelf. She snapped off the light, and darkness enshrouded them. He headed for the dim square of moonlight shining in the wide doorway. His feet, in a borrowed pair of Matthew's boots, snagged something and metal clanged. "Dammit, what'd you turn off the light for?"

Emily took his hand in hers. "Follow me," she said. "I won't let you run into anything."

Jefferson felt the suffocating hint of claustrophobia dissipate the moment her fingers slipped between his. A few more yards and they were out of the dark barn, standing beneath the midnight sky. Clouds obscured the moon and stars as they headed for the house. "Smells like rain," he said as he held open the screen door for her.

"Summer's almost over."

Jefferson quietly followed her through the house and up the stairs. His hip ached with a dull, throbbing ache. They stopped in the doorway of her bedroom. He saw the inviting expanse of her bed, warmly illuminated by the dim glow of the small lamp on the nightstand.

She tucked her hair behind her ear. "I won't push you about what happened, Jefferson," she said quietly. "It's your business, just like you said. I won't pry anymore."

She stretched up and sweetly kissed his cheek.

Had she been standing before him wearing nothing but a smile, he couldn't have been more unbearably aroused. There must be a particularly vile place in hell for men like him, he decided. Her hair was a ribbon of silk over the shoulder of her dinky little sweater. He reached out and ran his fingers through the rain of hair.

The sheen of her dark eyes beckoned.

He stepped into the room, and the door closed behind them with a soft click.

She moved over to the nightstand, reaching for the lamp.

"Leave it on."

"All right," she hovered by the side of the bed.

"Where are your pajamas?" The tip of her pink tongue touched her lower lip momentarily, and he felt the effect clear to his toes in the barely-fitting boots.

"Here," her hand blindly searched under the pillow and she pulled out a froth of white.

He abruptly turned and sat down on the wicker chair

in the corner of the room, vaguely surprised when it
didn't collapse beneath his weight. "Put it on," he suggested, studying the toes of Matt's boots.

She hesitated a moment and he wondered if he was
going to have to endure the sight of her undressing. But
she headed for the modest-size bathroom connected to
her room.

"You won't leave?" she asked softly.

"I won't leave."

She went into the bathroom and closed the door.

Jefferson sighed hugely and raked his fingers through
his hair. After a moment, he heard the water running in
the bathroom and reached for a boot. The twinge in his
back brought an oath to his lips and he sat back, deciding the boots weren't worth the effort.

The bathroom door opened and Emily stepped into
view. He recognized the ruffled nightshirt from that
night in Tristan's kitchen. It seemed like a lifetime ago,
but could've been counted in days.

The light from the bathroom illuminated the lines of
her slender waist through the white fabric. For the brief
second when she half turned back to shut off the light
he imagined that flat belly swollen with child. Her
breasts full. Heavy with milk.

The light snapped off and the momentary illusion was
gone. She approached him, a silver-handled brush in her
hands. She stopped a few feet away and ran the brush
through her hair. "Sleepy?"

He shook his head, visions of Emily, pregnant with
his child taunting him. "Here," he held out his hand
for the brush. "Sit on the floor."

"You're going to brush my hair?"

"Got a problem with it?"

"No," she said faintly. She handed him the brush

and sank down in front of him, tucking her legs beneath her.

Jefferson was glad she couldn't see the way his hand trembled before he lifted the brush to run it through her luxurious hair.

"Ah," she sighed pleasurably. "That feels wonderful."

"I remember this brush," he realized eventually. "It was my mother's."

"Mmm-hmm. Squire gave it to me a few years ago." Her head fell back against his knee. "The bristles have gotten softer, but it's still a beautiful brush." She fell silent as he continued stroking her gleaming hair. After a while she yawned, and he set the brush aside.

She looked back at him, her lids heavy.

"Come on," he said, standing up and pulling her to her feet. "Bed for you." He tossed back the bedclothes and tried not to watch her long legs climb onto the mattress.

He covered her up to her chin and snapped off the light.

"Jefferson? You said you wouldn't leave." Her hand caught his.

There was only one way he'd get through the night, he decided. "Scoot over," he said.

The sheets rustled while she moved and he lowered himself atop the bedding. With the pillows on the other side of her, and his weight pinning the blankets on this side, she was more or less cocooned.

"Jeff—"

"Shh," he whispered. Unerringly, his arm scooped around her waist and, blankets and all, tucked her backside against his front.

"You've still got your boots on," she protested.

He adjusted a pillow underneath his head. "Never mind. Go to sleep."

She shifted a bit. A pillow tumbled softly off the bed and a moment later, her hand slipped about his. She lifted it to her lips and kissed his knuckles. Then tucking their hands close to her heart, she slept.

Chapter Twelve

The dim light of dawn was peeking into her bedroom when Emily awoke. He'd been watching her sleep for quite a while. He'd memorized the cadence of her breathing. He'd known she'd awakened, even before she pushed the hair out of her eyes and peered up at him.

"Didn't you sleep at all?" she asked.

"For a while."

The bed creaked slightly when she turned toward him and propped herself up on her elbow. "Another bad dream?"

Surprisingly, he hadn't had his typical nightmare. He looked at her, sleepily rubbing her face. Perhaps not so surprisingly, after all. "No bad dream."

"I'm glad." She yawned and turned over, snuggling back against him. She yawned again and pulled his arm over her once more. "What's bothering you then?"

Jefferson adjusted the pillow beneath his neck. He

closed his eyes and absorbed the sweet warmth of her. It helped that she wasn't looking at him. He was the worst kind of coward, but if he was going to get this out, he didn't think he could do it with her pansy brown eyes looking up at him. Where he would see all that warmth inside her drain away. "I was a hostage in Lebanon for six months."

The only sign that she heard him was the tightening of her fingers over his and the cessation of her soft breathing.

He was glad for her silence. If he tried hard, he could pretend that she was sleeping. Not hearing him at all. He swallowed, lifting his hand to push on the knot of pain between his eyes. "My partner and I were there to arrange the escape of a political prisoner," he continued eventually. "Before Kim and I managed to get back out again, we were caught. Officially, we weren't there, so there could be no official action to get us out."

Emily sank her teeth into her tongue. "You don't have to tell me this."

He was quiet for so long she thought perhaps he'd decided he agreed, after all. "We planned our own escape." He made a rough sound. "Nineteen successful missions in a row, then two miserable failures. We failed going in. We failed coming out."

He'd done this sort of thing *nineteen* times? "But you're here."

"*I'm* here. Kim's not."

She turned over, crying inside at the stark expression in his eyes. How much this *Kim* must have meant to him. "Were you...partners for a long time?"

His chest slowly lifted. "Couple years."

She could take this, she reminded herself roughly. If Jefferson was brave enough to tell her the secrets he was obviously punishing himself for, then she had to be brave enough to listen. "You were close."

"We were friends," he admitted. "He shouldn't have died."

"He?"

He must have read her surprise. "Kim Lee. My partner. He left a young wife and son."

"Oh, Jefferson," she laid her palm on his cheek. "I'm so sorry."

He turned away, swinging his legs off the bed. "If I'd done my job better, it wouldn't have happened."

Emily sat up, too, aching to press herself against his stiff back. "What, um, happened to the person you went there for?"

"He returned to his country and is back in control of the local government. We got him to our contact before everything blew up in our faces."

The whole idea of sneaking in and out of countries was alien to everything Emily knew. She scrubbed her hands over her face, trying to think with some measure of coherence. "Why weren't you able to leave with him?"

"They were right on our butts. We had to get him out of the country, so Kim and I hung behind, stopping them from getting to the pick-up point before our guys had a chance to get off the ground." Jefferson only had to close his eyes to hear the gunfire; the whop-whop of the chopper's blades over their heads as he and Kim fought like fury to give their contact enough time to dart in and back out again, his cargo safely stowed inside.

He pressed the heels of his palms against his closed eyes, blocking out the vivid memory. "Kim should've been on that chopper."

Emily scooted closer to him. "Would you ever have left your partner behind?"

"No."

"Then why expect him to have behaved any differently from you?"

At least a half dozen people had told him that. His own logic told him that. But between his logic and his emotions, the idea continually short-circuited.

Her light touch drifted over his shoulder. "Is that when you got shot?"

"No." Now that he'd begun telling the sordid tale, he wanted to be finished with it. He wanted it out. Done with. Over. "We were overtaken," he continued. "I swear, they must have had three dozen men out there." At the time it had seemed like a hundred. But even against those odds, they'd fought. Until one of them got close enough to Jefferson to crush his assault rifle into Jefferson's hip. He hadn't been able to walk, but they'd dragged him on the ground back to their unit. Kim had been knocked unconscious and two soldiers had hauled him back by his feet.

He touched the scar on his jaw. "They kept us pretty subdued." He saw no reason to describe the beatings. Or the mental games their captors had delighted in playing. When he'd been conscious enough to do so, he'd tracked the days the best he could by scratching marks on the wall beside his filthy mattress. "Luckily they never resorted to pumping us full of drugs. They kept Kim and me separated for a couple months."

There wasn't a word on earth adequate to describe Emily's horror. She contented herself with threading her fingers through his.

"They were waiting for another team to try and get

us. Kim and I knew, though, that there wouldn't be any team.''

"But why not? Surely they'd try—"

Jefferson shook his head. "Too risky. Sending us in in the first place was as much of a move as they'd make. They wouldn't want to draw the attention that two strikes might've received."

"Our government is supposed to protect its citizens! Why wouldn't they—"

He sighed faintly. "I'm not with the government, Emily. Hollins-Winword Industries is a private-sector agency. They take on some of the challenges that the government deems too risky, no matter how desirable." He stood up and went to the window. "At a certain level, we have support of the armed services, but basically we're on our own. It's the rules of the game." His words were short. Matter-of-fact.

"Some game," she murmured, her thoughts whirling. "And you've been doing this all along? How on earth did you ever get into this? Does anyone else know? Squire or Sawyer, even?"

Jefferson thought of his surprise at Sawyer's presence at the private medical facility in Connecticut. He snorted. "Sawyer knows, but not because *I* told him." He tugged aside the curtain and looked out at the red glow of the sun just coming over the horizon. "I just sort of fell into it. I had a knack with languages. Knew about agriculture. About weaponry."

He vaguely remembered the way he'd felt when he'd been fresh and green and revoltingly new to the game. "At first, it was an adventure. Exciting. Seeing the world, you know. My specialty was fitting into the local scene." He heard Emily's surprised grunt. "Strange, I know. But—" he shrugged "—I'd go in. Set up the

strike. Get out. The pay was good.'' It wasn't until later
that he'd appreciated the work for its small measures of
justice in an all-too-unjust world. And not until much
later that he'd wondered at the futility of it all.

''All the things I've said I've done, I've done.'' He
wanted her to know that it hadn't all been a lie. ''I've
worked on bridge crews. I've worked on tankers. I've
taught farming techniques to indigenous people in a
dozen different countries. But Hollins-Winword has
been behind all of it. Placing us strategically with the
locals. So we were living among them. Biding our time
until it was necessary to do the job we were ultimately
sent there to accomplish.''

''This is like something out of a fiction novel,'' Emily
stared at him. She slowly ran her hands through her hair.
She didn't know what she'd expected to hear, but it
certainly hadn't been *this*. She wondered if she was really up to hearing the rest. ''So, how did you finally
escape?''

He scratched the corner of his eye. ''After a while,
our guards eased up. They probably figured that no one
was coming to get us. It cost manpower to keep Kim
and me separated—manpower that they could put to better use elsewhere. So they ended up sticking us in the
same cell. It took another several weeks before we had
the chance to make a break.''

Emily pressed her palm to her pounding heart. ''And
then?''

''Bad luck. We had the same guard every night. And
every night for weeks, this guy would squirrel away an
hour or so to visit his woman in the village. It was the
only time of the day when they didn't have us under a
gun. The cell had a dirt floor. Over the weeks, we dug
beneath the wall, hiding the spot under the bare mat-

tress. We just needed to get outside the village. We'd buried an emergency pack before we'd gone inside. Once we got to it, we'd have been able to notify our contact and arrange a pickup.

"The night we crawled out, the guard came back early. That guy, as soon as he saw the empty cell, knew his ass was in a sling. Before Kim knew what hit him, the guard stabbed him. Kim hadn't even finished crawling through the hole under the wall."

Emily didn't even try to stop the tears that sprung to her eyes. "And you?"

"It was him or me, Em. So far, everything had been quiet. I didn't know if Kim was alive or not, and I sure as hell didn't want the guard raising anyone else." He couldn't bear to see the revulsion in her eyes, so he kept looking out the window, his voice neutral as he mechanically relayed the details. "I broke his neck, took his keys and locked him in our cell. I managed to get Kim on my back and hightailed it out of there. I found the pack. Dug it up. It was right where we'd left it. Less than a mile from us the entire time we'd been held. A helicopter arrived within minutes.

"Before it arrived, though, our escape had been noticed. It wasn't hard for the guards to track us. Hell, we'd left a bloody trail leading straight to us. The chopper couldn't even land—just sent down a rope while it hovered. I harnessed Kim and grabbed hold. I was shot before we got twenty feet off the ground."

It was far too easy envisioning Jefferson, dangling from the end of a rope. It was probably a miracle that he'd not fallen when he'd been struck. She pressed her lips together. "And Kim?"

Jefferson was silent for a long, long minute. "He'd

lost too much blood. He died before we even got him into the chopper.''

Emily held back a fresh spurt of tears. ''His poor family.'' She untangled herself from the sheet and went over to him. ''No wonder you have nightmares,'' she murmured, slipping between his tense body and the window. He wouldn't even look at her. He just kept staring out the window. ''What about you? You'd been shot.''

''The pilot landed us on a naval carrier. They kept me stabilized. Eventually I ended up in Germany for a few surgeries.''

''How few?''

''Hip replacement. Some bones that had to be broken and reset. There's a pin in my knee.''

She seriously considered bolting for the bathroom before it was too late. ''We could have lost you and never have known why.''

His lips twisted. ''Pretty revolting tale, eh?''

''It's horrifying. And tragic. But it's over now.'' She watched the muscle tick in his jaw. ''Isn't it? You're not still working for that Hollins-Whateverworth, are you?''

''Winword,'' he supplied tonelessly. ''I'm on disability.''

''Do you plan to go back?''

''Nope.''

Thank God! ''What do you plan to do then?''

''Dunno.''

She sucked in an unsteady breath. ''As long as it doesn't take you away from me, I don't care what it is. Jefferson,'' she said as her voice broke. ''You *were* all alone, weren't you.'' Standing on tiptoe, she hugged him to her. If ever there was a man who needed hugging, Jefferson was that man.

Jefferson grabbed her arms and held her from him, giving her a small shake. "Don't you get it? I killed a man. Two, if you count that bastard guard." More, if you counted other casualties from his missions. She still was looking at him with those soft brown eyes. "I was *responsible*," he growled. "My partner died because of me. His little boy is growing up without his daddy. Because of me."

"Did Kim go on that—that mission unwillingly?"

"No," he growled.

"Then he had to have known the risks involved." She shook her head. "It's terribly sad about his wife and son. No, Jefferson, don't turn away from me!" She scrabbled for his arm. "You didn't kill Kim. The guard who stabbed him did."

"You don't understand."

"I think I do. You take your responsibilities so seriously. It's not a crime to share the burden once in a while. Good heavens, you could have been killed yourself!"

"That's just it. It should have been me. I was the lead man. I should have made sure the mission didn't fail. Kim had every reason to come back alive."

"And you didn't?"

Anger curled through him. Why couldn't she understand? "He had a family."

"So do you."

"He had a son," he bit out.

Her hand touched her stomach. "Perhaps you'll have a son, too."

The words were like a blow. It would be every undeserving wish fulfilled. "You wouldn't want to bring a child into the world with a father like me."

She swiped a tear from her cheek. "You're not going

to convince me to blame you for your partner's death. It seems to me that you've cornered the market of laying blame on Jefferson Clay.'' Her chin tilted defiantly. ''And why wouldn't I want a father like you for my children? You're the most decent, honorable man I know.''

''I broke a man's neck with my bare hands.'' He held his hands up. ''He wasn't the first,'' he added stiffly.

She didn't even hesitate. ''And you watched your partner die because of the wound that guard inflicted. You're alive, Jefferson. After all you've told me, I consider that a very great blessing.''

The back of his eyes burned. ''Why?''

''Because I love you,'' she said simply.

''Even after what I've said?'' Was that his voice? Hoarse. Shaking.

''Particularly after what you've said. You didn't have to tell me all this, Jefferson. But you did.''

''You weren't supposed to—''

''What? You thought you'd scare me off, perhaps? Jefferson,'' she said as she shook her head, smiling gently, even while a tear trailed down her cheek, ''when are you going to learn? I love you. *You.* Too serious. Too sensitive. And far too handsome for my peace of mind.''

He ground his teeth together. His head shook back and forth, denying.

''It's all right,'' she whispered, gliding to him and pulling his head to her shoulder. Such a strong man. And how he struggled with his emotions. She held his carved face between her hands and kissed his lips. ''It's all right now,'' she soothed. She kissed the scar on his jaw. And when the tear slipped from his shadowed eyes, she kissed that away, too. ''Come back to bed.''

He let her lead him to the tumbled bed. He let her pull off the snug boots. He even let her unbutton his wrinkled shirt and toss it onto the floor. When her fingers went to the buckle at his waist, however, he stopped her. "This is still Squire's house."

"Yes. It is," she agreed. "But this is Emily's bed," she added. "It was brought from *my* parents' home. And I want to share *my* bed with the man I love. I need to put my arms around him. And hold him. And be held by him in return."

She didn't reach for his buckle again. Just stood before him, waiting quietly for him to decide. And really, what decision was there? To walk away from her was to kill off a portion of himself.

Jefferson stood up, and the buckle jingled faintly as he unfastened it. Watching her closely, he popped loose first one button, then the next. "It'll be morning soon," he murmured.

"A new day."

"Squire is coming home today." He'd had years to accept his father's opinion. For her, she'd had only a few hours. "He won't like this. Are you prepared for that?"

In answer, she took his loose jeans in her hands and pulled them down his hips. "He's gonna have to learn to like it," she said decisively.

He automatically kicked the jeans from his feet and nearly swallowed his tongue when she whipped the nightshirt over her head and tossed it aside.

"He's been yammering about grandchildren for several years now. Maybe we should give him what he wants," she said.

It was inconceivable that she still felt that way. Even knowing the truth about him. A twinge worried at his conscience. He still hadn't told her about the fragment in his back.

"You are alive. And loved more than you could ever dream." She took his hand in hers and pressed his palm to her abdomen.

He saw the tears gleaming in her eyes. He wanted to give her her every desire. He wanted to give her the world. He'd given her his heart long ago, and she'd never even known it. But could he give her a future? Was it crazy of him to even consider it?

"Give me your child, Jefferson."

"Crazy," he murmured. But he folded her into his arms and gently kissed her lips.

Emily could have cried at the sweetness of his kiss. He couldn't have told her more clearly that he loved her if he'd actually said the words. The ground shifted beneath her feet and she weakly sank down to the mattress.

He followed her down, hauling her in one smooth motion across the full-size bed until she lay diagonally across it. He set about seducing her with gentleness. With unspoken love. In minutes she was arching against him, twining her legs in his, impatient for him.

"Slow down," he soothed, kissing the curve of her neck.

"I need you," she moaned against shoulder. *"Now."*

"Now?" His fingernails grazed the outside of her thighs. Suddenly he moved, sliding deep inside her. "Like this?"

She whimpered, her hips pressing into his. "Yes."

He lifted his head. Wanting, needing to see her face. Slowly he slid back, almost withdrawing. The sound from her throat was pure yearning.

He drove himself into her. Her eyes popped open, and

she gasped. Her breath grew short and choppy. "Like this?"

Her fingernails dug into his hips. "Yes."

He repeated the motion. Again. And again. Until burning color rode her cheekbones and her breath was a near sob. Eyes narrowed, he focused on the woman beneath him. He absorbed her. Her whole body was trembling. And he breathed her.

She struggled to lift her head. To kiss his lips. She did, but the uncontrollable sensations tightening within were overwhelming her. Her eyes flickered and he followed her gaze to that point where they joined. He looked up, just in time to see the tip of her tongue moisten her lip.

It was too much for him.

Her faith in him, undeserved though it was. Her compassion. Her goodness. It washed over him. As surely and insistently as his climax built. His forehead brushed her shoulder and he couldn't hold back a groan.

Suddenly, he felt clumsy. Uncontrolled. She deserved so much more than he could give her. But, amazing at it was, he was the one she wanted. Driven, he arched against her over and over.

"I love you," had she said it again? Or was the knowledge reverberating in his imagination?

Her hand touched his face, and he looked into her beautiful eyes. And for the first time in his life, he cried out as he gave his very soul to the woman he loved.

Jefferson slumped against her, and Emily held him close, tears leaking from the corners of her eyes to roll into her hair. Her breath was still ragged, but it was nothing compared to the harsh sound of Jefferson's. His arms slipped beneath her back, holding her in an achingly tight embrace. And she held him in her arms.

While a slow stream of tears trickled down his cheeks.

Chapter Thirteen

Sawyer and Daniel had driven into town to bring Squire home. Emily was on the front porch, a basket of freshly picked peas from Maggie's garden sitting beside her. She snapped them and dropped the sweet peas into the bowl on her lap. The pile of discarded pods was growing faster than the pile of shelled peas, though, since almost half of them ended up in her mouth rather than the bowl.

As soon as she saw the cloud of dust in the distance, she set aside the peas and went inside. "They're coming," she said.

Tristan set aside the computer printout he was studying and rose.

Jefferson was in the office with Matthew, going over some notes Matthew had been keeping. "They're coming," Emily said, poking her head in the doorway.

Matthew nodded and dropped the papers onto his desk. He smiled at her as he left the office.

Emily looked at Jefferson. He still looked tired. But the rigid strain around his eyes was almost gone. It would take a long while for him to recover emotionally from what he'd been through. But this morning had been a start. A good start. Her heart did a quiet little dance when the corners of his lips tilted and he held his hand out to her.

"You ready for this?" he asked when she slipped into his arms.

"Mmm-hmm. You?"

He grinned lazily, stealing her heart all over again. "Yup." He kissed her on the nose and headed for the kitchen. "Your fingers are green."

"I've been shelling peas," she said.

"And eating a few, too, if I remember correctly."

"Naturally. What good is it shelling peas, if you can't sample the fruit?"

"They're vegetables, angelface."

"Nah. Nothing that tastes that good could be a vegetable."

He just smiled faintly and pushed open the screen door, then followed her outside and around to the front of the house. Matthew and Tristan were already there, watching the dot in the distance take the form of a car. When the sedan finally pulled to a halt on the gravel drive, Emily's heart was thumping with anticipation. And nervousness.

She didn't want to upset Squire. But she wasn't going to forsake their happiness for his opinions. She and Jefferson had talked about it only long enough to agree that they couldn't shove their relationship in Squire's face. But they weren't going to hide it, either.

Not that she could quite describe yet what their relationship was, exactly. For the moment it was enough to know that he loved her. His touch told her that he did.

Though it would be nice to think that someday he would actually let the words pass his lips.

He caught her eye, and heat streaked through her. It was as simple as that. One look from him, and she was ready to throw herself into his arms. No matter who was standing around to see the sight.

The corner of his lip tilted. He knew what he was doing, darn it all! The car doors were opening, but she kept her attention on Jefferson for a moment, promising retribution.

Sweet retribution.

"Dang it, quit hovering over me." Squire's cantankerous complaint made her smile. A dimple deepened alongside Jefferson's mouth, and he watched his father shove open the car door. "I ain't dead," the man was saying.

"You're loud enough to wake the dead," a female voice retorted.

Jefferson recognized the nurse who'd spoken from the hospital as she rounded the car.

"Git away from me, woman."

The nurse, dressed in tidy tan slacks and a tailored silk blouse, lifted her hands, resigned. "You may call me *Mrs. Day.*"

Squire snorted. Using his big hand on the opened door of the car, he pulled himself upright. Until he towered over the woman. He looked down at her. "Git away from me, *Mrs. Day.*"

Somehow she managed to look down her nose at him. "I cannot believe I agreed to stay on here for a week."

Squire gave a bark of laughter. "I charmed you into it, darlin'. You know you couldn't resist."

Sawyer covered his eyes with his hand, and Daniel was quietly sneaking away from the scene.

"Where you goin', boy?"

Daniel shrugged. He patted his pockets and pulled out a crumpled pack of cigarettes. "Don't want to smoke around you, Squire. Bad for the lungs and all."

"Put them fool things away," Squire said. As if he hadn't been an avid smoker for a solid twenty years. "Them things'll kill you." He spotted Matthew. "You get that tractor fixed yet?"

Matthew nodded. "Yup."

Squire nodded, his eyes lighting on Emily. "Well, young lady. You got a hug for this old man?"

Emily couldn't resist him. She was still livid over the way he'd treated Jefferson. But livid or not, she loved the rascal. She slipped between Tristan and Mrs. Day. "Welcome home," she whispered, reaching up to hug him.

He kissed her forehead, then cupped her chin in his palm. Lifting her face to his eyes, he studied her. "Well, well. Don't you look mighty fine, Miss Emily. Life at the ranch has brought some color to your cheeks."

She nearly bit off her tongue. Her cheeks pink, she lowered herself back onto her heels.

Squire eyed her speculatively, then lifted his eyes to look at the assembly of his sons. "Damn, Jefferson. You look like a danged woman with that long hair. Get it cut why don't you."

With that, he leaned back into the car and pulled out his small bag.

"You can't carry that." Mrs. Day abruptly pulled it out of his hands.

"Hell, woman, I was carrying my own bag a long time before you came along, and I'll be carrying it a long time after you're gone. Now git out of my way. I want to go sit at my own kitchen table and drink some drinkable coffee."

She stood right in his path, unmoving. "One cup," she said. "Now give me that bag."

Sawyer made a strangled sound and slammed shut the driver's side. He quickly walked around the car. He took the bag out of his father's hand while the man was staring at his nurse. He walked by Tristan and Emily, heading for the back of the house. "They've been at it since we left Casper," he said beneath his breath. "Thought the man wasn't supposed to have any stress."

"What's that, boy?" Squire lifted his silver head. "Never known you to be a mumble mouth."

"Never known you to be rude to a pretty woman," Sawyer retorted.

Squire grunted, but a devilish glint was burning in his eyes. He looked down at his nurse for the next week. "Pretty women ought to be home tending their husbands." He tossed out the chauvinistic comment, testing for reaction.

Emily's eyebrows skyrocketed.

Mrs. Day looked Squire right in the face. And laughed. She laughed so hard her eyes watered. "Oh, please," she gasped breathlessly. "You'll turn my head." Still laughing, she slipped around him and reached for her own small suitcase.

"Tristan, don't stand there like a bump. Take the lady's bag."

He jumped to attention and reached for the suitcase. "It's easier to just go along with him," Tristan told the woman.

She arched an eyebrow and studied the lean length
of Squire Clay. "I'll bet," she murmured.

Squire cast her a long look. Emily watched it all with
amazement. Squire was attracted to his nurse! Never, in
her entire life, had she seen Squire look upon a woman
with that particular glint. Oh, she'd known he'd had lady
friends. But he'd never brought them back to the Double-C, as far as she knew. And now, the first time a
woman was with him, it was because she was his *nurse.*
A *Mrs.* nurse.

Squire threw his shoulders back and looked around.
"Good to be home," he said at last. He patted Emily
lightly on the cheek. "Go and fix some of that coffee,
would ya darlin'?" He glanced around and strode
around the house. "Yup. Sure is good to be home."

Tristan, Emily and Jefferson just watched his back.

"Wow," Emily finally said.

Jefferson dropped his arm over her shoulder and nodded.

Tristan turned to Mrs. Day. "You," he said admir-
ingly, "are a brave woman. A very brave woman in-
deed, and I am truly impressed." He extended his arm,
indicating that she should precede him. "How do you
take your coffee, Mrs. Day? With a shot of whiskey?
Or without?"

She straightened the collar of her blouse and smiled
serenely as she headed after Squire. "With, of course."

Alone beside the car, Emily leaned into Jefferson.
"That was interesting," she said.

"Tell me about it."

"He fancies her, doesn't he."

"Mmm-hmm."

She slipped her fingers into his belt loops. "Do you

know that there are now four women staying at the Double-C at one time? That's a first.''

"Yup." He halted her wandering fingers with a stern hand. "Stop it."

"What?" Innocently her velvet eyes looked up at him.

"That," he jerked away from her fingertips. "You're tickling me."

"No."

"Dammit," he muttered, trying not to laugh when she poked him. "You'll regret it."

"I doubt it," she pressed herself against his chest, making sure he felt the hard points of her nipples stabbing him through their clothing.

"Witch," he accused gruffly. Then he jerked again when she found that ticklish spot.

She giggled and danced away before he could get a good grip on her. "Maybe you'd better take a trip into town, *boy*." She darted to the left, then the right, evading his hands. "Git that danged hair cut."

"You're supposed to be in there fixing coffee," he said lazily, letting her romp around him like a frisky pup.

"Obviously Squire's feeling better." Emily twisted and scooted back when his fingers caught the hem of her loose T-shirt. "He was glad you're here. I could tell."

Jefferson shrugged. He wasn't going to think too hard on that, just yet. He allowed the shirt to slip from his fingers. She was quicker than he'd expected, though, and managed to circle behind him, unerringly finding that spot again.

He whirled around. "You're gonna get it."

"I hope so." She widened her eyes laughingly. She

dashed across the gravel drive toward the circled lawn beyond. "I *sincerely* hope so."

Her eyes were deep brown, but Jefferson could have sworn he saw the sun shining right out of them. He realized he was smiling like an idiot. She was standing a few yards away, her brow arched in challenge. "Oh, yeah," he promised them both. "You're definitely going to get it."

She was fast. He'd give her that. But he had longer legs. She squeaked and darted for the stand of trees. That was her mistake.

His arms pinned her between three closely growing trees. She was huffing, her chest making the most interesting of diversions beneath her soft shirt. "You have nowhere to go."

"Never say die," she vowed, her eyes sidling this way and that. But there was nowhere to go. Only forward. She reached for his waist and latched on, her fingers tickling for all they were worth.

His laugh was strangled. "Brat," he grabbed her waist and tipped her feet off the ground.

Squire paused before the wide picture window overlooking the front of the house. He watched his middle son. Watched him laugh and playfully wrestle with Emily. Watched them tumble to the soft green summer grass and catch their breath. He saw the moment when they went curiously still, and the way his son smoothed Emily's dark hair away from her ivory face. Before he turned away from the sight, he saw the way their lips met in a kiss. A kiss that was so pure and fulfilling, he practically felt the waves of their emotions rock the house.

Carrying his bag, he headed for his bedroom tucked

beneath the staircase. He closed himself in the room, and his boots scraped the wooden floor as he crossed to the bureau standing beneath the window that looked over the side of the house. He picked up the framed picture of a woman and looked at it for a long time. Remembering how he'd felt about the woman who'd given him five fine sons. His thumb moved across the glass, remembering how it had felt to run his fingers through that waist-length blond hair. How her rosy lips had tasted beneath his. "Sarah," he murmured his wife's name. "For a while there, I thought I was finally gonna join you."

After a long moment he carefully set the picture frame back in its spot. "I guess I still got some things to do yet. Or undo, I guess," he said. "But you already know that, don't you." He looked at the black-and-white photo for a long moment. Then he dropped his bag on the bed and headed back to the kitchen.

Emily was there, fixing the coffee he'd asked for. A grass stain marred her otherwise clean pink T-shirt. She was laughing at something Tristan was saying. The rest of the boys were sprawled in chairs surrounding the big table. Squire stood in the doorway, looking at his family, feeling ridiculously grateful and more than a little old.

The refrigerator door closed, and Mrs. Day came into sight. Her thick auburn hair was twisted in a knot at the nape of her neck, and when she leaned over to set the small container of milk in the middle of the table, her slacks tightened over her derriere.

Perhaps not so old, after all, Squire decided.

"Person tends to forget why we built this room so big," he said, walking into the kitchen. Tristan drew up his legs from the middle of the floor, and Squire pulled out his usual chair. "Seeing y'all here reminds my why."

Emily found a plate and arranged a batch of brownies on it. She set it on the table, next to the milk. She added a bowl of grapes and the sugar bowl.

"One cup," Mrs. Day reminded when he reached for the coffeepot Emily set on a hot pad beside his elbow.

"One cup," he mimicked. "I'll drink as much of this as I want."

"Not if you want me to stay the week, you won't," she said pleasantly. "And you made a deal with your cardiologist. You wouldn't want to back down on a deal, would you? If you have to suck coffee down all day, switch to decaffeinated."

His eyebrows lowered. "You've gotta be kidding."

Emily suddenly moved, and a cupboard door slammed closed.

He switched his attention to her. "You git bit by a bug or something?"

She shook her head and slipped into the chair between Jefferson and Tristan. "Nope." Not looking at him, she reached for the grapes and broke off a few.

He snorted. Then busied himself pouring the steaming hot brew into a mug. "Don't hover, woman. Set yourself down." He looked over at Daniel. "Scoot over son. Give the woman a place to park."

Daniel obliged, pulling up the spare chair that had always sat beneath the telephone hanging on the wall.

Mrs. Day sat in the spot Daniel usually held. Right at Squire's left elbow. He picked up the nearly flat saucer that Emily had placed next to his mug and poured the coffee from the mug. Without spilling a single drop, he lifted the coffee to his lips and sipped at the burning hot liquid. "Ah, Emily, my darlin' girl. You do know how to fix a cup of coffee."

Tristan started to laugh, abruptly cutting off the sound and shooting a glare at Emily.

"Don't be kicking under the table, Emily," Squire said without looking up from the coffee. "Ain't polite."

Matthew laughed and reached for a brownie.

"Now tell me," Squire said as he set the empty saucer down. "What all's been going on the past few weeks?"

Jefferson leaned back in his chair, toying with his mug of coffee as the conversation swirled around the table. He wondered absently whether Mrs. Day was able to follow the multiple discussions crisscrossing the table. It didn't seem to bother her, he decided, watching as she dribbled milk into her cup of coffee and sipped at it, her bright blue eyes drifting across the various faces around the table.

Emily's palm drifted over his thigh, and he caught her fingers in his hand, sending her a warning squeeze. He saw her smile behind the bottle of apple juice she lifted to her lips. He wiggled his toes inside his boot, aware that they were going numb again. Dammit. He shifted on the unreasonably hard wooden chair.

"You okay?" Emily looked at him.

"Stiff," he dismissed. His eyes lifted to see Squire watching him with his piercing eyes. Jefferson just looked back, and after a moment Squire looked down and poured himself another cup of coffee.

"I said one cup." Mrs. Day snatched the brimming drink away before he could pour it into the saucer.

Squire grimaced at her. "Bossy woman."

"Stubborn man."

Squire's lips tilted. "Yes ma'am. You surely got that

right.'' He gave a bark of laughter. He didn't try to have his second cup of coffee. A fact that all of his sons duly noted. ''Think I'll go sleep a spell,'' he announced, pushing his chair back with a scrape. ''Want t' be awake for whatever supper Maggie's cooking tonight. Been lookin' forward to decent food for weeks.'' He gave a nod that encompassed everyone at the table and walked out of the kitchen.

Tristan was the first one to speak. ''Impressed,'' he commented as he nodded across the table to Mrs. Day.

She gave him a bemused smile, her eyes on the doorway that Squire had just passed through. ''Your father is an...interesting man.''

Sawyer reached for a handful of grapes. ''You hear that? Squire's *interesting.*'' He popped a grape into his mouth and chewed it, reflectively. ''Never heard it put quite like that before.''

The telephone rang and Daniel scooped it off the hook. He spoke briefly and handed it to Sawyer, who listened for a moment then excused himself. ''I'll take it in the office,'' he said and strode out. Daniel listened at the phone long enough to know when Sawyer had reached the other extension, then hung up. Leaning over, he opened the cupboard door that Emily had so abruptly pushed closed.

He looked at the large new can of coffee sitting on the shelf. Grinning, he pulled out the can. ''Old devil never even knew it, did he?'' He held up the can, showing the label.

Emily buried her face in her hands. ''He'd have strangled me, if he'd have seen that. Put it away, would you?''

Mrs. Day reached for the coffeepot and topped off her cup. ''You might try pouring the coffee into a different container," she suggested mildly. "One that doesn't say *decaffeinated* on the label."

Jefferson's back twinged and he grimaced. He pushed back his chair and stood up. "Think I'll go for a walk," he announced.

Emily started to get up, but he stopped her with a light hand on her shoulder. She looked up at him. There was a faint white line around his compressed lips. Before she could voice her concern, though, he leaned down and kissed her full on the lips. Surprise held her in her seat.

"I won't be long," he said.

"Well," Matthew commented after the screen door had slammed shut behind Jefferson, "I guess we know which way the wind blows now."

Even Tristan was looking at her with a measure of surprise in his eyes. "Looks like you kissed and made up."

She flushed, clear to the roots of her hair.

Mrs. Day suddenly scooted her chair back. "Perhaps one of you could show me where I'll be sleeping? I'd like to unpack a few things."

Daniel hopped off the counter. "No problem. To tell the truth, you've got your choice. We have a spare room upstairs, and a spare room down here."

"Where is your father's room? I should stay as close to his room as possible."

"Down here then," he told her, showing her the way through the living room and past the staircase.

Left in the kitchen with only Matthew and Tristan, Emily fiddled with her empty juice bottle. She didn't think that Matthew would disapprove of a relationship between her and Jefferson. But, looking at his sober expression, she wasn't quite so sure anymore.

He must have read the apprehension in her eyes, because he simply poured himself more coffee and smiled faintly. "If you and Jefferson can make each other happy, I'm all for it," he said. "It's about time one of the Clay boys settled down."

Emily flushed all over again. Matthew made it sound as if wedding invitations would be going out in the afternoon mail. And even though she dreamed in her heart of hearts of being Jefferson's wife, the details of that were far, *far* from being worked out. It was ironic, really, considering Jefferson's lovemaking. And his very definite avoidance of birth control.

Tristan butted her with his elbow. "More Clay boys could settle down if they weren't so all-fired determined to dislike pretty, long-legged redheads."

Daniel returned and slid into Jefferson's empty chair. "What's this about redheads?"

"Nothing," Matt said firmly.

"Ahh," Daniel said, nodding sagely. "I can tell by the look in your eyes, Matt old man. This conversation wouldn't be about Jaimie, now would it?"

"Shut up."

Daniel rocked his chair back on two legs. "Man, you need to lighten up. She's just what—"

"Forget it. Jaimie Greene is a flighty, sassy, little—"

"Whatever she is, she's sure got your shorts in a knot," Daniel delighted in pointing that out. Tristan chuckled beneath his breath.

"We've another redhead at the Double-C," Emily hurriedly said. "Do you think she's got a husband waiting for her at home?"

"Nope," Daniel answered, his eyes still goading Matthew. "She's a widow."

"How do you know that?"

"I asked her."

"You asked her?" Emily blinked. "Lord, Daniel, what business is it—well, I mean— Oh, geez, I hope you didn't offend her."

"Nope. So, Matt, you going to give us all a break and just get it over with Jaimie or not? Or do we have to put up with your bad mood for the next six months?"

"Zip it," Matthew snapped. His chair scraped back as he stood up. His boots rang as he stomped out.

"Geez Louise, Daniel, what was that for?" Emily asked.

"Emily, have you noticed how uptight Matthew is? He's gonna work himself into the grave if he doesn't unbend a little. Seems to me that Jaimie's the perfect one to help him do it. A few hours in bed with her would do wonders for his mood. It sure worked with Jefferson and you."

Emily groaned and scooted back her chair. "I need some air," she announced.

Tristan shook his head. "Dan, old boy, you need to learn some finesse."

Daniel just shrugged. "Maybe. But am I wrong?"

"Probably not," Tristan admitted.

Emily skipped down the back steps, and the smile she'd been suppressing broke free. Daniel was incorrigible. And maybe his methods lacked something, but his heart was in the right place.

She wondered how far Jefferson had gone. His knee had obviously been bothering him when he'd left the kitchen. She really should have found out where he'd thrown away that cane. It was silly of him not to use it, when he obviously still needed the extra support.

She looked inside the tack room, but it was empty. His boots were still sitting on the shelf where he'd left them the night before. She started to walk toward the swimming hole, but abruptly turned back. She slipped a halter over Daisy's head and led the horse out of the stall, then hoisted herself onto Daisy's bare back and clicked her into a trot.

A sense of unease was growing in her, and before they were halfway to the swimming hole, she knew why. She reined in Daisy and hit the ground running.

Jefferson was lying in the grass, his eyes closed. If it hadn't been mown just the other day, she'd have missed him completely.

No, oh no, oh no! Her mind screamed as she skidded to her knees beside him. "Jefferson?"

Sweat dotted his forehead, and he slowly opened his eyes.

Her hands were frantically running over his legs. Automatically feeling for broken bones. "What happened?"

He slowly blinked. "Em?"

"I'm here," she leaned over him, pressing her palm to his forehead, running her fingers over his scalp. "Did you fall? Are you hurt?" It was a needless question. She could see the glaze of pain dulling his dark blue eyes. "What's wrong?"

He grimaced and crushed her hand in his. He closed his eyes, then opened them again, as if gathering his strength. "I can't feel my legs."

Emily's mouth ran dry. She sat back on her heels. "Oh, Lord." She looked at Daisy, only a few feet away. But there was no way she'd be able to get Jefferson up on the horse. If he should even be moved at all. "I have to get help," she said in a rush. "Just...just don't move, oh, geez, that was stupid." She bent over him and kissed his mouth. "Will you be okay for a few more minutes?"

"Yeah." His bruising grip eased up on her hand, and she bounded for the horse. "Em—"

She darted back down beside him. "What?"

His cloudy eyes searched hers.

She frowned. Wiped the fresh sweat from his forehead. "What?"

"Love you," he murmured.

A dart of pure panic pierced her heart. They were the words she'd wanted him to say. But his timing frightened her right out of her mind. Something was wrong here. Something was terribly, terribly wrong. Before she succumbed to the violent fear flooding her, she kissed his lips. Hard enough to bring some sense to her whirling thoughts. "I'll be right back," she vowed.

He closed his eyes. "Yeah."

She lunged for Daisy. Grabbing a handful of mane, she vaulted onto the horse's back and dug her heels into Daisy's flanks. She rode the horse right up to the back steps and jumped off, racing into the house, running smack into Tristan.

"Holy sh—" He grabbed her before she bounced off him into the kitchen cupboards. "What's wrong?"

"Jefferson," she gasped, her hands clutching his shirt. "He's hurt."

"Where?"

"About halfway to the swimming hole."

Tristan was already yelling for Matthew and Daniel. Mrs. Day and Sawyer came running, too. Within seconds they knew the problem and were springing into action. Daniel went for the truck. Sawyer went for the first aid kit, and Mrs. Day gathered up a collection of big towels from the mudroom.

Matthew was on the phone. "What do you mean we can't get the chopper here? No, dammit, I need it— *Yes,* fine. No, we'll get him there ourselves." He slammed the phone onto the counter. "What the hell do we pay taxes for," he growled.

Squire walked into the room. "What on God's green earth is all the fussin' about?"

Suddenly all motion ceased. Mrs. Day recovered first, pressing the towels into Emily's hands and telling her to go get in the truck. She quickly took Squire by the arm and pushed him in a chair before telling him briefly that one of his sons was apparently injured.

Squire popped up off the chair like a shot. "What the devil we sitting around for, then," he said. "Get the boy home. Is that old stretcher still in the bunkhouse?"

Tristan slammed out the door, already on his way.

Emily swayed in the doorway, her arms full of towels. "Don't go passing out on us, Emily," Squire warned sharply.

Dread numbed her thought processes. She heard Mrs. Day sternly order Squire to stay put, then felt the woman gently push her out toward the truck. Emily climbed up into the cab beside Daniel, sliding over to make room for Mrs. Day. She was absently aware of Sawyer vaulting into the truck bed, the square, white first aid kit in his hand, followed by Matthew.

Tristan trotted around the corner and tossed a stretcher into the truck bed, vaulting in after it.

"Go," he called.

Gravel spewed from beneath the tires as Daniel gunned the engine and set off for the stand of trees. It took mere minutes, with Emily pointing to the spot where she'd left Jefferson. Mrs. Day was out of the cab before the wheels had even come to a complete stop, and Emily was right on her heels. She raced through the grass, falling to her knees alongside Jefferson. He'd lost even more color, but his eyes were open.

She moved toward his head when Matthew and Tristan came up beside him, laying the stretcher on the grass. Mrs. Day had produced a stethoscope and was leaning over his chest, quietly questioning him. All Emily heard was something about his back.

After a moment Mrs. Day sat back, clearly unhappy with the situation. "At least you kept your knees bent," she murmured.

Jefferson grimaced. Simply turning his head seemed a monumental task. He looked straight at Sawyer. "Get me back to the house."

"That's not where you need to go," Sawyer replied.

Tired of watching the unspoken messages passing between the two men, Emily spoke. "What's going on here?" Jefferson's shadowed eyes turned her way, and her stomach dropped even further at the dull pain he couldn't hide. Biting her lip, she gently smoothed his hair away from his forehead.

"On the count of three, okay?"

Daniel and Matthew were at Jefferson's legs, and Tristan and Sawyer were on either side of his waist. "Emily, keep his head steady," Mrs. Day instructed.

"One, two," Emily gently cradled Jefferson's head and when Sawyer counted off three, she moved with the rest as they carefully slid him onto the stretcher. It had only taken a second or two and Jefferson had hardly moved, but fresh beads of sweat rolled off his forehead. She got out of the way as the brothers grabbed the handles of the stretcher and lifted. Jefferson muttered a dark curse, his fingers latching on to her hand like a vise.

"No hospital," he gritted as they slid him onto the truck bed. "Promise me, Em. No hospital."

She climbed up beside him, placing the rolled-up towels beside his head and beneath his knees where Mrs. Day instructed, then carefully moved around so that she could sit near his head. Daniel and Mrs. Day climbed into the cab, leaving the others to follow on foot.

"Jefferson, you need—"

"Promise me," he growled.

Her brows knit together. Using the hem of her T-shirt, she wiped the perspiration from his face. "All right." For now, she added silently.

Jefferson's eyes closed, relieved. He knew he could count on Emily. She might be small. She might be young. She cried far too easily and looked for the best in people when there was no best to find. But she had a core of strength inside her that would never fail her.

Even though it caused a fresh wave of pain to wash over him, he shifted his head until he could see her. The sun was shining brightly over them, turning her pale pink shirt to white. She looked like an angel. His lips were dry. "I'm sorry."

The soft fabric stopped its daubing. She leaned down and gently kissed his lips. "There's nothing to be sorry for."

The truck rolled to a stop and rocked slightly as Daniel and Mrs. Day climbed out. They waited a few more minutes for the others to catch up, and then Emily moved out of the way while they carefully transported Jefferson into the house.

It wasn't an easy task. The house, though roomy, clearly hadn't been designed to accommodate four large men bearing an equally large man on a stretcher. Squire stood out of the way, uncharacteristically silent, when Jefferson was carried past. There were corners to maneuver around and stairs to climb. But eventually, amid much grumbling and cursing, they lowered Jefferson onto the bed in the room he'd used since childhood.

Mrs. Day supervised the placement of pillows beneath his knees. Her hands quickly wound a tight tube from one of the towels and she carefully slid it beneath Jefferson's neck, while Matthew and Tristan pulled off his boots. Jefferson hissed, covering his eyes with his bent arm.

Sawyer came back in, bearing a wide, flat, cold pack. They managed to gently slide it beneath Jefferson's back. "Damnation," he muttered as the cold penetrated the worn fabric of his shirt. But it wasn't long before he overlooked the cold for the relief it brought.

The brothers seemed to breathe a collective sigh as they hovered around the bed. Jefferson held Emily's fingers tightly, and she sat on the faded, woven rag rug that covered a good portion of the wood-planked floor. She propped her chin on the mattress, careful not to jiggle the bed.

Mrs. Day brushed a strand of hair out of her eyes. "You need more care than we can provide here," she said.

From Emily's angle she could see beneath the arm that Jefferson still had over his eyes and could see his strained expression. "No hospital," he said tiredly.

"You had back problems before?" Daniel asked. "I have. Ever since that last accident I had on the bike. Racked myself up but good. I got the name of a good orthopedic guy in Gillette—"

"No."

Matthew leaned against the tattered wing chair that sat across from the foot of the bed. He crossed his arms. "You should see a doctor. A chiropractor. Something."

"No."

"Dammit, Jefferson, you—"

"*No.*"

Matthew sighed. "You always were a stubborn fool. The older you get, the more like Squire you become."

At that, Jefferson's arm shifted and he glared at his brother. "Bull."

Matthew smiled faintly. "Well, anyway, since you won't go to the mountain of medical help, maybe we should call someone out here." Mrs. Day was nodding in agreement.

Sawyer lifted his hand. "I'll call someone."

Emily frowned at the panic that edged into Jefferson's face. Her fingers were going numb, and she wiggled them slightly. "Jefferson—"

"I said no," Jefferson grimaced.

She bit the inside of her lip, looking at the other men. Sawyer's narrowed eyes studied Jefferson's prone body. Matthew and Daniel shared an unsurprised look. And Tristan was looking out the window, his expression thoughtful.

"I hope you change your mind," Mrs. Day finally said. She brushed her palms on her slacks. "I'd better see to Squire."

"See if you can change his mind, Em," Matthew said finally.

"I'm not changing my mind," Jefferson said distinctly. "Just let me be."

Daniel shook his head, following Matthew out the door. "More like Squire every day," he agreed.

Jefferson snorted faintly.

Sawyer tugged on his lower lip. "Jefferson, this is really a *bad* idea. A bad idea. You need—"

"I know what I need," Jefferson growled. "To be left the hell alone."

"But you said you couldn't feel your legs," Emily cried out.

Though his face turned a little green, Jefferson's foot moved. Merely a few inches. But it had moved. "It's getting better," he said, inflexibly.

"For how long," Sawyer asked, just as inflexible. He got no reply from Jefferson and, throwing up his hands in disgust, he left the room.

A weary sigh left Jefferson's dry lips. Emily slipped her fingers loose and stood up. "I'll bring you some water."

As soon as he heard Emily's light tread on the staircase, Tristan said, "She knows what you need without you even saying a word."

"Turn the screws a little tighter, why don't you?"

He shrugged and moved closer to the bed, so that Jefferson could see him without having to tilt his head. "Do you know what she needs? Without her telling you?"

"Not now, Tris."

"Then when?" Tristan crossed his arms. "When you're up and about again? That won't work, 'cause you'll probably just head out again."

"I don't have anywhere to head out for," Jefferson said grimly. Nor could he envision leaving Emily again.

"Not even that nice little condo you own down in South Carolina? Oh, that's right. You've signed it over to Kim Lee's wife. Lisa, isn't it? And the boy. What is his name? Oh, yeah. *Jeff.* Appropriately named after his honorary godparent."

Jefferson slowly lowered his arm and eyed his brother. "You've been busy." He waited for some sort

of explanation of how his baby brother had come by
that information, but none was forthcoming. "You've
got one thing wrong, though. Lisa is Kim's *widow*," he
finally said.

Tristan nodded. "True. Sometime we'll have to talk
about that, too." He idly scratched his ear. "So, how
about going to that little brick farmhouse. You
know...the one outside Stockholm?" He didn't give
Jefferson a chance to respond. "Or the flat in London?
The apartment in D.C.?"

"Enough," Jefferson snapped.

"It's time to finish what you started, Jeff. I know
you've sold those places. Over the last six months,
you've divested yourself of every piece of real property
you've collected around this bloody world. You've
closed every account, in every country, under every
alias you've used in the past ten years. Except for the
bank account you opened in Casper when you were
twenty years old, you're strictly cash and carry. The
only thing, as far as I know, that you haven't officially
done, has been to resign. If they'll even let you."

"They'll let me," Jefferson assured grimly. "They
don't have any use for half cripples. And infiltration
works better when your nerves don't splinter at the
sound of a phone ringing or a dog barking. How'd you
get the info? You been doing some hacking of your
own?"

Tristan shook his head. "No hacking," he said
slowly. "I've got clearance."

Jefferson could have laughed at the absurdity of it all.
If just the notion of laughing hadn't caused a zillion
darts of pain, he'd have done just that. One of these
days, he'd have to have a serious talk with Tristan about
the path he was apparently treading.

"The point is," Tristan went on, "that you've been systematically tying up all your loose ends. Like you're preparing for something. The question is, what?"

"Isn't that in your computer files somewhere?" Jefferson asked caustically.

Tristan took no offense. "Oh, I've got it figured out," he said. "It just took me until now to do it. People getting ready to die often put their affairs in order." He uncrossed his arms, hating that Jefferson hadn't corrected him. "I expect Sawyer knows there's a surgical team in Connecticut just waiting for you to say the word. That's who he wants to call, isn't it?"

Jefferson's jaw locked. "I'm not having the surgery."

"You're a damn, stubborn fool," Tristan said, shaking his head. He recognized Emily's light tread as she came upstairs. "A damn, stubborn fool."

"Hand me my bag there."

Tristan looked at the duffel. "Whatcha need?"

"Prescription," Jefferson said, barely managing to keep his eyes open. God he was tired. So tired.

Tristan unzipped the bag and ran his hand inside until he found the little brown bottle. He looked at the label, then twisted off the lid and dropped a tiny pill into Jefferson's hand.

Without water, Jefferson stuck the pill in his mouth and swallowed it just as Emily entered the room. She carried a covered container of water with a bendable straw sticking out of it. She held it to his lips while he drank. He tried to stay awake. He didn't want to frighten her any more than she already was. But the medication worked quicker than his stubborn will. In minutes, his head was swimming and the grinding, awful ache in his back began to dull.

Emily's fingers were laced with his when he closed his eyes, sinking into a painless gray oblivion.

In some corner of his mind, Jefferson knew that he was slipping in and out of consciousness, yet he was unable to do anything about it. Odd, fractured thoughts flitted through his mind.

He remembered his mother. The way she had smelled. The way she'd smiled at her young sons when they'd come tumbling into the house, muddy and disheveled after playing outside. The way her eyes would gleam whenever Squire entered the room.

A vision of Kim swam into his cloudy thoughts. He saw the pride in his partner's eyes when he'd spoken of his young wife. Of their child.

Squire entered the parade through Jefferson's thoughts. Squire, frighteningly silent and stark, watching his wife's casket being lowered into the ground, while in his arms he held a tiny baby tightly wrapped against the blowing snow. Squire, tugging a dark-haired, dark-eyed little waif into the kitchen one night and thrusting her into the midst of them.

Emily, sweetly lovely at sixteen. Innocently alluring at nineteen. He'd felt like a lech, watching her. Wanting her. It didn't matter that he'd always loved her. For the child she'd been. For the friend she'd become. For the mate he'd yearned for. He'd loved her. He'd known he would never hurt her. Could never hurt her.

So he'd stayed away. Until the call of Emily had been too strong and he'd been too weak to deny it, and he'd come back. Just to be near her. Just to look at her beautiful face. And pretend, in the tiny reaches of his mind, that that would be enough.

He knew better now. He knew that his only chance for peace was to keep her in his life. Keep her in his arms and in his heart.

Had he learned the lesson too late?

Chapter Fourteen

"You're a damn, stubborn fool," Sawyer said the next morning when he stopped in the room to check on Jefferson.

Jefferson grimaced at the effort it cost him, but he finished pulling on a clean shirt and turned to face his brother. "So everyone keeps telling me," he muttered. He was standing. Just. But at least he wasn't numb from the waist down. "I'm doing better."

Sawyer grunted. "For now maybe."

Jefferson gave up after fastening just two buttons on the shirt, and leaned his weight against the dresser. "Where's Emily?"

"Still sleeping."

"Good. She needs it."

"She sat up with you most of the night."

"All night," Jefferson corrected. While he'd been fitfully dozing, she'd kept him warm. She'd held water to his lips, and hours later, in the middle of the night, she'd gotten a second dose of medication down him.

The drug had done its job, and he was up on his feet again.

More or less.

"Obviously no one can make you change your mind about the surgery. If you're going to throw away the rest of your life, that's your business."

"Give it a rest, would you?" Jefferson raked his fingers through his hair, hating the cloudiness that clung to him because of the medicine. "You think this is easy for me? Christ! I'm sick to death of everybody telling me what a fool I am. How selfish I am. How stubborn. Hell, if it's not Squire riding me not to touch Emily, then it's Tristan digging around in my life or it's you bugging me about that damned surgery! Can't you just leave me be?"

Sawyer's lips thinned. "I'm not going to speak for Squire. Or for Tristan. Or any of the rest of them. But, for myself, I'd like to see you among the living for a good many years to come. And unless you change your mind about the surgery, that likelihood seems pretty slim."

"Come off it, Sawyer. My chances *with* the surgery are pretty damn slim." Moving at a snail's pace, he crossed over to the wing chair. His arms held his weight as he gingerly sank into the chair. "Why don't you go work on Tristan. I guess he's starting to paddle in some pretty deep waters."

"I'd hardly call it starting. He's been on the inside for more than a few years. His, ah, *talents* with the computer keyboard have been useful. And he's not an emotional mess right now."

Jefferson grimaced. Shows how much he knew about what went on in his family.

"What about Emily? Have you thought about her in all of this? What the surgery could mean for her?"

"I've thought about nothing *but* Emily."

"Have you told her? You know she expects a future with you. A *long* future."

"Back off." Jefferson had already made a decision about the surgery. During the long night hours with Emily in his arms, he'd made a few more decisions. But he was sick to death of having his brothers shoving their opinions down his throat.

Sawyer sighed. He raked his fingers through his hair, a man out of patience and out of time. "I wish I could stay here and get you to change your mind. But the fact is, I've gotta get back to D.C. There's a charter picking me up in Gillette in about ninety minutes."

"Guess you'd better get moving then."

"Dammit, woman, I don't care what you say. I'm climbing those stairs and that's final." Squire's roar could have been heard clear to the next county.

"Crazy old man," Sawyer muttered. He moved over to Jefferson and stuck out his hand.

Jefferson reached out and briefly shook his brother's square hand. "Watch your back."

Sawyer's lip twitched. "Always do. Give Emily a kiss for me," he said, heading for the door. "At least it's something I can be sure you'll do."

Squire appeared in the doorway, faintly out of breath from climbing the stairs that Mrs. Day had been determined he was not to climb. "You leaving now?"

Sawyer nodded.

Squire's lips pursed. "Don't wait for me to have another danged heart attack before coming home."

Jefferson saw the absolute and utter surprise in his brother's eyes when Squire reached out and hugged him. Clearly disconcerted, Sawyer stepped back. But he knew he had no time to spare. Lifting his hand in a brief goodbye, he left.

Jefferson and Squire just looked at each other. Finally Squire moved over to the bed. He shoved aside one of the rolled-up towels and sat down, sighing slightly as he did so. "Your brother's done well for himself."

Jefferson nodded slowly.

"Fact is, you've all done well for yourselves," Squire continued, ruminating. "Even little Emily, though I sure wish she'd give up on that danged job and come home where she belongs."

"She likes her work."

Squire grunted. "So, she could work around here. Matt does a fine job on the books, 'course. But truth be told, he hates that sort of thing. Rather be out in the sunshine, he would, but he's too damn stubborn to admit it."

"Seems to be a problem with this family," Jefferson muttered.

"Never did understand why she was so all-fired determined to leave here." Squire shot a look Jefferson's way. "Well—"

Jefferson wished his legs were a little more steady. He'd have walked out of the room right then. "What do you want?"

Squire squinted and tugged at his ear. "Comin' close to death changes a man," he said finally.

"I know."

"S'pose you do, at that." Squire lifted his chin in a typical nonverbal fashion. "Heard you got a problem with that back o' yours." Squire scratched his jaw, rubbing at the stubble he'd yet to shave. "Kinda hard for a man to make a baby when he's dead from the waist down."

Jefferson's eyes narrowed to slits. His hands tightened over the arms of the chair. "What game are you playing, old man?"

Squire shrugged. "Seems a shame to me, that's all."

"*What* is a shame?"

"Em's talked about babies since she was nineteen years old. Didn't want anything more, I'd guess. 'Cept maybe to have her own horse farm. Instead she ended up a bean counter, living way out in Califor-ni-ay." He shrugged. "Women. Go figure."

Jefferson blinked. "Let me get this straight. You're telling me that I'm the one who should give Emily a child?" It didn't matter that that was exactly what he'd already decided to do. "You told me not to set foot on this ranch unless I was sure I could keep my pants zipped around her. And now you're telling me you want me to get her *pregnant?*"

"I ain't saying nothing," Squire snapped. Hell, he'd decided he needed to right a terrible wrong, but that didn't mean it was all that easy for him.

"Bull," Jefferson snorted.

"Don't give me no lip, boy. I don't like it, and I won't take it. Not under my own roof. No sir."

"God, you're impossible," Jefferson growled. "It's a wonder any of us stay sane with your blood running through our veins."

"Don't go insulting your heritage, boy. Good stubborn Clay blood. That's what we got. Kept us going all these years, after your mama passed on, and it's gonna keep us going a whole lotta more years." He pushed himself to his feet. "Well, that's it. I got no more to say. Habits die hard, son. But they do die."

He walked to the doorway, then stopped and turned back, looking over the bedroom. "Good to see you under this roof, boy. It's been too long."

With that, Squire left him. Jefferson realized it was as close to an apology as he would ever get.

Emily wandered into the room, an oversize shirt covering her to her knees. In one hand she was carrying a bunch of paper. "Was that Squire I just heard? I thought Mrs. Day said he wasn't supposed to be climbing any stairs just yet."

"She said that all right," Jefferson murmured. "Come here."

She pushed her tumbled hair out of her still-sleepy eyes. "You're up."

"Yeah." Her tongue dipped over her lip in that movement that never failed to drive him mad. "Come here," he said again. As soon as she was close enough, he pulled her down onto his knees and carefully absorbed the feel of her warm bottom settling on his lap. He never wanted to forget that sensation. "There's something we need to talk about."

She looped her arms around his neck and laid her head on his shoulder. "I'm not sure I like the way this is starting out," she said softly. "There's something I need to tell you first." She plopped the papers she held onto her thighs. "About this."

He glanced at it, then looked a little more closely. "Where did this come from? Ah, hell, *Tristan*. Am I right? That little punk."

Punk was the most unlikely description she'd ever heard applied to Tristan Clay. But that wasn't the issue. "He gave this to me a few days ago," she said. "The morning after you and I...slept by the swimming hole." She fingered the dog-eared corner of the top page. "I didn't read it."

Had he been presented with an answer sheet to someone's behavior, he wasn't sure he'd have passed it up. "Why not?"

"I didn't think it would be right. I imagine Tristan read it, though. He's nosier than you, even." She shrugged, diffident. "I just thought you should know."

He took the papers, looking at them for a long moment. He sighed faintly and dropped them onto the floor beside the chair. "There was a time," he murmured, sliding her hair behind her shoulder, "when I would have completely blown up over this."

"Yes."

"Coming close to death changes a man," he said softly.

"What?"

But Jefferson just shook his head and lifted her lips to his. When they parted, he could have sworn there were stars shining in her eyes. "I love you, you know," he said.

Definitely stars. "I know."

Yeah, she had. All along. She'd pushed and prodded and slid beneath his skin, even when he'd been too stupid and too pigheaded to know it was exactly what he'd needed. "I'm sorry it took me so long to say it," he admitted.

"It frightened me," she whispered after a moment. "You said it, lying there in the field, yesterday. It was like you were saying goodbye to me or something."

"I don't ever want to leave you," he said roughly.

"Then don't."

He didn't even have to close his eyes to envision the

life they could have together. "I want to marry you," he said at last.

Her eyes grew moist. "You don't have to say that, just to please me."

He knew that. Just as he knew he'd planned to marry her, even before Squire had come in here, babbling about habits dying hard. "I'm saying it to please me. Emily Nichols, I want you to be my wife." He swallowed. "I want you to be the mother of my children. I want to sit across the breakfast table from you, with our son doing his homework at the last minute and our daughter stuffing cereal in her little face, but managing to spread more of it on the floor."

She smiled through her tears, recognizing her own words coming from his lips. "I want that, too," she breathed. "More than anything in this world."

"You're gonna call that Stuart guy this morning and tell him you quit that job?"

A hundred details spun through her mind. Bird. Her clothes. The few pieces of furniture she'd collected. She dashed away a tear and nodded without a qualm.

"I don't know where we'll live," he added. "I think there are too many Clays under this roof right now." Even after Squire's abrupt change. He saw her bite her lip. "I, uh, heard that George Dawson was thinking about selling his spread, now that his wife is gone. He doesn't have any kids to pass it on to. Dan was talking about it the other day. Dawson's got a fair quarter horse program going."

"That would take a lot of money," she murmured, visualizing the bordering ranch. It rivaled the Double-C in prosperity.

He could smile at that. "Angelface, I've got a lot of money." He couldn't resist kissing the O of surprise her lips had formed. "There's just one thing," he said after a long moment had passed. He tucked her head under his chin and held her close.

"What?" Her breath stirred the hair brushing his shoulders.

"I want to make love to you."

He felt her smile. "Sounds good to me."

"Every night."

"Even better."

"Yeah," he agreed, feeling his body stir just to speak of it. "But first, I gotta have a little surgery."

Epilogue

"He said a *little surgery*." Tearfully, Emily glanced once again at the big round clock hanging on the wall of the waiting room of the hospital in Casper. Between the row of hard, plastic chairs, she paced across the dull gray carpet. "What had he been thinking?"

Tristan reached for her hand when she paced by him for the fourth time. "Sit." He pulled her onto the chair beside him.

"He was thinking of you," Squire said, testy as he usually was around hospitals.

"But this is so dangerous," Emily muttered, rubbing her cold arms through her sweater. To think that she'd gone all that time thinking that he'd just been plagued with knee problems. And he'd let her think it, too, damn the man. She wasn't going to let him forget that in a hurry, she promised herself, stealing another look at the clock. Jefferson had been taken to surgery more than four hours earlier.

"What's taking so long?" She restlessly got to her feet again, and Tristan threw his head back against his seat, giving up on trying to keep her somewhat relaxed.

Gloria Day entered the waiting room, foam coffee cups in her hand. She moved beside Squire and handed him one.

"This ain't that decaffeinated stuff, is it?" He suspiciously lifted the lid. He supposed he could drink the piping hot stuff out of the cup.

"Of course not, darling," she said, patting his leg comfortingly. Squire's big palm covered hers. Her fingers were bare, but it was only a matter of time before Squire put his ring on her finger. Everyone knew it. Except perhaps for Squire himself. The man was exceedingly inflexible about some things.

"You know I can't stand drinking that decaffeinated stuff," he muttered, sipping the coffee. "This ain't bad for hospital coffee," he decided.

"Yes, dear." Without batting a blue eye, she looked at Daniel and Matthew, sitting in the seats opposite. She looked right at them, just daring them to laugh. There was only one way to handle this crew of men. She'd realized that right off the bat.

They shifted in their seats, Matthew turning his attention back to the agricultural magazine in his lap. Daniel absently patted his pockets, looking for the cigarette pack he'd once again abandoned a few weeks ago.

Emily stopped below the round clock and watched the second hand slowly revolve. "This is making me crazy," she complained. "Can't we find out how it's going?" She looked over at Gloria. "Couldn't they at least tell us how it's going?"

Gloria set aside her coffee. She rose, automatically smoothing down the legs of her finely tailored slacks. "I'll go see what I can find out."

"Thank you." Emily was so grateful, she thought she might start bawling again. She seemed to do that an awful lot lately.

Daniel shifted in the hard seat and stuck his legs out. "I can't believe they made Jefferson wait four months before doing this surgery."

Emily pinched the bridge of her nose. She'd thought it ridiculous too, but Jefferson's surgeon had made the final decision. Even though the surgeon had been urging Jefferson to have the surgery immediately, when Jefferson finally agreed, Dr. Beauman had decided to wait, after all. Something to do with wanting the fragment in a more promising position. *A promising position!*

She still couldn't believe that kid could possibly know what he was talking about. But Jefferson had been sure, only insisting that the surgery be done in Wyoming, and that's all that had mattered to Emily.

Gloria returned, smiling faintly, with Sawyer right on her heels. He was a formidable sight in his dark uniform.

Anxiously Emily hurried over to them. "Well?"

Gloria looked up at Sawyer. He dropped his arm over Emily's shoulder and turned her to see Jefferson's surgeon approaching. Emily thought she might faint, while it seemed to take forever for him to walk down the brightly lit hall. She was vaguely aware of Squire coming up to stand behind her, his palm closing over her other shoulder. Matthew and Daniel stood behind her, and Tristan towered over them all.

The surgeon stopped right in front of her, his eyes

smiling gently behind his round glasses. "It went well. He's going to be fine."

Emily sagged with relief. She looked up at Tristan, who winked. "Told you," he mouthed.

She turned back to Dr. Beauman. "When can we see him?"

"He's already asking for you," he said.

Emily looked back at her family.

"Git going," Squire said, urging her forward. The rest were nodding, all in agreement.

She quickly kissed Squire's cheek and then followed the surgeon through the swinging doors at the end of the hall. There was a confusing array of curtains and beds, but as soon as she saw a lock of dark gold hair, she headed toward it, forgetting all about Dr. Beauman.

She stepped beyond the curtain partially shielding both sides of the bed. Her eyes raced over his face and the shoulder-length hair that Squire still bugged him about. He was pale, and a tube ran from his wrist to an IV pole beside the bed. But his eyes were open and focused right on her.

"Hi."

Jefferson smiled slightly and held out his hand. "My clothes and stuff," he said, his voice hoarse from the tube that had been in his throat during surgery. "Open the bag up."

"Jefferson, you can't change clothes and walk out of here just yet," Emily said softly. But she retrieved the faded black duffel bag from the rack stretching between the wheels of his bed. One of these days that bag was simply going to disintegrate, right before their eyes. She unzipped it. "What do you want?"

"My ring," he said, eyes heavy. "They made m' take it off."

She looked inside the bag. Sure enough, lying right there on top of his black jeans and white shirt lay a gold band. She took it out and put the duffel bag back on the rack. He held out his hand, and she slipped it on his finger. He smiled faintly and held her hand, his thumb slowly gliding over the matching gold band on her hand.

"I'm not dead," he said after a moment. "Guess it worked."

Emily sucked in a shuddering breath. "Mmm-hmm. Dr Beauman, boy wonder, said you'd be fine."

The corners of his lips lifted slightly. He was silent for several minutes, while she looked her fill at his wonderful face.

"How you feeling?" he asked eventually.

She smiled, silly tears coming to her eyes again. "Fine."

Again that half smile of his. "Not sick?"

She shook her head. "Not today."

He drew a satisfied breath. "Good." He could feel sleep tugging at him, but he managed to keep his eyes open for a while longer. "Let me see."

She half laughed. "Jefferson—"

"Come...on...angelface," he insisted slowly.

Her cheeks pinkened. "Oh, all right," she finally said. She unwound the scarf at her neck and tossed it onto the foot of his bed. She put her hands on the hem of the bulky blue sweater that hung to her thighs. "Honestly, I can't believe I'm doing this."

The slash in his cheek deepened. She simply could not resist the man. Every single day it got worse. "Okay." She lifted the hem of the sweater, and after a quick look around, tugged down the waist of the black leggings she wore. Then she moved close enough for him to touch her.

Jefferson's eyes glowed beneath his heavy lashes. He felt woozy even moving, but he reached out and laid his palm on the firm, gently rounded belly she'd revealed. He slept with his hand on that growing belly every night. "Now," he growled, content. "Now...I can...go to sleep."

Emily leaned over, pressing her lips to his. "I love you, Jefferson Clay."

Bending over him, she rested her cheek lightly against his forehead. The hem of Emily's sweater fell back to her thighs. Covering the hand that still rested upon their growing child.

He was barely awake. But his words were clear. He told her often now. Several times a day.

They still thrilled her to her very core.

"Love you...too...Emily...Clay."

* * * * *

Dear Reader,

Here Comes the Groom is one of my favorite books. Allison and Kent, the heroine and hero, first appeared in *Mother of the Groom* (3/93), where they were supposed to marry, but in the end, they broke their engagement, and Allison took off to France.

Here Comes the Groom tells the story of what happens when Allison returns to Houston after the death of her race-car-driver husband. She now has a sick child, a bruised and hurting heart, and is a mature woman instead of a spoiled girl.

This was a wonderful book to write, not only because I loved Allison and Kent and wanted to see what would happen when they met again, but because Diana and Lee, who starred in *Mother of the Groom,* were two of my all-time favorite characters, and the chance to revisit their lives was just too tempting to pass up.

I hope you enjoy meeting these people as much as I enjoyed writing about them. If you get a spare minute, please visit my Web site at www.patriciakay.com and share with me your feelings about the story.

Happy reading!

Patricia Kay

HERE COMES THE GROOM
Patricia Kay

This book is dedicated to Loretta Kenny,
the kind of friend every woman needs,
and to the West Houston Chapter
of the Romance Writers of America
for their unwavering support over the years.

Special thanks to Marilyn Amann, Carla Luan,
Heather MacAllister, Alaina Richardson and
Sue Royer—critique group extraordinaire.

Prologue

It is too late to call back yesterday...
                                    Ancient Proverb

Allison Fornier tightened her arms around her two-month-old daughter. "Sleep, *mon bébé*," she whispered. "Don't be afraid. Soon we'll be home, and the doctors there will make you well. You'll see."

Marianne's tiny mouth tipped at the edges, as if she were smiling at her mother's words, and Allison's heart squeezed painfully. She cuddled the baby closer and stared blindly out the window of the Concorde jet as she blinked back tears.

There would be no more crying for Allison. She had already done her crying, and the crying hadn't solved anything.

Sighing deeply, she turned her gaze back to Marianne. Anyone giving the baby more than just a casual glance would realize something was wrong. There was a bluish cast to her nail beds and lips, and her skin color was dusky instead of creamy. These outward signs were an indication of serious problems involving Marianne's tiny little heart—a heart that didn't seem to work the way it should.

Allison still shivered every time she remembered Dr. Montand's solemn dark eyes, his grave tone of voice when he had delivered Marianne's sentence the day after her birth: "I am very sorry, Madame Fornier, but your daughter has a condition known as pulmonary atresia. Her body is compensating with collateral circulation to the lungs, but her pulmonary artery is too small, and not all the blood is being oxygenated as it should be."

Allison's throat had gone dry, and her heart had seemed to stop. "H-how serious is it, Doctor?"

"Very serious, I'm afraid. But we can correct the problem. It will require open-heart surgery, however." His eyes, liquid with compassion, had held her gaze.

"Open-heart surgery!" Just the thought scared Allison half to death. Marianne was so tiny. Open-heart surgery was so serious.

At first Allison hadn't wanted to believe Dr. Montand. How could this be possible? How could Marianne, so perfect, so beautiful, be in such danger? It couldn't be true. Dr. Montand *had* to be wrong.

But Dr. Montand hadn't been wrong. Dr. Deauville, the heart specialist who was brought in to oversee Marianne's tests, confirmed Dr. Montand's diagnosis. "Although we probably won't want to do the actual surgery until your daughter is a little older, we will monitor her carefully, *Madame*. If she shows signs of any deterioration at all, we may *have* to do the surgery. But first we would do a heart catheterization. This would show us how much blockage there is.'' His voice had softened. ''I realize all of this has been a great shock to you, *Madame*. Think about what I've said, and if you have any questions, please feel free to call me.''

Before he left the room, he had added slowly, ''I was very sorry to learn of your husband's death. All of France will miss him.''

After he was gone, Allison remembered the doctor's words. If he only knew how guilty his words of sympathy had made her feel. He, like everyone else, thought she was devastated by the death of Jean Luc Fornier, her dashing race-car-driver husband, who had died in a crash seven months earlier, when she was two months pregnant with Marianne. The truth was, Allison mostly felt relieved that she no longer had to keep up the pretense of a happy marriage.

But Marianne. Marianne was different. Although Allison could barely tolerate Jean Luc toward the end of their marriage, she desperately loved her daughter and would have gladly laid down her life for her. Panic filled her at the thought that Marianne was so seriously ill.

For six weeks after she brought Marianne home from the hospital, all had gone well. Then one day Marianne's color had worsened, and Dr. Deauville confirmed Allison's fears.

''It's time to do the heart catheterization,'' he had said.

Fear had clogged Allison's throat. ''But she's so little,'' she'd whispered. *And I'm so alone here.* ''I—I'd like to call my father.''

''Of course,'' Dr. Deauville had said. ''We don't have to do the test immediately, but we shouldn't wait too long.''

As the taxi sped Allison home to her apartment, she had done some hard thinking. She'd decided she didn't want to have the catheterization performed in Paris. She wasn't sure when her feelings about the city had changed. All she knew was that she no longer felt at home in Paris. She was afraid that from then on the city would always be associated with disaster in her mind. It was here that her marriage to Jean Luc had started to fall apart. It was here that she had received the news of his death. And it was here that the doctors had delivered their edict about Marianne.

After a long night of soul-searching, she had realized that what she wanted was to go home to Houston, no matter what she had to face when she got there. She had finally admitted she needed the comfort and security that only people who loved her could give her.

In the short time since she'd found out about Marianne's heart condition, she'd also discovered that many of the latest techniques concerning open-heart surgery had been perfected in France, but Houston also had world-renowned medical facilities, including top children's hospitals.

So, after conferring with the French doctors, she had decided she would take Marianne home—to the Children's Clinic of Houston. And the doctors there would cure her.

That decision had been made a week ago. Even though she had worked almost every available hour, it had still taken the better part of six days to get everything ready to leave. Packing, closing the apartment, storing the most valuable of the furniture and antiques, conferring with Jean Luc's attorney and banker, obtaining all the necessary records from Marianne's doctors—all took time and energy.

Madame Bergeron, the starchy housekeeper who had been with Jean Luc and Allison from the very first days of their ill-fated marriage, had cried when Allison said goodbye.

"Madame," Allison had said gently. "It's not too late. We can still get a passport for you. I would be happy to have you with me."

"*Non, Madame,*" the housekeeper had said, wiping her eyes with her apron. "As much as I love the little one, how can I leave my own grandchildren?" She had kissed Marianne's forehead. "But I thank you for asking me."

Saying goodbye to Jean Luc's mother had been just as painful, but in a different way. Genevieve Fornier had Alzheimer's disease and wasn't even aware that she was seeing her only grandchild, perhaps for the last time.

Finally everything had been taken care of, all obstacles overcome, and now here they were, on the Concorde jet, due to land at JFK airport in just under an hour. Allison wondered what her reception would be when she arrived in Houston.

She knew her father would be overjoyed to see her. She wasn't so sure about her father's wife.

Diana.

Allison still remembered the reserve in Diana's cool blue eyes when she and Allison's father had arrived in Paris for Jean Luc's funeral. Oh, Diana was too much a lady to say or do anything but the correct thing. She had put her arms around Allison and comforted her. She had seemed genuinely concerned for her well-being. But Allison hadn't been fooled. She knew Diana would never forgive her for what she had done.

And could Allison really blame her stepmother for

her feelings? Allison had been engaged to Kent Sorensen, Diana's son. But she had broken that engagement only days before their scheduled wedding and run away to Paris. A few days later, when the invited guests showed up for what they thought would be a wedding between Allison and Kent, they had instead witnessed the vows of Allison's father, Lee, and Kent's mother, Diana.

Allison sighed, remembering the chaos she'd caused. The heartbreak and misery.

Yes, Diana would be a very odd mother not to disapprove of Allison. Now that Allison herself had a child, she understood how fiercely protective mother love could be. She had a much greater understanding of Diana's feelings. One of the things she had resolved to do from the moment she'd decided to go back to Houston was to try very hard to build a good relationship with her stepmother.

Stepmother.

That meant Kent was now her stepbrother. Funny that this was the first time she'd ever thought of him that way.

She tested the word.

Stepbrother.

Would she ever feel an easy camaraderie with Kent? A brotherly sisterly fondness?

No, she thought. Her feelings toward Kent were not sisterly. And she didn't think they ever would be.

Allison closed her eyes, memories of Kent flooding her mind. She could still picture him as he'd looked the night of their wedding-rehearsal dinner. She could still see the pain and unhappiness clouding his blue eyes, the shock and disbelief. She could still remember the look on his face when he'd realized she meant what she'd said, that she wasn't going to marry him after all.

She had been so wrong.

She knew that now.

She had thought of Kent often over the years. Thoughts of him had sustained her through many of the last miserable months. He was the one bright spot in an otherwise dark horizon. At least she knew that by releasing him from their engagement, she had allowed him to follow his dreams.

And as she gazed out the window at the mounds of white clouds below, looking for all the world like drifts of snow, she hoped he was happy.

But most of all, she hoped he had forgiven her.

Chapter One

Allison adjusted the slats of the miniblinds so she could see the backyard deck while no one outdoors would be able to see her.

Even though her stomach was jumping with nerves, she couldn't help smiling when she spied her father. Who would have thought that Lee Gabriel—sophisticated, urbane Lee Gabriel—could ever be so happily entrenched in suburban living?

Today her father, who was fast approaching his fifty-first birthday—a fact that still amazed Allison—was decked out in a silly apron and a tall chef's hat. As she watched, he bent over the big gas barbecue grill, doing something to the ribs he and Diana would be feeding their guests today.

While he worked, her stepmother walked into view. Diana set a big bowl of something on the picnic table, then headed for Lee. As she came up behind him, she reached out and patted his rear end.

Lee turned and laughingly caught his wife in his arms. Although Allison couldn't hear them, she could see Diana laughing, too, as she tried to escape Lee's hands, which slid down her back to caress her own rounded bottom. She lifted her face, and Lee gave her a long, lingering kiss.

Just the way her handsome father and his lovely blond wife stood—so close together that their bodies seemed molded into one—spoke volumes about the way they felt about each other. Although they'd been married more than three years, their body language said they still wanted each other with the intensity of newlyweds.

Allison stared, mesmerized, at the scene below. She knew she should look away. She knew this was a private moment, that Lee and Diana thought themselves unobserved. But she couldn't. She was like a starving woman, staring through a glass window at an array of freshly baked pastries that were beyond her reach.

Loneliness twisted through her. Loneliness and something else. A deep yearning.

What must it be like to be loved so well? To feel so comfortable with your love that you could show it with such unabashed joy and desire?

You could have had that, too. You threw it away.

She let the blinds fall back together. Stop it, she told herself. Stop feeling sorry for yourself. Count your blessings. And like a litany, she did.

She was healthy.

She was young.

She had a family who loved her.

And she had Marianne.

Beautiful Marianne, who was now napping in the

nursery down the hall, a fact confirmed by the sound of her even breathing coming from the baby-room monitor Allison carried everywhere with her.

Marianne, who in a few short days would be entering the Children's Clinic of Houston for her heart catheterization.

Marianne, who Allison would not, could not, lose.

Remembering her baby daughter, Allison shook off her spurt of unhappiness over the past. There was no sense in spending even one moment of emotional energy on regrets. In the weeks and months to come, she would need every bit of her strength to help her deal with Marianne's medical problems.

Pull yourself together. Put on a cheerful face, go downstairs and help your father and his wife get ready to greet their guests, she scolded herself.

But even as she reminded herself what she knew she must do, she couldn't get rid of the butterflies fluttering around in her stomach. The butterflies caused by the knowledge that Kent had been invited to the Fourth of July celebration that would begin in minutes.

Would he come?

And if he did come, how would he act? Would he be happy to see her again? Or would he be cold and aloof? Maybe even angry?

Maybe he doesn't care at all. Maybe he no longer thinks I'm important enough to care about.

That thought hurt.

It hurt a lot, even though Allison knew she deserved whatever Kent wanted to dish out. When she'd first run away to Paris, she'd told herself Kent hadn't played fair with her. He'd led her to believe he was going to accept the associate law position with Keating & Shaw. Then, in the middle of their rehearsal dinner, he'd sprung the shocking news that he had changed his mind. He wasn't going to take the job and ensure their financial future. Instead, he planned to go ahead with his idealistic dream and open a storefront law office.

During the miserable weeks that followed, Allison told herself Kent was just as much at fault in their breakup as she was. And she even believed it.

But during her short-lived, disastrous marriage to Jean Luc, she quickly discovered it didn't matter how financially secure you were if there were no love and commitment to go along with it. It was only then that she had finally faced the truth.

She had traded substance for flash, gold for a cheap imitation, something solid for something that crumbled when you touched it.

She had done this.

She alone.

No one else.

She had lost Kent, tossed him away, and he had every right to despise her.

But even as Allison told herself these hard truths, she prayed he didn't really despise her. Maybe she could never have his love again, but she hoped, she prayed she could win his friendship. She needed a friend. She would know how hard a job that would be by this first meeting. She hoped she could get through it without falling apart.

As she had several times already, she wondered if Diana had purposely arranged for her and Kent to meet for the first time surrounded by a lot of people. After all, Diana was a kind woman. She would know how awkward and ill at ease both Kent and Allison would feel when facing each other for the first time since their breakup. She would want to try to smooth the way if she could.

Well, it was time to stop stalling. Allison picked up the baby monitor and started toward the door, then turned to take one more look at herself in the full-length mirror. She was dressed casually in army green walking shorts and a matching jungle-print blouse. As she smoothed her hair and stared at herself in the mirror, she wondered what Kent would see when he looked at her. She wondered if he would notice the changes that had taken place over the past years. She had taken great care with her makeup, wanting to hide the telltale smudges under her eyes—the smudges that advertised how little sleep she'd been getting lately.

Allison didn't want anyone, especially Kent, to feel sorry for her. Satisfied that she looked as good as she could, given the circumstances, she tiptoed into the adjoining room, took one last peek at Marianne, who slept soundly, then headed for the backyard.

Kent downshifted and impatiently tapped his fingers against the steering wheel of his white Corvette in time to Michael Bolton's rendition of "When a Man Loves a Woman." He eyed the car in the lane next to him—a Jeep filled with laughing girls clad in bathing suits and skimpy shorts. One of them, a beautiful dark-haired girl with come-hither brown eyes, winked at him.

Kent smiled cynically. Yep. They were all alike. The Corvette did it every time. Like Allison, money turned them on.

Allison.

His jaw tightened. Until yesterday he hadn't been sure he would even go to the Fourth of July party his mother and stepfather were hosting. Then, defiantly, telling himself not to be a coward, he'd invited Christina Sargent—another lawyer with his firm and someone he'd been dating for a while—to go to the party with him.

Normally Kent enjoyed spending time with Lee and his mother, but that had been spoiled now that Allison was back in Houston and living with them. Now he wouldn't be able to drop in for a cup of coffee or a beer. Now he would no longer feel relaxed and comfortable in their home.

Even his mother realized that everything had changed.

"You'll come to the party, won't you, Kent?" she'd asked, and he had heard the underlying tension in her voice.

"I don't know."

"You've got to get this meeting over with sometime."

"Yeah, I know."

"She's having a tough time right now, Kent. And she's a part of our family—like it or not."

"Yes, I guess you're right." How could he argue with the truth of his mother's statement? He was sorry that Allison's husband was dead and that her baby was sick. Of course he was. He wasn't insensitive or vindictive. Just because she'd discarded him like yesterday's garbage didn't mean he wished her bad luck. But he couldn't pretend he was happy to be forced into a family harmony that wouldn't exist as long as she was around.

Like it or not, his mother had said.

Well, he would never like it. As far as he was concerned, Allison Gabriel Fornier could have stayed on the other side of the world forever.

He wondered what his mother thought about all of this. That telephone conversation, which had taken place two days ago, had been the first time Diana had ever made a reference to the situation between him and Allison since Allison's hurried flight to Paris three and a half years earlier. Diana and Lee had gotten married at the ceremony that was intended to be Kent's and Allison's, shocking all of their friends and family with the unexpected turn of events.

Kent couldn't help grinning as he remembered that crazy day. Although he'd been in a state of near-paralysis over Allison's desertion, he'd still been happy for his mother. The press had had a field day, writing about the Sorensen-Gabriel wedding. They'd chortled over how the Sorensen turned out to be Diana instead of Kent, and the Gabriel turned out to be Lee instead of Allison. For days afterward there had been speculation over what had happened to cause the abrupt change, but Kent's family and friends had rallied around him and no one talked.

Kent knew they talked among themselves, though. But everyone, including his mother, seemed to understand that he couldn't talk about it. Couldn't talk about Allison. Not if he wanted to keep his emotions under control. Not if he wanted to heal.

So Diana carefully avoided the topic. Oh, she'd casually mentioned Allison's wedding to that big-shot Grand Prix race-car driver, Jean Luc Fornier, but she'd had to. She knew their marriage would be splashed all over the papers. And occasionally, but always in Lee's company, Diana would drop news of Allison in the conversation, so Kent was kept up-to-date on what was going on in Allison's life.

But she'd never alluded to their former relationship. Once Allison was gone and the wedding was off, Diana acted as if Kent no longer cared.

Kent had tried hard to foster that impression with everyone. It was different now, naturally, but for the first few months it had been very difficult to pretend indifference. Then, as the months passed, it got easier. But when Allison married Jean Luc, only four months after running out on Kent, Kent had had another bad spell. He'd lain awake many nights envisioning her with Jean Luc. Envisioning them making love. The fact that Jean Luc was famous, that his handsome, dark face had routinely been plastered all over the national magazines and newspapers so that Kent could easily picture them together, made the whole situation all the worse.

For a long time there had been an awful ache way down in his gut. He kept remembering how Allison had never let him make love to her. All during their engagement, she had insisted they wait until their wedding night. At the time he'd thought she just had high standards. That she wanted their wedding night to be special. That *she* was special. It had been tough, but he'd tamped down his passion. Now he realized what a fool he'd been. Allison had probably been withholding sex because he had refused to do what she wanted him to do.

Kent told himself he didn't care.

He told himself he was much better off without Allison.

He told himself she had never loved him, that all she had wanted was money and prestige, and when she thought she wasn't going to get them, she'd taken off without a backward glance.

She was cold and hard-hearted. A calculating little witch. She had never loved him at all.

He ignored the relentless voice that said Allison had never made any secret of what kind of life she expected when the two of them married. She had never approved of his idea to open a storefront law office and work there exclusively, to spend his days serving the underprivileged of Houston. She'd told him his plan wasn't practical, that they could not live on love alone. And when her father had arranged for Kent to receive an offer from Keating & Shaw, one of Houston's most prestigious law firms, and had suggested that Kent could combine the two—work days for the law firm, and with several other young lawyers do the *pro bono* work part-time—Kent had even admitted the suggestion was a sensible compromise.

He was all set to accept the offer.

But the day before their rehearsal dinner, he got cold feet. For so long he'd dreamed of the storefront office. For so long he'd thought of himself as some kind of white knight. He just couldn't relinquish those dreams.

He couldn't compromise. With him it was all or nothing.

So Allison had broken their engagement, in front of their families and friends, in the most painful way, and then she'd fled to Paris.

And now she was back.

Resentment and anger welled into his chest. He clenched his jaw. Damn! Why did her baby have to be sick? Why did she have to come back to Houston? It wasn't as if he could avoid seeing her. After all, as his mother had pointed out, they were related. Her father and his mother were married, which made him and Allison—what? Stepsiblings?

Kent grimaced. That was almost funny. Allison was his stepsister.

He wondered if she was still as beautiful and as sexy as she had been.

Now why are you thinking about that? Who cares? As Kent turned into the driveway of Christina's townhouse complex, he told himself he didn't care. It made no difference to him whether Allison was gorgeous or ugly, shapely or skinny, sexy or prim.

He didn't give a damn.

Allison Gabriel Fornier no longer had the ability to upset him in any way. He would go to the party today. He would pay a lot of attention to Christina, who was his date for the day, and he would be coolly friendly toward Allison, just as if she were a casual acquaintance.

He would show her—and everyone else—that she was no longer important to him.

Lee looked at his watch. It was almost noon. "They should start arriving soon, don't you think?"

Diana smiled at him. She had just carried a stack of earthenware plates outside and placed them on the picnic table. "I told everyone any time after noon."

Lee lifted the lid of the gas grill again. Boy, those ribs looked good. He turned them, then basted them with his homemade barbecue sauce. "I'm glad it's a nice day," he said. For some reason, the powers-that-be had smiled on them, and instead of its customary one-hundred-plus, the mercury was only expected to reach ninety-two degrees today. Even the humidity wasn't too bad, considering this was July in Houston.

"Would you like something to drink, honey?" Diana asked.

"What've you got?"

"Fresh limeade, cold beer and all kinds of soft drinks."

"I'll have a glass of the limeade." Lee accepted the

glass, then sank down into one of the comfortable redwood chairs dotting the deck. He looked at Diana, who sat perched on the edge of one of the long benches flanking either side of the picnic table. She looked particularly beautiful today, he thought, in her dark blue bathing suit and matching long skirt, which showed her tall, lush figure to advantage. At forty-seven, Diana was a strikingly attractive woman with gorgeous eyes, a beautiful smile and sleek blond hair. If anything, she was even lovelier now than the first day he'd seen her almost four years ago. He grinned, thinking about that meeting. He had gone with Allison to celebrate her engagement to Kent Sorensen and to meet Kent Sorensen's mother. Little did he dream that he would be meeting his destiny.

As he studied her, Diana stared out at the pool, her forehead knitted in thought.

"Diana, love, quit worrying," Lee said. "It's going to be all right."

Now she fastened her clear blue gaze on his. She sighed. "I hope so."

"They're both adults. They can handle this."

She shrugged. "I know they're adults but... Oh, I don't know. I've never been convinced that Kent was over Allison, and Allison...well, she seems awfully fragile right now. I'm concerned about her, too."

Lee felt a quiet pleasure at her words. He knew Allison was not one of Diana's favorite people, even though, to her credit, she had never once said so, and he realized his wife had tried very hard to be fair to his daughter. "She'll be okay," he said with more assurance than he actually felt. He was concerned about Allison, too. "She may look fragile, but she's a strong woman. Besides, she's just worried about the baby."

"Honey, I know. We're all worried about the baby."
She sighed again, staring out toward the pool. Beyond
the covered deck, the kidney-shaped pool sparkled aqua-
marine in the brilliant sunshine. "I pray everything will
be all right."

"Yes, me, too." The baby's test was scheduled for
early Wednesday morning, just five days away.

Diana was silent for a few moments, then she said,
"I'm not even sure Kent's going to show up today."

"He'll come. He'll be too curious about Allison to
stay away."

Now her direct blue gaze met his again. "You're hoping they'll get back together again, aren't you?" she
said quietly.

Diana never failed to surprise Lee. And here he'd
thought his secret wish had been well hidden. "Would
that bother you?"

Her gaze never wavered. "I don't know. She hurt him
a lot." A hint of sadness darkened her eyes. "He's
changed because of it."

Lee didn't know what to say, but he was saved from
saying anything because just then he heard the first car
pull into the driveway. Almost simultaneously the back
door opened and Allison, looking much too thin and
tired to suit Lee, walked outside.

They'd been talking about her. She could see it in
their faces as they both turned to look at her.

"Is the baby asleep?" Diana asked, giving her a welcoming smile.

Allison nodded. She heard the clunk of a car door
slamming shut, then footsteps. All three of them looked
toward the back gate. Allison's heart thundered in her
chest. She licked her lips.

The gate opened.

Allison sighed with relief as she realized she'd been given a reprieve. It wasn't Kent entering the back gate. It was Diana's sister Carol, followed by two of her children and her husband. For the next half hour, new arrivals kept the momentum going: Diana's mother; her other sister, Jackie, with her two children; Lee's secretary, Britta, and her handsome husband, Bengt; two of Lee's associates; a couple of agents from Diana's real-estate office; and then Sunny Garcia, Diana's best friend and the manager of her office.

"Allison, I was so sorry to hear about your husband," Sunny said.

"Thank you." Allison had always liked Sunny, a perky redhead with an infectious grin.

"Where's the baby?"

"She's sleeping right now."

"Oh…" Sunny's forehead creased in disappointment. "I wanted to see her."

"Oh, you will, Sunny," Diana interjected. "Allison will bring her down later. Marianne won't sleep more than an hour or two."

"So how does it feel to be a grandmother?" Sunny asked.

"It feels wonderful," Diana said. "Marianne is a heartbreaker."

Allison wanted to hug Diana. No matter how Diana felt about her, she obviously loved Marianne. Their gazes met, and Diana smiled. Just then there was the thumping sound of another car door opening and closing, then more footsteps walking up the drive. Both Diana and Allison turned toward the gate.

Allison forgot to breathe as Kent, preceded by a leggy blonde who was laughing up at him, walked through the gate. Allison knew the exact moment he saw her, for the smile slid off his face. Time stood still as they stared at each other. Allison's mouth was dry. She wanted to say something, but she couldn't. Then, taking the blonde's hand, Kent walked toward her.

"Hello, Allison," he said. He smiled, but the smile didn't reach his eyes. "It's been a long time."

"Hello, Kent." She struggled to keep her voice as casual as his had been. "It's good to see you."

"Thanks." His blue eyes, so like his mother's, glinted in the sunlight. "It's good to see you, too." He turned toward the blonde. "Christina, this is Allison Fornier, my stepsister. Allison, this is Christina Sargent."

The blonde's gaze darted to Kent as if what he'd said had surprised her. Then she recovered and smiled at Allison, giving her a quick, appraising look. Allison met the blonde's gray-eyed gaze as Kent's words thrummed in her mind. *Stepsister.*

"It's nice to meet you," Christina said. She extended her hand, and Allison shook it. Then, her gaze sliding back to Kent's, Christina said, "I had no idea you had a stepsister. You've never mentioned her."

"She's been living in Paris," Kent said, avoiding Allison's eyes.

To Allison's intense relief, Diana walked over.

"Hi, Mom." The warm smile he gave her was like a knife twisting in Allison's heart. The thing she had always loved most about Kent was his incredibly warm smile. He put his arm around Christina, and the knife twisted deeper. "This is Christina Sargent. Christina— my mother, Diana Gabriel."

"It's very nice to meet you," Diana said. "You work

with Kent, don't you? I remember him mentioning your name.''

''Yes,'' Christina answered.

For a brief moment Allison thought about how Christina hardly looked the type to work at a storefront law office, but she was too nervous about seeing Kent again to examine the thought more closely.

After a few moments of chitchat, Diana said, ''Why don't I introduce Christina to everyone?'' She led the blonde off, leaving Allison alone with Kent.

Awkwardly Allison and Kent faced each other again. Allison's heart was beating so hard she was sure everyone could hear it. A welter of emotions rushed through her as she studied Kent: happiness, pain, confusion, regret, tenderness, fear.

He looked wonderful—deeply tanned and very handsome in dark swimming trunks and a white knit shirt. He looked exactly the way she had always pictured him, yet there was something different about him.

She tried to decide what the difference was. His dark hair was shorter than she remembered it and more stylishly cut, but that wasn't it. He looked older, of course, not so much the fresh-faced all-American boy, but more mature and filled out than he had been. But that wasn't it, either.

''I'm sorry about your husband,'' he said.

Allison swallowed against the pain that had lodged in her throat. Her hands trembled, and she clasped them together. ''Thank you,'' she managed to say.

Something flickered in his eyes, something she wished she could believe was understanding, but it was gone so fast she couldn't be sure. ''I hear your baby's sick,'' he said awkwardly.

She nodded. ''Yes.''

"I was sorry to hear that."

"Thanks." Oh, God, she hadn't felt this awkward and stupid since she was twelve years old. She wondered if he felt half as unhinged as she did.

"You're thinner," he said, looking her over.

Suddenly Allison wished she hadn't worn shorts. "Yes, well…" Why couldn't she think of something intelligent to say? What was the matter with her? She forced her mouth into a smile. "You know what they say—a woman can never be too thin or too rich."

His gaze met hers again. Now it was filled with… what? Disgust? Allison cringed inside. Her feeble attempt at humor had been a mistake. A big mistake. She was sure he had interpreted her stupid remark as a dig at him—a reminder that once financial security had been more important to her than him.

"The storefront must be doing well," Allison said, desperate to change the direction of their conversation.

Kent frowned. "What do you mean?"

"Well…um…your mother said that Christina works with you, so I thought—"

He stared at her. "I no longer have the storefront. I sold it."

Allison could almost feel the color draining out of her face as shock rippled through her. "You no longer have the storefront…." she repeated slowly. "Wh-where *are* you working?"

For one long moment he didn't answer. Then, with an odd expression in his eyes, he said, "I'm an associate with Keating & Shaw."

Just then the gate opened again and Sunny's daughter, Nikki, followed by a pleasant-looking, stocky man, entered the backyard. "Kent! Hi!" Nikki walked straight over to where Allison and Kent were standing.

"Hi, Nik," he said.

Still stunned by Kent's revelation, Allison fought to regain control of herself while watching Kent hug Nikki, then kiss her cheek. He grinned down at her, keeping his arm around her shoulders. Envy pricked Allison's heart. He hadn't so much as touched *her* hand when he'd greeted her. Finally Nikki disengaged herself and turned to her.

"Allison! It's good to see you again!" she said, a big smile lighting her face.

"Hello, Nikki. It's good to see you, too."

With no hesitation at all, Nikki leaned forward and hugged Allison. The hug surprised Allison. God knows, they'd never been friends, and even though Allison was sure Nikki was happy about the breakup of Kent and Allison's engagement, she hadn't expected a warm welcome from Nikki. When two women loved the same man, it was impossible for them to be friends. And Nikki had loved Kent as much as Allison loved him. In fact, Allison wouldn't have been surprised if Nikki had shown up at today's party on Kent's arm.

"I'd like you to meet my husband, Glenn Prescott. Glenn, this is Allison Fornier." Nikki smiled proudly.

Allison hoped she'd disguised this second shock, for she had had no idea Nikki was married. Somehow she'd thought Nikki would always be in love with Kent.

"Nice to meet you," Glenn Prescott said, extending his hand.

He had a firm handshake and soft hazel eyes. He gave Allison a friendly smile, and she could feel herself responding.

They made small talk for a few minutes, then Nikki excused herself to go to talk to her mother. Glenn and Kent gravitated toward the rest of the men, who had congregated in a group and, if the bits of conversation Allison overheard meant anything, were discussing yesterday's Astros' game.

Allison walked over to the other end of the deck and sat on the railing. She wished she were anywhere but here. Trying to pretend this was just a normal holiday gathering, trying to pretend that there had never been anything between her and Kent, trying to pretend she was comfortable around him—all had her stomach in knots. Fingering the baby monitor, she wondered how soon she could escape, maybe say she had to go check on Marianne.

As the thought crossed her mind, Kent's clear laugh rang out, and the yearning Allison had felt earlier returned. It settled deep into her belly, throbbing with a dull ache.

At that moment Kent turned his head, and across the distance separating them, their gazes met and locked. Something hard and bright shimmered in the depths of his eyes, and just before he looked away, Allison realized what it was.

Hate.

He hated her.

Chapter Two

He wanted to hate her.

He had fully intended to hate her.

Instead, Kent's heart had twisted at the sight of her. Gone was the bright, assured, sassy woman he'd once known. In her place stood a woman who looked fragile and vulnerable. A bone-deep sadness haunted the depths of Allison's golden brown eyes. A sadness Kent wished he could ignore. A sadness that made her look older than her twenty-six years.

Inwardly he grimaced. Obviously the death of her husband had hit her hard. Kent realized that up until this moment, he'd harbored a secret hope that her marriage to the hotshot racer had been one of expediency instead of love. Now he knew it wasn't.

How could she fall in love so fast? So soon after breaking *their* engagement?

Because she never loved you at all, you idiot.

His jaw hardened as his gaze swept over her body. She'd lost too much weight. And he didn't think she'd done it on purpose, despite her flippant remark about no woman being too thin or too rich.

Even in the face of these changes, she was still beautiful. Covertly he studied her, cataloging the differences the years had made.

Her hair was shorter but still lustrous and thick, a rich dark brown streaked with gold. He'd always teased her about her hair and eyes being a matched pair.

Those eyes. Kent had dreamed about her eyes too many nights to count. Even sorrowful, they were captivating—sultry, thick lashed and a dreamy shade of topaz.

Same tip-tilted nose.

Same cleft chin, inherited from her father.

Same high cheekbones.

Same slightly exotic look.

His gaze dropped to her mouth. That mouth sure brought back some memories. Memories he'd rather forget. Full and lush, her lips invited a man's kiss.

Kent tried to push the thought away, but his mind kept returning to it. He kept remembering the kisses they'd shared. He could still taste her, the sweet, dark recesses of her mouth. The way his blood would pump when they kissed and touched. How much he'd loved her and wanted her.

And how she'd continually refused him.

Remembering, the pain he'd so successfully submerged had threatened to erupt again.

Damn, he thought. *She means nothing to me. Why am I dredging up all this ancient history?*

Even as he told himself all this, he couldn't look away. And he couldn't stop the memories.

She looked different, yet so familiar. They had been apart three and a half years, but the months they'd been together seemed like yesterday as they came rushing back. Images he'd once thought were long dead resurfaced.

Allison laughing up at him.

Allison looking so sexy and beautiful at their engagement party that Kent's mouth had gone dry every time he looked at her.

Allison, eyes bright with tears, at their rehearsal dinner, where she'd broken their engagement then disappeared from his life.

Jesus, she'd gotten under his skin. He'd loved her so much. And she had nearly killed him when she walked out on him.

Forget all that. It's over.

He tried not to look at her sitting by herself. But his gaze kept returning to her. He pretended to be engrossed in the men's discussion of last night's Astros' game, but his eyes and mind kept straying in her direction.

"Kent, are you going to stand here and talk sports all day?"

Kent turned at Christina's comment. She smiled at him, her gray eyes smoldering as they swept his face possessively. For the first time since he and Christina had begun dating, Kent felt a faint twinge of annoyance. "Sorry," he said, turning toward her. "Is there something you'd like to do?"

"Why don't we swim?" she suggested. "I wore my suit under this." As she spoke, she began to unbutton her red jumpsuit. When she stepped out of it, she was clad in a wispy black bikini that showed her tall figure to advantage. She smiled over her shoulder as she walked toward the pool. Kent watched her as he rid himself of his knit shirt and shoes.

Christina was, like him, an associate with Keating & Shaw, and a month ago they had both been assigned to a big case under Colin Jamieson, one of the senior partners. Because their role in the case involved extensive research, they had been thrown together a lot.

Kent had been attracted to Christina from the first. And she made no secret of her interest in him. So it had seemed natural that after a long day's work, they would go out for dinner together. And still more natural to end the evening at Kent's condo or Christina's town house.

Kent had enjoyed the time he'd spent with her. She was smart, beautiful and entertaining. She was also aggressive and had a sharp legal mind. She stimulated him, both personally and professionally.

Christina was, in fact, everything he could possibly want in a woman. At this very moment she was lying on her back in the glistening water, beckoning him with her lazy smile.

He wondered if Allison was watching.

He knew it was petty, but he wanted her to see that he had done very well for himself. That he hadn't been sitting around mooning over her.

He walked toward the pool, casting one last glance over his shoulder before diving in.

As the minutes passed, Allison wished desperately for a reason to leave the lively crowd. She felt miserably uncomfortable since seeing that cold expression in Kent's eyes. It had been bad enough before he'd arrived. Then she'd only wondered what his reaction to her would be.

Now she knew.

And knowing was infinitely worse than speculating.

She tried not to look at him again after that one revealing glare he'd given her. Yet she couldn't seem to keep her gaze or her thoughts away from him.

And when his date approached him and said something, and Kent smiled in response, something inside Allison had contorted painfully.

Once Kent had looked at her that way.

Once he had smiled at her that way.

Once his heart had belonged to her.

It was all she could do to keep sitting there, acting as if she didn't care what Kent did, pretending not to watch as Christina took off her red jumpsuit and walked seductively toward the pool.

Watching Kent watching Christina was like having someone stick a knife into her; the pain was just as sharp. And when he began to walk toward the pool to join the beautiful blonde, Allison could stand the torture no longer. She stood abruptly and walked toward the back door with the intention of going inside to check on Marianne, even though there were no sounds from the baby monitor.

"Allison, I'm dying to see your baby."

Allison turned at the sound of Nikki's voice. She smiled. "I was just going to go inside to check on her. Do you want to come?"

Nikki grinned. "You bet."

Allison studied her companion as they walked into the house together. Nikki Garcia Prescott, like Kent, had changed since Allison had last seen her. The changes were for the better. Her sleek dark hair was cut in an attractive pixie style that suited her small face, and she'd learned how to apply makeup and dress more attractively. She also acted more confidently than she had three and a half years ago. Allison wondered if marriage had given her that contented, self-assured air. "I was surprised to meet Glenn," Allison said. "No one told me you'd gotten married."

Nikki smiled happily. "We've only been married for eleven months."

"He seems awfully nice." Allison led the way upstairs. "How'd you meet him?"

"We work together."

By now they'd reached the baby's room, and Allison put her finger to her lips. "If she's still sleeping, I don't want to wake her," she whispered.

Nikki nodded.

Allison gently pushed the door open, and they tiptoed over to the crib. As they approached, Marianne stirred, and her eyelids fluttered open.

"Oh," Nikki said softly. "She's beautiful...."

Something constricted in Allison's chest as she gazed down at her baby. She wondered if she would ever look at Marianne without feeling awed that this exquisite creature belonged to her. She turned off the monitor, then leaned over the crib. "Hi, sweetie."

Marianne rewarded her with a smile, and Allison choked up. At two months Marianne had just begun smiling, and each time she did, Allison felt this same, almost embarrassing emotion. She'd had no idea she would love her baby so fiercely. Before she'd gotten married, she had occasionally thought about having children, but she hadn't realized how miraculous it would be. Now that she had her daughter, she couldn't imagine life without her.

She picked up the baby, holding her warm little body close for a second, inhaling the sweet baby smell.

"Oh, can I hold her?" Nikki asked, her eyes shining eagerly.

"Just let me change her first." Allison walked toward the changing table, and Nikki followed her.

"She's wonderful," Nikki said, shyly touching Marianne's head.

Allison took off Marianne's diaper and dropped it into the diaper pail. She reached for a fresh diaper. "She is, isn't she?"

"My—my mother told me about her heart." Nikki gently rubbed Marianne's head. "But she doesn't look sick."

"Except for her color." Allison believed in putting people at ease, so she tried to be matter-of-fact when she talked about Marianne's problems.

"Even her color isn't that noticeable."

"No. Not today. But sometimes it is." Allison deftly cleaned Marianne and put on the new diaper. "We have to keep her as quiet as possible."

Nikki nodded. "You know, Allison, I really admire you."

"Me?" Allison resnapped Marianne's knit outfit. "Whatever for?"

"You just seem so capable, and…well, you've survived everything so well."

"I guess I put up a good front." She lifted the baby and handed her to Nikki. "I have my bad days, believe me."

"Well, you've done the right thing coming home. I know Diana and Lee are happy you're closer." Nikki cuddled Marianne, and Marianne's big eyes fastened on Nikki's face.

"Some people aren't so happy," Allison muttered before she could stop herself. Oh, great. Why had she said that?

There was silence for a moment. Then Nikki asked, "Are you referring to Kent?"

Allison nodded.

"Well, it's really none of my business, but... Oh, shoot. It really is none of my business."

Allison grimaced. "No. Go ahead. Say whatever it is you were going to say."

Nikki shook her head.

"Come on, Nikki. I'm the one who brought up the subject. I can take it."

Nikki's green eyes were thoughtful as they studied her. "Well, you can't really blame Kent if he still harbors some bitterness toward you."

"No, you're right."

"You hurt him a lot," Nikki said, her voice soft.

"I know." Allison sighed deeply. "It's funny. After I went to Paris, I fully expected Diana to write me and say Kent had married *you*."

Nikki's gaze met hers again. "I guess for a while I hoped that would happen, too. But it wasn't meant to be. He was never in love with me, and he never will be." Then she smiled, her eyes softening with happiness. "And now, of course, I'm so glad because I met Glenn, and he's wonderful."

Allison returned her smile. "You're lucky." *I wasn't so lucky, but that's my own fault.*

A few minutes later Allison heated a bottle for Marianne while Nikki held her and cooed to her. Marianne, who usually complained loudly when it was time for her feeding, seemed mesmerized by Nikki's soft drawl and kept rewarding her with smiles.

"Her eyes are beautiful," Nikki said. "Wonder if they'll stay blue?"

"I don't know. Her father had blue eyes, so they may." One of the reasons Allison had been attracted to Jean Luc initially was because his eyes had reminded her of Kent's. She knew that now. She hadn't known it at the time.

"You must miss him a lot."

Allison shrugged. She refused to lie and say she did. She was sorry Jean Luc was dead, because no man should die so young. She was sorry he'd never know his beautiful daughter. And she was sorry they'd made each other so unhappy.

But she didn't miss him.

When the bottle was ready, Allison took Marianne from Nikki. "I'm going to go sit in the rocking chair in the den and feed her."

"Oh, bring her outside! Everyone wants to see her."

"I'll bring her out when I'm through." Allison didn't feel like explaining that she always started out by breast-feeding Marianne and didn't want to do that in front of dozens of people. The bottle would just be supplementary because she didn't have enough milk to satisfy the baby.

"Promise?" Nikki said.

"Yes. I promise."

Kent wondered when Allison had left the party. One minute she was there, the next she wasn't. He swam toward the edge of the pool. He'd had enough of the water, he decided.

After climbing out, he toweled himself dry and reached for his knit shirt.

"The ribs are almost ready," Lee called from the grill. "Is anyone hungry?"

This question was met with a chorus of cheers and affirmative answers. Kent scanned the patio again, then headed for the cooler where the beer was stashed. Reaching down, he took out a can and popped the top. As he took a long swallow, he saw Nikki emerge from the back door of the house.

Smiling, he walked over to her. He didn't see enough of Nikki. They'd been best friends since their toddler days when Nikki's mother had baby-sat him while his mother attended real-estate school. And their friendship had only strengthened over the years. Nikki had been the sister he'd never had. All through their school years they'd done homework together, told each other their troubles and shared each other's triumphs.

Nikki had taught Kent how to dance.

And Kent had taught Nikki how to drive.

Rarely had a night gone by that they didn't talk on the phone.

It was only after Kent had started college at the University of Houston and Nikki went to work that they began to drift apart. Each made other friends. Somehow Nikki didn't seem to fit in with Kent's crowd, and he felt out of place with her cohorts from work.

Still, their friendship was the kind that when they did see each other, there was never any awkwardness between them.

No, Kent thought. The awkwardness had begun about five years ago when Kent was twenty-three and Nikki was twenty-two. That's when her feelings toward him had changed. Instead of friendship, she had fallen in love with him, and Kent had not felt the same way. He had loved her, but he hadn't been in love with her.

When he met Allison and fell in love with her, that had really put a strain on his relationship with Nikki, for Allison hadn't liked Nikki, and that dislike was obvious. He'd never been sure how Nikki felt about Allison. She'd acted as if she liked her, but maybe that was strictly for his sake. Funny, he thought, that he'd never asked her.

Now, though, things had come full circle. Allison and Kent had broken their engagement, and Allison had left Houston. Nikki had met Glenn and gotten married and was obviously very happy. Nikki and Kent were once more best friends. And now Allison had reentered their lives.

"So, I haven't seen you for a while," he said as he reached Nikki's side. "What've you and Glenn been doing?"

She smiled up at him. "Can I tell you a secret?" Her green eyes, one of her prettiest features, Kent thought, sparkled.

"Sure. You know you can."

"Glenn and I are expecting a baby." Her eyes glowed with happiness.

"Gee, Nik, that's great!" Kent felt a sudden twinge of envy, which he quickly forced away.

"Yes, we're absolutely thrilled. But don't say anything, okay? It's too early to tell people, but, well, you're like a brother to me, so I had to tell you."

Kent hugged her.

"Should I be jealous?" asked a male voice behind Kent.

Kent turned. Nikki's husband, Glenn, stood there, a big smile on his face. "I'm the one who's jealous. Your wife just told me your great news."

Glenn beamed and slipped his arm around Nikki. "Yeah, we're pretty happy."

"Oh, honey, I just saw Allison's baby," Nikki said, "and she's so beautiful!" Her sparkling gaze met Kent's. "Don't you think so, Kent?"

"I haven't seen her yet."

"You haven't?" She gave Kent an odd look.

He kept his face carefully blank. "Nope."

"Well, you'll get your chance soon. Allison said she'd bring the baby outside after she finishes feeding her."

Kent nonchalantly looked toward the house. The back door remained closed.

"So, Kent, who's your date?" Nikki asked.

"Christina? We work together." He avoided her gaze. She was altogether too damned perceptive.

"She's a lawyer?"

"Uh-huh. We're assigned to the same case right now."

"Have you been dating her long?"

"For about six weeks, I guess."

"Is it serious?"

"Boy, you're nosy," he said, grinning at Glenn, who stood quietly smiling.

"She is, isn't she?" Glenn said, giving Kent a conspiratorial wink.

Nikki playfully punched Glenn on the arm. "Come on, Kent. Don't be mean. I just want everyone to be as happy as we are."

"You mean you just want to see everyone married," Glenn said.

"Oh, give me a break," she said, laughing. Then she turned to Kent again. "Well, is it?"

"Is it what?" Kent teased.

"Kent!"

"No, it's not serious," he said, relenting.

"Christina sure is great looking," Glenn said.

"Now wait a minute..." Nikki said. "You're married, remember?"

"Maybe married, but not dead," Glenn retorted. Then he looked over Kent's shoulder. "Speaking of your date, here she comes now."

Kent turned around. Christina was headed their way. She still wore her bathing suit, but she'd wrapped a blue beach towel around her body, sarong style. Kent noticed how several of the men ogled her as she walked by. She smiled as she reached them. "Don't you want to get something to eat?" she asked Kent.

Just as Kent started to answer, the back door opened, and Allison, carrying her baby, walked out. Nikki turned. Within minutes Allison was surrounded by people exclaiming over the baby. Nikki and Glenn drifted away, and Kent and Christina were left by themselves.

"I still can't get over the fact that you've got a step-sister and never told me," Christina said, her eyes on Allison.

Kent kept his voice light. "There are probably lots of things I haven't told you."

"But I know we've talked about your family. You told me all about your mother. You even told me about Nikki. Why didn't you tell me about Allison?"

Kent shrugged. "Subject just never came up." He forced himself not to look in Allison's direction, but it was difficult because of all the excitement her appearance with her baby had generated.

Christina gave him an odd look. "Why do I get the feeling there's something more here than meets the eye?"

He frowned. "You're imagining things."

"Am I?"

"Yes." Because he wanted to change the subject, he suggested, "Why don't we get something to eat?"

Ten minutes later, plates laden with barbecued ribs, baked beans, coleslaw and rolls, they found a couple of empty lawn chairs and sat down.

Not long after, Lee walked over and sat down next to Christina. "I haven't had a chance to talk to you," he said to her. "I understand you work with Kent."

Christina smiled. "Yes."

"You must be a very good lawyer."

"I am."

Lee laughed. "I like that. No coy answer. No false humility."

She shrugged. "I don't believe in hiding my light under a bushel."

That was certainly true, Kent thought.

"Good for you," Lee said.

Kent smiled as he listened to the exchange. He admired and respected his stepfather. He had liked him from the first moment he'd met him. Of course, at the time he'd thought Lee was going to be his father-in-law. As he remembered that day, Kent's attention wandered from the conversation, and his thoughts once more drifted to Allison. Out of the corner of his eye, he could see her, flanked by his mother and Nikki's mother as she walked to the edge of the patio and sat in one of the redwood deck chairs.

"Well, enjoy your food," Lee said about ten minutes later as he got up and walked away.

They finished eating, Kent forcing himself to listen to Christina's chatter and not look in Allison's direction. Then, because he knew the longer he waited the more difficult it would be, he said, "I think I'll go over and meet my little stepniece."

"I'll go with you," Christina said, "although babies really aren't my bag."

Kent knew that. Christina had made this same remark several times in his hearing.

They walked over to where Allison was sitting just as Kent's mother stood up. She smiled at him, and he smiled back. Nikki's mother, Sunny, also stood, saying, "Well, it looks as if you've got some other people who want to see the baby. Here, Christina…it is Christina, isn't it?"

"Yes," Christina said.

"You can have my seat," Sunny continued.

"And you can have mine," Diana said to Kent.

Kent hadn't intended to sit down. He'd had some idea of walking up, giving the baby a quick once-over and walking away again. But he sat.

His gaze met Allison's. "This is Marianne," she said, her voice soft. Slowly he looked at the baby.

"Hi," he said, leaning closer.

Marianne's huge eyes turned toward him. She studied him gravely.

"Hi, there," he said again, feeling a little silly because he didn't know how to act.

Marianne smiled, waving her little fists in the air.

Kent's heart turned over. Mesmerized, he reached out to touch her hand, and she closed her tiny fingers around his thumb. The feel of warm baby was like no other he'd ever experienced.

"What do you think of her?" Allison asked.

Eyes still on Marianne, he said, "She's beautiful."

"How old is she?" Christina asked.

Kent had almost forgotten Christina was there.

"She's almost two months old," Allison replied, turning toward Christina.

Christina gave the baby a cursory look. "She's very pretty," she said. "Your father told me you were married to Jean Luc Fornier. I'm sorry about what happened to him."

Kent looked at Allison. She avoided his eyes. "Thank you," she said.

"I really gave Kent the business for not telling me you even existed. I still can't believe it. He has a stepsister married to a famous race-car driver, and he never even mentions it."

At that moment Kent wanted to strangle Christina. He was saved from having to say anything when Lee's secretary, Britta, walked up to them and began cooing over the baby.

"See you later, Allison," Kent said. Standing, he said to Christina, "You coming?" Without waiting for her, he walked straight toward the cooler.

By the time he'd opened a beer and taken a long swallow, he'd gotten control of his emotions.

"What's the deal between you and your stepsister?" Christina asked. "Is there bad blood between you?"

"Why do you ask that?" Kent said. Just to prove that he could, he met her gaze evenly.

"I don't know," Christina said slowly. "I just got a funny feeling while we were talking to her. It's as if you don't like her much."

"I like her fine."

Christina shrugged. "The two of you seem awfully stiff together."

Kent's jaw hardened. Damn it all. He didn't want to get into it, but he knew if he didn't tell Christina some of the background between him and Allison, she'd find out sometime, anyway. And then she'd attach even more importance to Kent's not telling her than she already had. Not only that, she'd think Allison still mattered to Kent. He took another swallow of beer. "Okay. I might as well tell you. Allison and I used to be engaged to each other." As he spoke, he met her gaze squarely.

Her jaw dropped. She didn't say a word for a moment, then her eyes narrowed. "And you didn't think it was important enough to tell me?"

Kent shrugged. "It's ancient history."

She stared at him. "What else haven't you told me?"

"I don't know why you're making such a big deal out of this," he countered. "We didn't have an amicable parting of ways, okay? So I'd rather not talk about it, okay? That's why I didn't tell you. Okay?"

"Fine," she said tightly.

Anyone looking at her would be able to tell she was angry. Suddenly Kent was ashamed of himself. Just because he still hadn't come to terms with his feelings for Allison didn't mean he should take it out on Christina. "Hey," he said softly, touching her shoulder. "I'm sorry. Maybe I should have told you, but like I said, Allison and I…well, things are awkward between us. I guess they always will be."

"Are you still in love with her, Kent?"

He looked into her cool gray eyes. "No."

"Are you sure? Because if you are, tell me now."

"I'm not. Allison and I are completely finished."

"I hope you're telling me the truth."

Defiantly, hoping Allison was watching, Kent bent down and gave Christina a lingering kiss. "Now do you believe me?" he asked when he lifted his head.

He ignored the small voice inside that asked, *hey, buddy, who are you trying to convince?*

Chapter Three

"Great game, Kent."

Kent zipped up the cover over his tennis racket and grimaced at Bobby Halloran, his old college roommate. "Maybe for you. But I sure have had better days."

Bobby laughed. "Well, if you're looking for sympathy from me, buddy, you're barking up the wrong tree. I've been on the losing end too often. It's about time I won a match!" He waved. "See you next week."

"Yeah."

Kent tossed his gear into his car, climbed in, started the engine and pointed the Corvette toward home. He couldn't wait to jump in the shower after his sweaty exercise in futility. As he drove, he thought about the game. He and Bobby had played tennis together early every Sunday morning since both were freshmen at the University of Houston. Normally Kent enjoyed their game. But it was hard to enjoy what had happened to him this morning. He'd missed easy returns, double-faulted several times during his serve and practically handed Bobby the match. For some reason, his concentration had been shot.

Who was he kidding, anyway? He knew damned well why he hadn't been able to concentrate today. Ever since the party at his mother's house on Friday—the party where he'd come face-to-face with his past—his mind had been on one thing and one thing only.

Allison.

He kept reliving the months of their engagement. Remembering all the things that had happened between them. Replaying old conversations. Rehashing old hurts. Wondering if there was anything he could have done differently.

God, he was sick of it. What was done was done. Why couldn't he leave it alone?

Because she came back, that's why. As long as she wasn't around, you could pretend none of it mattered. But now she's here, and you can't pretend anymore.

"I don't care about her," he muttered angrily. Someone behind him hit his car horn, and Kent jumped. He was stopped for a red light. The light had turned green, and he hadn't even known it. He jammed the car into gear and took off with a peal of rubber.

For the rest of the way home, he forced himself not to think about anything except what he would do for the remainder of the day. He usually spent some portion of the weekend with Christina, but she had gone to San Antonio to visit her parents this weekend. She'd invited him to come along, but he'd declined. Going to meet a woman's parents implied a serious relationship. And Kent wasn't sure he was ready to have Christina *or* her parents make that assumption.

So what should he do now that he had a free day? He could go into the office. Lord knows, he always had plenty of work to do there. But he didn't feel like working today. He'd been doing too much of that lately, what with his new assignment and the firm's insistence on every associate billing a certain number of hours per week.

Kent frowned. Billable hours was one aspect of working at Keating & Shaw that still bothered him. He wondered if other firms engaged in the practice of padding. He'd been pretty naive when he was hired and had questioned Ben Keating's order to bill a minimum of sixty hours per week. When Kent had commented on the order to one of the other associates, saying he didn't see how anyone could work sixty-hour weeks every week, it had been explained to him that if he made a one-minute phone call, he was to bill a quarter hour, which was the smallest amount of billed time allowed. With that guideline, a lawyer could put in fifty actual hours but bill eighty.

For the past year and a half, Kent had obediently followed the firm's guidelines, just as every member of the firm did. Yet the practice continued to disturb him. Still, he said nothing because he wanted to keep his job. Eventually he hoped to make partner. If that meant he had to compromise, so be it. That was the way of the world, as he'd learned the hard way. Compromise. Negotiate. Make deals.

So he kept his mouth shut, his nose clean, and did what he was told. Let someone else be a squeaky wheel. Squeaky wheels did not make partner. Squeaky wheels either got fired or they got assigned to the most boring, routine cases and remained in their small, stuffy cubicles forever.

Kent wanted a corner office with a big window. And he wanted to work on exciting, career-making cases. No more playing at Don Quixote for him. His hard work and cooperative attitude were beginning to pay off, too. Several months ago he'd been assigned to a big personal-injury case involving one of Keating & Shaw's most important clients—Emmett Wilder. Suit had been brought against Wilder by Shelley Petrowski, the widow of Greg Petrowski, who had been killed while testing the Wild Rider, a motorcycle designed and manufactured by Wilder's company.

Kent had been thrilled to be assigned to work with Colin Jamieson, the senior partner in charge of the case. Kent knew that a case like this was the kind of assignment that made a new associate's career. Do a good job, impress Colin Jamieson and Kent would be on his way toward his partnership.

But despite his enthusiasm for the Wilder case, he still didn't feel like working today.

Well, if he didn't work, what should he do with the rest of his day? Catch up on his reading? Drop into Dusty's and watch the Astros' game with a bunch of the guys? Yeah, that sounded good. And on the way, he could stop at his mother's and leave the new wills he'd prepared for her and Lee at their request.

You don't have to do that, he reminded himself. Lee said he'd come by your office and pick them up. Are you looking for an excuse to see Allison again?

Kent ignored the taunting voice. Of course he wasn't looking for an excuse to see Allison again. Lee did so much for him that he simply wanted to save Lee some hassle.

Uh-huh. And the moon is made of green cheese.

Kent gritted his teeth. He'd be damned if he'd com-

pletely change his life just because Allison was now
back in Houston. Why should he have to avoid his
mother's house? Why should he have to do anything
different from what he'd been doing?

He would take the wills over there, he thought defiantly. And if he did happen to see Allison, he would
simply say "hi" and nothing else. He would continue
to show her how little importance her existence held for
him.

Because if he didn't go, if he let Allison's presence
in his mother's home deter him from his normal routine
or stop him from dropping in as he was accustomed to
doing, then he would be giving her control of his life.

Allison decided she would put on her bathing suit and
go lie in the sun for a while. Marianne had just gone to
sleep for her afternoon nap, Diana had gone out for one
of her rare weekend appointments to show houses to a
client, and her father was working on his computer in
the study.

Armed with the baby monitor, a book, sun block and
a beach towel, Allison walked out to the pool. Head
protected by a big straw hat, she donned her sunglasses,
stretched out on a chaise lounge and opened her book.

About forty-five minutes later, she wondered if perhaps she'd had enough sun for one day. Maybe she
should cover up or go inside. Just as the thought formed,
she heard a car pull into the driveway. She glanced up
briefly, then shrugged. Her father would take care of
whoever it was. But a few minutes later she heard footsteps coming toward the back of the house and then
someone opening the back gate.

She sat up and looked around. A tremor slithered
down her spine as Kent stepped onto the deck.

He stopped. "Hi," he said.

"Hi." She stood, reaching for her beach towel. She was glad he wasn't close enough to see how her hand trembled as she clutched her book. She held her towel protectively in front of her, feeling her near-nakedness and wishing she didn't feel so exposed. She also wished she'd listened to her instincts and gone inside five minutes ago.

Yet even as the wish formulated, she couldn't suppress a tiny spurt of pleasure as she looked at him. She'd always enjoyed looking at Kent, always thought he was one of the nicest-looking men she'd ever known. He wasn't movie-star handsome, but his appeal was timeless and pure male. Today he wore khaki walking shorts with lots of pockets and a pale yellow knit shirt, both of which set off his tan and emphasized his solid, athletic body. Large wraparound sunglasses covered his eyes and hid his expression from her. In his left hand he carried a dark briefcase, which should have looked incongruous with his casual outfit but didn't.

"I rang the doorbell, but no one answered," he said. He gestured with the briefcase. "I brought some papers over for Lee and Mom to sign."

Allison, still feeling awkward, walked slowly toward him. "That's funny. Dad's inside. He was working in the study last time I saw him."

"Where's my mother?"

"She's out showing houses."

"Oh. I guess I should have called first. But you said Lee's here?"

"Yes. I—I'll go find him for you, if you like."

"No, that's okay. I've already bothered you. I can go find him myself." But he made no move to go.

"I'm going in, anyway. I think I've had enough sun for today," Allison said.

He removed his sunglasses, and his clear blue gaze slowly inspected her. "You always did sunburn easily," he said softly.

Heat suffused Allison as their gazes locked. Unspoken thoughts shimmered in the air between them. Remembrances of past intimacies, of shared experiences, of happy times together, flooded Allison's mind, and she knew Kent was remembering, too. Her heart picked up speed, and she wished she could give voice to her regrets. She wished she could say something, anything that would clear the air between them.

Just then the back door opened, and the moment was gone. Her father walked outside. "Kent!" he said. "Was that you ringing the doorbell?"

Kent smiled, the first time he'd smiled today, and pain welled into Allison's chest. She would give anything to have Kent smile at her that way again, with spontaneity and warmth and pleasure. "Yeah," he said. "Where were you?"

"Trapped on the phone. I'd just placed a call to Pieter Koenig in Amsterdam and was waiting for him to come on the line. Sorry about that."

"That's okay. I brought the revised papers we talked about."

"You didn't have to do that. I told you I'd come and pick them up at your office."

Kent shrugged. "I'm on my way to Dusty's, so it was no trouble at all."

Lee grinned. "You still hanging out at that saloon?"

Kent chuckled. "Yeah. Some things never change."

Today everything Kent said reminded Allison of the past. She remembered the one time he'd taken her to

Dusty's, a favorite haunt of his law school days. She hadn't been crazy about the place, and she'd made no secret of her dislike. He hadn't taken her again. Oh, God, she'd been such a snob then. It was a wonder he had ever loved her at all. Suddenly she couldn't bear to stand out here in his company another moment. "I— I'll leave you two to discuss your business," she said, avoiding Kent's eyes. "I'm going in."

"I'm not staying, so don't let me run you off," Kent said, his tone stiff. He removed a manila folder from his briefcase and handed it to her father.

Her gaze darted to his. "You're not running me off." But the expression in his eyes told her he knew she was lying. And when her gaze drifted back to her father, she knew he knew it, too. "I told you. I've been in the sun too long."

Kent didn't answer, but she could feel his eyes on her as she walked to the back door. She opened it. "Be sure to sign these in the presence of two witnesses who are not related to you" were the last words she heard Kent say before she closed the door behind her.

"Kent, are you paying attention?"

Kent looked at Christina, who sat across from him in the law library. "Yeah, sure, did you say something?"

Christina rolled her eyes. "I not only said something, I said it *twice*." She frowned. "You've been preoccupied all day. What's wrong with you?"

He shrugged. "Just tired, I guess."

Her frown deepened. "Tired? But you said you didn't do anything this weekend. You didn't even work."

Was it his imagination, or was her tone accusatory? "I've put in more than my share of hours since we started work on this case. I think I'm entitled to a week-end off.''

"You don't have to get so defensive. I just made a comment, that's all.''

"Sounded more like an accusation to me.''

"What *did* you do while I was gone?''

Jesus, she was beginning to act as if she owned him. "I told you. Nothing much.''

"But what, specifically?'' She tapped her gold pen against the open reference book sitting in front of her. Her long, painted nails were the exact shade of red as her suit and her lipstick. Always perfectly turned out, Christina exuded confidence and power. For some reason, this fact irritated him today, when earlier this had been something that he'd admired. "Did you play tennis with Bobby? Did you go out Saturday night?''

He stared at her. Her gray eyes stared back. Women, he thought in disgust, he was beginning to feel they weren't worth the aggravation. What was her problem? She'd never quizzed him like this before. And he didn't care for it. Not one little bit. He forced himself to keep his voice mild. "I didn't know I had to give you a report. What do you want? A detailed summary? Shall I write everything down? Eight fifty-five, left for the tennis game. Nine-fifteen, started the game.''

Her eyes narrowed. When she spoke, her voice was tight. "You don't have to be so sarcastic, Kent. I just asked a simple question.''

"First I'm defensive, now I'm sarcastic. Make up your mind.''

Her jaw hardened, her eyes glittering like smoky diamonds. Hard, smoky diamonds. "I don't care for your tone of voice.''

He shrugged.

"You can be a real bastard when you try, you know that?"

He smiled. "All this name-calling isn't very professional, Christina. I just don't happen to like this interrogation." Still calm. Still cool.

"I'll ignore that crack about me not being professional," she snapped. "And if you don't want to tell me what you were doing, fine. Don't tell me."

"I thought we had an understanding. I don't run your life, and you don't run mine."

"Did you go over to your mother's this weekend?"

Oh, so that was it. "As a matter of fact, I did." He'd be damned if he'd explain further.

Her smile was wry. "I thought so."

"Look, I don't know what in hell you're thinking, but whatever it is, you're wrong. The only reason I resisted giving you a blow-by-blow account of my weekend was because I was trying to make a point." The point being, you do not own me. Yet.

"Oh, I got your point," she said, fury written all over her beautiful face. She laid down her pen. "Your point came through loud and clear. Now could we please get back to business? We have a lot more work to do before we can call it a day. Or would you prefer I finish up so you can go and do whatever it is you're doing that you don't want to discuss?"

Kent decided he would not rise to her bait again. "Good idea," he said. "Where were we?"

She looked as if she wanted to say something else. Instead, she shrugged and said, "We were deciding which of us should track down and interview the members of the design team for the Wild Rider and which of us should interview Petrowski's friends and family."

"Why don't you take the family, and I'll take the design team?" Kent suggested.

"Why?"

"You're better at interviewing family than I am."

"I'm also better at ferreting out dirt."

Kent winced. What she said was true. Christina had a nose for dirt. Whenever a potential witness had something to hide, she usually sensed it. So it wasn't surprising she was suspicious about his feelings for Allison.

Kent, on the other hand, wanted to believe everyone. You'd think, after his disastrous experience at the storefront, he would be more cynical and less apt to take people at face value. Well, hell, he *was* more cynical, but he still had a long way to go before he could match Christina. His tendency to want to believe the best of people was a bone of contention between them. More than once she had accused him of being squeamish. Of not having the guts to go for the jugular.

Sometimes Kent wondered if she was right. Take the Wilder case, for instance. No matter how many times he told himself all his loyalty should lie with Emmett Wilder, who was, after all, his firm's client and the one paying the bills, Kent found himself identifying with Shelley Petrowski. He had never even met the woman, had only seen pictures of her at her husband's funeral, but the pictures had haunted him. He couldn't understand how anyone seeing the young widow with her tear-streaked face, holding tightly on to the hand of her three-year-old daughter and cradling her infant son in her other arm, could be anything but sympathetic.

He sighed. It wasn't his job to worry about Shelley Petrowski. It was his job to find evidence to back up Emmett Wilder's claim that his company was not at fault in Greg Petrowski's unfortunate accident.

"Honestly, Kent, you're doing it again!" Christina said, exasperation dripping from her voice. "What is your problem today?"

"Sorry. I was thinking about the case."

"What about it?"

He shrugged. "Nothing. Just thinking about who I'll talk to first." There was no point in telling Christina his doubts. She wouldn't understand. In her mind, everything was black or white. Either something was important because it would help your client's case, or it was irrelevant because it wouldn't. Period. End of discussion. There was no room for gray areas in Christina's thinking. And she would be quick to tell him there was no room for gray areas in his thinking, either.

Later that afternoon, in his office, Kent rubbed his forehead wearily. He really should stay late tonight. He'd goofed off enough this weekend.

But once again he didn't feel like working. He wanted to go home, change into comfortable clothes, have a cold beer and plop down in front of the TV set. Mindless stuff. He began to cram papers into his briefcase. He would compromise. He'd leave now, but he'd try to get some work done at home tonight.

Just as he snapped his briefcase shut, his intercom buzzed. "Mr. Sorensen," his secretary said, "Mr. Gabriel is on line one."

"Thanks, Loretta." Kent punched the button for line one. "Lee?"

"Hello, Kent. Sorry to bother you at work."

"That's okay." He wondered what his stepfather wanted. He rarely called Kent at work. "Is everything okay with the wills?"

"Yes, yes, everything's fine with the wills. That's not why I called. I wanted to talk to you about something, and I happened to be thinking about it right now so decided to call you while it was on my mind."

"Sounds serious."

"Not serious, but it's important. At least to me." Lee hesitated for a moment, then said slowly, "It's about Allison."

"Oh?" Kent said cautiously. Allison was a subject he preferred not to talk about, especially with Lee. He had successfully avoided thinking about her today. And that's the way he wanted to keep it.

"Ordinarily I try to stay out of yours and Allison's personal lives...."

Kent waited. He remembered when once that hadn't been true.

"But these are unusual circumstances," Lee continued. "Look, Kent, I'm not going to beat around the bush. I can see that you're constrained around Allison. It's been obvious to both me and your mother that you haven't forgiven or forgotten what happened between the two of you."

Kent stiffened. "Well, I'm sorry you feel that—"

"Now don't get defensive," Lee said. "I'm not blaming you for anything."

"Sure sounded that way to me." Kent knew he was reacting badly, but he couldn't seem to help himself. After all, he wasn't the one who had run out on Allison. He wasn't the one in the wrong here. *She* was the one who had caused all their problems, so he had a perfect right to be angry.

"Come on, Kent, be fair," his stepfather said mildly. "You know your mother and I love both you and Allison. But right now Allison needs our help and support more than you do. She's going through a difficult time and she doesn't need more stress in her life. She needs less.''

''Meaning?''

''Meaning your attitude isn't helping things. If it's obvious to me and your mother that you're still holding a grudge against her, don't you think Allison realizes it, too? It was obvious to me yesterday, seeing the way she acted when you came to the house, that she *does* feel your animosity. Do you really want her to have more to worry about and feel guilty about than she already does? Can't you be a little understanding and put your personal differences aside?'' Lee's voice took on a gentle, chiding tone. ''Allison needs all her resources to deal with Marianne's problems. She needs her family behind her. Supporting her.''

''Maybe it would be best, then, if I just stayed away from the house completely.''

Lee didn't answer for a long moment. Then he said slowly, ''Well, that wasn't exactly what I had in mind. Look, Allison really needs a friend right now. I was hoping that instead of staying away, you would make a real effort to be that friend.''

Kent took a deep breath. ''Sir, you know I respect you. You know I'd do just about anything for you. But you're asking too much this time. If you think I'm upsetting Allison, I'll stay away. But that's all I can do. Because there's no way she and I are ever going to be friends.''

Chapter Four

Allison looked around Marcy Bartlett's kitchen. Marcy and Joel had completely redone the old West University house they'd bought two years ago. In keeping with the Colonial design, the kitchen was red, white and blue and had an old-fashioned country flavor.

Marcy had been Allison's best friend since they'd met at camp as ten-year-olds and recognized a kindred spirit. Allison had missed Marcy during the years she'd spent in Paris. They hadn't had much contact, mainly because Allison hadn't wanted Marcy to know how unhappy she was.

Today both women were seated at the large round maple table that dominated the room. They had large glasses of iced tea in front of them, and Marcy had set out some thin slices of lemon pound cake. As they talked, Marcy held Marianne.

"Hi, cutie," she said softly. "Are you gonna give me a smile?"

The baby cooed.

Allison felt like hugging Marcy. Some days Marianne's color was worse than others. Some people were scared off by it and were afraid to handle the baby. But Marcy was a natural and treated Marianne as if there weren't anything wrong with her. Nikki had been the same way, and Allison was grateful.

"I love your kitchen," Allison said.

"Thanks." Marcy grimaced, her nose wrinkling. "This kitchen's my consolation prize."

Allison frowned. "Consolation prize?"

"Uh-huh. Because I can't get pregnant, and Joel wanted to take my mind off that depressing fact."

"Oh, Marce, I didn't know...." Allison said softly, her heart going out to her friend, whose freckled face and normally bright eyes both held traces of pain. "But listen, it just takes some women longer than others—"

"I know. But we've been trying for three years."

"Oh." Here Allison had been envying Marcy because she had a devoted husband whom she adored, a home of her own and a settled life. All of which proved you could never really tell anything about anyone from the surface. Outwardly it might look as if a person had everything going for them. Inwardly they might be uncertain or unhappy or any one of a dozen negative emotions. "Have you thought about adoption?"

"Yes, Joel and I have talked about it, but, well, Joel's an only child, and his parents are kind of hung up on us having a baby of our own."

Allison nodded sympathetically.

Marcy shrugged, her light blue eyes thoughtful. "I haven't given up hope. And if I don't get pregnant, I'm going to push to adopt." She turned her gaze back to Marianne. "I want a baby so badly. You're so lucky to have Marianne." She nuzzled the baby's forehead. "She's so beautiful, even though she's sick." Then her face took on a stricken look. "Oh, Allison, I'm sorry! I completely forgot about Jean Luc."

"That's okay. Believe me, I am lucky to have Marianne, and I know it." She hesitated, then hurriedly, before she could change her mind, said, "I—I haven't told anyone else this, but Jean Luc and I didn't have the best of relationships."

"Oh?"

Allison sighed, looking away from her friend's penetrating gaze. "I guess I married him on the rebound. And you know what they say about marrying in haste...."

"You sounded as if you were in love with him when you called me to tell me you were getting married," Marcy said softly.

"I know now that I was simply dazzled by him. He was so good-looking, so dark and dangerous and sexy. And he paid attention to me. He made me feel really special. I needed that. My ego was bruised after what happened with Kent."

Marcy nodded. "I wondered when the conversation would get around to Kent."

Allison swallowed. She hadn't meant to mention Kent's name. Or had she?

"Have you seen him yet?"

Allison nodded. "Twice." She fiddled with her iced-tea glass, drawing circles in the condensation. "My dad and Diana had a barbecue on the fourth, and he came...with a gorgeous blonde on his arm. And then yesterday he stopped by the house, and I saw him for a minute."

"And?"

"And what?"

"How did you feel?"

Allison thought about lying. But that wasn't why she'd introduced the subject, and she knew it. She wanted to tell Marcy everything she couldn't tell her father. Or her stepmother. Or anyone else. She wanted her friend to give her advice. To tell her everything would be all right. And it seemed fitting to confide in Marcy, because she and Joel, who was Kent's best friend, had introduced the two of them. Ironically, Allison thought with a start, at a Fourth of July barbecue. Why had that fact just occurred to her?

"I—I felt awkward and nervous and miserable. My—my heart was beating like a tom-tom, my hands were sweaty, and my throat was dry. I felt like crying, and I didn't know what to say."

Marcy grinned. "Gee. Is that all? And here I thought you might have cared!"

Allison laughed, but she could feel tears forming at the back of her eyes, and she blinked several times to try to keep them at bay. But she couldn't, and suddenly, without warning, she began to cry. She bit her bottom lip, furious with herself, and scrabbled around in her pocket for a tissue. "Damn," she said. "What's wrong with me?"

"Oh, honey," Marcy said. "You're still in love with him, aren't you?"

"No!" Allison dabbed at her eyes, then blew her nose. "I'm not still in love with him. I—I just... Oh, shoot, I don't know! I feel so strange around him. It—it hurts to see him." She swallowed, concentrating on keeping the tears back. "Oh, this is so stupid. I don't know why I'm acting like such a fool."

Marcy laughed again, but her eyes were filled with sympathy. "Allison, can I ask you something?"

Allison blew her nose again. "Of course."

"Do—do you ever regret what you did?"

Allison sighed, looking down at her hands for a moment. "You mean running out on Kent?"

"Yes."

Allison's gaze met Marcy's once again. "Yes, I regret it. I regretted it from almost the first moment I did it."

"Then why? Why didn't you just turn around and come back? You know he wanted you to."

"Oh, God, Marce, I don't know! I was young and stupid and stubborn and pigheaded. Who knows why anyone does anything?" She twisted the tissue in her hands. "And I guess I felt that Kent didn't love me enough."

"Didn't love you enough! How can you say that? Kent was absolutely bonkers over you. Why, Joel and I have talked about it a million times, how Kent was so nuts about you he couldn't see straight."

Allison shrugged. "Obviously he didn't love me enough to take the job with Keating & Shaw."

"But, Allison, the same could be said for you. You didn't love him enough to marry him no matter what he decided to do."

Allison nodded. "I know. Don't you think I've told myself the same thing dozens of times? I was selfish and wrong." She sighed heavily. "Unfortunately I can't go back and change things."

"It's a dirty, rotten shame that things turned out the way they did. You two were so good together. I just couldn't understand why you couldn't work things out."

"I don't know. I guess I felt I came second, and maybe Kent felt that way, too."

"I don't think you came second with Kent. It's just that he was so idealistic. He'd dreamed of opening his storefront law office for years, and he couldn't relinquish that dream."

"Yet barely four years later, he's done just that," Allison said. Suddenly the unhappiness and confusion and, yes, betrayal, she'd been feeling ever since learning of Kent's abandonment of his storefront practice nearly overwhelmed her. "Why did he do it, Marcy? Why was he unable to do for me what he did later, anyway? All these years I've been feeling so guilty…so sorry about hurting him, but at least I could take comfort from the fact that his life was on the right track…that he was doing what he was always meant to do. And then I come home and discover he's gone to work for Keating & Shaw after all!" She fell silent, overwhelmed by the futility of it all. Why had they both had to suffer? Had everything been in vain?

Marcy, eyes compassionate, said slowly, "I don't know, Allison. Things change. Maybe your leaving Kent made him see things differently."

Allison rubbed her head. "It doesn't matter now. It's no use second-guessing. It's all over with. Nothing can change the past. Now I've got to stop thinking about Kent and what happened between us and concentrate on Marianne."

Marcy looked down at the baby, whose eyes were drifting open and shut. "She's sleepy," she whispered.

"I know. I think I'd better be going."

"Oh, don't go yet!"

"I'd better." Allison stood. "And Marce?"

Marcy looked up.

"Please don't mention any of what I said about Kent to Joel."

Marcy frowned. "I wouldn't do that—"

"Yes, you would." Allison knew that Marcy and Joel told each other everything. "But promise me that this time you won't."

Marcy seemed about to say something else. Instead, she sighed. "Okay. I won't."

"Promise."

"Cross my heart."

Allison chuckled over their childhood pledge and reached for the baby.

Kent spent the day tracking the whereabouts of the six-member design team for the Wild Rider. Four of the designers were still employed by Wilder's. He made a check mark by their names. He would set up interviews with them for later in the week. He knew the plaintiff's attorney would subpoena all of them for depositions, so he felt it was important to woodshed them first—slang for coaching them privately, as in taking them behind the woodshed and telling them what to say.

One of the designers had died of a heart attack two months earlier. Kent crossed his name off the list.

That left one—the senior member of the team—Armand Brasselli. In checking Brasselli's personnel file, Kent saw the man had retired in January and moved to Poway, California. There was even an address in the files because Brasselli was collecting early retirement. Kent made a note to ask his secretary to try to set up a time when Kent could fly out there to interview him.

After that he made a list of all the possible questions the designers would be asked by the opposition. Once he had talked with the designers, he would help them formulate answers, as well as tell them what not to say. Since the plaintiff's case was based on the theory that Wilder had known there was a design problem, Kent figured the design team would play a big part in the trial.

By the end of the day, Kent left the office with a satisfied feeling, knowing he'd accomplished a lot.

Tuesday night he met Joel Bartlett, who worked for the rival firm of MacAllister, Amann and Royer, for drinks at their favorite downtown pub. As usual Joel was sitting at the bar, and Kent slid onto a bar stool next to him.

"So how was your day?" Joel asked.

"Busy. What about you?"

Joel shrugged. "Boring." He drank some of his beer. "I'm thinking about looking for another job."

Kent frowned. "Why? There's only one other firm in town that compares to yours, and that's mine. Why change?"

Joel sighed. "I don't think I'm cut out to work for a big law firm. I want to do a lot of different kinds of things, and you know how it is with the big guns. New guys like us just do grunt work. Same old, same old. All day, every day."

Kent nodded sympathetically. Boredom was a common complaint among his contemporaries from law school. It took a lot of years of grunt work and proving yourself before you were allowed to handle anything even remotely challenging. He knew he was lucky to be on the Wilder case. At least the case itself was interesting, even if he probably would not be assigned anything other than research and interviewing.

"Why don't we start our own firm?" Joel offered.

"No way," Kent said. "I was an entrepreneur once, remember?"

"That was different. Think about it, Kent. You, me, Michael. The three of us together—why, we'd be unbeatable!" Joel's eyes shone with enthusiasm.

Kent just shook his head. He was sitting in the catbird seat at Keating & Shaw. He would soon be in the six-figure income bracket. Starting a firm of their own would mean struggling for years. Although…he had to admit the thought of working with Joel and Michael Berry, another young lawyer they'd hung around with all through law school, held a lot of appeal. At one time he'd have jumped at the chance to do something like this. But now, well, he'd learned his lesson. "No, I don't think so. We'd be giving up a sure thing for a shot in the dark," he said. "I don't want to risk it."

"Yeah, you're probably right," Joel said morosely. "Marcy'd probably kill me if I mentioned it. Now that we've bought that house, we need every penny I earn."

Kent nodded.

They fell silent for a few minutes, then Joel said, "So Allison's back, I hear."

"Yeah." Kent did not want to discuss Allison. Maybe if he didn't elaborate, Joel would drop the subject.

"Have you seen her?"

Kent sighed. Joel wasn't going to drop the subject. "Yeah, I've seen her," he said reluctantly.

Joel started to say something else when the bartender walked up to them. "What'll you guys have?" he asked, wiping the bar in front of them.

"I'll have a light beer," Joel said.

"Me, too," Kent said.

"So how'd she look?" Joel asked when the bartender had served them and walked away.

Kent shrugged. "Older. Thinner." He kept his voice as noncommittal and impersonal as he could. He wanted nothing so much as to talk about something else. Anything else.

"Yeah, well, that's understandable. She's had a rough time. Even so, I'll bet she's still gorgeous."

Kent shrugged again. "I guess so."

"You guess so! You suddenly grow a pair of blinders?" Joel chuckled at his sally. Then his smile grew sly. "I can't believe you're that indifferent. You never were before."

"Yeah, well, times change."

"Not that much."

"*I've* changed."

Joel took a swallow of beer, then he grinned. "Like I said, not that much." He nudged Kent. "Come on. Tell me the truth. You're not as immune as you pretend to be."

Kent ignored him and drank some beer himself.

"She came over to visit with Marcy yesterday...." Joel said slowly. He drank more beer and grabbed a handful of peanuts from the dish in front of them.

Kent refused to rise to the bait. He said nothing.

"Marcy said she's different."

Why couldn't Joel talk about something else? "Yeah, well, we've all changed. Say, did you see the Astros' game last night?"

"Nope." Joel ate a few peanuts. "Marcy said Allison's really grown up. Matured."

Kent sighed heavily. He turned to Joel, fixing him with a steady look. His friend looked back. "Joel, I know what you're trying to do, and it's not going to work. I don't want to discuss Allison. Now, can we talk about something else?''

"Oh, jeez, sorry, buddy. I wasn't thinking, I guess. If the subject makes you uncomfortable, sure, we can talk about something else.''

If Kent hadn't known Joel so well, he might have believed that bland innocence in his expression and his tone of voice. "The subject doesn't make me uncomfortable. I just happen not to be interested.''

"Hey, no problem. Don't get riled up.''

"I'm *not* riled up!'' Kent said with more force than he'd intended. "Why does everyone persist in trying to shove the topic of Allison down my throat?'' Kent took a swig of beer. "Damn it!'' he said as he set the bottle down. "I couldn't care less what she says or does.''

Joel raised his eyebrows.

The lively strains of a Clint Black song filled the silence between them. Why Clint Black? Kent wondered. Was everyone and everything conspiring to remind him of Allison and their past relationship? Clint Black had always been one of her favorite performers, and Kent had taken her to see him in person once. It had been a wonderful evening, and at the end of it, when they'd kissed good night, she had said, "I love you so much, Kent. You're so good to me.''

Kent sighed again. Joel was right. He was bothered by Allison, and he didn't like it when anyone discussed her. "Listen, Joel, I'm sorry,'' he said. "I guess I'm touchy where she's concerned.''

"It's okay. I understand.''

"No, I'm not sure you do.'' Hell, how could Joel understand when Kent didn't understand himself?

"Listen. If you don't want to talk about her, it's okay.

But, you know, you're going to be thrown into her company whether you want to be or not.''

"I know, and I've got to learn to handle it better.'' He tapped his fingertips on the bar. "Lee called me yesterday. He asked me to try to mend fences with her. He said she's really going through a bad time right now.''

"Yeah. Marcy told me.''

"So what else did Marcy tell you?'' In spite of his protestations to the contrary, Kent wondered if Marcy and Allison had discussed him.

"Nothing much.''

"Oh, come on. Marcy tells you everything.''

Joel's eyes were impossible to read in the darkness of the bar. "Well, not this time. In fact, she was suspiciously closemouthed.'' He grinned. "So suspiciously, I finally asked her about it. You know what she said?''

"No, what?''

"She said Allison had made her promise not to tell me about their conversation.''

Later, as Kent lay in bed and tried to fall asleep, he kept thinking about Joel's statement and wondering what it was the two women had discussed that Allison didn't want Joel to know.

"I called Kent yesterday,'' Lee said as Diana slipped into bed beside him.

"Oh? What about?''

"I wanted to talk to him about Allison.''

Lee could feel her stiffen beside him. "What about Allison?'' she asked quietly.

"I just told him Allison could really use a friend about now.''

There was silence for a moment, and Lee could almost hear the wheels turning in Diana's mind. "I'm not sure it's realistic to think Kent and Allison could ever be friends, Lee," she said slowly.

"If Kent makes an effort, they can be."

She turned on her side to face him and gently touched his forearm. As it had never failed to do in the three and a half years they'd been married, her touch sent a tingle of pleasure through him. "Honey, do you think it's fair to put that kind of pressure on Kent?" She paused. "I know why you did it. You think Allison's under too much stress, and you want to make things easier for her. Well, I do, too, but none of her problems are Kent's fault, you know."

He laid his hand over hers. "I know that. But if they're ever going to be comfortable around each other, Kent will have to make the first move."

"Well...what did Kent say when you talked to him?"

"At first he tried to deny that there was a problem between them."

"And then..." Diana prompted.

"He said pretty much what you said. That he and Allison could never be friends."

He could feel her shrug.

"I was hoping maybe you'd talk to him," Lee suggested.

"Me! Absolutely not. This is none of our business, Lee. I understand why you felt you had to try. After all, Allison's your daughter, and it's natural for you to be concerned about her, but don't expect me to get involved."

"I thought you cared about Allison."

She stiffened. "I do care about Allison. But I also care about Kent. She hurt him once, Lee. And once is more than enough."

Allison couldn't sleep Tuesday night. All she could think about was that at eight o'clock the next morning, Marianne would be prepped and already half-asleep in preparation for the heart catheterization.

Diana and Lee had both arranged to be off all day and were planning to accompany Allison and Marianne to the hospital. Allison would always be grateful for their support. Right now she wasn't sure how she would have survived if she hadn't had them to count on.

All day she'd tried not to think about the test. All day she'd tried not to think about what she would do if Marianne's prognosis wasn't good. All day she'd tried not to think about how she would survive if Marianne didn't make it.

Allison didn't want to think these gloomy thoughts. She had always believed in the power of positive thinking. But she was also a realist. She always had been. In fact, her pragmatic approach to life was what had caused her problems with Kent.

Kent was a romantic. Allison wasn't. All her romanticism had evaporated when her mother had died when Allison was just a teenager. Allison had adored her effervescent, beautiful mother, and when her mother had told her that she'd been diagnosed with breast cancer, she'd downplayed the significance of the diagnosis. She'd told Allison that the malignancy would be removed and all would be well.

All hadn't been well.

The malignancies couldn't all be removed. The spread of the cancer had been too fast and too pervasive.

Marianne Gabriel had only lived two months after her surgery.

And Allison had never been the same. As she stood beside her father while her mother's coffin had been lowered into the ground, she'd realized that all the positive thinking and romantic notions in the world wouldn't do a bit of good when faced with the harsh realities of life.

But no matter how many times Allison told herself this, she simply couldn't imagine life without her baby daughter. She refused to think about how she'd cope if the worst happened.

The worst won't happen, she told herself fiercely. *I won't let it happen.*

At six-thirty Wednesday morning, Allison and Marianne were safely ensconced in the back seat of Diana's Mercedes. The trip to the medical center only took twenty minutes. By seven o'clock Allison was signing the admission papers, and Marianne was whisked off to begin preparation for her test.

At nine o'clock Marianne was wheeled into surgery, and Allison, Lee and Diana were seated in the waiting room.

At ten o'clock, after several cups of coffee, Allison gave up all pretense of reading the magazine in her hands and anxiously watched the clock.

At ten-thirty Dr. Richardson, the heart surgeon, finally entered the waiting area. "Mrs. Fornier?"

"Yes." Allison stood, clasping her purse tightly. Her mouth had gone dry. The doctor looked so solemn. Her heart suddenly stopped beating. Within seconds her father and Diana had joined her, one on either side. Dr. Richardson nodded to them, then turned his dark gaze back to Allison.

"Is Marianne all right?" Allison asked. *Please, God. Please let her be all right.*

"Yes. She's fine right now. However, the test showed that the blockage of the pulmonary artery is as I anticipated. Your daughter will definitely need open-heart surgery to correct this problem."

Even though Allison thought she'd been prepared for this edict, her heart began to pound and her knees suddenly felt weak. "Wh-when?" she managed to ask.

Allison's father laid a comforting hand on her shoulder, and Diana slipped her arm around Allison's waist.

"Well," Dr. Richardson continued, "right now we'll wait and watch. The older she is, the better her prognosis. But she'll require careful monitoring. The most crucial problem would be congestive heart failure. If her color should worsen or she should have trouble breathing, you should, of course, call us immediately."

Allison listened as the doctor went on to explain that Allison would have to keep the baby as quiet as possible because every time Marianne got too excited or upset, her oxygen level would go down, compounding her problems. The French doctors had said much the same thing, but then she hadn't wanted to listen. Now she had no choice.

"H-how long will Marianne have to stay in the hospital now, Doctor?" she asked.

"There are a couple more tests we want to do tomorrow morning. But you can take her home after that."

He went on to say that Marianne would be in recovery for about an hour, then, if all was okay, she would be brought back to her room in the Pediatric ICU.

The rest of the day passed in a blur. Allison did what she was told to do, but all she could think about was the upcoming heart surgery and the severity of Marianne's problems. She felt as if a tremendous weight were pressing down on her chest as a great fear overwhelmed her. All afternoon she sat in the waiting area, and when she was allowed into Marianne's room for ten minutes each hour, she stood by Marianne's crib and watched her sleeping daughter. When her father or her stepmother talked to her, she answered, but her answers were automatic. Her entire attention was focused on the baby.

Marianne stirred off and on during the afternoon but didn't wake entirely until about four o'clock. Allison wished desperately she could hold the baby, but as long as Marianne was attached to so many tubes and wires, that was impossible. In addition to the cardiac monitor and intravenous, the baby was being given oxygen by nasal cannula—two little prongs attached to her nose. It hurt Allison to look at her, and countless times during the day she wished she could switch places with the baby. She would gladly have endured all the pain to save Marianne from suffering any more than she had already.

About five-thirty Lee and Diana headed for the cafeteria again, but Allison didn't want to go. She knew she'd never get food down. With a weary sigh she walked to the window of the waiting area, which overlooked a courtyard. Down below she could see several people sitting on a stone bench under a small redbud tree. Dotted in clusters around the courtyard were bunches of white-and-purple periwinkles. The July sun beat down, firing the courtyard with bright light.

Everything looked so normal outside. No one out there gave any indication that they might be thinking of the life-and-death struggles going on inside these stone walls. Lost in her thoughts, Allison gazed out the window.

"Allison…"

She whirled around to stare at Kent, who stood in the doorway. For a moment she was speechless. "Wh-what are you doing here?" she blurted. Immediately she wanted to kick herself. "I—I'm sorry. I didn't mean that the way it sounded. I was just so surprised to see you. How'd you get in?" Even the waiting area outside the Intensive Care Unit was limited to family members.

He smiled ruefully, advancing into the room. He was dressed in a charcoal pin-striped suit, white shirt and dark red tie. She realized he'd probably come from work. "I told them I was your brother," he said. He shrugged. "It wasn't really a lie."

Allison nodded, still stunned by his appearance.

"How's Marianne doing?" He inclined his head toward the double doors leading into the ICU.

"So far, she's doing okay." They were both still standing, facing one another. "Listen, why don't we sit down?" she suggested.

Once they were seated, Kent said, "Where're Lee and my mother?"

"Eating dinner in the cafeteria."

"Oh." He studied her, his blue eyes solemn. "How are you doing?"

Allison shrugged. "I'm okay." She went on to explain what Dr. Richardson had told them.

"That's tough," Kent said softly, and the sympathy in his voice touched her.

"How'd you know where we were?" Allison finally asked.

"I called my mother's office, and Carla told me." Carla was Diana's receptionist.

"It—it was good of you to come." She lifted her gaze until it met his.

His eyes held an expression she didn't understand. She could feel her heart beating too fast.

"Kent, I—"

"Allison—"

They both spoke at once.

"Yes?" she said.

"No, you go first," he said.

There were so many things she wanted to say. So many things she didn't dare say. "I—I'm sorry for everything," she said, blurting it out before she lost her nerve. "I'm sorry I hurt you."

He stared at her. His eyes were so blue. They reminded her of an October sky, clear and bright and intense. She wished he'd say something.

"Do—do you think you can ever forgive me? Is it possible for us to be friends?" She was determined to settle this here and now. If he could never forgive her, it was better to know it.

"I don't know," he finally said. "But I'm—I'm willing to try if you are."

Something warm and sweet rushed through her at his words. "Oh, Kent," she said, "except for Marianne getting well, there's nothing I want more in this world."

Chapter Five

For the next couple of days, Kent couldn't get his conversation with Allison out of his mind. He kept remembering the way she'd looked when he'd seen her in the hospital. The dark shadows that looked like smudges under her eyes. How haunted her expression was. How much he had wanted to take her into his arms and comfort her.

He told himself his reaction was perfectly normal. That anyone, seeing how worried Allison was, seeing how tiny and helpless Marianne looked, would have felt the same way. He also told himself the only reason he'd gone to the hospital at all was that he hadn't wanted to disappoint Lee. Ever since their conversation, when Kent had said he could never be Allison's friend, he'd felt like a jerk.

He knew she was at fault in their breakup. He knew he was perfectly justified in his answer to Lee's request.

He even knew Lee was being a bit unreasonable in making the request.

Still, Kent had felt like a jerk.

So he'd gone to the hospital. And ever since, he hadn't been able to get the twin pictures of Allison and Marianne out of his mind.

He knew Marianne had gone home Thursday. He had casually called his mother on Friday and worked the conversation around to the baby. Diana had said yes, the baby was home and seemed to be doing fine. She'd explained what the doctor had told Allison about keeping her quiet.

"I was thinking of stopping by to see her," he said.

"That would be nice of you," his mother said.

He tried to gauge her reaction. Was she in favor of his visiting or not? He couldn't tell.

"Can you think of anything I could buy for the baby?" he continued. "I thought I'd bring her something."

His mother thought for a minute. "A cuddly stuffed animal?" she suggested.

On Saturday Kent decided to go into work early. He planned to work until about two o'clock, then go shopping for something for the baby. He would take the gift over to his mother's house on his way home.

When he arrived at work at eight o'clock Saturday morning, Christina was already there. She grinned at him, a gleam of triumph shining in her eyes.

He pushed aside his irritation. He and Christina had been playing this unacknowledged game for weeks— each one trying to beat the other one into the office. It seemed to Kent that no matter how early he got there, Christina was always there first. Kent had finally decided that being the victor in this subtle game of one-upmanship wasn't worth the aggravation, so now he came to work when he was ready to come, no matter when he thought Christina might be there. If she wanted to spend her time trying to best him, fine. Obviously she felt she had something to prove. He didn't.

"Sleep in?" she asked lazily. She was leaning back in her chair, her long legs propped up on the conference table. Today she wore tight jeans and a striped knit top that hugged her body. Weekends were always casual at the office. Kent was wearing jeans, too, along with a dark cotton shirt and deck shoes.

"No," he said.

"I tried to call you last night." Swinging her legs down, she leaned forward and propped her elbows on the table. Papers were spread out in front of her.

"I know. I got your message." Kent tossed his briefcase on the table.

"Why didn't you call me back?" The question was voiced casually, but Kent knew it wasn't a casual question.

"I got home late." He knew she was dying to ask where he'd been. He refused to volunteer the information. It was none of her business. They were not engaged or anything close to it. "I'm going to go get a cup of coffee. Do you want some?" he said.

"No." She looked about to say something more, but she didn't.

Acting as if everything were perfectly normal, he walked out the door and down the hall to the coffee room. He'd be damned if he was going to let Christina make him feel guilty. He had nothing to feel guilty about. He poured himself a cup of coffee, added two sugars and stirred. He leaned back against the countertop and took a sip. He'd give her a few minutes before going back to the conference room.

"Hey, Kent, how's it going?"

Kent looked up, smiling at Paul Castleman, another of the younger associates at the firm. "Hey, Paul! It's going great. How's it going with you?"

Paul shrugged. "Okay, I guess. But I'm bored. I wish I'd get assigned to something exciting like the Wilder case. They've still got me doing deposition summaries on the capitol land-lease deal. You're a lucky son of a gun, you know that?"

Kent grinned. "You sound like Joel Bartlett. He said the same thing last night."

"So," Paul asked, "do you think you'll get to do any courtroom work?"

"Are you serious?" Associates never got to do courtroom work, and Paul knew it. The best Kent and Christina and Paul and others like them could hope for was an interesting case, because they would always be assigned to do legwork, which meant research and interviewing. Courtroom work was always done by the senior guns in the office. Kent was always amused when he watched TV shows where young lawyers in a firm actually got to try cases in court because he knew that kind of thing never happened in real life. It was simply there for dramatic effect. In truth, a young lawyer's life was usually very humdrum and monotonous.

Although—and he had no intention of telling Paul this —Colin Jamieson *had* dangled a carrot in front of Kent's nose more than once since he'd been assigned to work under him, saying things like "maybe we'll let you get your feet wet on this case because we've got plans for you, and this will be good experience." But Kent knew better than to disclose that kind of information. Envy, jostling for position and back-stabbing were not unknown among the associates. There was no sense in shooting himself in the foot before he ever got out of the gate.

He and Paul talked for a few more minutes, then Kent headed back to the conference room. Christina looked up as he reentered. "I thought you got lost or something."

"Nope. Just ran into Paul Castleman."

For the next couple of hours, they worked quietly. About eleven o'clock Christina closed the reference book she'd been perusing and stretched. "I'm hungry," she announced.

Kent looked up. "Me, too. My stomach's been growling for at least an hour."

Christina grinned. "I know. I heard it. Want to send out for pizza, or should we go out for lunch?"

"We'd better send out because I've got to leave about two o'clock." Although he told himself he didn't have to explain, he added, "I've got some things to do this afternoon."

To his intense relief, she didn't question him. He watched as Christina stood and walked to the far end of the room, where she picked up the receiver of the phone sitting on the mahogany sideboard.

After a minute she asked, "What kind should I get? Pepperoni and mushroom?"

"Yeah, that sounds good."

Once the pizza was ordered, she rejoined him at the table. "They'll be here in about twenty minutes."

"Good." He reached for the reference book he'd been studying.

"Have you got plans for tonight?" she asked.

"Uh, no."

"Do you want to come to my place for dinner? I'll fix steak and onion rings," she said, naming one of his favorite meals.

"I...uh...sure."

She smiled happily. When two o'clock came, she bid him a cheerful goodbye. "I'll see you at seven," she said, blowing him a kiss as he gathered up his things.

As Kent walked out the door, he wondered why he felt so little enthusiasm for the coming evening.

Allison tucked Marianne into her crib in the pretty blue bedroom Diana had designated as the nursery and thought how glad she was they hadn't kept Marianne more than one night at the hospital. She'd hated the hospital atmosphere and was very glad to be home.

It was funny. She'd only been staying at her father's house for ten days, but she already thought of it as home. More so than she'd ever thought of her Paris apartment with Jean Luc.

Determinedly she pushed the thought of Jean Luc from her mind. Every time she thought about her late husband, she started to feel guilty again. And she didn't want to feel guilty. She'd finally started to feel better about herself now that she had apologized to Kent. She hoped he'd meant what he'd said about trying to rebuild a friendly relationship. She had half hoped he would stop by Thursday night when they got home from the hospital, but he hadn't. Maybe he would come by this weekend. She hoped so.

She smiled, thinking of Kent. He'd been so nice to her at the hospital. She wondered about his change in attitude. It had come so abruptly. One day he was cold and aloof around her. The next he had come to see Marianne and stayed talking to Allison for more than an hour.

What had happened to make him change? Allison suspected her father might have had something to do with Kent's attitude. She knew it would be entirely in character for her father to have talked to Kent about her. But that was all right. Anything that would help eliminate the awkwardness between them was welcome.

She was still thinking about Kent as she walked slowly downstairs, out to the big, high-ceilinged kitchen with its open beams and gleaming copper pots and dozens of plants.

Her father was the cook in the household, and he took great pride in his kitchen. Although he held a job of heavy responsibility as executive vice president of sales for Berringer, International, he had been known to cut a late meeting short because he was planning to make something complicated for dinner and wanted to get home and get started. Diana always laughed when she told people about Lee and his prowess in the kitchen. "That's why I married him," she would say, giving him a loving glance. "Because he kept me so well fed and I didn't want to go back to frozen dinners."

As Allison entered the kitchen, her father looked up. He was slicing onions at the counter. "Baby still sleeping?"

Allison nodded. "I thought maybe she'd wake up by now, but she's still conked out."

"Well, she's been through a lot in the past couple of days." Lee dumped the onions into a pot, added a little water and set the pot on the stove. He turned on the burner, then walked back to the counter, where he proceeded to peel and slice another large onion.

"What're you making?" Allison said. She sank into a chair at the table.

"French onion soup." He grinned at her. "I thought we'd have open-face cheese sandwiches, salad and the soup."

"Sounds wonderful." But Allison had had no real appetite for food in months.

"I'm trying to fatten you up," her father said.

"I know." He was concerned about her weight loss, and Allison wished she could reassure him. *My appetite will come back the minute I know the baby's out of danger.*

Just then the doorbell rang.

"Honey, would you get that?" Lee requested.

Allison nodded and got up, walking toward the front door. As she entered the spacious foyer, she could see a man's outline through the smoky glass panels on either side of the massive double walnut doors. As she got closer, she was sure the man was Kent. Her heart accelerated as she opened the door and he smiled down at her.

"Hi. The gate was locked so I had to come to the front door like real company," he said. He held a large wrapped package in his hands.

She returned his smile. "Come on in." Suddenly she was glad she'd worn her apricot sundress today. She knew the color looked good on her. "Dad's back in the kitchen."

"Where's Mom?"

"She went shopping with your grandmother."

Kent rolled his eyes. "I'll bet she was thrilled about that. You know what a pain Gran can be."

Allison chuckled. She and Kent had been engaged long enough for her to understand that Diana and her mother had a real love-hate relationship. Barbara Kent was a garrulous, cranky woman who was never satisfied with anything her children did or did not do for her. Once Diana had said in Allison's hearing that if her mother said ''jump'' and her daughters did, she'd then complain that they'd deserted her.

Kent followed her back to the kitchen. "Hey, Lee," he said. "You on kitchen detail again?"

"Always," Lee said. He was adding cans of beef broth to his soup pot. "Your mother really cracks the whip if I shirk my duty."

Allison smiled at the idea of anyone cracking the whip with her forceful father. Still, if anyone could do it, it would be Diana.

"Would you like something to drink?" she asked Kent.

"Have you got any iced tea?"

While she poured him a glass of tea, he sat at the kitchen table, stretching his long legs out in front of him. He set the package on the table.

Allison gave him a covert glance, admiring the way his dark cotton shirt fit his broad chest and the way the fabric of his jeans molded to his thighs.

"So Mom took Gran out, huh?" he said.

Lee grimaced. "Under duress, I might add."

Kent turned to Allison, who had reseated herself at the table. "Speaking of grandparents, how're yours doing?"

"They're fine. They're on safari in Africa right now."

"I would've thought nothing would keep them away now that you're back home."

Allison knew Kent was referring to the fact that her maternal grandparents, Howard and Jinx Marlowe, doted on her. She was their only grandchild, and from the time she was born, they had thought the sun rose and set on her. "They'd already left on this trip by the time I decided to come home."

"When are they due back?" Kent asked.

"They'll be back next Sunday, and I can't wait to see them." Her grandparents really were pretty special, she thought.

"What about your Aunt Elizabeth? She still living here in Houston?"

"Sort of. Right now she's in New Zealand."

"New Zealand! What's she doing there?"

Allison grinned. "She's got a new boyfriend. He owns a chain of newspapers in New Zealand, and she's his houseguest." Her Aunt Elizabeth was her mother's only sister and Allison's only aunt. At one time Allison had hoped her father and her aunt would get together, but that hope was dashed when Lee fell in love with Diana. Now, though, Allison was glad things had worked out the way they had. She finally realized that no one was ever going to replace her mother, and it had been foolish of her to think anyone could.

"Did you work today, Kent?" Lee asked. He carefully measured Worcestershire sauce into his soup, then added black pepper and salt.

"Yes, until about two. Then I had some errands to run and thought I'd stop by here before going home. See how Marianne is doing." He turned to Allison again. "Where is she?" He reached for the package. "I brought her something."

"Oh, thank you," Allison said, pleased by his thoughtfulness. "She's sleeping. She seems to be doing a lot of sleeping since she got home."

Disappointment clouded his eyes.

A rush of happiness flooded Allison at the realization that Kent cared about Marianne, that she was beginning to be important to him. "Do you want to go upstairs and see her?" she asked.

His eyes brightened. "I'd love to."

"Can I open the present first?"

"Sure."

Allison carefully unwrapped the box, discarding the pale yellow paper and ribbon. She parted the tissue paper inside. A gasp of pleasure escaped as she lifted out a beautiful mobile of baby animals in pastel colors. Smiling, she wound the mobile. The pure, sweet notes of "Someone to Watch over Me" floated in the air.

Her gaze met Kent's, and she smiled. "It's beautiful. Marianne will love it."

Five minutes later they stood side by side, looking down into Marianne's crib. Allison was acutely conscious of the warmth of Kent's arm brushing hers and the intimacy of being here, in the darkened nursery, with him.

Marianne slept on her side, her tiny fists clasped together under her chin. Her breathing was feather light, and her eyelashes rested like layered silk against her cheeks. Allison wondered what Kent was thinking. She wondered if he ever thought about the fact that Marianne could have been their baby, if Allison hadn't broken their engagement. Allison thought it. All the time.

Very gently Kent reached inside and touched her hand with his forefinger. Marianne stirred.

"Oops, sorry," he whispered. "I wasn't trying to wake her up."

"I know," Allison whispered back. "It's okay." They stood looking at the baby for a few more minutes, then, in silent agreement, turned and walked quietly out of the room.

Once they were safely outside, Kent said, "She's a wonderful baby."

"Thanks. I think so, too."

"You're lucky to have her."

Allison looked up at the wistful note in his voice. Their gazes met, and there was something about the expression in his eyes that caused Allison's heart to start beating like a piston again. For a long moment they said nothing, then the moment passed and they continued on their way downstairs.

Kent stayed for almost an hour. For most of that time, they sat in the kitchen and watched Lee finish up his dinner preparations. Then Kent glanced at the kitchen clock. "I'd better get going," he said, standing. "It's after five."

"Why don't you stay for dinner?" Lee suggested. "There's plenty."

Kent's glance slid to Allison. "I—I can't," he said with what sounded like real regret to her. "I've got plans."

He has a date, Allison thought, knowing she was right. He was probably taking that Christina somewhere. She fought to keep her expression neutral and said brightly, "Well, thanks for stopping by. And thank you again for the mobile."

Within minutes he was gone. But Allison couldn't banish him from her thoughts. All night long she kept wondering what he and Christina were doing at that exact moment. Then she'd get mad at herself. Did she really want to know?

Later that night, after Marianne was in bed for the night and Allison was lying in her own bedroom down

the hall, she wondered if Kent and Christina would
spend the night together.

The thought that they might gave her the emptiest
feeling—a feeling she knew she had no right to have.
She had no claims on Kent. She had broken their engagement a long time ago, and he did not belong to her.
He would never belong to her. So she might as well get
used to the idea that he would make love to other
women.

She wished with all her heart she had allowed him to
make love to her when they were engaged. At least now
she'd have those memories.

She finally fell asleep. But her dreams were filled
with images of Kent. She pictured them as they had
been on the night of their engagement party. After the
party was over, they'd walked in the backyard of her
grandparents' estate. The two of them had ended up in
the gazebo at the back of the property. It had been beautiful out, clear and warm, with millions of stars twin-
kling in the navy night. They had kissed and touched,
and their kisses had become more heated, their breathing
more rapid. Allison had finally pulled away, and soon
after Kent had gone home.

But this time, as she relived the night in her dream,
when Kent wanted to make love to her, she didn't push
him away. They made love right there, on the floor of
the gazebo, with the moonlight shining through the lat-
ticework and dappling their bodies, which soon became
slick and hot and quivering with desire.

This time, when Kent touched her, she touched him
back. When his fingers found the sensitive peaks of her
breasts, she arched into his touch and begged him for
more. When he found her most intimate places, she
didn't push him away.

And when their passion reached its zenith, Allison moaned and cried Kent's name, waking herself up.

For a long time afterward, she couldn't fall back asleep.

Chapter Six

Kent wearily sank onto the bar stool. Joel wasn't there yet, but Kent knew he'd be along in a few minutes. Their Friday-night beer together was a standing ritual, much as Kent's Sunday-morning tennis game with Bobby Halloran had become.

Sure enough, less than five minutes later Joel plopped down on the seat beside him. "Man, it's hot out there!" he said. He mopped his forehead with his handkerchief. "I sure will be glad when summer's over."

"You say that every summer," Kent said.

The bartender walked up, and Joel placed his order, then turned to Kent. "You look tired. Rough week at work?"

"Not as far as work goes."

"So what's the problem?"

Kent hesitated, but only for a moment. He grimaced. "Christina."

Joel raised his eyebrows. "I thought things were really cooking between you two."

Kent sighed. "They were, but now they're getting... complicated. I...uh...I haven't spent much time with her the past couple of weeks, and she's sore."

"She'll get over it."

"Unfortunately until she does, it's affecting our working relationship."

Joel took a swallow of his beer. "Didn't I tell you it was a mistake to get involved with someone you work with?"

"Yeah, and I wish I'd listened."

"You know, there was a time when you were really hot to trot as far as Christina was concerned. Nothing was more important than seeing her."

"Things change."

Joel gave him a thoughtful look.

"I know what you're thinking," Kent said, "and you're wrong."

"How do you know what I'm thinking?"

"Allison has nothing to do with this," Kent said. But he couldn't quite meet Joel's eyes, and he wondered what his friend was thinking. "My attraction to Christina has just run its course."

Joel raised his eyebrows. "Okay."

Kent gave him a defiant look. "Well, that does happen, you know!"

"I didn't say it didn't."

Kent stared into his beer bottle. "I thought you were my friend," he said morosely.

Joel chuckled. "I am your friend."

"Then why're you giving me such a hard time?"

"I'm not giving you a hard time. I'm just trying to

get you to face the truth. That's what friends are supposed to do.''

"No, they're not. They're supposed to be sympathetic. Say things like 'Yeah, you're right.'''

"Yeah, you're right," Joel said obediently, but there
was laughter in his voice.

Kent continued to stare glumly at his beer. He wished
he could convince Joel that he was wrong. Hell, he
wished he could convince *himself* that Joel was wrong.
Whether Kent wanted to admit it or not, Allison was
the main reason his feelings for Christina had changed.
Not that he was in love with Allison or anything. It
wasn't that. It was just that Allison's return and his re-
membrance of the way he'd felt about her had simply
emphasized to him that he didn't feel the same way
about Christina. He sighed again. "You know," he said
slowly, "maybe I should make a break with Christina."

"I agree," Joel said. "If you're no longer interested
in her, you should."

Kent grimaced. "She's not going to like it."

"No, she probably won't."

"Do you have to agree with everything I say?"

Joel laughed. "Make up your mind. A few minutes
ago you wanted me to agree with you."

"A real friend knows when to agree and when to
disagree," Kent mumbled.

"He's just mad because it turned out I was right all
the time," Joel said, grinning at Sam, the bartender, who
stood a few feet away, not even trying to pretend he
wasn't listening to their conversation.

Sam nodded sagely. "Some guys can't admit they
made a mistake."

Kent stood, pulling a couple of dollars from his
pocket and slapping them onto the bar. "That's it," he

said. "I'm not going to sit here and be insulted. I'm going home."

Joel's laughter followed him out of the bar.

Allison wasn't sleeping well. Each night before going to bed she would tell herself she wasn't going to worry and she wasn't going to dream. Yet each night, as she lay in bed and waited for sleep to claim her, she worried. And after she finally fell asleep, she dreamed.

These dreams weren't erotic, as was the one she'd had about Kent. These dreams were filled with turmoil and left her shaken and troubled.

Over and over she relived the last weeks of her marriage to Jean Luc. They were weeks filled with bitter fights and hurtful words, weeks she wished she could wipe out of her mind forever, weeks she wished had never happened.

If only she could go back and live the weeks again, so that now when she did dream about her dead husband, the dreams would be poignant and sad, but wouldn't leave her riddled with guilt.

Especially painful was the last time she had seen Jean Luc alive. He had been packing to rejoin the racing circuit in Seville, and Allison, who had been looking for a good time to tell him about her pregnancy, decided to help him by refolding his shirts. She could see he had thrown them into his suitcase with no regard for how they would look when he unpacked them.

Jean Luc was shaving; she could see him through the partially opened bathroom door. Allison lifted the shirts out of the suitcase and laid them on the bed. One by one she neatly folded them and tucked them back into the suitcase.

Then she eyed his toiletries case, which was sitting

open on the bed. She remembered that she'd purchased some of the English soap he liked so much the last time she'd gone shopping. She rummaged through the closet until she found the package. She removed one of the small, wrapped bars and put it into his toiletries case. As she withdrew her hand, a small plastic-wrapped package caught her eye.

She stared at it. Her heart began to pound in her chest as its meaning became clear to her.

Condoms.

Jean Luc had put a package of condoms in his toiletries case! Suddenly everything that was wrong in her marriage and her life erupted within. Breathing hard, she yanked the offensive packet from the toiletries case and charged into the bathroom. She pushed the door open so hard it hit Jean Luc in the back, and he cursed.

"What the devil—" Blood welled on his cheek where he had nicked himself.

"Just what were these doing in your toiletries case?" she demanded, shoving the packet under his nose. "Why would a married man need condoms on a trip where he won't be accompanied by his wife?" Her voice was shaking with fury.

Instead of apologizing or making up some excuse, Jean Luc raised his eyebrows in that infuriatingly superior way of his and said, "What I choose to pack is no business of yours."

"No business of mine!" Without thinking, she raised her hand and slapped him as hard as she could.

His blue eyes glittered with fury as he caught her right wrist in his strong hand. "Don't ever do that again," he said through gritted teeth, "or I won't be responsible for what happens to you."

"You—you...bastard!" Allison sputtered, so angry

she couldn't find words to express how she felt. His casual dismissal of their marriage vows, his blatant disregard for her feelings, his refusal to even pretend he was sorry—all sickened her.

He continued to grip her wrist so hard it hurt, and the tendons of his bare arm stood out like ridges on a washboard. Voice full of contempt, he said, ''Perhaps American women can call their husbands names and strike their husbands at will, but Frenchmen won't stand for such behavior. I suggest you go into the bedroom and calm yourself down.''

Allison stared at him. She had known Jean Luc didn't love her the way she had once thought—hoped—he would. But this cold indifference, this total absence of feeling on his part, caused her heart to freeze. Suddenly all her fears were confirmed. Her marriage was a total sham.

To think she had been going to tell him her news. She had actually hoped that knowing they were going to have a child would make a difference to him, would magically heal her diseased marriage. Now she knew nothing would make a difference. Jean Luc didn't love her, and she didn't love him. Worse, he didn't respect her.

And she didn't respect him.

Allison's remaining innocence completely disappeared that day. She didn't answer Jean Luc, and after a moment he loosened his hold on her wrist. Allison rubbed it, then turned and, head held high, walked slowly out of the bathroom. She would not give him the satisfaction of running away. She walked out of the bedroom, down the hall and into the library, shutting the door behind her. She walked to the long casement window that overlooked the small park across from their apartment building. It was raining—a soft autumn rain—and through the wet glass she watched the people on the street below. Their colorful umbrellas bobbed as they walked along the leaf-strewn boulevard. Across the street, standing up against the wrought-iron fence that rimmed the park, a flower vendor—oblivious to the rain—hawked her wares.

As Allison stared out the window, she decided that when Jean Luc returned from Seville, she would tell him she wanted a divorce. She refused to consider what she would do if he said no.

An hour later he was gone. He never said goodbye. She heard the muffled noise that meant he had carried his bags into the foyer. She heard a low conversation between him and Madame Bergeron, their housekeeper. Then, minutes later, she heard the doorbell and, glancing down, saw a taxi stopped in front of the building.

She watched through the window as Jean Luc and the driver emerged, watched as they loaded Jean Luc's bags in the taxi, watched as Jean Luc climbed in the back and watched as the taxi sped away down the street.

Jean Luc didn't look back once.

After his taxi was no longer in sight, Allison walked back into their bedroom and, dry-eyed, looked around. She knew that she and Jean Luc would never share their canopied bed again. They would never be a couple again. Their marriage was over. She knew she should feel awful. Yet she didn't. All she felt right then was relief that she could finally admit to herself that she didn't care.

In fact, she hoped she'd never have to lay eyes on Jean Luc again.

Two days later she was notified of Jean Luc's death. The sensible, rational part of her brain told her it wasn't her fault Jean Luc had been killed. But the other part—the emotional, irrational part—told her that maybe, just maybe, if she had told him about the baby, if they'd had a loving parting instead of a bitter one, if Jean Luc had known he was going to be a father—he would have been more careful.

And worst of all, if she hadn't wished never to see him again, maybe he would still be alive.

She knew she was being ridiculous. She knew she hadn't caused his race car to crash and burn. She knew his death wasn't her fault.

Still, she felt guilty. She felt guilty because she hadn't been able to love him the way she should have, and maybe that was why he couldn't be faithful to her. Perhaps he had sensed that her feelings weren't what they should be.

She had never told Jean Luc about Kent.

But she wondered if he'd known, anyway.

On the day of the race, had he been thinking about their fight? Was that why his concentration had slipped? Was that the reason he'd crashed? On and on her thoughts whirled with questions to which there were no answers.

Since then, no matter how many times she told herself none of it was her fault, a tiny part of Allison had always felt responsible for Jean Luc's death. Just as she now felt responsible for Marianne's problems.

So she hovered over Marianne, and the tension she felt transmitted itself to the baby, causing a negative effect. She cried more than normal, and even when sleeping, whimpered from time to time.

Allison knew this was bad for Marianne, but she felt powerless to change things. She just couldn't stop worrying. And nothing her father or Diana did to try to distract her worked.

Even the two visits Kent made to the house in the weeks after Marianne came home didn't seem to help because they were such impersonal visits. He dropped in. He asked about the baby. He was thoughtful and concerned about her welfare. But that was it. He and Allison were never alone together, and they made no progress toward establishing a more personal relationship.

She didn't think they ever would.

On Saturday afternoon, two weeks after Marianne had come home from the hospital, Allison, Lee and Diana were relaxing in the TV room when Kent stopped by on his way home from work. He walked into the middle of a discussion between Allison and her father—a discussion where Lee was urging her to get out more.

"What's the matter?" Kent asked.

"She's hovering over the baby too much," Lee explained. "She needs to get out of the house."

"I agree," Diana said gently. "It's not good for either you or Marianne to spend all your time with her. Why don't you call Marcy? Maybe go out to dinner and a movie?"

"No, really, I'm okay," Allison protested. She felt uncomfortable continuing this discussion in front of Kent.

"You're not okay," her father insisted. "All anyone has to do is look at you to see how stressed you are." He turned to Kent. "Don't you think so, Kent?"

Kent nodded thoughtfully. He seemed to consider a moment, then said, "Why don't I take you out to dinner tomorrow night?"

Both Allison and Diana stared at him. Lee grinned. "That's a great idea!" he said happily.

"You don't have to do that," Allison said. Her heart was thumping madly, and she wondered if she was blushing, because her face felt hot. Oh, Lord. What if Kent thought she had been maneuvering to get him to ask her out? She could have strangled her father.

"I know I don't have to," Kent said. He glanced at his mother, whose expression was noncommittal.

Allison thought she knew what Diana was thinking. "I can't leave Marianne," Allison said hurriedly.

"Of course you can," Lee said.

Finally Diana stirred herself. "Why can't you?" she asked. "Your father and I are here. Don't you trust us to watch her?"

Kent waited expectantly, and Allison wondered if pity was all that had prompted the invitation. She hoped he hadn't felt obligated to ask her, after what her father had said. What should she do? She desperately wanted to go. But part of her was afraid to. And it wasn't just fear of leaving Marianne, either. It was fear of the unknown. Fear of what would happen. Fear of what might be said. She swallowed nervously. "I...of course I trust you," she said to Diana. "I—"

"It's settled then," her father said. "You're going."

Allison's gaze met Kent's, and he smiled.

She knew she was lost.

All day Sunday Allison counted the minutes until seven-thirty, the time set for Kent to pick her up. Now she had something new to worry about.

What to wear.

She tried on outfit after outfit, discarding them mostly

because nothing fit her properly any longer. Finally she settled on a forest green silk dress with a short, flared skirt, cap sleeves and a deep V neckline. With it she wore her thick gold necklace, a gold bangle bracelet and the heavy gold hoop earrings her Aunt Elizabeth had given her. And tonight, because it was a special night, she wore the large emerald ring her grandparents had given her for her eighteenth birthday.

She looked at herself in the mirror at least ten times, smoothing back her hair, touching up her makeup, wondering if her green eye shadow was too faint, then deciding it wasn't.

Finally seven-thirty came. After giving Marianne another kiss, she relinquished the baby to Diana's waiting arms, then walked slowly downstairs to meet Kent.

He stood in the wide foyer and watched her come down the stairs. He was wearing light gray dress slacks, a dark blue sport coat and a white shirt open at the collar. His dark hair was carefully brushed, and he looked casually elegant and so handsome he took her breath away.

When she reached floor level, he smiled down at her. "Hi."

Her silly heart decided to play leapfrog in her chest. "Hi," she said, knowing she sounded breathless and wishing she could be more casual and cool about this date. Stop thinking of it as a date, she told herself. You know why he invited you to dinner. He feels sorry for you. No more. No less.

Diana had walked downstairs, too, and held Marianne in her arms. Kent touched the baby's nose. "Hi, cutie," he said. "How're you feeling tonight?"

"She's had a good day today," Diana said.

Allison met Diana's gaze. "Now, if she should happen to—"

Diana interrupted her with a short laugh. "Allison, would you quit worrying? I know what to do."

"You know where Dr. Richardson's number is, don't you?" Allison persisted, already sorry she'd said she'd go tonight.

"Yes, I know where the doctor's number is." Diana rolled her eyes at Kent. "Would you get her out of here before she drives me crazy?"

With a laugh he took Allison's arm and steered her out the front door. The heat of the day still hovered in the air of the late-July evening. An army of cicadas sang as they walked to Kent's car, and the air was filled with the scent of newly mown grass. In the distance Allison heard the shouts of several children at play. Overhead, the sky had turned that hazy shade of lavender that signaled twilight, Allison's favorite time of day. She'd always thought that the world was a softer, more forgiving place at twilight, filled with a sense of peace that was missing at other times.

Her arm tingled where Kent's warm hand touched it, and when he opened the passenger door of the Corvette and helped her inside, she felt all shivery. So many memories came flooding back as he got into the car and she was surrounded by the scent of his after-shave, a subtle blend that reminded her of ocean breezes and warm sand. How many times had they been together like this in the intimate confines of a car?

"This is a nice car," she said as Kent turned the key in the ignition, put the Corvette in gear and began to back out of the driveway.

"Thanks. I like it."

"Um, where are we going?" she asked as she tried to quell her nervousness.

He shifted again, and the car shot forward. "I made reservations at Brennan's." There was an underlying tension in the casual admission. "I hope you don't mind."

"Why should I mind?" But she knew why. He had asked her to marry him after a dinner at Brennan's. She knew he was referring to that evening—remembering it, just as she was. "I love Brennan's," she added, wanting to dispel the sudden tension. Yet she wondered why he would purposely evoke it. Why pick Brennan's when there were so many other restaurants dotting the city? Did Kent want her to remember? She swallowed nervously. Oh, God. Why had she agreed to come tonight? What was going on?

They didn't talk much during the remainder of the drive downtown. Instead, Allison looked out her window and concentrated on relaxing. As usual, there were hundreds of joggers running in Memorial Park as the Corvette cruised down Memorial Drive. As they neared downtown, Allison admired the Houston skyline off to the right—an inky silhouette against the amethyst sky. She had always thought the city's skyline could hold its own against any city's, including some that were more renowned. She particularly enjoyed the modernistic twin peaks of the Pennzoil Building and the Dutch Renaissance look of the NCNB Building.

"Impressive, isn't it?" Kent said, breaking the silence.

"Yes."

"Glad you're back?"

Allison sighed. "Yes, I am. I just wish it were under happier circumstances." She wished she had nerve enough to ask him if he was glad she was back, too. Once she might have, but she had changed since that earlier, more self-assured time. Now she felt too uncertain of Kent's feelings and motives. Except for momentary flashes of emotion, he had given her no indication he was interested in anything except a family-type friendship between them.

Silence fell between them again, and Allison gazed out the window until they drew abreast of Brennan's.

"I see a parking place up the street," Kent said. "Do you mind walking? I don't trust these guys who valet park cars."

Allison grinned. Men were the same the world over when it came to their cars.

That quivery feeling of part excitement, part nervousness, returned as Kent helped her out of the car and kept his hand on her arm until they entered the restaurant. Another flood of memories engulfed Allison as she stood in the dimly lit entrance foyer and they waited to be seated. She glanced at the bowl of pralines sitting on the high table to their left, remembering how Kent had laughingly taken three of them as they exited the restaurant that night years ago.

"Kent!" she'd said, scandalized.

"What did I do?" he'd shot back, grinning with a little-boy innocent look that half exasperated, half enchanted her. "Nobody saw me," he whispered in her ear as they'd walked into the star-encrusted night.

Oh, I was such a fool to leave him.

"This way, please," the hostess said, breaking into Allison's poignant memory. She led them into the main dining room to her right.

Ten minutes later they were seated next to each other at a window table, overlooking the street. At least this was different, Allison thought in relief. The night they'd become engaged, they'd been seated at a window over-looking the inner courtyard.

For the next five minutes, Allison struggled to relax and deliberately avoided Kent's eyes. As the service people swirled around them, she wondered if Kent felt as uncomfortable as she did. She was grateful when their waiter came and took their drink order and gave them menus. That gave her something to look at, and she pretended to study the menu.

When their drinks arrived, Allison sipped at her wine, still avoiding Kent's gaze. She tried to think of some-thing innocuous to say. She and Kent would never dis-pel the awkwardness between them completely. She'd been fooled into thinking they would because she'd grown comfortable around him at the house.

But this. This was different. This was old turf. Turf that stirred memories that should be kept buried. Mem-ories that could do nothing but hurt her because they so sharply reminded her of what she'd lost.

"Allison?"

Slowly, reluctantly, Allison lifted her gaze and looked into Kent's eyes.

"This was a mistake, wasn't it?" he said.

Allison's heart went *thump, thump, thump.* She wet her lips.

"I shouldn't have brought you here. Do you want to leave?"

His eyes gleamed in the lamplight, never leaving her face. She shook her head. "No. I'm okay."

"Are you sure?"

"Yes." She would make sure she was okay. She would not embarrass herself or him. She was a woman of the world, wasn't she? She could handle this. She had handled much worse.

Still holding her gaze, he nodded. "Okay. But after dinner, I think we'd better talk."

"Talk?" Now her heart was going double-time: *thump-thump, thump-thump, thump-thump*.

"Yes. I think we've got some scores to settle, don't you?"

Chapter Seven

Scores to settle.

All through dinner, Allison thought about what Kent had said. She had known they would have to talk eventually. Just because she'd apologized didn't mean she was off the hook. Kent deserved a complete explanation of what had happened three and a half years ago, and she'd always known she'd have to give it to him.

It was going to be hard to talk about the past, but it really was best to get everything out in the open. That would be the only way they could possibly go forward.

She was almost relieved when dinner was over. She had hardly tasted her pasta-and-shrimp dish, even though Brennan's was famous for its Creole- and Cajun-inspired food.

Finally they were ready to leave. As they walked out together into the warm, humid night air, Kent said, ''I know a little piano bar where it's pretty quiet and we can talk. Is that okay with you?''

''Yes, that's fine.''

Half an hour later they were seated across from each other in a dark booth. Allison had just called home and after being assured by Diana that Marianne was sleeping and doing fine, she had rejoined Kent. Now they looked at each other. Kent didn't say anything. Gathering her courage, Allison said, ''You're still angry with me, aren't you?''

He cupped his hands around his glass of Baileys liqueur and looked down. He shrugged. ''I'm trying not to be.''

''I know. And I appreciate that. But I feel your anger. And really…I—I guess I don't blame you. I know I hurt you. But, you know, Kent, I'm not sure I'm solely to blame for what happened.''

His gaze slowly met hers.

Before she lost her nerve, she plunged on. ''I've thought about this a lot. I know I was selfish and self-centered, and I know I was a fool to have run off like that, but I think there was a basic problem between us that had nothing to do with what kind of job you accepted.''

Now she really had his attention. She could see it in the way he sat a little taller and in the way his eyes had locked with hers.

''What kind of basic problem?'' he said.

''I don't think we ever really listened to each other.''

He seemed to consider her statement for a moment, then said slowly, ''Would you explain that?''

''Well, think about it. You were talking. I was talking. But did we really hear what the other one was saying?''

He shrugged. "Maybe not." He twirled his glass in his hands, and Allison's gaze was drawn to them. She admired the way they looked—strong and solid, with long fingers and neatly trimmed nails. She thought about all the times those hands had touched her. And all the ways. Casually. And not so casually. She remembered how good they'd felt, how much she'd welcomed his touch. As the memories flooded her, she wished…no. There was no sense wishing. What was past was past. They couldn't go back in time.

"You hurt me, you know," he said, still rotating the glass. "I was a real mess after you left." His direct gaze held hers, and his hands stilled.

The moment trembled between them. There was so much to say. So much pain to heal. So much to atone for. Allison's chest felt tight as the weight of the past pressed down on her. Striving for calm, she murmured, "I was a real mess, too."

"Why?" he said, urgency and bewilderment in his voice. "Why did you just take off like that? Why wouldn't you talk to me? I tried to see you, you know."

"I know." Allison was fighting tears. She took a deep breath, hoping it was too dark in the bar for Kent to know how close she was to breaking down. She mustn't break down. She mustn't.

"Your grandmother said you didn't want to talk to me." All the bitterness and pain he must have felt at the time pulsed in his voice.

She had been staying with her grandparents at the time of their breakup. She remembered that awful morning. "I didn't."

"But why not? I've never understood that." His gaze pinned hers.

He had such honest eyes. They demanded a corresponding honesty from her. "I—I think I was afraid to see you."

"Afraid of *me?*"

"No, no, not afraid of you! Afraid of my own weakness as far as you were concerned."

"I don't understand."

"I'm not sure I do, either." How could she explain her flawed reasoning? She'd mulled it all over so many times, and she still wasn't sure she understood it completely. Trying to formulate her answer, she sipped at her Kahlúa.

Finally she said, "It's complicated, but I've thought about this a lot. I was so set in my idea of the way our life would be. I pictured you working for Keating & Shaw...making lots of money."

She spoke slowly, thoughtfully. This was so important. She had to try to make him understand the way her brain had worked. "I had it all worked out. I pictured myself coming to watch you work in court. Meeting you downtown for lunch. I saw us living in a beautiful house, with me giving elegant dinner parties. I could just see all of our friends...your associates and their wives...coming and going. The two of us getting written up in B. J. Barrette's column."

Kent's face twisted in the semblance of a smile.

She sighed. "You know...up-and-coming young lawyer and his wife. I had it all planned. The perfect marriage. The total package." Allison bit her lip. "I had been prepared for a life like the one I've described all of my life. And when you talked about opening the storefront office, I just couldn't see it. I thought...I don't know what I thought."

Their gazes met and held. She closed her eyes briefly, then opened them again. His eyes hadn't wavered. Be honest, she reminded herself. "Okay. I do know what I thought. I thought you'd change your mind."

He looked at her for a long time. Piano music and the muted conversations of the other patrons of the bar surrounded them. Finally he spoke. "And I thought you'd change yours."

"Yes! That's what I've been trying to tell you. Neither of us was really listening. I couldn't see your vision. And I know now that you couldn't see mine. Anyway, I didn't want to give up that picture in my mind. I didn't want to concede, in any way, that you might be right to follow your dream. I didn't want to compromise. So I closed my eyes to reality...." She laughed without mirth. "Isn't that funny? I'd accused you of being a romantic and prided myself on my realism, and there I was, completely ignoring reality and indulging my own foolish, romantic dreams."

"Allison—"

"No. Let me finish. I kept telling myself you would see the error of your ways. That if you really loved me, you'd take the job with Keating & Shaw." Again, she met his gaze squarely. "And then, when I went to Paris, I told myself that if you *really* cared, you'd come after me."

What was he thinking? she wondered as her words flowed between them, pulsing in the air like static electricity.

"I thought about coming after you."

The quiet admission caused her heart to leap. "You did?"

He nodded. "But I guess pride kept me away. I told myself you didn't really love me if you could throw away what we had so easily."

Pride.

Yes, she thought. Pride got in my way, too. She had taken a stand and couldn't back down. Oh, God. What a mess we made of things. We hurt each other so much. And for what?

"Kent," she said haltingly, "there's something I have to ask you."

"Ask away."

"Why did you give up your storefront practice?"

He grimaced. "It's ironic, really. It didn't take long for me to realize your father was right all along."

"What do you mean?"

"Once he told me that I had some kind of romantic dream of being a modern-day Don Quixote. And he was right. I did. You say you had a picture in your mind. Well, I did, too. Only my picture was very different from yours. I saw myself as the champion of the down-trodden. Riding in on a white horse and taking on all comers. Defending innocent people who couldn't afford high-priced lawyers. Going up against the establishment and winning. Truth and honor besting the big guys." He laughed, the sound derisive and cynical. "Talk about being naive! Jesus, it's no wonder I got shot down!"

It hurt her to hear him. For so long she had comforted herself with the thought that his dream had come true. She didn't want to know that even when your intentions were completely unselfish, things could sometimes go wrong. Right didn't always come out on top. "What happened?"

He shook his head, then drained his glass of Baileys. "Well, my disenchantment with the storefront wasn't sudden. It came gradually...over a period of two years. I don't know. I got so tired of plea bargains and deals. Drugs and poverty. It all began to seem so hopeless to me. As if no matter what I did, nothing would ever change. You know, gridlock is the name of the game. And then came the straw that broke the camel's back.''

Allison waited quietly.

''I took on this case. A young girl named Jessie. She'd been accused of selling crack. She was a single mother, two small kids. She brought the kids with her when she came to see me. They looked so pathetic with their big eyes and scared faces. Jessie pleaded with me. 'I'm innocent,' she said. 'I can't go to jail. Who'll watch my kids?' The kids were clinging to her hands, looking at me. And Jessie—'' he made a sound of disgust, a cross between a laugh and a snort ''—you should have seen her. She looked like a kid herself. Hell, she is a kid. She was a mother at fourteen. Even now she's only twenty-one. Well, anyway, the police had no real evidence against her. Everything they had was circumstantial. Damned incriminating, but still circumstantial. Anyway, to make a long story short, I got her off. Afterward I found out she really *had* been selling crack. In fact, I found out she had no intention of stopping. She bragged about it. Was proud of how she'd fooled everyone, including me.''

His gaze met Allison's again. ''When I found out that I'd worked my tail off for a woman who didn't give a damn about her kids or anything but selling enough crack to keep herself supplied, I just lost it. I couldn't believe it. I'd put everything—heart and soul—into defending her. I'd believed her. Believed in her. And all the time she'd been lying to me. I mean, who needed it? I finally wised up. If I was gonna bust my ass, I might as well be making money while I was doing it.''

Allison wanted to reach out and take his hands in hers. Even when she'd berated him for his idealism, that quality was one of the reasons she'd loved him so much.

Why didn't I realize it before? she asked herself. "So you went to work for Keating & Shaw after all."

"Yep. Like I said, I finally wised up."

"Do you like working for them?"

"Yeah, I like it fine," he said quickly. Too quickly, she thought. "Of course, I've had to readjust my thinking."

"In what way?"

"Well, now I'm on the side of the big guys usually."

"And how do you feel about that?"

"I feel fine about it. Why shouldn't I? I'm doing what a lawyer is supposed to do—protecting my client's interests. That's what they pay me to do."

Allison nodded, but she heard the note of defensiveness in his voice. "What kinds of cases have you worked on?" Somehow she just couldn't picture Kent getting fired up about defending big oil companies or the like.

"All kinds. Right now I'm assigned to a personal-injury case against one of our biggest clients."

"Tell me about it."

"Are you really interested?"

"Yes, I am." She needed to know. She needed to see if her instincts were right, if he was just pretending to be happy.

Allison listened carefully as he told her about Emmett Wilder and the suit that had been brought against him. She listened not just to Kent's words, but to all the nuances of his tone and all the things she imagined he wasn't saying.

"Anyway," Kent finished, "we're still in the process of discovery, so right now I'm going over all the records relating to the design of the bike and preparing to interview the members of the design team. We don't want any surprises in court.''

''I'm assuming there was a flaw in the design of the bike.''

''Yes. That's why Petrowski crashed.''

''Do you think Wilder knew about the flaw?''

''He says he didn't.''

''What if he *was* guilty? Could you still defend him?''

''Well, he's not, so the question isn't relevant.''

''But just for the sake of argument, what if he was?''

''It's my job to give my client the best possible defense. No more. No less.''

''Guilty or not?''

''Guilty or not.''

Allison stared at him. ''That—that doesn't sound like you.''

''What doesn't sound like me?''

''I—I just never imagined you could feel that way. That you could defend someone, guilty or not.''

''Allison, that's what a lawyer does.'' He laughed, a short, harsh sound. ''What did you think when you were urging me to go to work for Keating & Shaw? That I'd be defending little old ladies who got hit by trucks? The truth is, most lawyers are defending big companies who want to keep their losses at a minimum.''

''But Kent...how can you feel good about defending someone who is making money off someone else's misery?''

''Hey, if it weren't for misery, there'd be no lawyers!''

Allison couldn't prevent what she knew was a stricken look from crossing her face.

"Oh, hell," he said with a sigh. "That's just an old, tired joke. I was only kidding. Don't look like that."

Allison hated the cynicism she heard in his voice. This was not the old Kent. This was not the Kent who could no more defend a guilty man than he could torture an animal. She wasn't sure she even knew this Kent. It was going to be very hard for her to accept the changes in him. From white knight in blue jeans to a take-the-money-and-run guy in an expensive suit. Surely, buried deep beneath this new, hard shell was the Kent she had known and loved—the compassionate, warm, caring man who wanted to save the world. She had to believe this was true. She *did* believe this was true.

People have let him down. Too many people, including me. That's why he pretends not to care. He cares. He's just put up walls to protect himself. Slowly the hope grew that maybe, since she'd been one of the ones who'd been responsible for the walls, she could be a major catalyst in bringing the walls down again.

"So now that I've told you about me, why don't we talk about you?" he said.

Allison had been afraid the conversation would get around to her. But fair was fair. He deserved his turn. "What do you want to know?"

"Why did you marry Fornier? Did you love him?"

Allison bowed her head so she didn't have to see his eyes. Now was the moment of truth. "I thought I did." When Kent didn't answer, she looked up. "I married him on the rebound."

He nodded slowly.

"It—it wasn't a very happy marriage. And I blame myself for that."

"Do you want to talk about it?"

She shook her head. "No. It's over with. I made a

mistake, but Jean Luc is dead, so there's really no sense in dredging it all up again.'' She knew he deserved more than this inadequate explanation, but she just couldn't talk about her marriage tonight. Maybe after Marianne's surgery. After the baby was well. After Allison no longer felt so guilty. Maybe then she'd be ready to open herself up and let Kent see all her scars.

Keeping her face carefully blank, she picked up her purse from the seat beside her. ''It's getting late, Kent. I should be getting home. I don't want to leave Marianne too long.'' She knew if she brought Marianne's name into the conversation, Kent would give her no argument.

''Okay, sure.''

As they walked out into the velvety night air, Kent said, ''I'm glad we talked.''

Allison drew a deep breath. ''Yes. Me, too.'' But they weren't through talking. She knew it. And she knew he knew it, too.

Kent drove slowly. He didn't want the evening to end. Tonight, for the first time since Allison's return, he felt almost relaxed in her company. He was very glad they had made a beginning at clearing the air. He still wasn't sure he understood her reasons for running away the way she had, but at least they were talking to each other again. Really talking.

Allison had changed, he thought as he glanced at her profile. She had matured. She had left Houston a girl; now she was a woman. He guessed that wasn't surprising after all she'd been through. He liked her new maturity. Wistfully he wondered if things would have been different if they'd met now instead of years ago.

As if she sensed his look, she turned, smiling slightly.

He'd inserted a CD by Harry Connick, Jr., and the mellow jazz floated in the air between them. He smiled back.

It was nice having her here in his car. Like old times. He smiled wryly. Well, not exactly like old times. When they'd been engaged, she had usually insisted that he drive her little sports car—a present from her Marlowe grandparents—instead of his battered old Honda. He guessed if he'd been thinking with his brains instead of his hormones, he'd have realized that Allison would never be contented with anything but the best.

Even the ring he'd given her had symbolized the differences between them. He had intended to give her a small but tasteful diamond, but the look on her face when she'd seen the array of modest stones had changed his mind for him. And fast. He'd ended by buying her a one-and-a-half-carat ring that he could ill afford. In fact, he'd used a large portion of his seed money for the storefront, which meant he'd had to start up his business with much less capital than he'd hoped.

He still had that ring. He'd intended to take it back, knowing Sedgewick Mason, the jeweler who'd sold it to him, would have given him a full refund. Sedgewick was a friend of his mother's. But somehow he never had. He wondered what Allison would say if she knew. She would probably be astounded at his sentimentality. Maybe not, though. After all, as she'd pointed out, she had once accused him of being a hopeless romantic, whereas she prided herself on her more pragmatic approach to life.

His thoughts continued in this vein until he turned onto the street where Lee's home was located. It wasn't very late, but most of the large homes, which sat far back on the wooded lots, were dark. Kent pulled into the long driveway and stopped just outside the gate. Lee had purchased the house before he and Diana married, and he'd once told Kent he especially liked its location—at the curve of a cul-de-sac that backed up to Buffalo Bayou.

Kent helped Allison out of the car, and after unlocking the gate, they walked together into the walled courtyard and up to the double walnut doors. The two lamps mounted on either side of the massive doors bathed them in pools of gold as they stopped under their soft glow.

The heavy scent of summer roses filled the air, and through the tall pine trees that dotted the grounds, a full moon spilled pearls of light. In the woods bordering the bayou, Kent could hear the rustle of small feet—probably chipmunks or squirrels, he thought, although once his mother had come face-to-face with a skunk at the back of their property. He chuckled, remembering Lee's laughing description of Diana's shriek and headlong flight into his arms.

"What are you grinning about?" Allison asked.

"Oh, just remembering when my mother saw a skunk out here."

"Out here!" She moved instinctively closer, looking around in obvious alarm.

He laughed again, but he felt a warm pleasure at her basic assumption that he would protect her. Without thinking, he placed his hands on her shoulders, feeling the warm, firm flesh under the thin silk of her dress. Suddenly a sizzling awareness arched between them, and Allison slowly raised her head.

In the golden light her eyes shone like polished stone. Her scent, something fresh and light as raindrops, drifted around him. Her face, partly in shadow, partly illuminated, looked so familiar and so achingly lovely. Her mouth—a mouth that had always begged to be kissed, with its full, sensuous lips—was slightly open, waiting. Inviting. Tempting.

His hands tightened on her shoulders, and he felt her tremble.

He wanted to kiss her.

He knew he shouldn't.

He knew nothing would be solved or changed or worked out by giving in to this powerful physical attraction he still felt for her.

He also knew she wanted him to kiss her.

He lowered his head, and the moment his lips met hers, the moment he tasted the unique essence that was Allison, he was lost. He folded her into his arms and kissed her as if there would be no tomorrow. He kissed her like a dying man who was eating his last meal and intended to extract the last drop of satisfaction and enjoyment from it. He kissed her as if he would never have a chance to kiss her again.

And she kissed him back. She never resisted him at all. She wound her arms around his neck and welcomed him. She gave herself so sweetly and so thoroughly that his blood pounded through his veins and his heart galloped in his chest and his entire body felt dazed and drugged and discombobulated.

They clung to each other, and he could feel the soft curves of her body aligned against his and his body's corresponding reaction. His hands roamed her back, then dropped to cup her rounded bottom and pull her tightly against him so she could feel how much he wanted her.

He might never have pulled away. He might have continued kissing her and touching her until there was

no question of stopping. But when he forced her awareness of his arousal, she abruptly pulled away. She was
breathing hard, and Kent felt as if he'd been hit by a
train.

"Kent, I—I don't think we should do this."

Still stunned and shaken by feelings he'd thought
he'd put behind him, he said stiffly, "I guess I misunderstood. It won't happen again."

"Please, Kent, don't be angry. I—I just need some
time. I'm too confused about everything and too worried
about Marianne. I can't handle anything else right
now."

Kent knew she was right. He wanted to stay aloof.
Act as if he couldn't care less that she had withdrawn.
Again. But he heard the genuine misery in her voice.
And he knew she was being honest with him. Sighing
with regret, he kissed her cheek gently, resisting the
impulse to run his lips over its petal-soft surface.
"You're right, of course," he said. "I was out of line."

"No! I don't want you to think that. You weren't out
of line. I—I wanted you to kiss me. But…everything is
happening too fast. I need time to think. And I think
you do, too."

Chapter Eight

Allison lay awake a long time. She relived every moment of her evening with Kent, especially the kiss he'd given her and the strength of her reaction to it.

She had never dreamed she would feel that way again. She had never imagined that Kent—with one plundering kiss—would unleash all those needs and desires that had lain so long unfulfilled. She had never believed that the physical attraction she'd always felt for Kent could be so easily rekindled.

One kiss.

One stunning, earth-moving kiss.

She almost laughed. Would have laughed if there'd been anything to laugh about.

She still loved him. And she still wanted him. But giving in to this want, to this love, would be madness. Because even though they'd made a beginning tonight, they had not worked out all the old problems. There was still a lot of hurtful stuff between them. And until they understood it and could overcome it, starting a physical relationship would only complicate matters.

And Allison did not need another complication in her life. Marianne and her physical problems were complication enough. Marianne had to be Allison's only consideration right now. Allison and Kent and their troubled past and uncertain future could drain none of Allison's needed energy.

So, regretfully, as much as Allison might want to explore whether she and Kent could ever regain what they'd lost, she knew she'd been right to call a halt tonight. She simply couldn't take on a highly charged emotional involvement. For now, anyway, they had to cool it. She resolved to tell Kent her decision the next time she saw him.

But right before she fell asleep, she admitted to herself that it was going to be hard—very hard—to keep to her good resolutions.

When Kent arrived home after his dinner date with Allison, he saw the message light blinking on his answering machine. He pressed the Play button, then began to undress.

"Damn you, Kent! Where are you?" Christina's angry voice filled the room. "Did you forget we were using the Astros' tickets tonight?"

Kent stopped in the process of unbuttoning his shirt. Holy sh— He broke off the thought as Christina's tirade continued unabated. After a string of curses he'd never heard her use before, he heard the click as she hung up. He sank into the nearest chair and closed his eyes. He couldn't believe it, but he had completely forgotten he and Christina had made plans to use the firm's box seats for tonight's Astros game. He hadn't seen her all day yesterday, and she hadn't reminded him on Friday. But that was no excuse. They had talked about it earlier in the week. He couldn't imagine how he could have forgotten.

Oh, boy. He was really going to get a piece of her mind tomorrow. He wasn't looking forward to it. And he could just imagine what she'd say if she knew he had taken Allison out instead.

He opened his eyes, staring sightlessly at the far wall. He couldn't tell her. He would have to lie. But should he lie? Only pond scum lied about something like that. Wouldn't it be better to be honest? Take his lumps? He'd been thinking he should break off with Christina, anyway, and wasn't this the perfect time to do it? She could yell at him, call him names and save face. She could break off with him, instead of vice versa.

Or maybe not. Maybe he should tell part of the truth but not let her know who his date was.

He was still trying to decide which approach was best when he finally fell asleep hours later.

"Where the hell were you?" were the first words Christina said on Monday morning. Her voice was tight and controlled, barely a whisper, because they were standing in the hall outside the conference room, surrounded by dozens of their associates. They were all waiting for the Monday-morning meeting to start.

"I'll tell you later," he said. "I'm really sorry," he added.

She wasn't moved by his apology. She narrowed her eyes and glared at him.

All during the meeting, he could feel her watching him.

Later, in the privacy of his small office where she'd followed him after the meeting, she faced him. "Well?"

He wet his lips. "I...uh..." He took a deep breath. "Look, I feel like a real jerk, but I forgot."

"You forgot," she said through gritted teeth. Her gray eyes looked like slate—hard and flat and cold. Her chest was heaving under her royal blue suit coat. "You forgot," she repeated.

He nodded. "I'm sorry," he said again.

"Where were you?"

"I'd gone out to dinner."

"Alone?"

This was the moment of truth. "No. I had a date."

Two bright red spots of color appeared on her cheeks. "You had a date," she said softly. "You forgot about me and made another date."

Kent cringed. "Yes." Whatever she said or chose to do, he deserved it.

She stared at him for what seemed like hours, but in reality was probably only a minute. Kent met her stare and waited. "Nobody treats me like this," she said, her voice shaking. "It's that ex-fiancée of yours, isn't it? I knew the moment I saw her she was bad news!" Her eyes narrowed. "The only thing I've got to say to you, Kent, is that you're going to be sorry. Very sorry!"

And then she stalked out of his office.

All day long Kent fought the urge to call Allison. After he finally stopped thinking about Christina and how justifiably angry she had been, he began to relive the previous evening, especially the heated kiss he and Allison had shared.

He had kissed a lot of women since Allison left him years ago. None had made him feel the way he'd felt

last night. Oh, he'd been turned on by some of the
kisses. Physically turned on. But no one except Allison
had ever had the power to turn him on emotionally.

That knowledge scared the stuffing out of him. Because that meant he was not over Allison. That meant
she still had control over him. Once before, he'd let her
control him, and it hadn't worked out. And it had hurt
like hell when she'd ditched him. Did he really want to
let himself be in a position for her to hurt him again?

Did he have a choice?

You always have a choice.

All day, in between phone calls and reading and dictating, his thoughts were threaded with bits and pieces
of the previous evening.

He was still thinking about Allison when, late in the
afternoon, he got a call from Marcy Bartlett, Joel's wife.

"Hi, Marce! How are you?"

"I'm fine. How're you doing?"

"Great. Just great."

"Listen, Kent, Joel and I are having a small dinner
party Friday night. We'd like you to come."

"What!" he said in mock indignation. "Is Joel re-
neging on our standing date for a beer after work?"

"Yes," Marcy said with a laugh. "Under protest, of
course. But seriously, can you come?"

"Who else is coming?"

"Well…" She hesitated just long enough for Kent to
realize she was up to something. "Oh, fiddle. You'll
find out anyway. I've invited Allison."

He smiled. Matchmaking. Marcy was matchmaking.

"You'll come, won't you, Kent?"

Oh, hell, he wanted to go. "Yes, sure. I'll come."

"And Kent?"

"Yeah?"

"It might be nice if you gave Allison a ride."

* * *

Allison hoped she looked all right. She didn't know what was wrong with her that she was so undecided about what to wear lately. Normally she felt confident of her clothes sense and her judgment. But now, where Kent was concerned, she was suddenly all indecisive and girlish.

She'd chosen a soft pants outfit in a creamy, soft fabric with matching bone-colored flats and gold jewelry. It was, after all, just a dinner at Marcy and Joel's.

Nervously Allison waited for Kent's arrival. When he'd called earlier in the week to ask if he could pick her up and take her to the dinner, at first she'd said, "Maybe it would be best for us to go separately." But she hated driving alone at night, and after all, there was no harm in accepting a ride, was there? It wasn't as if she were going to go to bed with him or anything.

"You look nice," Diana said when Allison walked into the living room a few minutes later.

"Thanks."

"Would you like a glass of wine, honey?" her father asked. He and Diana sat opposite each other on matching love seats. Diana had a glass of wine in her hand, and Lee was drinking something from an on-the-rocks glass. A plate of pâté and crackers sat on the coffee table between them.

"No, I don't think so. Kent should be here any minute."

The words were no sooner out of her mouth than she heard the clunk of a car door outside. Her stomach fluttered as Diana said, "I think I hear him now."

A few seconds later the doorbell rang, and Allison, nervously smoothing down her pants, walked out to the foyer. Her heart skidded up into her throat as she opened the door and Kent smiled down upon her.

"Hi," he said, giving her an admiring glance.

"Hi." Would the sight of him always make her feel this way? She wondered if long-married couples still felt this giddy sensation when the object of their affections came into sight. God, she hoped not. She couldn't imagine how anyone could stand this constant state of edginess, this perpetual nervousness. She felt unhinged, and she wasn't sure she liked the feeling.

"Where are the old folks?" Kent said with a conspiratorial wink.

Allison grinned, and her stomach settled down a bit. "They're in the living room."

"Guess I'd better pay my respects."

"I heard you call us 'old folks,'" Diana said when Kent and Allison entered the living room. She raised her face as Kent leaned down to hug her and kiss her cheek. Lee stood, and the two men shook hands.

"Do you have time for a drink before you go?" Lee asked.

Kent shook his head. "Better not. Marcy said dinner at seven-thirty." He glanced at the mantel clock. "And it's already after seven."

A few minutes later they left. As they drove down the curving street leading to lower Memorial Drive, the sun was lowering in the west, and the world was bathed in amber and scarlet. Allison's tension had returned now that she and Kent were alone again, and she concentrated on taking even breaths to try to dispel it. She wondered if Kent felt the same way. The silence between them was beginning to be uncomfortable. To combat it, she said, "Tonight should be fun, don't you think?"

Kent smiled, giving her a brief look, then turning his attention back to the road.

Wasn't he going to help her out at all? Why didn't he say something? "Marcy said she'd also invited Gail and Michael Berry." When Allison and Kent were engaged, Gail and Michael had rounded out their group of special friends. Michael, like Joel and Kent, was a lawyer, and Gail, an artist, worked for a big ad agency.

"I know."

"Do—do you see them often?"

"Not as often as I'd like." There was an odd note in his voice.

What did that odd note mean? "I guess you're all too busy," Allison offered.

"It's not that. It's…" He hesitated, drumming his fingers against the steering wheel. They were stopped for the light where Memorial Drive met the Loop. "Well, they're married, and I'm not."

Allison didn't answer. She knew he was thinking exactly what she was thinking. We could have been married. We could have been a part of this special group for years now. Another thought, one Allison had had many times, followed naturally. Marianne could have been Kent's baby. Our baby. Once more the heartache that always seemed to be hovering just under the surface rushed through her. Who knows? Maybe Marianne wouldn't have been born with a problem if she had been Allison and Kent's child. Oh, God. She had to stop thinking these black thoughts. They helped no one. They accomplished nothing except making her feel worse about herself and her poor judgment than she already did.

A silence fell between them again, and in the ten or so minutes it took to reach Marcy and Joel's West University home, Allison struggled to regain her composure.

When they arrived at the Bartletts', they pulled into the driveway and parked behind a dark green Jaguar. "The Berrys are here," Kent said.

"I can see he's doing well, too," Allison commented as she eyed the Jaguar.

Kent, who had just turned off the ignition, looked at her. His brow was furrowed. "We work damned hard for our money," he said.

Oh-oh. There was a definite note of defensiveness in his voice. "I know," she said hurriedly. "I didn't mean to suggest you didn't." She made a mental note to be careful. Kent was obviously sensitive to remarks about how much money he made. She saw his sensitivity as another clue that he wasn't entirely comfortable with the way he was making his living, no matter what he said.

She was very grateful they had arrived at their destination. Once they were inside the Bartletts' home and surrounded by their friends, Allison felt herself relaxing. She could see Kent was more comfortable, too.

"It's so good to have you home again, Allison," Gail Berry said, giving Allison a smile.

"I'm glad to be here, believe me." She smiled at Gail, a classy-looking brunette who wore huge round glasses with bright red frames and was given to dressing in flowing skirts and dresses in vivid primary colors matched with long, trailing scarves.

The three women were sipping at a predinner cocktail in Marcy's living room. The men had disappeared into Joel's study, where he was presumably showing off his new computer.

"Are you and Kent an item again?" Gail asked, her dark eyes bright with curiosity.

Allison looked at Marcy. "No, but I think Marcy wishes we would be."

Marcy grinned sheepishly. "I admit it. I'd love to see them get back together." She leaned forward and said in a conspiratorial whisper, "I think he's still in love with you."

Allison could feel her face warming up. To cover her confusion, she lifted her glass to her lips and sipped. "We're just friends," she said, but she could feel her heart beating too fast. Despite what Marcy hoped, Allison knew her decision to keep her relationship with Kent one of friendship only was the right one.

Gail and Marcy exchanged a coy look.

Allison was saved from having to say anything more by the reappearance of the men. They were laughing as they walked into the room, and Allison looked up. The thought flashed through her mind that of the three of them, Kent stood out. It wasn't just that he was better looking than either Joel, who was smaller and more serious looking, or Michael, who was short and a little overweight. Kent had more presence. There was a quality about him that was hard to define, but Allison knew that anyone looking at him would know he was a bright and shining star who would make his mark on the world.

Pride swelled her heart as she looked at him. For one crystal moment their gazes met and clung. Then Joel, laughing, said something, and the moment was gone.

"Allison, you're awfully quiet tonight," Michael said about halfway through dinner. He was seated on her right, Joel on her left. Kent was diagonally across the table.

"Am I? I'm sorry." She had been dreaming about

the past again, imagining what her life would be like if she and Kent were now married, as their friends were.

"She's got a lot on her mind," Marcy said.

Michael nodded. "Yes, Gail told me about your baby."

"I was hoping you'd bring her tonight," Gail said.

"It's best not to take her out unless I absolutely have to. She's supposed to be kept as quiet as possible," Allison explained.

"I'm dying to see her," Gail said.

"You're welcome to come over anytime," Allison said.

Gradually the conversation drifted to other things, but the mention of Marianne and her problems was a reminder of what Allison had decided earlier.

She was going to cool it with Kent.

And she would tell him so on the way home.

Chapter Nine

Some things were easier said than done.

Three times on the way home Allison had tried to introduce the subject of their relationship. She would open her mouth, all set to say what she had been thinking, then she would lose her nerve. The trouble was, when she was around Kent, all she could think about was how she felt about him.

No. Be honest, she told herself. The real trouble was, down deep she didn't want to cool it with Kent.

It was that kiss. If only she could wipe that kiss out of her mind. Too many times tonight, as she'd looked at Kent's mouth or his hands, she'd remember that kiss.

She wondered if he had thought about the kiss, too. Had it meant anything to him at all? Had there been any of the emotions she was feeling behind the kiss? Or with Kent, was it just that same potent physical attraction they'd always felt for one another? With the old Kent, she would have known what he was feeling. But this new Kent was another story. Maybe he kissed everyone the way he'd kissed her.

Like that blonde. She wondered if he was still seeing Christina. Kissing her the way he'd kissed Allison. Envy knifed through her and with it a feeling close to despair because she knew she had no right to be envious. Kent was free to kiss whomever he pleased, whenever he pleased. He was also free to make love to anyone at all. Allison had no claims on him. *So what are you waiting for? Why don't you get it over with? Tell him what you decided about cooling it.*

She stared out the passenger-side window as the music from a Paula Abdul CD played softly. Why did life have to hurt so much? Why was everything so…hard? For a moment she wished she were eighteen again, when her biggest problem was what color dress to wear for graduation. Wouldn't it be wonderful if she could do everything all over? And this time she'd do it all right.

But then, if she were eighteen again, she wouldn't have Marianne. She sighed deeply, closing her eyes against the night lights of the city. No. She didn't want to be eighteen again. She wouldn't trade Marianne for anything.

"That was a big sigh," Kent said.

Allison opened her eyes and turned toward him. She tried to smile, but a smile just wouldn't come. Once again tears hovered just beneath the surface. Oh, she was sick of feeling so weepy!

"Is something wrong?" he asked. "Didn't you have a good time tonight?"

"I had a great time tonight. And, no, nothing's wrong." Quit acting like a wimp, she told herself. And for the rest of the ride home, she forced herself to talk about the evening. Kent told her a couple of stories about Michael and Joel, and Allison even found herself laughing.

But as they pulled into the driveway at her father's house, all her earlier tension returned. What if Kent tried to kiss her again tonight? What would she do? *You should have told him your decision on the way home,* she scolded herself.

When Kent came around to her side of the car and helped her out of the Corvette, just the simple touch of his hand on her arm sent all kinds of messages to her brain—messages that Allison did not welcome because she knew they would only make things more difficult for her. But she was powerless to stop them. Powerless to stop the shivery awareness. Powerless to stop the aching need that rippled through her as Kent walked her to the door.

Tell him. Tell him.

They were standing in the courtyard once again. Like a replay of the previous weekend. Allison looked up. "Kent, I—"

The words died on her lips as he reached out and took her hand in his. The simple contact set her heart to pounding. "Listen, Allison," he said. "All week I've been thinking about what you said last Sunday night, and you're right. Anything but friendship between us would be a big mistake." He hesitated, and his words hung in the air between them. "Just as it was last time."

Something hard knotted in Allison's chest, and she pulled her hand away. She knew he was only reinforcing what she herself had said. And she knew he was right. She had been planning to say exactly the same thing. So why did the words hurt so much?

Somehow she managed to keep her voice steady as she said, "I'm glad you see it that way. Well, thanks for the ride. I enjoyed the evening." It took everything she had, every ounce of strength, to smile, but she did it. "Good-night, Kent." Then, before he could say more than a soft good-night in return, she turned and inserted her key into the lock, opening the door quickly.

Then she walked inside and shut the door behind her.

Kent spent a hellish weekend. Ever since Allison's return, nothing had gone right in his life. He'd alienated Christina, and now, for some stupid reason, he felt as if he'd done something wrong with Allison, too. He kept replaying his conversation with her on Friday night after Marcy and Joel's party. Why had he gotten the impression that he'd said something he shouldn't have said?

By Monday morning he decided he was not going to think about women at all. Period. He was swearing off all women—at least for the duration of the Wilder case. He'd been neglecting his work because of his entanglements, and that would have to stop. It would stop.

Determined and purposeful, he went to the office early and began the laborious task of reading his share of the R & D notes on the Wild Rider.

Late Monday afternoon, while looking through the last notebook, Kent abruptly stopped reading. He stared at a notation about a third of the way down the page. That couldn't be right. He blinked twice, then focused on the line he'd just read. He read it again: CONT TO CK W.R. F/PRBLM W/STRG. AB.

Kent read the cryptic message aloud. He'd looked at so many pages of notes that he pretty much understood the shorthand used by the design team. He began to translate. "Continuing to check Wild Rider for problem with…" With what? The steering?

Chilled, he looked at the date again—the previous November. One month before the Wild Rider was test ridden by Greg Petrowski. One month before the steering mechanism had failed and Petrowski had been killed.

Continuing to check?

The note was initialed "AB." Armand Brasselli, the head of the design team. The man Kent's secretary had been trying get an appointment with so that Kent could interview him, but who, so far, she'd had no success in reaching.

That phrase, *continuing to check*, really troubled Kent, because according to Emmett Wilder, there had been no problem at all in the preliminary testing of the steering. So why would the designer be *continuing* to check something with which they did not have a problem to begin with?

Kent frowned and swiveled his chair so he could prop his feet on his wastebasket. Had Armand Brasselli made other notes about the steering? Earlier notes? If so, why hadn't they shown up? And why hadn't Emmett Wilder mentioned them? Had Wilder lied to the firm? It was a disturbing thought.

Was it possible Wilder hadn't known about the ongoing tests? Kent searched his memory, trying to remember exactly what Wilder had said when Colin Jamieson had interviewed him. Kent had been present that day, and to the best of his ability to recall the questions and answers, Wilder had said he had been involved in the day-to-day tests and there had been nothing amiss.

Christina had searched the earlier test notebooks.

Could she have overlooked something pertaining to the case?

Kent wondered if she was in her office now. She had been avoiding him the past week. And when she hadn't been able to avoid him and they did end up in each other's company, she was totally impersonal—all business. That suited Kent. He would have hated to rehash their differences. He also figured that, given time, Christina would get over most of her anger, and they could work their way into a better relationship. They'd better, because the firm wasn't that big. They were bound to be thrown together many times in the future. He knew he was lucky that for now, while her anger was still fresh, they were working on different aspects of the case, so it hadn't been a problem to keep their distance.

But this discovery of Brasselli's note could be important. He'd better find Christina and ask her if she'd noticed anything else along these lines.

He walked down the hall to Christina's office. The door stood open, but she wasn't there. He walked in, found a yellow pad of self-stick notes on her desk. He scribbled her a note and left it stuck to the back of her chair where she couldn't fail to see it.

As he left her office and walked back down the hall to his own, he ran into Colin Jamieson. "I was looking for you, Kent," Jamieson said, forehead knitted. "I need you to go to Conroe tomorrow and take a deposition from Dr. Yost."

"Okay." Kent mentally juggled his schedule. "What time?"

"He said to be there at two. Call his office and let the receptionist know you're coming."

"Okay," Kent said again. "Uh, listen, there's something I wanted to ask you about. Can you come into my office for a minute?''

Jamieson's frown intensified, and he looked at the expensive watch on his right wrist. ''I only have three minutes.''

Kent almost smiled, but didn't quite dare. To Kent's way of thinking, the older man was just a little too full of his own self-importance. It hadn't taken Kent long to discover Jamieson also had absolutely no sense of humor. ''It won't take long. I just want to show you something I found in going through the R & D notes on the Wilder case.''

''What is it?'' Jamieson said impatiently, following Kent into his small, crowded office. Kent walked around behind his desk and picked up the notebook he'd been studying earlier. He handed it to Jamieson, opened to page twenty-three.

''Look at the notation on line ten,'' he said.

Jamieson studied the notation for a long moment, then, with an inscrutable look on his face, he handed the notebook back to Kent. ''What about it?'' he said, his tone clearly stating that Kent was wasting his valuable time.

''Don't you think it's a little odd that Armand Brasselli should say he was continuing to check a problem, most probably with the steering, when according to Emmett Wilder, there were no problems with the steering?''

Jamieson shrugged, but his dark eyes carried an expression that was not as casual or indifferent as his gesture. ''I think you're making too much of nothing,'' he said. ''Forget about it.'' His voice carried a warning note that Kent would have had to be deaf not to hear.

''But you can't call this notation nothing. Brasselli

PATRICIA KAY   449

was referring to something,'' Kent insisted even as he
knew Jamieson would not like being contradicted.

"I do call it nothing," Jamieson said coldly. "The
plaintiff's attorneys have already been over these notes,
and they didn't question it." He smoothed back the
sides of his already impeccably groomed salt-and-
pepper hair. "Now, I'm going to be late for my appointment if I don't get going." He turned. "And don't
forget to call Dr. Yost's office."

Dismissed, Kent thought. Well, hell, why worry about
this if Jamieson thought it was nothing? After all, Jamieson was the senior partner, not Kent. Jamieson had
the courtroom experience, not Kent. And Jamieson was
calling the shots on this case.

Not Kent.

"Kent's birthday is next Wednesday, and I'd like to
give him a birthday party. What do you two think?"
Diana asked.

It was the Tuesday after Marcy and Joel's party. Allison, Lee and Diana had just finished dinner and were
sitting around the kitchen table.

Lee smiled. "I think that's a great idea."

Allison wasn't sure she agreed, but her reasons were
not ones she wanted to try to explain, so she smiled and
said, "Me, too. Were you thinking of a surprise party?"

"Well, yes, I was," Diana said. "I thought I'd invite
him for dinner. You know. A family celebration. And
when he gets here, he'll find all his friends are here,
too."

Allison agreed to help Diana plan the party, and for
the next week, during which she did not see Kent at all,
she kept to her word. Throughout the week, she wondered what Kent was doing. Each night she imagined

him and the beautiful Christina together. She tortured
herself with images of their kissing the way she and
Kent had kissed.

The brightest spot of the week came on the day Diana
and Allison were writing out the invitations. Christina's
name was not on the list. As if it wasn't important at
all, Allison said, "Did you forget about the girl Kent's
been dating? You know…Christina?"

Diana shrugged. "No, but when I talked to Kent the
other day, I very casually brought up Christina's name.
It's a good thing I did, because Kent said they're no
longer seeing each other."

Allison's heart went *zing* after which she immediately
berated herself. Why should it matter to her whether
Kent was seeing Christina or not?

But it did matter, and she knew it. She actually began
smiling again, and by the day of the party, she was
actually looking forward to the evening.

She gave Marianne her bath early that afternoon, and
by five o'clock Allison was soaking in a tub full of
scented bubbles while the baby lay happily in her crib
watching her musical mobile. Allison had left the bathroom door open, and as the music drifted in the air, she
remembered the look in Kent's eyes when he'd presented her with the gift for Marianne.

At five-thirty Allison began dressing for the party.
Since coming back to Houston, she'd actually gained
back about six of the fifteen pounds she'd lost, and she
knew she looked better.

At six she was ready to go downstairs. The guests
had been told to come at six-thirty. Kent had been invited for seven. Allison took one last look at herself in
the full-length mirror. She had chosen to wear a casual
summer outfit—black split skirt and a fitted, short black-

and-white diamond-print jacket, paired with sheer black stockings and low-heeled black patent leather pumps. With the outfit she wore a clunky silver bracelet and black-and-silver diamond-shaped earrings. She smiled at herself, deciding she was happy with the way she looked.

Diana had insisted on hiring the teenager who lived across the street to sit upstairs with Marianne so that Allison could relax and enjoy herself at the party. After giving instructions to the girl, Allison fluffed her hair one last time, then walked slowly downstairs.

A few of the guests had already arrived, among them Diana's mother, Barbara Kent, and her youngest sister, Jackie.

"Hi, Allison," Jackie said.

Allison smiled at the pretty blonde. She really liked Jackie, who had a perky personality and a nice smile for everyone. She'd had a tough time after her divorce a few years back, but she was doing well now.

"Hello, Allison," said Barbara Kent.

"Hello, Mrs. Kent." After hesitating briefly, Allison walked over and gave Kent's grandmother a hug. Although Allison knew Diana and Barbara were often at loggerheads, she had always liked the cantankerous woman. "It's good to see you again."

For the next fifteen minutes, one guest after another arrived, including Marcy and Joel, Gail and Michael Berry, Nikki and Glenn Prescott and Nikki's mother, Sunny. In fact, most of the people Allison had seen at the Fourth of July barbecue had all been invited to the birthday celebration, with the exception of Christina and Lee's and Diana's co-workers. In their places were some of the people Kent worked with, none of whom Allison knew.

By ten minutes to seven, all the guests had arrived. Lee had made arrangements with several of his neighbors to hide the cars in their various backyards or driveways, so Kent wouldn't be suspicious when he drove up.

Everyone took their places in the living room, and Diana closed the louvered doors that led into the foyer so Kent wouldn't see them when he arrived.

Allison looked around at the thirty-some guests as they all whispered and laughed among themselves. As she did, her gaze met Marcy's, and Marcy grinned at her. Joel, who was standing next to Marcy, his arm around her shoulders, winked.

Precisely at seven o'clock, the doorbell rang. "Shh," said Carol, Diana's sister, and the crowd fell silent. From behind the louvered doors, Allison heard Diana open the door, heard her say "Hi, Kent! Happy birthday," and his cheerful answer.

"Where're Lee and Allison?" Kent asked.

Allison kept her eyes on the closed doors, not trusting herself to meet anyone else's gaze.

"They're having a drink in the living room. Let's go in."

Allison held her breath, knowing everyone else in the room was doing so, too.

Diana opened the doors, and Allison, along with everyone else, shouted, "Surprise!"

Kent's mouth fell open.

Allison's heart felt full as she watched the emotions flicker across his face—first surprise, then delight. He grinned and advanced into the room.

As he greeted people, Allison watched him. He looked even more handsome than usual, she decided, in well-pressed tan slacks, an open-necked burgundy cotton shirt and dark brown loafers.

Eventually he reached her. "Did you have a hand in planning this?" he asked, smiling down at her.

"Yes, I helped, but it was all your mother's idea." She returned his smile. "You really were surprised, weren't you? I was afraid you might guess what she was up to."

"Nope. When she asked me to dinner, I thought, yeah, that would be nice, and never gave it another thought."

"Well, happy birthday."

"Thanks."

They stood there awkwardly, and Allison knew Kent felt just as uncomfortable as she did. There was so much she wanted to say, but she had no right to say any of it. "Where's the baby?" he finally asked. "Sleeping?"

"She may be by now. Diana hired Judy from across the street to watch her tonight."

He nodded, and another awkward moment of silence followed. Then, just as Allison was about to excuse herself to go help Diana in the kitchen, a good-looking, tall man about Kent's age walked up to them. Allison couldn't remember his name, but she knew he was a co-worker of Kent's.

"Hey, Kent! Great party, huh?" he said.

"Hi, Steve. Yeah, it is." Kent turned to Allison. "Have you two met? Steve Trumbull, Allison Fornier— my stepsister."

"Stepsister, huh?" Steve said, laughing. "Boy, some guys have all the luck!"

Allison smiled, but she wanted nothing more than to escape. She felt too vulnerable right now, too exposed. She wondered if she'd ever be able to handle her feelings for Kent in a way that would allow her to be around him without worrying that everyone else in the room would know exactly what was going on inside her. Finally she made her excuses and walked back to the kitchen, where Diana, along with the caterer she'd hired for the evening, was arranging hot hors d'oeuvres on a large crystal platter.

For the next hour Allison busied herself by tending to the guests. Then, when she felt she'd done all she could to help and really needed to circulate, she spied Marcy and Joel standing off to one corner of the family room that opened onto the kitchen. A few minutes later she joined them.

Marcy hugged her. "So you finally decided to take a break."

"You sure look pretty tonight," Joel said, giving her an admiring glance.

"You'd better watch it," Marcy said. "I'm getting jealous!"

At just that moment, Kent walked up. He smiled at her, then turned to Joel. "Why didn't you tell me about this party?" he asked.

Joel grinned. "I don't tell you everything."

"Oh, yes, you do."

Marcy said, "Hey, he'd better not!"

They all laughed.

"So, what's new at work?" Kent said, turning back to Joel.

As the men began to talk about their respective law firms, Allison chatted with Marcy. But a few minutes later her attention was caught by something Kent was saying.

"And so I decided to ask Colin Jamieson about it."

''Why? Did you think there might be something wrong?'' Joel asked.

''Well, not only that, but I was worried about what the plaintiff's attorneys might think. Jesus, this could have blown huge holes in our case!''

''What are you talking about?'' Marcy asked.

Allison was glad Marcy had asked the question. Her curiosity was aroused, too.

Joel looked at Kent, and Kent shrugged. He turned to include the two women in the conversation. ''I was just telling Joel I'd discovered something that made me think a client of ours might not be telling the truth.''

''On the Wilder case?'' Allison asked.

His eyes met hers. ''Yes.''

''So what did Jamieson say when you asked him about it?'' Joel asked.

''He said not to worry about it.''

''That's all?''

''Yep.''

''So are you just going to forget about it?''

''Hell, why not?'' Kent said. ''I don't get paid to question a senior partner. You know that.'' Then he laughed. ''And I happen to like getting paid. That means I keep my mouth shut.''

''But, Kent,'' Allison said, ''if you think something is wrong, you can't just sit by and ignore it, senior partner or not.''

He stared at her.

''Well, you can't.''

''Why can't I?''

''Because it's wrong, that's why!'' She knew this was the wrong time and the wrong place to question his decision, but she couldn't seem to help herself. She didn't like his cynical reply to Joel's question.

"You're the last person I'd imagine who'd feel that way," Kent said.

Allison tried not to feel hurt. He had good reason for thinking this, and she knew it. "And you're the last person I'd imagine who'd let money stand in the way of what's right." As soon as the words were out of her mouth, she knew she shouldn't have said them.

His eyes narrowed. "Can you believe it? Self-righteousness from the original take-the-money-and-run girl."

Stunned by the cruelty of his remark, Allison could only look at him. Suddenly she realized just how much she'd been fooling herself in thinking she and Kent could ever build any kind of relationship again. His stinging indictment of her told her exactly how much anger he still harbored against her. He had never forgiven her, and he never would.

Chapter Ten

Fighting tears, Allison turned and walked away. But not before she heard Marcy say "That was a little cold, don't you think?"

Blindly Allison headed for the powder room. A few seconds later Marcy fell into step beside her. She squeezed Allison's shoulder.

Allison held on to her emotions until they were both in the tiny powder room with the door closed. Then she sat down on the closed toilet seat and buried her face in her hands. She was shaking. "Oh, God, Marce," she said. "He despises me."

"Oh, honey, he doesn't despise you!" Marcy knelt in front of her and gently pulled her hands away from her face. She held them tight. "You know what I think?"

Allison shook her head. She was trying very hard not to cry. Above all, she didn't want anyone else at the party to know she was upset. Knowing how protective her father was, especially now during Marianne's illness, she wanted to avoid a scene where she envisioned his berating Kent. She'd caused enough trouble in this family. She didn't want to be the source of yet another crisis.

"I think Kent is unhappy about the choices he's made," Marcy said, "but he's too stubborn to admit it. Joel has told me about talks they've had, and all is not as wonderful at Keating & Shaw as Kent would have us believe. That's why he lashed out at you. Because you said what we were all thinking. And because Kent feels exactly the same way down deep."

"Do you really think so?" Oh, she wanted to believe Marcy. Marcy was saying what Allison had been thinking, but she'd been afraid, way down deep, that it was wishful thinking. But if Marcy and Joel thought so, too...

"Yes, I really do."

"And you don't think he hates me?"

"No. In fact, I think just the opposite. I think he's still in love with you." Her blue eyes were soft with compassion. "That's why your implied criticism hurt. That's why he struck back. He cares about what you think."

If only Allison could believe Marcy's theory was true.

"Now come on," Marcy urged. "Wash your face. Put on more lipstick. Smile! And let's go out there and knock 'em dead!"

Allison gave her a wobbly smile.

"Good! That's much better."

Allison took a shaky breath. She did feel better.

"Everything's going to be okay," Marcy said as they both stood.

"I hope you're right."

"I am. You'll see."

After Allison walked away and Marcy went running after her, Kent said, "Why is it okay for Allison to say anything she pleases, but when I retaliate, I'm cruel?"

Joel shrugged. "Well…"

Kent put down the empty glass he'd been holding and shoved his hands in his pockets. He looked down at his feet. Although he felt justified in his anger at Allison for criticizing him in front of his friends, he knew he should never have said what he did. Now he felt like a first-class heel.

He sighed. Why had he said what he did? Had he wanted to hurt Allison?

As a lawyer, he knew a case could be made for him. After all, she had hurt his feelings, too. Still, he knew the reason he'd gotten so mad was that she'd only given voice to the doubts that plagued him late at night when he was alone. Doubts he didn't want to acknowledge.

Joel nudged him. "The girls are coming back," he said.

Kent looked over his shoulder. He saw Allison, but she didn't look in his direction. Instead, she turned and walked into the dining room. A moment later Marcy rejoined them. She gave Kent an accusatory look, but she didn't say anything.

"Excuse me," Kent said. "I think I'd better go apologize." He headed toward the dining room. Would Allison forgive him? he wondered.

Just then a new song began to play, piped through the house on the built-in stereo system. When Kent reached the dining room, where the large dining table had been pushed into one corner, he saw that several

couples were dancing. Allison stood in the arched doorway leading into the L-shaped living room. Kent
threaded his way through the dancers until he reached
her side. Walking up behind her, he touched her shoulder. "Allison."

She stiffened.

"I...would you dance with me?"

She turned, raising her face to his. Her beautiful
golden brown eyes studied him gravely. "Why?"

"Because we have to talk."

She looked at him for another long moment, then,
with a small sigh, she said, "All right."

She felt so small and defenseless in his arms. So soft
and feminine. And still so fragile. How could he have
lashed out at her that way? Especially in light of her
personal situation. Why was it that she could always
manage to make him forget everything, so that he acted
in ways he normally wouldn't?

He pulled her close as they began to dance, and he
could feel the shudder that raced through her body.
"I'm sorry," he whispered against her fragrant hair. "I
had no right to say what I did. You didn't deserve it.
Can you forgive me?"

She pulled away a little bit and looked up at him. She
nodded. "And—and I'm sorry, too."

His arms tightened around her. "You spoke the
truth."

She didn't answer for a minute. "You spoke the truth,
too."

Kent wished they were alone. He wished.... But they
weren't alone. And wishing wouldn't change the facts.
"Are we still friends?"

"Yes."

But as he drew her close again, he knew they were

both kidding themselves. It wasn't friendship he was feeling. And he didn't think she was feeling friendship, either.

That night as Allison lay in bed, she remembered every moment of the party. She kept thinking about what Marcy had said. Was Marcy right? Was Kent still in love with her? Was that why he'd been so quick to turn on her when she'd criticized him so thoughtlessly?

Allison knew she wasn't blameless in what had happened. She'd had no right to infer Kent wasn't doing the right thing. No right to judge him. After all, she had certainly made some poor choices in her life.

He'd asked if they were still friends. She'd answered yes. But even as she was agreeing, she knew she wasn't being truthful with him. What she felt for Kent was much more than friendship.

She was in love with him.

She had been in love with him for a long time.

She was afraid she would always be in love with him.

And she didn't know what to do about it.

After a night when he didn't get much sleep, Kent decided he would try to talk to Colin Jamieson one more time. He told himself this decision had nothing to do with what Allison had said to him.

First thing Thursday morning, Kent approached Jamieson's secretary. "Lisa, I'd like to see Mr. Jamieson this morning, if possible."

Lisa looked at Jamieson's appointment book. "You're in luck. He's got a few minutes open around eleven."

"Put me down."

At eleven o'clock Kent headed back to Jamieson's

office. After keeping him waiting fifteen minutes, Lisa finally ushered Kent into the large corner office that afforded a spectacular view of Houston's skyline. Sunshine flooded the office, and the sky looked blue as far as the eye could see. Rank definitely had its privileges at Keating & Shaw.

"What is it, Kent?" Jamieson said, looking up from some papers on his desk. He didn't offer Kent a seat.

Invitation or not, Kent sat in one of the two leather chairs positioned in front of Jamieson's desk. He leaned forward. "I've been thinking about that notation I found. You know, the one about the tests on the steering mechanism of the Wild Rider."

Jamieson's eyes hardened.

Refusing to be intimidated by Jamieson's lack of encouragement, Kent plunged ahead. "I'm really bothered by that notation, and I'd like your permission to investigate it further."

"No."

Kent struggled to hold on to his temper. Getting angry wouldn't help his cause, nor would it help his position in the firm. "Sir, I think there's a possibility Wilder is lying to us. Don't we owe it to ourselves to find out the truth? I was planning to interview Brasselli anyway—"

"Now, dammit, Kent," Jamieson said, his face becoming red, "I said 'no.' So don't push it. You're out of line, and I want you to drop the subject. Do you understand?"

"But I—"

Jamieson's eyes narrowed. "I don't want to hear another word about this." His voice carried an implicit warning.

"But, sir, I think—"

"I don't give a damn what you think! And questioning my judgment is not the way to make partner, young man. I hope you realize that.''

Kent bit back the sharp retort that threatened to erupt. ''Couldn't you at least mention that discrepancy to Ben Keating? See what he says?'' Ben Keating was the managing partner of the firm and one of its founders. He was also a good friend of Lee's and had been instrumental in Kent's job offer from the firm.

Through clenched teeth Jamieson said, ''This is my case, Sorensen. My case. Not yours. Not Keating's. I make the decisions here. Have you got that?''

''Yes, I—''

''Now,'' he continued coldly, ''do you want to stay on this case or not?''

Kent knew the real question was do you want to stay on with this firm or not? ''Yes. I do.''

''Fine.'' Jamieson looked back down at the papers on his desk. ''We're finished, and I'm very busy.''

''Yes, sir.'' Kent knew he should apologize, but he simply couldn't bring himself to say the words. He was backing off. That was enough.

Thursday night Marianne took a turn for the worse. In the space of just a few minutes, her color turned dark blue, and Allison, after hooking up the emergency oxygen supply, called Dr. Richardson's beeper number.

Within minutes the doctor called her back. After Allison explained the situation, he said he would send an ambulance. ''I'll meet you at the hospital. Don't panic. She'll be all right as long as she's got the oxygen.''

White-faced, Allison, Lee and Diana stared mutely at each other as they waited for the ambulance to arrive. All Allison could do as she watched the baby labor to breathe, was pray. *Please, dear God, let it be okay. Let*

*my precious baby be okay. Please don't take her away
from me. I know I haven't done much of anything ad-
mirable with my life, but please, please, don't punish
Marianne. She doesn't deserve it.*

On and on she prayed.

Promising.

Begging.

Bargaining.

She paced and prayed. She looked out of the window
and willed the ambulance to go faster.

Finally the ambulance arrived, sirens screaming as it
raced down the quiet street. Two paramedics rushed in,
and Allison watched as they gently lifted Marianne and
carried her downstairs and outside. Within minutes they
had her hooked up to the oxygen supply in the ambulance.

"You can ride back here with her, ma'am," said the
youngest looking of the paramedics. His freckled face
was grave.

"We'll follow you," her father said, giving her a hug
then boosting her into the back of the ambulance. Before
the door closed, Allison's gaze met Diana's. She saw
the fear in Diana's eyes and knew it was a reflection of
what her own eyes must show.

The ride to the hospital went by in a blur. Allison
held on tight, her eyes never leaving Marianne's little
body. She watched Marianne's chest rise and fall, rise
and fall, as the same litany of prayer ran through her
mind. The siren's wail sliced through the night as the
ambulance careered toward its destination.

When they pulled up under the canopied emergency
entrance, Allison scrambled out of the vehicle and allowed the paramedics to do their job. Two nurses were
ready for them as they entered the brightly lit receiving

area. While the nurses took over, Allison answered questions and signed forms.

Within minutes Dr. Richardson joined her. "We're transferring the baby to pediatric ICU," he said. "I'll examine her there."

As the hospital personnel began to wheel Marianne off, Lee and Diana walked through the door. "Thank goodness," Allison said. "I hated to leave here, knowing you were coming, but they're taking her to pediatric ICU."

"Let's go," Lee said, putting his arm around her. Diana took her hand, and they walked together behind the crib on wheels.

Allison was glad for their support. She was afraid that once she was alone, terror would overcome her. This crisis, coming after such a long period where Marianne had done so well, seemed worse because they had been lulled into thinking the baby wasn't as sick as the doctors had originally suggested.

Now Allison knew she was.

And the knowledge terrified her.

Ten minutes later Marianne was settled into an examining room in the unit, and Allison, Lee and Diana were instructed to wait outside in the hallway. "Or you can go out into the waiting area," a kind redheaded nurse said, pointing to the double doors that led outside the section.

"No," Allison said. "We'll wait here." There were no chairs in the hallway, so they stood in a silent, tight little group. Every once in a while, their gazes met, and Allison had to look away. She couldn't stand seeing the fear her father tried to disguise or the compassion in Diana's blue eyes.

As the seconds ticked away, Allison continued her

prayers. Her eyes watched the doorway as she imagined what was going on inside the room. They waited and waited for what seemed like hours to Allison.

Finally Dr. Richardson came out of the room. Allison held her breath, fear clogging her throat.

He met her gaze. "That crisis point I warned you of has come, Mrs. Fornier. I wish we could have waited until Marianne was a little older, but we can't."

"Do you mean the open-heart surgery has to be done now?" Allison's voice sounded strange to her, as if it were coming from a great distance.

Diana took her hand again, squeezing it comfortingly.

"Yes," Dr. Richardson said. "We'll make sure she's kept stabilized through the night, and we'll do the surgery first thing in the morning."

Allison bit her bottom lip to still its trembling. *Oh, God. Oh, God. Please, God.*

"Let's go out to the waiting area where we can sit down and I can explain everything to you," the doctor added. "By that time, the release forms should be ready for you."

A nurse wearing the name tag Marilyn Flack explained the various forms to Allison. "Now, about blood," she said.

"Blood?" Allison said.

"Yes. Your daughter will need blood during the surgery. Are you willing to take blood provided from the hospital blood bank, or do you prefer using your own donor?"

Allison looked at her father and Diana. "I don't want a stranger's blood." She turned to the nurse. "I'll give her blood."

"Or I will," Lee said.

The nurse looked at Marianne's chart. "Your daughter is AB-negative, Mrs. Fornier. What's your blood type?"

"A-positive."

"I'm afraid you're not compatible."

"Not compatible! But I'm her mother!"

"That doesn't matter. Was her father AB-negative?"

"I don't know."

"He must have been. I'm afraid the only blood types compatible with your daughter's are AB-negative or O-negative."

Stricken, Allison again looked at her father and step-mother. Lee shook his head. "Like you, I'm A-positive."

"So am I," Diana said.

Allison swallowed. "I—I guess we'll have to use the blood-bank supply." But the thought scared her. She knew labs tested blood thoroughly, but today, with AIDS and its attendant horrors, it frightened her to take even the smallest chance with blood from an unknown source. But what choice did she have? Marianne had to have blood.

Thirty minutes later the papers were signed. "Why don't you go home for the night, Mrs. Fornier?" the doctor asked.

"No! I want to stay here with Marianne," Allison said.

"You're going to need your rest," Dr. Richardson insisted. "Tomorrow is going to be a long day."

Allison shook her head stubbornly. "I'll lay down here, on one of the couches."

Dr. Richardson sighed, meeting her father's gaze. "All right," he finally said. "I'll ask them to give you a pillow and blanket."

"Diana," Lee said, "why don't you go home and get some sleep? I'll stay here with Allison."

"No," Diana said. She smiled at Allison. "If you two are staying, I'm staying, too."

And so the three of them began the long night's vigil. They didn't do much talking. Each was lost in his or her own thoughts.

Lee thought about his little girl and how he wished he could lift this burden from her shoulders.

Diana thought about how much she had grown to love Allison and little Marianne.

And Allison thought about how Marianne was the best part of her and how, if she could, she'd trade places with her.

The clock ticked away the minutes, and they waited.

At seven o'clock Friday morning, Kent's phone rang. "Kent Sorensen," he said as he lifted the receiver.

"Kent? When I tried your condo and there wasn't any answer, I was hoping you'd be at work."

It was his mother.

He tensed. "Mom? What's up?" Diana never called him this early.

"Marianne was rushed to the hospital last night," said his mother's strained voice.

Kent's heart rate shot up alarmingly. "What happened?" He tried unsuccessfully to push his fear down. "Is she all right?"

He heard his mother sigh. "Yes, for now, anyway. She turned so blue, Kent. It was so frightening. It happened so suddenly, about nine o'clock last night. I know Allison was terrified, but she managed to get the emergency oxygen hooked up to the baby, then she called the doctor. He sent an ambulance, and we all came down here to the hospital. We've been here ever since."

"But Marianne's okay?"

"Well, no, not okay. Just stabilized. They're going to do the open-heart surgery this morning. She's scheduled to go into the operating room at nine."

"Oh, man," he said. "Is Allison doing all right?"

"As well as can be expected. She's worried sick, of course. And, well…"

"What?"

"Well, last night we found out Allison's blood isn't compatible with Marianne's, and neither is Lee's or mine, so they'll be using blood from the blood bank. Allison's worried about that, and the truth is, so am I."

So was Kent. "What kind of blood do they need?" Maybe one of his friends could supply blood for her.

"She's AB-negative. Either that or O-negative."

Kent's heart leaped. "I'm O-negative! Did you forget?"

"I—I guess I did," Diana said slowly.

"I could give blood."

"Oh, Kent! Would you?"

"What kind of question is that? Of course I will! Notify the nurses or doctors or whatever you have to do. Tell me where to go, and I'll be there in thirty minutes!"

Dr. Richardson allowed Allison to see Marianne for a few minutes before they wheeled her into surgery. The baby had already been given an injection, and she was asleep. Allison's eyes filled with tears as she stared down at Marianne's small body swathed in hospital green and covered by white cotton blankets. An intravenous tube was taped to her tiny hand. She looked so little. So helpless.

Her feathery eyelashes lay against her cheeks, and most of her face was obscured by the nasal prongs covering her nose. Allison bent over and kissed Marianne's forehead, then stood watching as the nurses wheeled her away.

She joined her father and stepmother in the waiting area outside the surgical unit. The large wall clock read 8:57.

"How did she look?" Diana asked.

Allison pressed her lips together. Tears threatened to erupt. All she could do was nod and swallow hard.

"Oh, honey…" Diana said. Both she and Lee got up and put their arms around her.

Allison couldn't control the tears any longer. She didn't want to cry. She'd fought against crying for hours because she was afraid once she started she wouldn't be able to stop. But now her strength seemed to have completely disappeared, and the tears gushed.

Lee gently walked her to the leather couch in the corner and sat her down between them. He kept his arm around her shoulders, and Diana pushed a tissue into her hands.

"I—I'm sorry," Allison said. She swiped at her eyes, then blew her nose. She took a couple of long, shaky breaths. The tears hadn't stopped completely, but at least they weren't coming in torrents any longer.

"Don't apologize," Diana said.

Her father just squeezed her shoulders.

At that moment Allison looked up and saw Kent. A piercing mixture of pain and happiness shot through her as she took in the worry lines furrowing his forehead, the concern flooding his blue eyes and the wonderful fact of his presence.

He walked straight over to her, and she stood. And then, without seeming to care that they were in a public place, that his mother and her father were sitting there watching them, that they were supposedly nothing more than friends, he put his arms around her and tucked her head under his chin.

"Kent," she whispered. "You came."

"Nothing would have kept me away," he said. "I knew you needed me."

And with those words, something hard and tight inside Allison seemed to uncoil and loosen, and she knew that at least some of her prayers had been answered.

Chapter Eleven

"**Y**ou mean you gave blood?" Allison asked. Kent had just explained about Diana's early-morning call. "Your mother didn't tell me!"

"Well, if anything went wrong, I didn't want to get your hopes up," Diana said. She smiled.

"Oh, Kent. That's wonderful. How can I ever thank you?"

"I don't need any thanks. I care about Marianne, too," he said softly.

Then he took her hand and led her to one of the couches. The four of them settled in to wait. Kent held her hand the whole two hours they waited. At any other time, Allison would have wondered what Diana and Lee were thinking. Right now nothing except Marianne seemed important.

At eleven o'clock, just as Allison was beginning to

get really anxious, Dr. Richardson, surgical cap pushed back on his head, walked into the waiting area.

Allison took one look at his weary face set in grave lines, and her heart zoomed into her throat. Kent's hand tightened, and for a moment no one said a word.

Then, as if a silent cue had been given, all four rose to their feet and waited. Allison held her breath, heart pounding.

Then Dr. Richardson smiled, his gaze meeting hers. "Marianne's going to be all right," he said. "The surgery was successful."

Allison's knees nearly buckled beneath her. "Oh, thank God," she said. "Thank God." And then the four of them were all laughing and talking at once.

During the days that followed Marianne's surgery, Allison spent most of her time at the hospital. It was terribly hard on her to see Marianne hurting, because recuperation after open-heart surgery was painful for anyone, and for a baby, who didn't understand what was happening, it was especially difficult. But Marianne, like most babies, bounced back quickly. Within days she was smiling up at Allison, and even though Allison knew the baby's tiny chest still hurt, the pain didn't seem to cloud her sunny disposition.

By Wednesday, five days after the surgery, Marianne was able to take a bottle and she was moved out of pediatric ICU and into a private room in another wing. Allison loved the new room, a colorful red, yellow and green. By the time the flowers and stuffed animals and other gifts that had been sent to the baby were put in the room, it almost looked as if it were Christmas. Marianne seemed to love all the color and stayed awake for longer periods of time.

Allison had a lot of company at the hospital. Diana and Lee came nightly. Sunny and Nikki came. Joel and Marcy came. Michael and Gail Berry came. Her grandparents, who had returned from their safari, came twice.

And Kent came.

Allison knew that she and Kent had reached some kind of turning point the day of Marianne's surgery, and she also knew that once the baby was home again, they would have to talk about their feelings.

Until then she tried to put her emotions concerning him on the back burner. But sometimes, when Marianne was sleeping, Allison would drift into that half state of wakefulness and dreaming where she would conjure an idyllic setting that had no bearing on reality: a two-story white house with a picket fence around it and climbing roses adorning it. Inside the house would be a family—a mother who looked like Allison, a father who looked like Kent and several rosy-cheeked children, the oldest of whom was a little girl who looked the way Allison imagined Marianne would look when she got older.

Only one thing happened to disturb Allison's dreamlike state. One day, while sitting in the lounge at the end of the hall from Marianne's room, Allison was in the middle of one of her romantic fantasies when a young, dark-haired woman walked into the lounge and sat down across from her.

Allison mentally gave herself a shake and smiled at the woman, who gave her a shy smile back. The woman looked familiar to Allison, but she couldn't place her or think where she might have seen her before.

For a while the two of them leafed through magazines, but several times Allison could feel the woman's gaze upon her, and finally she laid her magazine on the coffee table between them and said, ''Hi. I'm Allison

Fornier, and my daughter is recovering from surgery." She inclined her head toward Marianne's room.

"Hello," said the woman in a soft voice with a slight Spanish accent. "I am Yolanda Gonzales." She smiled, her dark eyes friendly but still shy. "My son, Roberto, is also recuperating from an operation."

They began to talk, and a few minutes later Yolanda said something about Dr. Richardson.

"That's it!" Allison said. "I saw you in Dr. Richardson's office!"

"Oh, yes. I remember," Yolanda said.

That was the beginning of a friendship that built rapidly over the space of the next couple of days. Allison learned that Yolanda was a single mother, struggling to get her teaching degree while working full-time as a secretary. She lived with her grandmother, she explained, who watched Roberto for her. Roberto, who was eight months old, had been born with a hole in the wall between the two upper chambers of his heart—a condition that required surgery to fix. He had had the surgery the day before Marianne had had her surgery, and he was now recovering rapidly.

Allison grew to like and respect the other woman, who had a plucky spirit and had overcome many obstacles in her young life. She couldn't help comparing her own silver-spoon existence with Yolanda's economic struggles.

Gradually, as the two women talked, Yolanda's story unfolded. She had fallen in love with a young man named John Guerrero, who came from a family much higher placed on the social and economic ladder than Yolanda's, and John's parents had disapproved of her. "They thought John was better than me because I have no education and my parents were laboring-class people.

They forbid John to see me, and because he worked for his father, he was afraid to defy them openly.''

"Oh, that's terrible," Allison said.

"But John and I were seeing each other secretly," Yolanda admitted. "He was trying to figure out a way for us to marry."

"What happened?" Allison asked, caught up in the other woman's drama.

Yolanda's eyes filled with tears. "I—I still cannot believe it myself. John was alone in his father's liquor store when two men came in with a gun. They robbed him, then they shot him. He died on the way to the hospital." Now the tears ran down her cheeks. "I didn't even know about it. He was dying, and I never knew!"

"Oh, Yolanda." Allison's heart constricted with pity. "How awful."

"I waited and waited for him. He was supposed to come to my house after work, and he never came. I—I was afraid to call his house." She wiped at her eyes with a tissue. "I couldn't sleep that night. I kept worrying and wondering. And then, the next morning I heard about it on the news."

"Oh, God," Allison said.

"And do you know what is the worst thing?" Yolanda said.

"No, what?"

"John never knew I was pregnant. He never had the joy of knowing he would be a father."

"Marianne's father never knew about her, either," Allison said softly.

Yolanda sniffed. "Really? Why?"

And so Allison confided in Yolanda, as the other had confided in her. She told her all about Jean Luc and their marriage. She even found herself telling her about Kent.

"Ahh," Yolanda said, dark eyes shining. "Now I understand why he looks at you in a certain way."

Allison could feel herself blushing. Yolanda and Kent had met the previous evening, when he stopped by to see Marianne on his way home from work.

When, on Sunday, nine days after Marianne's surgery, Dr. Richardson released Marianne, Allison hated to call an end to her budding friendship with Yolanda.

She hugged Yolanda and said, "Let's keep in touch."

"I would like that," Yolanda said.

They exchanged addresses and phone numbers. When Lee and Diana arrived to take her and Marianne home, Allison hugged her new friend again. "I'll call you soon," she promised.

Kent decided the San Diego Airport was one of the scariest he'd ever flown into. A white-knuckle flier anyway, he was certain the jet couldn't possibly avoid hitting one of the buildings in downtown San Diego as they made their approach. Miraculously, though, the pilot managed to set the 727 down without a mishap.

This was Kent's first visit to San Diego, and as he drove the rental car up Highway 163 toward Escondido and Poway, he admired the spectacular vistas, so different from the flat terrain of Houston.

He wondered what kind of reception he would get from Armand Brasselli. When Kent's secretary had finally gotten in touch with Brasselli, the former designer had been resistant to talk to Kent. Loretta persisted, though, and finally Brasselli had agreed to see Kent.

Kent had taken the first flight to San Diego. Less than thirty minutes from now, he would meet Brasselli. Fleetingly Kent remembered the closed look on Colin Jamieson's face when Kent had said he wanted to ask Brasselli about the terse notation concerning the "continuing" tests on the steering mechanism—if that's what the note had meant. Kent had not been able to uncover a single other reference to any ongoing tests—to the steering mechanism or any other part of the Wild Rider. And when he'd finally talked to Christina about the subject, she said she'd seen nothing at all in the notebooks she'd studied.

Kent knew Jamieson would not be happy if he found out about Kent's trip to San Diego. Routine questioning of Brasselli could have been handled via a phone call. And routine questioning was all Kent had been authorized to do.

But Kent wanted to see Armand Brasselli's face when Kent introduced the subject of the notation. In fact, Kent had copied that page of the notebook and brought the copy along with him so that if Brasselli for some reason denied knowledge of it, Kent could produce the proof that the notation had actually been made.

Kent exited Highway 163 at the Poway exit and turned right, following the twisting four-lane road around the mountain and into Poway proper. Without any difficulty, he found the condominium complex where Brasselli and his wife lived. As Kent pulled into the entrance to the hillside community of pink stucco units garlanded with deep-red-and-purple bougainvillea, Kent mentally prepared himself for the impending interview.

Brasselli answered the door himself. He was a stocky, dark, good-looking man who appeared to be in his late fifties. He was dressed in shorts, sneakers and a T-shirt.

The T-shirt stretched over some impressive muscles. "You Sorensen?" he demanded. He didn't smile.

"Yes." Kent did smile and extended his hand.

Expression warming slightly, Brasselli took his hand and they shook. Brasselli's grip was powerful. Kent wondered if the man lifted weights and vowed he would get back to some serious exercising himself. Soon.

Brasselli ushered Kent into a sunny, multiwindowed living room furnished in a comfortable, southwestern decor. Kent liked the look of the place with its russet-colored tile floor and open spaces. He sat on the sand-colored sofa in response to Brasselli's gesture and absentmindedly petted the head of a friendly yellow Lab who had materialized at his side.

"Would you like a drink?" Brasselli asked. "Beer? Scotch? Iced tea?" He looked at the dog. "Benjamin, don't make a pest of yourself!"

"How about a glass of water?" Kent said. He smiled down at the dog. "He's not a pest."

The Lab wagged his tail. When Brasselli returned to the living room with Kent's glass of water, he gave the dog a curt order, and the Lab walked a few feet away and settled down in a patch of sunlight.

A few minutes later Kent pulled out his small tape recorder.

Brasselli's eyes narrowed. "What are you doing that for?"

"I'm going to record our interview," Kent said matter-of-factly. He pulled his notes from his briefcase.

"Why?"

"Because I don't take shorthand, and I don't want to make any mistakes when I transcribe my notes later."

Brasselli thought about that for a minute, then said, "I told your secretary I don't know anything useful."

"Let me be the judge of that," Kent said. "Sometimes witnesses think they don't know anything when they actually do. Besides, you will definitely be called as a witness by the plaintiff. We need to know what to expect."

"Well, let's get this over with. I'm supposed to play golf at three o'clock."

Kent looked at his watch. It was just after one. "No problem." He met Brasselli's gaze. "Ready?" When Brasselli nodded, Kent turned on the tape recorder and spoke into the mike, giving the date, time and case reference. "Now, Mr. Brasselli, were you involved in the initial design of the Wild Rider?"

"Yes." Brasselli settled back in his chair.

"Can you tell me what your position was?"

Brasselli began to detail his involvement and responsibilities as the head of the design team.

Kent continued with routine questions about the progression of the design. After twenty minutes of questions and answers, Kent said, "In going over the R & D notebooks on the testing of the Wild Rider, I came across a notation you made last November." Casually he opened his briefcase and extracted the copy of the page containing the note. The note itself had been highlighted in yellow. "Take a look at this please, and translate the notation for me."

Brasselli, face impassive, accepted the paper. He studied it silently. The room was very quiet—the only sounds were those of the traffic on the highway below and the occasional thump of the dog's tail as he eyed them from his vantage point nearby.

Kent waited.

Finally Brasselli looked up. He shrugged. "It's nothing important."

"Even so, would you translate it, please?"

Something flickered in the depths of Brasselli's dark eyes. "I'm not sure I remember what this note meant."

"Try."

"Okay." Brasselli looked down at the paper again. "I'll try. Uh…continuing to check Wild Rider…"

Kent nodded. He'd figured out that much himself.

"…for problem with…"

Kent held his breath.

Brasselli looked up again. "Strength."

"Strength?" Kent didn't even try to hide his skepticism. "What does that mean?"

"You know, fork strength."

Kent met the man's gaze steadily. "You're sure?"

"Positive." Brasselli's dark eyes never even flickered.

"Because," Kent said slowly, "if this note didn't refer to fork strength and instead was related to *steering*, we'd have a serious problem, wouldn't we?" The word steering hung in the air between them.

"Well, it doesn't," Brasselli said, his answer clipped and final sounding.

"Would it surprise you, Mr. Brasselli, to learn that the crux of the suit being brought against Wilder's involves a faulty steering mechanism? *Knowledge* of a faulty steering mechanism?"

"Oh yeah?"

Brasselli's pretense of ignorance didn't fool Kent. He knew the man had known. He also suspected Brasselli was lying about the notation. He only wished he could prove it. "Yes."

"Did you have any more questions?" Brasselli asked. He very casually laid the copy of the notation on the table beside him.

"No, I don't think so." Kent turned off the tape recorder. "Thank you for seeing me." He returned his notes to his briefcase. "I'd like that copy back, please."

Brasselli said, "Oh, yeah, sorry."

Kent could have sworn his innocence was feigned.

But on the flight back to Houston, as Kent thought about the interview with Brasselli, he wondered if he'd imagined Brasselli's culpability. Maybe Kent was so hung up on the idea that Emmett Wilder was lying he had read something more into Brasselli's answers and expressions than had actually been there.

And even if Kent was right and Brasselli and Wilder were both lying, if he couldn't prove it, what difference did it make?

Kent returned to the office on Thursday. He'd only been gone one day. At eight-thirty Thursday morning, his intercom buzzed and Loretta said, "Mr. Jamieson wants to see you in his office."

"Now?" Kent had an appointment in fifteen minutes.

"He said right now."

Had Jamieson somehow learned about the interview with Brasselli? Kent wondered as he walked to Jamieson's office.

"I thought I told you to drop the matter of that note," Jamieson said without preamble as Kent entered his office.

Kent girded himself for what he knew was coming. "Yes, you did."

"Then why the hell didn't you?"

"I don't know what you mean."

"You know damn well what I mean!" Jamieson said. "You went out to San Diego and interviewed Armand

Brasselli and asked him about that notation. Now, don't try to deny it, because Brasselli himself told me."

Brasselli himself told him! If ever Kent had needed proof that there was something fishy with this case, Jamieson's disclosure clinched it.

"I'm warning you, Sorensen," Jamieson said. "And this is your last warning. Forget about this. Because if you don't, if I hear one more thing that you've done or said to stir this up again, you're history around here." He yanked a folder from the top of his In box and opened it. He began to read.

What the hell was going on? Kent decided then and there that he would not try to make any excuses. "I had always intended to interview Brasselli in person. I'm sorry if you think I should have told you ahead of time. I never imagined you'd object to being thoroughly prepared for trial. Brasselli will damned sure be called as a witness by the plaintiff. I was only doing my job. *Sir,*" he added.

Jamieson did not answer. In fact, he didn't look up.

Kent walked out of the office, ignoring the secretary's wide-eyed stare. Obviously she'd heard everything Jamieson and Kent had said. Kent grimaced. Knowing Lisa, by noon everyone in the firm would know about the confrontation.

Sure enough, later that morning Christina, giving him a smug look, said, "You'd better watch your step, Kent. I have a feeling your days here may be numbered."

Kent gave her a hard stare. Enough was enough, and Christina was beginning to get on his nerves.

For the rest of the day, while working on other things, Kent kept thinking about Armand Brasselli and Colin Jamieson's reaction to a perfectly legitimate interview and the cryptic notation itself. Was he being unreasonable about this? Was Jamieson right? Should he just forget all about it?

Finally, after going around and around and coming up with no answer that satisfied him, he decided he would stop by his mother's house after work and talk to Lee. He respected Lee's judgment and his integrity, and he'd be interested in hearing what the older man thought.

He'd intended to be on his way no later than seven o'clock, but it was nearly eight before he actually left. Then he decided to make a quick stop at his condo and change clothes. Thirty minutes later he'd changed into jeans and a dark blue cotton shirt and was heading out the door again. By the time his car was cruising up Memorial Drive toward the Loop, the sun had disappeared in the west, and dusk had settled over the city.

He had not seen Allison since she'd brought Marianne home on Sunday. He had purposely avoided going to the house because he knew Allison, as well as he, needed some time alone. They had spent several emotional hours together at the hospital—hours where they'd made a quantum leap in their relationship—and he wanted to give her time to think about it before he saw her again. But now he was going to see her.

He wondered how she'd act. Would she be happy to see him? He wondered what she'd think if he told her what he was preparing to tell Lee. At least she couldn't accuse him of sitting by and doing nothing, the way she had the night of his birthday party.

By the time he reached the house and pulled into the driveway, the night sky no longer carried any traces of the setting sun. Indigo shadows fell across the hood of the Corvette as Kent climbed out of the car and walked to the gate. It was locked, so he pushed the buzzer mounted into the brick wall, and a few moments later the speaker box crackled into life.

"Yes?"

It was Allison's voice. Kent said, "Allison, it's me, Kent."

"Oh—oh, just a minute." A second later he heard the click, which meant she'd released the lock on the gate. He opened it and walked through, closing it carefully behind him. By the time he got to the front door, she'd opened it. Light spilled out onto the walkway, and Allison, partially hidden from his view, stood behind the opened door. He walked inside, then turned to face her.

His breath caught, and for a moment he wasn't sure he'd ever breathe again. All he could do was stare at her. He wouldn't have been surprised to find that his eyes had bugged out of his head.

She was dressed for bed. Clinging to her curves was a pale peach satin peignoir trimmed in peach lace, covering, Kent was sure, a matching nightgown. The shimmery material fell sensuously over her hips and legs to just skim the floor. Peeping from beneath the hemline were bare feet with pink polished toenails.

As Kent's gaze traveled the length of her body and back up, he could see a pulse beating in the hollow of her throat, and he could also see the outline of her nipples clearly defined under the revealing fabric. His heart began to beat faster, and he couldn't tear his eyes away from her.

When he finally looked up and their gazes met, he could see she was as disconcerted as he was. Her cheeks were flushed, and she stammered a little when she said, "I…uh…I didn't expect anyone, so I…" Her voice trailed off, and she hurriedly shut the door and crossed her arms protectively across her breasts.

Kent found his voice and was surprised that it sounded normal. "I'm sorry. I should have called, I guess. I came to see Lee."

"He's not...they're not here."

"Oh. When will they be back?"

Allison's flush deepened. "Th-they're gone until Sunday night. They went to New Orleans."

"New Orleans! I just talked to Mom yesterday morning, and she never mentioned it."

"I know. My dad had unexpected business there, and on the spur of the moment, Diana decided to go with him. Then they thought they might as well stay the weekend, too." She was clutching the sides of the peignoir as if afraid it would suddenly fall open, and Kent knew she was mortally embarrassed by her state of undress.

"Damn. I really wanted to talk to your father." They were still standing, facing each other in the foyer, and Allison didn't seem to have any inclination to move. Suddenly unsure of what his next move should be, Kent wavered between saying he guessed he'd be going and walking into the living room and sitting down.

"Listen, Kent, I...uh...you're welcome to stay and visit awhile, but I think I'll just go upstairs and put on something else." She started toward the stairs.

"No, Allison, wait. It's okay. You don't have to do that. I'm only going to stay a minute. In fact, if you want me to, I'll leave now." God, she looked beautiful. He couldn't bear for her to take off the peignoir set. He could look at her dressed like that every moment for the rest of his life.

"Well..." She hesitated, indecision clouding her

lovely eyes. She sighed. "Okay. Come on in the living room. I just poured myself a glass of wine. Do you want some?"

He smiled. "Sounds good." He'd prefer beer but decided not to push his luck. He followed Allison into the living room and tried not to notice how the sleek material of her peignoir molded to her sweet little bottom. His pulse had gone haywire, and his jeans felt uncomfortably tight. To cover up his growing agitation, he said, "How's Marianne doing?"

"Oh, she's doing wonderfully!" Allison answered happily. "She's asleep. I put her down about thirty minutes ago."

Allison walked to the bar at the end of the room and uncorked a bottle of wine. She began to pour him a glass.

Kent looked around. He could see that she had been sitting at one end of the white sofa because her wineglass and the baby monitor were nearby and an open magazine lay on the cushions. He sat at the other end of the sofa and concentrated on getting his emotions and his raging hormones under control.

She walked back, handed him the glass of wine and sat on the other end of the sofa. She carefully pulled her peignoir closed, but if she were trying to look more modest, it was a losing battle.

Kent thought he had never seen her look more desirable or feminine. Her cheeks still had that flushed color that told him she was embarrassed to be caught half dressed. Her hair, worn in its usual casual style, curled damply around her face as if it had been freshly washed. She wore no makeup; there was only a hint of color on her full lips. As he watched, she caught her lower lip between her teeth and chewed on it—something he knew was a nervous habit.

Finally she looked at him. "Why did you want to see Dad?"

Kent hesitated, then told her everything, including his doubts about the truthfulness of the things he'd been told—both by Colin Jamieson and Armand Brasselli, as well by Emmett Wilder. "Anyway, Jamieson told me to drop the whole thing." He hesitated. "I'm thinking of going to Ben Keating, though. Telling him everything."

"You should, Kent. You can't just drop it. Not now. You know there's something wrong."

"It's not going to do me or Shelley Petrowski a hell of a lot of good if I get fired," he said reflectively.

"You won't get fired. Your instincts are right. I know they are. Go to Ben Keating. Tell him what you suspect. I'm sure he'll back you up."

"Keating might tell me exactly what Jamieson told me."

"Kent…" Allison's eyes looked like liquid gold as she faced him. "Do you really want to work for a firm that practices that kind of law? Can you live with yourself if Wilder really did know there was a design flaw and let Greg Petrowski test the motorcycle anyway? It sounds to me as if there's a cover-up going on."

Kent nodded. She was saying exactly what he'd been thinking. "You're right."

She smiled then, a blazingly beautiful smile, and something tightened in Kent's chest as their gazes met and held. Kent suddenly became aware of how quiet it was and, even though the room they were sitting in was enormous, of how very intimate it felt lit only by the soft light of two lamps.

He stood, and without thinking or planning, he suddenly found himself standing over Allison and reaching for her hand. Without hesitating, she placed her hand in his and allowed him to pull her up and into his arms.

She raised her face. She was breathing fast, and he knew she was feeling all the same chaotic emotions he was feeling. He looked into her eyes, silently asking a question, and read the answer in the depths of her golden brown irises.

He bent his head, and his lips met hers—at first gently, then with more intensity. He wrapped his arms around her, feeling her softness meet his hardness. His heart thundered in his ears, and his blood pounded through his veins as Allison's mouth opened under his.

He drove his tongue deep into the heated recesses of her mouth, and he could feel her body trembling as she responded. He could hear her heart racing, could feel the soft swell of her breasts against his chest and the firm flesh of her back and small, rounded bottom as his hands roamed up and down her body, pulling her ever closer.

He wanted to brand her, to possess her, to make her irrevocably his.

He tore his mouth from hers, dropped his lips to the sweet hollow of her throat. He inhaled her scent, tasted her silky skin with the tip of his tongue. "Allison, oh, Allison. I want you."

She stiffened, and Kent went rigid. Suddenly all the times in the past rose up to haunt him. All the times they'd kissed and touched. All the times she'd pulled away just as Kent reached the peak of his passion. Just when he wanted her the most.

She was pulling away again.

He'd been fooling himself. She hadn't changed. She

would never change. Once more she was going to send him home in the night, aching and miserable.

And then, so softly he almost thought he'd misunderstood her, she whispered, "Oh, Kent. I want you, too."

He stared down into her eyes—those beautiful eyes that had looked so sad for so long. "Are you sure?" he asked, his voice sounding rough to his ears.

She smiled, and the brightness of joy shimmered in her eyes, pushing away the last traces of sadness and sending a corresponding joy shooting through Kent.

"I've never been more sure of anything in my life."

Chapter Twelve

Allison thought her heart was going to burst as Kent kissed her. Suddenly her entire world went out of control, as if instead of spinning on its axis, it had tumbled out of the groove and was careening wildly through space. She was a chaotic mass of feelings—a euphoric mix that stunned her with its intensity. And when he touched her, all her long-buried needs erupted.

Then he said he wanted her, and for one long moment her needs were stilled as she absorbed the importance of his words. Now was the time to pull back if she had any doubts at all. Now was the time to call a halt if she wasn't sure. As his hands gripped her shoulders, she could feel the stillness in him. She knew her answer, the next few seconds, would determine the course of the rest of her life. Would Kent be forever relegated to the past? Or was he going to be part of her future?

Suddenly all the regrets, all the mistakes, all the sadness receded, leaving only a certainty that she belonged with Kent.

She always had.

And she always would.

And so she told him she wanted him, too. And her heart was filled with a blinding joy, a brilliant light that pushed out the darkness and sorrow and regrets of the past. When Kent swooped her up into his arms and began to climb the steps, Allison knew she was finally doing something right.

Kent carried her into her bedroom and set her down, but he still kept his arms around her, as if he were afraid if he let her go she might change her mind. She reached up and held his face with one hand on either side. They looked at each other for a long moment, then he bent his head and kissed her. This kiss wasn't as greedy as the one he'd given her downstairs. This kiss said he knew more would come so he could afford to take his time. This kiss promised and enticed, and when it was over, Allison was shaking with need and the force of her turbulent emotions.

Smiling down at her, Kent began to unbutton his shirt. Still a little shy about the mechanics of lovemaking, Allison wasn't quite sure what to do. Tentatively she reached over to help him, and she heard his quick intake of breath as her fingers grazed his chest.

More boldly she pulled his shirt open and slowly ran her palms over his warm skin, feeling the strength and power under the steady rise and fall of his chest. His chest was smooth, with only a few whorls of hair down the middle. Allison leaned forward and kissed him. She could feel his heartbeat under her lips as he gathered her closer.

He buried his face in her hair, whispering, "Allison. I've dreamed of this for so long."

She lifted her face to gaze into his eyes, which looked as dark as the midnight sea in the dimly lit room. "I know. I have, too."

They kissed again, and then she helped him remove the rest of his clothes until he was clad only in his briefs. She wanted him to take those off, too, but she still felt too shy around him to say so. Still, she couldn't resist touching the waistband, and that was all the hint it took. Kent hurriedly removed the briefs and then straightened.

Allison's breathing accelerated. He was so magnificent. So splendid. So completely male. She was awestruck by the beauty of his body. Why had she never realized just how beautiful a man's body could be? she wondered.

And then he was undressing her. Untying the sash of the peignoir and allowing the wispy material to slide off her shoulders and fall in a shimmery pool at her feet. Allison shivered as his fingertips grazed her collarbone then slowly trailed down to touch her breasts. She arched into his touch. He continued to caress her, touching her first with gentle fingertips that whispered erotically over her satin nightgown, and then bending to continue worshiping her body, but this time with his lips and mouth. The barrier of the nightgown intensified Allison's arousal, and she trembled under the onslaught of feelings.

Finally, just as she thought her knees would no longer support her, Kent reached down and lifted the nightgown over her shoulders, and the last barrier between them was gone.

Later, after he'd led her to the bed and they were lying next to each other, he began to touch her again, stroking her body and kissing her mouth at the same time. And Allison, who wasn't sure how much of this sweet torment she could stand, began her own exploration of him.

"Yes, yes," he said as she closed her palm around him, feeling his heat and strength, trembling in anticipation of the moment she'd dreamed about and thought would never come. She loved the feelings he was awakening in her, feelings that she never knew would be so powerful. She loved the way he touched her, each intimate stroke an affirmation of his need for her and hers for him. It was so good to finally allow herself to let go and just feel, to think of nothing except this man and this moment.

She never closed her eyes. She wanted to see him as he made love to her. She wanted to know what he was feeling. She had waited so long for this, and she wanted to experience every second to the fullest. She loved it when he moaned as she touched him. She loved it when she felt him tremble. And she loved it when his hands were no longer so gentle but became demanding and insistent.

She smiled when Kent said, "I can't wait any longer." She opened to him, welcoming his thrust, reveling in the feeling of completeness and unity as he pushed farther, settling deep inside her.

They began to move together, finding the rhythm that was theirs, fitting their bodies together in a timeless dance of love.

He thrust.

She received.

He inserted.

She surrounded.

He pushed.

She lifted.

Their moves were intricate yet simple. Primitive yet delicate. Ageless yet wondrously new.

Allison felt as if she were on a Ferris wheel, inching her way to the top as her heart pounded faster and her breath became more labored and her body tensed in expectation of the free-fall to come.

And then she reached the top, and for one breathless moment she trembled there at the edge of the world. Kent, too, seemed to still, then with one mighty thrust, he spun her off into the universe with him.

She wanted to cry.

She wanted to laugh.

She wanted to shout.

She wanted this feeling to go on forever. As his life force spilled into her, she kept her legs tightly wrapped around him, and she looked deeply into his eyes. ''I love you, Kent,'' she whispered. ''I've always loved you.''

The look on his face caused her heart to squeeze painfully. And then he kissed her. And kept kissing her. Her mouth. Her eyes. Her nose. Her throat. And over and over he said, ''I love you. I love you. I love you.''

Much later, after tiptoeing down the hall and peeking in at Marianne, who was still sleeping soundly, they made love again—slowly and sweetly—savoring each moment while whispering words of love to each other.

And afterward, as they held each other, they talked. ''Did you love Jean Luc?'' Kent asked, and Allison knew he needed to know.

''No. At first he excited me and made me feel special. But I never loved him. And I think he knew that. I think that's why..." She broke off. She didn't want to talk about her marriage tonight. Not tonight.

Kent's arms tightened around her. "We don't have to talk about it now."

She understood that eventually they would have to. And that was okay. As long as it wasn't tonight.

Still later she said, "When I found out you'd gone to work for Keating & Shaw, I felt as if someone had kicked me in the stomach."

His body tensed against hers. "But why? Isn't that what you wanted me to do?"

"Yes, but after I married Jean Luc, after everything in my life fell completely apart, the one thing that kept me going was knowing I'd done the right thing by releasing you from our engagement. It made me happy to know that at least *you* were happy. That you were following your dream. And then, to find out you weren't...I felt betrayed." There. She'd said it. Now she tensed, waiting for his answer.

It was a long time in coming. Finally in a low, thoughtful voice he said, "Somehow nothing worked out the way I thought it would. Without you my dream seemed hollow." He laughed without mirth. "You've heard that old saying, haven't you? The one that goes 'be careful what you wish for...'"

"'...because you may get it,'" Allison finished softly.

"I think that's what happened to us." He kissed her ear, his warm breath sending a pleasurable tingle down her spine. "I think we both got what we thought we wanted, and it turned out to be different from what we'd imagined."

"We were both too young."

"And too self-centered."

"No, I was the one who was self-centered," Allison said.

"I have to take my share of the blame, too," Kent insisted. "I refused to see that you were just being practical. That we needed more than love to live on."

"But we would have managed! I know we would have. I should have trusted you."

"Things would have still turned out the same. I still had some hard lessons to learn."

Allison decided he was being gallant in trying to accept blame, and she should allow him that gesture. She loved that about him. That he wanted to make her feel good about herself. Well, finally maybe she would be able to feel good about herself. Because now it looked as if she would be given a second chance.

With his fingertip he traced the line of her chin, then brushed his fingers over her lips. "Allison, do you think we've grown up enough to make a success of our relationship this time?"

The question trembled in the air. Allison held her breath, and in the muted light she met Kent's gaze. His eyes glowed, and her heart began to beat in slow thuds as the importance of his words permeated her body.

"Can we try again?"

"Try again?" she said, afraid to let her hopes go as far as they wanted to.

"Yes. Try again." He smiled down at her. "I want you to marry me. Will you?"

Allison blinked back tears as she whispered fiercely, "Oh, Kent! Yes, yes. I'll marry you!"

His kiss was like a benediction and a promise, and as Allison wound her arms around him and held him close, she vowed she'd never let anything come between them again.

* * *

Early Friday morning Kent went home, showered, shaved and dressed for work. Then he packed an overnight bag and tossed it into his car. He would spend the weekend with Allison. They would wait together for Lee and Diana to return and tell them about their engagement.

He hummed all the way to work. Even the prospective talk with Ben Keating—a talk he'd promised Allison he'd initiate first thing this morning—couldn't dampen his glowing happiness.

He hadn't felt this good in years. Memories of the previous night tumbled through his mind, and as he entered the office, he was smiling.

"My, don't you look happy this morning," said Barbara, the receptionist.

Kent headed straight for Ben Keating's office.

"I'm sorry, Kent, Mr. Keating is on vacation."

Even this news couldn't dampen Kent's spirits for long. "For how long?"

"He'll be back Wednesday."

As Kent headed for his office, he decided he could wait until Wednesday. And then, because nothing could keep his thoughts away from Allison for long, he began to count the seconds until he'd see her again.

Things were meant to turn out this way, he thought. If he and Allison had married years ago, neither would have been ready. They had both matured. Both learned lessons. Kent knew he was much better equipped to care for her and Marianne than he would have been before—both financially and emotionally.

And care for them he would. Allison and Marianne were now the two most important things in his life, and he would do anything he had to to safeguard their future.

* * *

Allison couldn't wait until Kent came back on Friday night. All day long, as she fed and bathed and played with Marianne, she thought about Kent and their love-making.

Poor Jean Luc, she thought. She had never ever felt about him the way she felt about Kent. Jean Luc's love-making had never moved her the way Kent's did. Everything between her and Jean Luc had been superficial—all flash, no substance. No wonder their marriage had been a disaster.

Except for Marianne. She smiled as she cuddled the baby. She guessed everything had worked out the way it had been meant to work out. If she and Kent had married four years ago, not only would she not have had Marianne, but she and Kent wouldn't have been ready to build the kind of life she knew they could have.

All day long she dreamed rosy dreams about how she would help Kent regain what she had cost him. How together they could make something wonderful out of the mistakes of the past. How, working side by side, they would build a future based on all the values Kent had once held dear. Values she was certain he still held dear.

And eventually they would have a child—a little sister or brother for Marianne to grow up with.

Allison touched her stomach. Maybe even now she was pregnant with Kent's child. Oh, that would be wonderful!

Finally six o'clock came. Allison was ready, trembling, eager. While Marianne had napped that afternoon, Allison had gotten everything ready, feeling wicked even as her heart fluttered with excitement and anticipation.

And then Kent was there, his eyes bright, his smile warm. The moment he closed the door behind him, he pulled her into his arms and kissed her greedily. "I missed you," he said, kissing her again and again. "Let's go make love," he whispered into her ear.

"We can't yet. The baby's awake."

He laughed and looked around. "Where is that little cutie?"

Allison's heart expanded. She could hear the genuine love in his voice. She gestured toward the living room. "In there. Sitting, waiting in her little chair."

While Kent played with Marianne, Allison watched him. Every once in a while his eyes would meet hers, and they'd share a warm, intimate look. He was good with the baby. She liked him and responded to him. He would be a wonderful father.

Later, while Marianne, who had already been fed, lay nearby in her stroller, Allison and Kent ate their dinner. Allison had fixed baked chicken and rice and served it with salad and rolls. They laughed and talked and Kent told her about having to wait until Wednesday to talk to Ben Keating. They drank some wine, and after dinner he helped her clear off the table and load the dishwasher.

Then together they got Marianne ready for bed. Kent sat and watched while Allison rocked the baby to sleep. Then quietly they carried her upstairs and placed her in her crib. Allison switched on the baby monitor, then turned to Kent.

He smiled, reaching for her hand. "Is it my turn now?" he murmured as they walked out of the room together.

She smiled and nodded.

He put his arm around her and turned her toward her bedroom.

"No," she said. "I have something else in mind." She felt like a kid on Christmas day. She couldn't wait to see his face when he saw what she'd done. Taking his hand, she led him into the master bedroom suite. When he frowned, she said, "Don't worry. Come on."

He followed her into the adjoining master bath. Ever since Allison had first seen this bathroom, she'd wanted one like it. The bathroom was enormous—almost as large as a bedroom—and in the center of it was a huge sunken tub. Overhead was a large skylight, which was now glowing orange from the evening sun.

As Kent, eyes questioning, watched, Allison turned on the taps. Smiling, she poured scented oil into the steaming water. Then she picked up the book of matches sitting on the vanity and began to light the candles in the dozen or so crystal holders placed around the room. She looked at him over her shoulder. "What are you waiting for?" she said.

Kent thought he'd died and gone to heaven when Allison, eyes bright with excitement, joined him in the tub. She lowered herself into the water and leaned back against him. The hot water and scented oil and flickering candles, combined with the feel of her against him, caused Kent's heart to try to explode out of his chest. His hands trembled as he stroked her slippery skin.

She laid her head back, and he closed his eyes. She felt better than anything he'd ever experienced before. The fact that he loved her, and she loved him, that she'd planned this, all added to his pleasure.

He cupped her high, firm breasts, feeling the hard nubs grow even harder as he teased them, and his own body quivered in response. "You feel so good," he whispered in her ear.

"I love when you touch me," she said.

They stayed in the tub a long time. They kept draining the cooled water and adding more. They touched and kissed and brought each other to the peak of pleasure more than once.

And then later they went to Allison's bedroom, where they slept in each other's arms.

On Saturday they took Marianne outside and settled her in her chair, shaded by an umbrella, and they lay in the sun and swam in the pool and cooked hot dogs on the grill.

Saturday night they sent out for Chinese food. Kent helped Allison bathe Marianne and put her to bed. Then, of course, they went to bed themselves.

Sunday morning they had a long, leisurely breakfast, after which they cleaned up the house together, played with the baby and settled in to wait for Lee and Diana to come home.

"They said they'd be home about three," Allison said.

"Before they come, there's something I want to give you," Kent said. He smiled at her, then reached into his pocket.

Allison frowned a little when she saw the jeweler's box. He could almost hear her thought processes, the questions running through her mind: When did he have time to buy a ring? Why didn't he ask me to come with him?

He watched her face as she opened the box. He knew the instant she realized the ring was the one he'd given her during their first engagement. He could see her hands were shaking as she lifted the ring from its satin bed.

"Oh, Kent," she said. She raised her face, and her eyes were bright with tears. "You kept it. All this time, you kept it."

"Let me put it on you."

When Kent saw the ring sparkling once more on Allison's hand, his chest expanded with pride. That ring belonged there. This time it would remain there.

Then he kissed her because his heart was too full to speak and because he wanted to.

Afterward she smiled up at him. "No wonder I love you," she said, her voice not quite steady. "You're incredibly sweet to me."

"It's easy to be sweet to you." He smoothed a strand of hair back from her face and thought about how much he loved her. Tears still shimmered in her eyes.

"What if I'd never come home? This ring is worth a lot of money. You should have taken it back."

"Aren't you glad I didn't?"

And then they kissed again. Finally Allison said, "We'd better stop. My father and your mother will be here soon."

Lee and Diana arrived home about twenty minutes after three. They came in the back door, and Kent and Allison, along with Marianne in her jumper chair, were sitting in the kitchen waiting for them.

"Hi, Kent," Lee said, setting down the two suitcases in his hands. "We saw your car out back."

Kent stood. Allison remained seated, hiding her hands in her lap. She didn't want her father or stepmother to see the ring until after they'd told them about their engagement.

"Have you been here long?" Diana asked, walking into the room.

"Did you have a good time?" Allison interjected. She knew Kent would not want to answer his mother's question. At least not right now.

"We had a wonderful time," Diana said, but her eyes were bright with curiosity as she looked first at Allison and then back to Kent.

"New Orleans is a great place," Lee said. "The only problem is, we ate too much." But his expression was quizzical, too.

"What's going on?" Diana asked. "You two look very pleased about something."

Kent looked at Allison. She put her hands on the table. The diamond was impossible to miss.

Diana's mouth fell open. Lee's face broke into a huge grin. Kent started to laugh and walked around to where Allison was sitting. She stood, and he put his arm around her.

"We're getting married," he said.

Allison knew her father was happy for them, but she wasn't sure how Diana felt. She watched her stepmother's face carefully. And then Diana smiled, and Allison felt weak with relief.

Just then Marianne cried out, and they all turned to look at her. She laughed and stuck her fist in her mouth. And then they were all hugging and talking at once.

"This is the way things were always meant to be," Lee said, hugging Allison.

Marianne cooed as if to say she agreed with that sentiment, and Allison was sure that this time nothing could happen to mar her happiness.

Chapter Thirteen

Allison floated through the next couple of days on a rosy pink cloud. Even the fact that it was difficult for her and Kent to be alone couldn't affect her happiness for very long.

It was especially difficult for them to make love. And now that they'd finally consummated their love, it was really hard not to be able to express it whenever they wanted to.

But they managed.

Allison smiled, hugging herself. The previous night—Tuesday—Diana and Lee had offered to watch Marianne, and Kent fixed dinner for Allison at his place. They'd hardly eaten any of the dinner. They'd tried, but they couldn't keep their hands off each other. Finally, laughing a bit guiltily, they'd abandoned their steaks and given in to the powerful emotions raging through them.

Allison squirmed as she remembered how they hadn't even made it to Kent's bedroom. Instead, they'd hurriedly undressed each other and made love right there on the dining-room floor.

She'd loved it.

And that in itself amazed Allison. She'd always thought of herself as rather prudish. Oh, she'd been wildly attracted to Kent during their first engagement, and she'd wanted to make love with him, but she'd never imagined that she could be so abandoned. So— so *wicked*. She'd never been that way with Jean Luc. And Jean Luc had been a skillful and knowledgeable lover. But somehow, when Jean Luc made love to her, she'd always known exactly what was happening, as if she were an observer and not a participant. Her mind would think, now he's touching me there and I'm supposed to feel thus and so. And she would. But she had always been in control of her emotions. Never once had she slipped over the edge. Never once had she given herself completely.

Allison daydreamed away most of Wednesday morning thinking about making love with Kent. She had finally realized that the reason she would never let Kent make love to her during their first engagement was that deep down she was never certain of his commitment to her. She had never been sure he would be able to make the choices necessary for them to have a good life together. If only she'd been able to see that the choices Kent made were the right choices.

She frowned. If only she didn't feel so responsible for Kent's defection from the storefront practice. For the cynicism and disillusion he felt.

It was so ironic that she finally understood what Kent had tried to tell her, and he no longer seemed to care.

Well, all that would change now. Allison was sure that now that they were back together, Kent would regain some of his idealism and eventually would even want to go back to the storefront—at least on a part-time basis.

Actually it might be very nice if Kent could stay at Keating & Shaw, as well. Her father had once explained to her that it would be much easier for Kent to accomplish the kinds of things he wanted to accomplish with the storefront once he'd built a name for himself with a firm like Keating & Shaw. A big firm had all kinds of resources behind it and could actually enhance Kent's work with the storefront. Kent would have the prestige and exposure of high-profile clients and still do the important work of the storefront.

We could have our cake and eat it, too!

Thinking about this, Allison looked at her watch. It was almost noon. She wondered if Kent had been able to talk to Ben Keating yet. She mentally crossed her fingers. Hopefully the talk would go well. She couldn't wait to find out what Ben Keating had had to say.

At eight o'clock Wednesday morning, Kent had called Ginny, Ben Keating's secretary. She'd informed him that, yes, Mr. Keating was back in the office, but he was extremely busy and couldn't possibly see Kent today.

"I only need five minutes," he said.

"He doesn't have five minutes." Her voice had taken on that don't-you-understand-how-important-he-is tone that always amused Kent. For some reason, most of the secretaries in the firm were competing in some kind of unacknowledged game of my-boss-is-more-important-

than-your-boss, and they never missed a chance to re-
inforce their superiority.

"Look, Ginny, this is important. Don't play games
with me, okay? Let me talk to him." Now that he'd
decided to talk to Ben Keating, he didn't plan to wait
another day.

He could hear the rustle of paper, and he imagined
her looking at the great man's calendar as she pondered
whether she should grant this favor to the lowly serf. A
few minutes later she came back on the line. "If you're
here exactly at ten minutes to twelve, I'll see that he
works you in for a couple of minutes before his lun-
cheon engagement." This was said in a tone of great
condescension.

"I'll be there." Now he could afford to be nice.
"And thanks, Ginny. I really appreciate this."

At ten minutes to twelve, Kent stood outside Ben
Keating's closed office door. Two minutes later the door
opened, and Keating beckoned to him.

"Kent," he said. "Come on in." He smiled.

Kent smiled back. He liked Ben Keating. Had liked
him from the very first time he'd met him.

Kent followed Keating into the sunny office with its
view of southwest Houston. Keating, a tall, distin-
guished-looking, gray-haired man with sharp, dark eyes,
seated himself behind a beautiful old carved mahogany
desk. "So what can I do for you, Kent?" he asked. He
gestured toward the whiskey-colored leather chairs
grouped to one side of his desk.

Kent sat and crossed his legs. "Well, sir, something's
come up on the Wilder case that disturbs me."

"Oh?"

Kent explained what he had discovered when reading
through the R & D notes. "It appears to me that the

design team knew there were structural problems with the steering. If I think so, it's a sure bet the plaintiff's lawyers will think so. And once they get their hands on that, our case is down the tubes.''

"Did you talk to Colin about this?"

"Yes, sir. And he brushed me off. You know we've got to produce all those documents within two weeks, and if we don't have a better explanation for that note than Brasselli gave me, or at least something to show they resolved the problem—whether it was with the fork strength or the steering mechanism, as I suspect—those sharks will eat Brasselli for lunch in his deposition. Not to mention what they'll do to us in front of the jury.''

After he'd finished, Keating pursed his lips and studied Kent for a few minutes. "Listen, son, Jamieson is one of the sharpest and most respected trial lawyers in the state. If he doesn't think there's anything to worry about, I'm afraid I have to respect his many years of trial experience and bow to his superior judgment.'' He paused. "And so do you.''

"I understand that, but—"

"Furthermore," Keating said, his voice a little sterner than it had been, "you've already been told all of this. By Colin Jamieson, who is, after all, the attorney in charge of this case. Now, I'll overlook your breach of etiquette in coming to me because you're young and you're relatively inexperienced, but I don't want it to happen again. From now on anything you have to say can be said to Colin.''

Kent knew better than to persist. Ben Keating had made himself clear. A wise employee knew when to retreat. Kent thanked Keating for his time and went back to his own office.

All afternoon he fumed. He was caught between a

rock and a hard place. Frustrated and angry, he reviewed his options. He could forget about that damned notation and get on with his assignment, which was what he'd been ordered to do.

Ordered! That still rankled.

Or he could ask to be removed from the case. If he wanted to keep his job, he'd drop this hot potato. Because if he asked to be removed from the Wilder case, he might as well resign from the firm, for he would be signing his own death warrant. He would have no future with Keating & Shaw.

Kent didn't call until nearly five o'clock.

"Did you talk to Ben Keating?" Allison asked.

"Yes."

"What did he say?"

"I don't want to talk about it over the phone. I'll tell you tonight." His voice softened. "It's okay if I come over tonight, isn't it?"

Allison laughed happily. "Of course. Do you want to have dinner with us? My father's making stuffed flank steak. He told me to invite you."

After they hung up, Allison wondered about Kent's reticence when she'd asked about his conversation with Ben Keating. Maybe things had not gone well.

Later that evening, after they'd had dinner with Lee and Diana and put Marianne to bed, they walked outside and sat on the deck where they could talk privately. They didn't turn on the outdoor lights or the pool lights, and the darkness wrapped itself around them. Off in the distance heat lightning streaked the sky, and Allison wondered idly whether it might rain later. "So tell me about Ben Keating," she said.

"Well, he said essentially the same things Colin Jamieson said."

"What do you mean?"

She heard Kent's sigh. "I mean he told me to back off. He told me I was completely out of line in coming to him."

"Oh, Kent!" Allison couldn't believe it. She had been so sure Ben Keating would see that Kent was right about this and Colin Jamieson was wrong. "What are you going to do now?"

He didn't answer for a moment. Then softly he asked, "What do you think I should do?"

She wanted to tell him what she thought. But something, some odd reluctance she couldn't identify, told her not to. "Kent, I can't make your decision for you. I tried that once, remember?"

"Will you support my decision, no matter what it is?"

Allison's heart skipped a beat as she realized what he was asking her. As she realized for the first time that maybe the old Kent really was gone forever. "Yes," she answered. She could live with whatever he decided. She loved him and he loved her. That was what was important. But down deep she knew there was no reason to worry. Kent couldn't have changed so much. He would make the right decision.

Wouldn't he?

On the Saturday night after their engagement, Allison received a call from Yolanda Gonzales, her friend from the hospital. She'd already talked to Yolanda several times since Marianne's release, and she was worried about Yolanda. She seemed depressed, even though— like Marianne—Roberto had made a rapid recovery from his surgery. Allison, wanting to cheer up her new friend, invited Yolanda and Roberto to come along on a picnic she and Kent had planned for Sunday afternoon.

Sunday turned out to be a very hot day, but Allison figured it would still be nice in Memorial Park. Marianne, who looked better and better every day, cooperated by taking a long nap early in the day and waking up an hour before Kent arrived.

By three o'clock they were on their way.

"How do you like this car I rented?" Kent asked. "I'm thinking of buying one like it."

"But what about your Corvette? I know how you love it."

"A Vette isn't exactly a family car, and now that I'm going to have a family…" He smiled and reached over to touch her hand.

"But we could get a family car for me to use, and you could still keep your Corvette," Allison insisted. "I was planning to buy a car, anyway." She and Kent had not discussed money yet, and Allison wondered how he would feel about the fact that she had an awful lot of it. She'd had a trust fund, set up by her Marlowe grandparents, before marrying Jean Luc. But now, because Jean Luc had been heavily insured, she was wealthy.

"We'll see," he said. "We don't have to decide anything this minute."

Thinking about the money, Allison felt a bit uneasy. Kent had a lot of pride. He might not want to use any money he considered Jean Luc's. Never one to borrow trouble, Allison put the uncomfortable thought out of her mind. She'd cross that bridge when she came to it.

She glanced at Kent. She wondered what he was thinking about. She wondered if he'd come to any decision about the firm and his future there. She wanted to ask him, but she still felt that strange reluctance she'd felt the other day. Surely it wouldn't be long before he came to the same conclusion she'd reached.

But what if he doesn't? What then?

Firmly, telling herself everything would be all right, she put that thought away, too.

It didn't take long to get to the park. Even though it was a blistering hot day, there were hundreds of people there. Even the jogging trail that followed the curves of Memorial Drive was full.

"Look at all those people running in this heat. Are they crazy?" Kent said as they pulled onto the main road leading into the park. "It must be one hundred degrees right now."

"They're gluttons for punishment, I guess." Allison had never been able to figure out the allure of running, even when the weather was nice. But now? In the worst heat of the afternoon? She'd take a nice aerobics class in an air-conditioned room any day. And if she was going to be outdoors, an early morning tennis game or a brisk swim in cool water was much more sensible, not to mention tolerable.

"Where's Yolanda meeting us?" Kent asked.

"By the tennis courts." Allison hoped they would be able to find Yolanda easily. She needn't have worried. Yolanda, with Roberto in a little portable stroller, was waiting exactly where she said she'd be.

Fifteen minutes later the five of them were settled on a quilt under the shade of an enormous ash tree. Roberto, eyes wide as he watched everything, sat in his stroller, and Marianne gurgled happily in her jumper chair.

Allison leaned back, thinking how much she would have hated doing something like this a few years ago.

A picnic in the park would not have held any appeal at all. But now, with her new maturity and Marianne's birth, everything seemed entirely different to her. Her gaze drifted to Kent, who, arms propped on his knees, watched as a couple of little boys cavorted with their dog, a friendly golden retriever. They kept throwing a stick, and the dog would bound off, retrieve it and bring it back, tail wagging.

Kent fit this atmosphere perfectly, she decided, envisioning many more Sunday afternoons spent in just this way.

She looked around. The park was filled with people having fun, laughing and talking, eating and playing. Somewhere close by, someone was playing the radio. The station had to be an oldies station, Allison thought, because all the tunes seemed to be vintage rock and roll. The catchy music added to her sense of happiness and well-being.

Now her gaze wandered to Yolanda and stopped. Some of Allison's pleasure faded as she realized Yolanda didn't seem very happy. There were worry lines in her forehead, and her dark eyes were clouded as she stared off into space.

"Is something wrong, Yolanda?" she asked.

Yolanda looked around. "No, no, it's nothing," she said. She darted a glance at Kent.

Kent, after exchanging a look with Allison, said, "You can talk in front of me."

Allison smiled at him. He was such a kind man. Jean Luc had not been kind.

"John's mother has found out about Roberto," Yolanda said, her gaze meeting Allison's. "She has contacted me."

"Is that so bad?" Allison asked. She turned to Kent.

''The John she's referring to is Roberto's father. He died before Roberto was born.''

Kent's gaze flicked to Marianne, and Allison knew he was thinking, just like her father. She nodded sadly. She wondered if that's why she had been drawn to Yolanda from the start. Because their situations, so dissimilar in some ways, were so similar in this one important part of their lives.

''John's parents hated Yolanda,'' Allison continued, wanting Kent to understand her friend's fear. ''They thought he and Yolanda were no longer seeing each other, so when he died, they had no idea Yolanda was pregnant.''

Kent nodded. ''Well, is it so bad that they know about Roberto now?''

''Yes!'' Yolanda said. ''You don't know them, Kent. They are ruthless people. And John was their only child. If I thought they would just want to be part of Roberto's life, that would be one thing. After all, I am not without sympathy for them. I lost John, too, so I understand their grief.'' Her eyes took a bleak look, and Allison's heart contracted with pity. ''But they wouldn't be content to just share Roberto. They would want to own him, just like they tried to own John. I am very frightened.''

''Kent, what do you think she should do?'' Allison asked.

He shrugged. ''There's nothing to do. It would be different if they'd made some kind of move, but they haven't.'' He looked at Yolanda. ''Have they? Have they said anything?''

She frowned. ''No. They've just said they want to see him.''

''Well, then you have to make a decision.''

''I don't want them anywhere near Roberto,'' Yolanda said fiercely. She put a protective hand on Roberto's head, and in response, he stuck his fist in his mouth and sucked noisily.

"Tell them that, then."

"But what if they insist? Can they force me to let them see him?"

Kent shrugged. "If they can prove Roberto is their grandchild. Can they?"

Yolanda nodded miserably. "I—I put John's name down as the father on the birth certificate."

"Oh, Yolanda!" Allison said, although she understood Yolanda's reasons. She had loved John. She had never dreamed his parents would see the birth certificate.

"I know," Yolanda said. "I was stupid. I didn't want them to know about the baby, but I never thought...." She gazed off into the distance, shoulders drooping, misery stamped all over her.

Allison reached over to take Yolanda's hand. "Don't worry, Yolanda," she said softly. "It'll be okay. They can't force you to do anything you don't want to do."

Yolanda looked up. "I'm afraid of them. They have so much money. They have such good lawyers. John used to tell me about their lawyers."

Allison looked at Kent. An idea formed. "Kent," she said slowly. "You could call John's parents for Yolanda. You could tell them how she feels. Maybe if you called—you know, the voice of authority—they'll back off."

Kent shook his head. "I don't think—"

"Oh, please, Kent, would you?" Yolanda pleaded. Hope shone from her eyes.

Kent shot a look at Allison. A look that told her he

was not pleased with her offer of his help. Sighing, he said, "All right. I'll call them for you."

Allison smiled. "Thank you, Kent," she said.

"Yes, Kent. Thank you," Yolanda echoed. "And God bless you."

Later, remembering the conversation, Allison decided it was fate that Yolanda had needed Kent's help. Perhaps by helping her, Kent would finally see where he belonged. Perhaps Yolanda's plight would remind him of all the thousands of other people who felt helpless in the face of insurmountable problems and inadequate resources.

Yes. That's exactly what would happen. Then he would once more be the Kent he used to be. The Kent she wanted him to be again.

Chapter Fourteen

Kent wished he'd never agreed to call John Guerrero's parents. But it had seemed so important to Allison that he help Yolanda, and he had wanted to please Allison. He thought Yolanda was making a mistake, though. He understood her fear of the Guerreros, but life would be so much easier for her if she would just call them and try to work out something that would make them happy.

He had tried to tell her this, but she had been adamant. So he'd agreed to call them for her.

He placed the call at ten Monday morning, deciding he might as well do it now and get it over with. A soft-voiced woman answered the phone, saying, "Guerrero residence."

"I'd like to speak with Mrs. Guerrero, please." Kent had decided that he would talk with Ann Guerrero instead of her husband, because she had initiated the contact with Yolanda.

"Who is calling, please?" asked the soft-voiced woman.

"Kent Sorensen. I'm an attorney calling on behalf of Yolanda Gonzales."

"One moment, please."

He heard a muffled conversation in the background and deduced that the woman who'd answered the phone had placed her hand over the receiver while she told Ann Guerrero who he was. A few seconds later a firm, no-nonsense voice said, "This is Ann Guerrero. What can I do for you, Mr. Sorensen?"

"I'm calling at the request of Yolanda Gonzales, Mrs. Guerrero."

"Why couldn't she call me herself?" Now Guerrero sounded belligerent.

Kent kept his voice neutral. "I'm sorry, Mrs. Guerrero, but Miss Gonzales prefers to have no direct contact with you."

"I see. And what about my request to see my grandson?"

Kent had promised Yolanda he would try to bluff Guerrero, even though he was sure the bluff wouldn't work. "She's considered your request to see her son, but she's decided to deny it."

"Does Miss Gonzales really think that I will just roll over and go away? Conveniently forget about my grandson?" Her voice was tightly controlled, but Kent could hear the underlying fury. "If that's what she thinks, she's sadly mistaken, Mr. Sorensen. My husband and I have no intention of going away. We have a right to see our son's only child, whether Miss Gonzales likes it or not!"

"I'm sorry, Mrs. Guerrero. I know this is not what you wanted to hear. However, Miss Gonzales is Roberto's mother. And she's made her decision.'' Kent purposely did not refer to Roberto as Mrs. Guerrero's grandson. One of the first things a lawyer was taught was to never reveal anything you weren't required to reveal.

For the first time since Ann Guerrero took his call, some of her control slipped. ''Well, you can tell that—that…woman…that she has not heard the last from us!''

After they'd hung up, Kent called Yolanda at work and relayed the conversation to her. ''I don't think she's going to drop this, Yolanda,'' he warned. ''She sounded like the kind of woman who would call her lawyer today and instruct him to take you to court and try to get a judge to grant her visitation rights.''

''But Roberto is *my* son. Can she do that?''

Kent heard the panic in Yolanda's voice. He felt sorry for her, but there was no sense in giving her a false sense of security. ''It's been done before.'' Successfully, too, he thought.

''And what happened in those cases?''

''According to Texas family law, if the Guerreros can prove it's in the best interest of the child for them to have a part in his life, the court can rule in their favor.''

''Oh, no! Kent, what will I do? They have money and connections.''

''Well, don't panic yet. There's no reason to do anything until they make a move. You should just be prepared. I'll talk to a friend of mine whose firm does a lot of *pro bono* work of this type. His name is Joel Bartlett, and I think you'll like him. I'm sure he'd be happy to represent you if you need a lawyer.''

''I don't want anyone else,'' she said, desperation edging her voice. ''I want you.''

''Yolanda, I'm sorry. I work for Keating & Shaw,

and frankly I know you can't afford our rates. Joel is a good friend of mine, and he'll do a good job for you.'' He hesitated, then decided he'd give her his best advice. ''Look, Yolanda, I know how you feel about the Guerreros, but why don't you talk to them? Wouldn't it be better for everyone concerned if you could work out something with them? Wouldn't it be better for Roberto? Is it really fair to deny him a relationship with his grandparents?''

''No. No. Because I know what would happen. They would gradually take Roberto away from me, just as they tried to take John away from me. They don't approve of me, Kent. They think they're better than I am. And even if they didn't take Roberto, they would try to turn him against me. I don't want him to have anything to do with them.''

Kent sighed. He was afraid that in the end the Guerreros would prevail, anyway, no matter what Yolanda wanted. As she had said, they had both money and clout. Yolanda had neither. On top of that, she was just managing to eke out a living for herself and her son. And he knew she had a fairly large medical bill to pay. A judge might think he was doing her a favor if he allowed the Guerrero grandparents to be a part of Roberto's life, especially if they offered financial help.

Well, he'd done what he could to help and advise her. Allison would be happy.

Allison wasn't happy. She stared at Kent as he repeated his conversations with Ann Guerrero and Yolanda. ''But, Kent! Why couldn't you represent Yolanda?''

''I told you. I couldn't take her case outside of the firm. And she can't afford our prices.''

"But surely Keating & Shaw do some *pro bono* work, too. All the big law firms do!"

"Yes, a small portion of our business is devoted to *pro bono* work, but I'm not currently assigned to that section. In fact, I'm not slated to serve in that capacity until sometime next year."

"But couldn't you talk to—"

"Allison, look, it's not just that." He ran his hands through his hair in a gesture of frustration. "I don't want to get involved in this."

"But why not?" She couldn't believe what she was hearing. Why, the old Kent would have jumped to Yolanda's defense. The old Kent loved representing the underdog. The old Kent would have been chomping at the bit.

"Because I no longer take on lost causes."

"Lost causes? You mean you think this would be a hopeless case?"

"Yes. I think she'll lose if the Guerreros decide to press the issue. After all, they *are* Roberto's grandparents, and they have a right to be a part of his life." He took a swallow of the drink she'd prepared for him, then added, "And as long as we're being truthful, I might add that I agree with that."

"You agree with that! Kent! You know what Yolanda told us. You know how those people tried to break her and John up. You know what they're like. They're ruthless and cruel."

"Allison, everyone makes mistakes. Maybe they were doing what they thought was best for their son. Don't you have any sympathy for them? Their only child is dead, and all they have left of him is Roberto."

"You're making them sound like saints."

"No. They're not saints. I know that. But they are

human beings. I just think, for everyone's sake, Yolanda should first try talking to them.''

"If she should decide to follow your advice, would you represent her then?"

He sighed wearily. "No. But I'm sure Joel will."

"I—I don't understand." She'd been so sure Yolanda's plight would set Kent back on the track he'd forsaken. "I thought you'd want to help her. In the old days—"

"This isn't the old days." His voice hardened. "I have a different kind of job now. Different priorities."

"I—I can't believe you really feel this way."

"Well, believe it, because I do. Hell, I'd have thought you'd be happy about the fact that I want to provide you and Marianne with a secure future."

"But, Kent—"

"Damn it, Allison, nothing you say is going to change my mind about this. Now can we just drop it?"

Stung by his answer, she said, "I suppose the next thing you're going to tell me is that you've decided to stay on the Wilder case."

He set his drink down on the redwood table next to him. He stared at her. "I haven't decided about the Wilder case yet. But I thought we'd agreed that whether I stayed with it or not, you'd support me."

"But I never thought—"

"Oh, I see," he said coldly, his eyes narrowing. "You never thought I wouldn't see things your way, did you?"

"That's not fair, Kent! I just meant—"

"I know exactly what you meant. You thought I'd come around to your way of thinking. You always think I'll come around to your way of thinking. You know,

Allison, you tried to manipulate me once before. It didn't work then, and it's not going to work now!''

With a sinking heart, Allison realized Kent still harbored bitterness toward her. Despite his love for her—and she didn't doubt that he loved her—he hadn't completely forgiven her.

Still, she couldn't give up. She couldn't pretend she was happy about the way he'd changed. Furthermore, she didn't believe he really had changed. All this cynicism, all this indifference, was just a barrier he'd thrown up to avoid being hurt again. Eventually, when he trusted her enough, when he trusted *life* enough, the old Kent would emerge. All she had to do was be patient.

But after Kent left to go home, doubts began to creep into Allison's mind. And late that night, right before she finally fell asleep, she admitted to herself that she was afraid.

At nine-thirty the following morning, Kent wearily rubbed his forehead. He felt frustrated and irritated after arguing with Allison over Yolanda's situation and his own situation here at Keating & Shaw.

He guessed he wouldn't have been so sharp with her if he hadn't been feeling so many doubts himself. He wished he knew what to do about the Wilder case.

The Wilder case.

Over and over he'd thought about that damned notation. He didn't know why it kept cropping up in his thoughts. No one else at the firm seemed to think it was a problem. Armand Brasselli said it had to do with the fork strength of the bike and had nothing to do with the steering. Nowhere else in all the dozens of test notebooks was there any mention at all of a problem with the steering. So why was he still doubting?

While his mind was thus occupied, there was a sharp knock on his door. Then it opened, and his secretary walked in, closing the door behind her. "Mr. Sorensen, Jackson Clemente and Tracy Higgins are here."

Kent frowned. "Already? They weren't scheduled to come until tomorrow." Clemente and Higgins were with the law firm representing Shelley Petrowski. The motion for production of documents on the Wilder case had been filed the previous week, and Clemente and Higgins had made arrangements to examine the documents the following day.

"Well, I guess somebody got their signals crossed, because they're here now," Loretta said.

"Oh, hell. And Jamieson's in Galveston today." Great. Now when they discovered the notation that Brasselli had made, Kent would be the one who would have to try to downplay its significance. Who would have to pretend it wasn't a hole in the defense.

"Yes, Jamieson's gone. That's why Lisa sent them to you," Loretta said.

"Okay. I'll get them set up. Have you notified Christina?"

"Yes," Loretta said. "She's on her way. Where do you want them to go? The conference room?"

"Yes. And Loretta? Call Lisa and ask her to come to the conference room, too. If Clemente or Higgins want copies of any documents, I want her to make them. That way she can assure Jamieson that everything was done according to hoyle."

Although it was Keating & Shaw's responsibility to allow the plaintiff's attorneys access to all documentation pertaining to the case—as well as to allow them to copy anything they wanted to copy—they also had a right to oversee the entire process. In other words, Keating & Shaw had the right to protect themselves and their evidence from either destruction or disappearance.

Ten minutes later Jackson Clemente and Tracy Higgins were busily examining the first of the documents, all of which had already been assigned their Bates numbers—an identification numbering system set up by the court. This system made each document easily identifiable and simplified the presentation of the evidence introduced during the trial.

Lisa, Jamieson's secretary, sat at one end of the conference table, and Christina sat at the other. Kent wondered if it were really necessary for him to be there, too. He walked down to Christina's end and said sotto voce, ''Are you planning to stay here the whole time?''

''Yes. Why?'' Her gray eyes studied him coolly.

He knew she was still nursing a grudge over his treatment of her, but he guessed she was entitled. He made his voice pleasant. ''Well, it's just that I have some things to do. I thought, if you're agreeable, I could take care of some of my work while you're in here, and this afternoon you can do something else, and I'll take over here.''

She leaned back in her chair and said, ''I'll stay the entire time.''

''That's not necessary. We can split it up.''

''Maybe I don't want to split it up. Maybe I think the Wilder case is the most important thing I have to do.'' Then, with a sly smile she said, ''Colin asked me to be present.''

Colin? Since when had she graduated to a first name basis with Jamieson? Continuing to keep his voice low, he said, ''If you want to take charge of this, fine. But if anything happens—'' he gave her a meaningful look ''—call me immediately!''

Her smile turned smug. "Don't be such a worrywart, Kent," she murmured, casting a glance in the direction of the two lawyers, who weren't paying any attention to them as they organized their work. "Believe me, everything is under control." Her eyes glittered as her gaze met his.

After Kent returned to his office, he kept remembering the smug look on her face when she'd said everything was under control. How could everything be under control when that damned notation existed? And why had she used that particular phrase? He knew it was probably just coincidence that she'd used that particular choice of words, but he couldn't shake the feeling that there was something not quite right about Christina's remark.

He told himself he was reading something into her remark that wasn't there. He told himself she was just needling him because she knew he'd had some misgivings over that notation, and she liked the fact that Jamieson and Keating had not agreed with him. He told himself she liked pretending she was in the know and he wasn't.

Still…he couldn't shake his apprehension, if that's what it was.

For the remainder of the morning, Kent deliberately put his misgivings out of his mind and dictated a batch of letters and a deposition. When he finished, it was nearly noon. Christina hadn't called him once.

He decided, despite her assurances, he would check on things in the conference room. Maybe Christina had changed her mind about staying with Clemente and Higgins the entire day and would want to be relieved for lunch. If so, he would ask Loretta to get him a sandwich, and he would eat in the conference room.

When he got to the conference room, Jackson Clemente had just pushed his chair back. He stood. "I think Tracy and I will grab a bite to eat before we continue," he said, looking first at Kent, then at Christina. "Either of you two want to join us?"

"Thanks, but I've got plans already," Christina said, standing, too.

Kent was relieved. The last thing he wanted was to spend his lunch hour in Christina's company. "Sounds good," he said to Clemente.

They decided to go to Treebeard's, which was one of Kent's favorite lunch spots, even though the food was heavier than he knew was sensible for lunch. The only other problems with Treebeard's were the noise level and the crowds of people who always packed the place to the rafters.

Once the three of them had gotten through the cafeteria-style serving line and were settled at their table with plates of red beans and rice—Treebeard's specialty—Clemente, a short, swarthy man with intelligent, dark eyes, buttered a piece of corn bread and said, "So, counselor, how's the defense coming along?"

Kent laughed. "Nice try, counselor. The defense is coming along just fine."

Tracy Higgins, a young associate about Kent's age, grinned. "That's what they all say," she quipped. Kent liked Tracy. When he'd been working out of his storefront, he'd run into her several times in court. She was bright and personable. Just the kind of lawyer he'd have liked to work with.

Clemente chewed his bread, then said with a wink, "We're gonna win this one, you know. You won't even get to the fifty-yard line.'' He smiled. ''So what are you gonna do about that?''

Kent rolled his eyes. Clemente was an ex-football player who peppered everything he said with football terminology. ''As my father would say, when in doubt, punt.''

Tracy laughed again and poked Clemente with her elbow. ''Notice how Kent's learned all the lawyer tricks?''

''Lawyer tricks?'' Kent said.

''Yeah, you know. Never answer a question directly.''

''I thought our motto was Always Answer A Question With Another Question,'' Kent countered.

''That, too,'' she said.

They made small talk throughout the rest of lunch. But as they were walking back to the office, Clemente said, ''You know, Kent, I was really surprised to hear you'd gone to work for Keating & Shaw.''

''Oh? Why?''

Clemente shrugged. ''Well, you were really making a name for yourself when you had your storefront. And you never seemed like the Keating & Shaw type.''

''What type is that?'' Kent hated the stiffness he heard in his voice, but he was getting mighty sick of people acting as if he'd committed a felony by leaving the storefront.

''Oh, hell, you know. Razor-cut hair, expensive suits, power ties, sports cars, the right address…''

Kent forced a casual-sounding chuckle, because Clemente's remarks were a little too close for comfort. ''I suppose you're going to pretend to be above all that.'' He gave Clemente's Italian loafers, expensive European suit and diamond tie pin a pointed look.

Clemente grinned. "I never said I was perfect."

Tracy said, "Oh, quit giving Kent a hard time. Let's get a move on. We've got a lot of work to do this afternoon."

But Kent couldn't get Clemente's words out of his mind. Did everyone think he'd made a mistake going to work for Keating & Shaw? He knew his mother had been disappointed, of course, but she'd never said anything. That was one of the things he liked best about his mother—her belief that people should make their own decisions and lead their own lives. She had always supported him, no matter what he did.

He frowned. That was what he wanted in a wife, too. That was what he wanted, *needed*, from Allison. And that was what Allison had said she would do. But would she? If push came to shove, would she?

Allison spent the day looking at houses. She left Marianne with her great-grandmother Marlowe, and Sunny Garcia took her around to see the houses she'd lined up.

"Kent said the two of you had decided on the West University area," Sunny said as they started out from Diana's office on upper Memorial Drive.

"Yes," Allison said doubtfully. Kent liked West U. Well, she did, too, but she thought the area was too expensive, especially since she knew Kent didn't want to use any of her money. But Joel and Marcy lived in West U., and Kent seemed set on it, so Allison had reluctantly agreed.

After looking at half a dozen houses, Allison fell in love with the seventh—a refurbished Colonial on a wooded lot. It was more money than Allison thought they should spend, but she had to admit that the house was perfect for them. It had four bedrooms and two full bathrooms upstairs, and a living room, dining room, kitchen, half bath and a small room that could be used as a study downstairs.

All the original moldings had been refinished, and the floors were the original hardwood. Allison especially loved the *porte cochère* and the glassed-in sun porch that extended across the back of the house.

As she and Sunny walked through the upstairs, Allison could just picture Marianne in one of the two smaller bedrooms that faced the back of the lot, which was south. The room would be sunny and bright the entire day, just right for a little girl. And the other bedroom would make a perfect playroom.

She sighed. If only Kent would allow her to use some of her money, they'd have no problem buying the house, no matter what he ultimately did. Still...what difference did it make, really? Even if he was adamant about doing this on his own now, when he finally came to his senses regarding the firm, if they were already committed to buying this house, he'd have no choice but to use her money.

Allison smiled to herself. "Sunny," she said, "I think I'll call Kent this afternoon and tell him about this house. Can you make an appointment for both of us to come back here tonight?"

Christina was already seated in the conference room when Kent, Clemente and Tracy Higgins walked in. For some reason, even though Kent told himself not to let her get to him, her insistence on staying there during the afternoon needled him. But two could play her little game, he decided.

"I'm going to get some coffee. Would anyone else like some?" he asked.

Christina eyed him from her vantage point at the end of the long table. "Thank you, I'd love some."

"Coffee would be nice," Clemente said.

"And I wouldn't mind a diet soda," Tracy said.

Lisa, who was also back from lunch, stood. "I'll help you, Mr. Sorensen."

When they returned with everyone's drinks, Kent sat across the table from the two rival lawyers. He pulled his appointment book out of his briefcase and pretended to study it. Out of the corner of his eye, he saw Christina staring at him. He wondered if she would get up and leave. She didn't.

Throughout the afternoon he watched and waited. When Tracy picked up the first of the R & D notebooks, he slid a glance Christina's way. She wasn't looking at him.

At three-thirty both Clemente and Tracy were deep into the R & D notebooks. Clemente closed one with a slap and handed it to Lisa. "I've marked the pages I'd like copies of," he said.

Lisa took the notebook and headed toward the copy center.

Clemente picked up the next notebook in line. Kent saw the cover dates and knew it was the notebook containing Brasselli's notation. Without alerting Clemente to the fact that this particular notebook interested him, Kent kept a surreptitious eye on the other lawyer as he slowly read his way through the pages.

Kent counted the pages silently. When Clemente turned from page twenty-one to page twenty-two, Kent held his breath. He watched as Clemente read down page twenty-two. The next page was the important page. The one with Brasselli's note on line ten.

Clemente turned to the next page. He began to read. Kent's heart accelerated.

Then suddenly Clemente frowned. He muttered something and turned the page, then turned back again to the previous page. He looked up.

"Is something wrong?" Kent asked. He wasn't looking at Christina, but he could feel her listening.

Tracy looked up, her hazel eyes curious.

Lisa stopped in the midst of collating some copies.

The room settled into quiet.

Then Clemente, dark eyes clouded, said, "There seems to be a page missing here."

"A page missing…" Kent repeated. He frowned, too. "Let me see."

Clemente handed the notebook to him.

Kent looked down. On the left was page twenty-two. On the right was page twenty-five. Pages twenty-three and twenty-four were gone.

Brasselli's notation was gone.

Kent looked up. He met Clemente's gaze. Then he turned to Christina.

Her cool gray eyes held that same smug look. That look that said, Didn't I tell you everything was under control?

Chapter Fifteen

Although dozens of thoughts raced through Kent's mind, he kept his face and voice impassive and only mildly curious. "Hmm. That's funny. I never noticed a page missing. Well..." He shrugged nonchalantly. "You know how they put these bindings together...." He examined the binding of the notebook and saw it was loose. He handed the notebook back to Clemente. "It probably just fell out. We'll look for it."

Clemente's face could have been cast from stone as he leveled his gaze at Kent. Kent willed himself not to think about the importance of the missing page. Later. In the privacy of his office he would think about it. But not now.

Finally Clemente spoke. "See that you do look for it."

Somehow Kent got through the rest of the afternoon. He avoided Christina's eyes because now was not the time to confront her, either. But at five o'clock, when Clemente looked at his watch and suggested, "Why don't we finish this up tomorrow?" he breathed a sigh of relief.

Once the two lawyers were gone and Lisa had returned to her office, he stood and walked to where Christina still sat. "What's going on?" he demanded.

"About what?"

"Don't give me that innocent look. You know damned well about what!"

Christina smiled with her cat-that-ate-the-canary look firmly in place. "Don't get so excited, Kent. I told you. Everything's under control."

His eyes narrowed, and he fought to control his temper. "What happened to page twenty-three?"

"Who knows? Like you said, those bindings are awfully loose."

"Did Jamieson remove it? Or did you?"

"Why, Kent!" Her tone was all innocence. "Removing evidence is against the law, and you know it."

"Yes. I know it. And so does Ben Keating."

Now that smug look evaporated, and a hardness took its place. "Do you also know what happens to young associates who try to make trouble for senior partners?"

"Is that a threat?" he countered.

"If I were you, I'd think long and hard before I went to Ben Keating. Remember. It'll just be your word against Colin's word that there even *was* a page twenty-three in existence."

Kent remembered the copy of page twenty-three that was still jammed somewhere in his briefcase. The copy that Armand Brasselli had tried to keep. The copy that would prove someone in this firm had tampered with evidence.

The copy that he could show Ben Keating.

* * *

Allison left a message for Kent at three o'clock, but he never called her back. She tried calling his office again at five-thirty, thinking he might be working late. Sunny, as instructed, had set up an appointment to look at the house at eight o'clock. Allison hoped she wouldn't have to call Sunny back and cancel, but if she didn't reach Kent, she might have to.

At six o'clock the phone rang. It was Kent.

"Hi," he said.

She immediately knew something was wrong. "Hi."

"Are you busy right now?"

"No, I—"

"I'm coming over. I'll be there in half an hour."

Allison started to say something about her message and the appointment to see the house, but he hung up before she could. She stared at the phone, her heart beating faster. What was wrong? She paced around for the next twenty minutes. What had happened to make Kent sound so ominous, so abrupt? Had there been a confrontation at work?

By the time Kent arrived a little after six-thirty, Allison was nervously imagining all sorts of things. And the sight of him, face tight and drawn, didn't set her at ease, either.

"Where are the folks?" he asked as he walked in. He was still dressed in his suit, but he'd loosened his tie and had obviously been running his hands through his hair.

"They were going out for dinner."

"Where's the baby?"

"She's at my grandmother's. That's why I called you, Kent. I made an appointment—"

"Allison, something happened today."

Immediately she stopped talking. "Come into the living room."

She listened as he told her about Jackson Clemente and Tracy Higgins and what they were doing at Keating & Shaw. And when he got to the part about the missing notebook page, she gasped. "Oh, Kent!"

"Christina denied knowing anything about it. In fact, she reminded me that I would be committing career suicide to accuse a senior partner of tampering with evidence, especially when I had no proof at all."

"But didn't you tell me you'd copied that page?" She was sure he had when he'd told her about his interview with Armand Brasselli.

"Yes." His gaze met hers.

"Well, then…you *do* have proof. Kent, you have to go to Ben Keating. This is terrible!"

His eyes, usually so clear and blue, looked as if the sun had gone out of them as they looked at her. "I don't have proof."

"I don't understand.…"

He smiled without mirth. "The copy is gone."

"The copy is gone!"

"Yep. Vanished without a trace."

"Kent! They took it!"

"Very probably."

"Wh-where was it?"

"It had been in my briefcase."

"How could they have taken it from your briefcase?"

"Easy. I leave my briefcase laying around my office all the time. When I'm at lunch. When I walk down to the copy room. When I'm in someone else's office. Anyone could go into my office and take something out of my briefcase."

Allison was appalled by this turn of events, but a tiny part of her was actually rejoicing, for now Kent would have no choice. He would have to leave the firm. And then everything would be the way it was always meant to be. She waited for him to echo her thoughts.

Instead, he leaned back on the couch and closed his eyes. "Jesus, I'm tired," he said. "I sure could use something to drink."

Allison stared at him.

A few seconds later he opened his eyes. He frowned. "Okay, sorry, I'll get myself a drink." He started to get up.

"I'll get you a drink, Kent. That's not the problem."

"Then what is?"

"Are you just going to forget about what happened today?"

"I suppose you think I should charge into Keating's office and start throwing accusations around."

"Yes. Of course I do. Tell him what's happened. He can't ignore this, Kent! And if he does, quit! You don't want to work there if this is the kind of thing that happens."

He stiffened. "You make everything sound so easy. But you're not the one sitting in my chair. It's my career that's on the line. And I don't intend to jeopardize my entire future out of some misguided sense of honor. Remember, I'm taking on a lot of responsibilities soon. I'm going to have a wife and a child to support."

"You can't just drop this, Kent. We'll manage. I've got money. Kent, just think! You can open the storefront again."

"I'll never touch a penny of your money. I told you that four years ago and I still feel that way. And about the storefront. How many times do I have to tell you?

I have no intention of opening the storefront again. That part of my life is over!''

"You can't mean that.''

Abruptly he stood. His eyes were no longer clouded. Now they blazed with blue fire. "My mind is made up, Allison, so let's just drop it, okay? I'm staying with Keating & Shaw, and I'm keeping my mouth shut about this missing page. It has nothing to do with me.''

"Nothing to do with you! It has everything to do with you!'' A coldness settled around her heart as she slowly stood to face him. "What's happened to you, Kent?'' she asked sadly. "I don't even know you anymore.''

His jaw hardened. "What the hell do you expect from me, Allison? I'm doing the best that I can. Isn't my best good enough for you? Are we back to that again? I can't seem to please you, no matter what I do. You always want more than I'm capable of giving.'' He walked to the front window, then swung around to face her again. "Make up your mind. Either accept me as I am, or we break it off now. Permanently!''

If a heart could actually break, Allison was sure hers would be cracking the same way an eggshell cracks. She couldn't accept Kent on these terms. She couldn't. This wasn't the Kent she knew and loved. And unless that Kent returned, unless he was true to himself, there would be nothing for them to build a future on. "I'm sorry, Kent,'' she whispered. "I'm so sorry.'' Tears burned behind her eyelids, and she tried to keep them from falling as she tugged at the ring on her finger.

On legs that threatened to buckle, she walked the few feet separating them and handed him the ring. Her fingers shook as he slowly opened his hand, never breaking eye contact, to accept it.

She bit her bottom lip to still its trembling and felt the hot tears sliding down her cheeks.

He swallowed once. Then, face white, fists clenched, he turned and walked away from her.

When he opened the front door and walked out, letting the door close behind him, Allison sank to the floor and cried and cried until there were no tears left.

The next week was the worst week of Allison's life. Worse than the week after she'd broken her first engagement to Kent. Worse than the week she realized she didn't love Jean Luc and he didn't love her. Worse than the week when she'd been told about Marianne's illness. Worse because this time there was no hope at all.

Her beautiful, wonderful dream was over.

Kent was gone. The Kent she had loved for so long didn't exist anymore. And she was to blame. All of this, all his problems, all their problems, could have been avoided if she'd only been mature enough years ago to realize what she'd had.

She couldn't hide her unhappiness. Diana and her father realized immediately that something had happened. Even if they hadn't had the obvious clue of the missing ring, they'd have only had to take one look at her stricken face to know.

Two days after the breakup, her father said, "Come on. Let's go for a ride and talk."

It was tempting to dump everything on her father's shoulders, but Allison knew she had to stop doing that. She was an adult, and she needed to solve her own problems. So she answered regretfully, "No, Dad. I appreciate your concern, but this is something I have to work out for myself."

After thinking about it, she called her grandmother Marlowe and asked her if she and Marianne could move into the guest house on their property. Her grandmother was delighted, and that night Lee and Diana helped her move.

Once Allison and Marianne were ensconced in the little house, she thought how ironic it was that she should end up here, where four years ago everything had begun. She and her father had occupied the guest house when they'd first returned to Houston from their long sojourn in Europe, and shortly thereafter she'd met Kent.

How things had changed. Four years ago she was a young, spoiled, self-centered girl. Now she was a woman, and she hoped she'd learned something.

That night, after Marianne was asleep, Allison sat in the living room and began to think.

For two days after Allison had broken their engagement, Kent had been numb. He went to work and he went home. But nothing really penetrated his numbness.

On the third day, after thinking and thinking about what had happened and everything that led up to it, Kent knew that he'd been kidding himself for a long time. Allison had been right. This time she'd been right. And maybe all along he'd known she was right but hadn't wanted to admit it.

Maybe you just wanted to punish her.

The thought chilled him. Was that it? Was that it all along? Had he been stubbornly clinging to his position because he didn't want to give Allison the satisfaction and forgiveness she'd asked for? Because he wanted her to continue feeling guilty over their first breakup?

Sighing, he got up and paced around his office. No

matter what his reasons were or had been, one thing was clear. He had to talk to Ben Keating. He couldn't live with himself if he didn't at least make an attempt to right a wrong.

No matter *what* happened to his future with the firm.

"Oh, Allison, I'm so sorry about you and Kent," Marcy said. The two of them were sitting in the living room of the guest house, with Marianne lying on a quilt Allison had placed on the floor beside them. Sunlight streamed over her, and she kicked happily.

Allison nodded. She had calmed down somewhat since her confrontation with Kent. She still ached inside. She still cried sometimes. But she had been doing a lot of soul-searching since Kent walked out. Trying to think how to begin, she picked at a thread on the couch. "You know, Marce, I've been thinking."

Marcy's soft eyes watched her face intently.

Allison hesitated. She wanted to say this right, so that Marcy would understand, but it was difficult because she was only just beginning to understand everything herself. "Do you think that the reason I've been so obdurate about Kent leaving Keating & Shaw and reopening the storefront is that I've been looking for absolution?"

Marcy frowned. "Absolution?"

Allison nodded. "I know it sounds weird but yesterday…all of a sudden…it just came to me. Maybe in all this I've felt so guilty about what happened years ago that I've lost sight of what's really happening now. Maybe in some twisted way I felt that if only Kent would quit his job with Keating & Shaw and reopen the storefront, I would no longer have to bear the burden for what went wrong between us."

Marcy slowly shook her head up and down. "You know, you might have something there."

Allison bit her lip. "Oh, Marce. What have I done?"

Kent walked purposefully down the hall. Ben Keating's secretary looked up from her computer. "Hello, Mr. Sorensen."

"Is Mr. Keating in?"

"Yes, but he's busy right—"

"Is someone in with him?" Kent asked, too determined to get this over with to wait for her to finish her sentence.

"No, but...Mr. Sorensen! You can't just go in there!" She leaped up.

Kent ignored her, continuing to head straight for Keating's door. He knocked once, then opened the door into Keating's office. The older man, who had been dictating, stopped in midsentence and set down the mike. "Kent? What's the meaning of this?"

Kent shut the door and walked straight to the desk. He didn't sit down. "I don't know if you're aware of this, sir, but Jackson Clemente and Tracy Higgins were here the other day to examine the documents on the Wilder case."

"Yes, I know—"

"Do you also know that while looking through the R & D notebooks, Clemente discovered a page missing from one of them?" Kent paused for one heartbeat. "The page containing the notation by Armand Brasselli? The notation I questioned?"

Keating frowned. His eyes darkened. He pursed his lips, his frown deepening. "No," he said slowly. "No, I wasn't aware of that."

"Someone in this firm removed that page, Mr. Keating. Someone who didn't want Clemente or Higgins to see it."

"That's a very serious accusation, Kent."

"I know that, sir. And I don't make it lightly. Believe me, I don't."

"Tampering with evidence is a crime," Keating said, voice soft, as if he were thinking aloud. He turned his chair slightly and stared off into space.

"Yes, it is."

Silence pulsed around them as Keating continued to frown. Kent could almost hear the wheels turning in the older man's head. After a long moment Keating cleared his throat and looked back up at Kent. "Sit down, Kent," he said.

Kent sat.

Keating picked up his phone. "Ginny, call Colin Jamieson and ask him to come to my office, please." He paused a moment. "Yes, now."

While they waited, neither man said anything. Keating seemed lost in thought, and Kent looked out the window. The only noises in the room were the ticking of the grandfather clock standing in one corner of Keating's office and the muffled ring of telephones outside the closed door. Outside the wall of windows behind Keating's desk, large white cumulus clouds floated by.

Finally there was a tap on the door. Kent tensed.

"Come in," Keating said.

Colin Jamieson, looking dapper and confident in a dark pin-striped suit paired with a teal green tie, walked in. He frowned when he spied Kent. "What's up, Ben?" he asked.

"Come on in, Colin, and close the door."

Jamieson did as instructed, then walked to the desk.

"Sit down, Colin. Kent has told me something that disturbs me."

"Oh? And what might that be?"

Kent marveled at the man's acting ability. Jamieson had to know what was coming, yet he managed to look innocent, as well as sound justifiably arrogant.

"Kent tells me that a page is missing from one of the R & D notebooks in the Wilder case. Did you know about this?"

Jamieson shrugged. "Christina Sargent mentioned something about it." He gave Keating an inscrutable look. "Something about the binding being loose, I think. It's not important."

Keating's gaze darted to Kent. "You didn't say anything about a loose binding. You said someone had removed the page."

"Someone *did* remove the page," Kent said.

"Now, wait a minute—" Jamieson said.

Ben Keating interrupted him. "Colin, hold on. Let me handle this, please."

Jamieson subsided, but not before shooting Kent a look that said Kent was going to pay for this.

"Kent," Keating said, "do you have any proof at all of this claim of yours?"

"No, Ben, I don't." Kent purposely used Keating's first name. "But Jamieson knows, and I know, and Christina knows, and I think you know that it's just too much of a coincidence that the one page that might contain something incriminating—something that could shoot holes into our defense—just happens to disappear before anyone but us has had a chance to see it."

"Now see here," Jamieson sputtered.

Kent kept talking. "If that's all that had happened, I

might think it was an accident, that the binding really was loose. But that's not all.''

''What do you mean?'' Keating asked.

''Yes, what do you mean?'' Jamieson echoed, his tone belligerent.

''Two things. When I first mentioned this notation, Jamieson lied to me. He told me the plaintiff's attorneys had already looked at the R & D notebooks and saw nothing to question. They hadn't. And…'' He paused. ''And I made a copy of that page,'' Kent added softly.

Keating raised his eyebrows.

Jamieson's lips tightened, but he said nothing.

''And someone stole the copy out of my briefcase,'' Kent finished.

Keating stared at him, then slowly swiveled his gaze to Jamieson, who nonchalantly inspected his nails. ''Do you know anything about this, Colin?'' Keating asked.

Jamieson looked up. ''Absolutely not. And I resent being called a liar. I never said the opposition had already looked at those notebooks.''

Kent couldn't believe how the man could lie. Just sit there and lie with a straight face. He wondered if Ben Keating believed him. He wondered if any punishment would be doled out. He doubted it. Colin Jamieson was a senior partner with the firm. There was no proof of wrongdoing. It was only Kent's word, after all. The word of a young associate with no track record against that of a senior partner with a long history with the firm.

Kent stood. Both Keating and Jamieson looked up. The grandfather clock continued to tick. The clouds outside continued to sail by. Life continued to move on.

Kent took a deep breath. Suddenly he felt freer than he'd felt in a long time. He ignored Jamieson and addressed himself to Keating. ''Ben, I don't know what you're going to do about this. I suspect nothing, but that's your problem, not mine. Personally I have no interest in being affiliated with a firm that condones this kind of thing. Effective immediately, I resign. I'll have an official letter of resignation on your secretary's desk before I leave today.''

And then, knowing that he'd done the right thing, he turned and walked out.

He didn't look back.

After Marcy left, Allison decided that the only way she would ever know if there was still hope for her and Kent was to make the first move.

She picked Marianne up, grabbed her diaper bag and carried her to the main house. When her grandmother answered the door, Allison said, ''Gran, I have two favors to ask.''

''What are they, honey?'' Jinx smiled, her green eyes welcoming.

''Will you watch Marianne for a couple of hours?''

''Of course.'' Jinx held out her arms. ''Come here, sweetheart. Your great-grandma loves to watch you!'' Marianne chortled as Jinx took her and held her close.

''And Gran? Do you think I could use your car?''

Kent stared at Lee. ''When did she move out?''

''Yesterday.''

''She's staying at the guest house again?''

Lee's eyes, which were so much like Allison's, held a cautious expression. ''Yes.''

''Thanks.'' Kent dashed back to his car, got in and started the engine. He pointed the Corvette in the direction of the Marlowe property.

* * *

Allison drove slowly down her grandparents' street. Maybe she should have called Kent first.

No. She would drive to his condo, and she would wait there until he came home.

When she got to the end of the street, the light was red, so she stopped. Out of the corner of her eye, she saw the white Corvette turn onto the street, and as it drew abreast of her, she recognized Kent.

At the same moment he looked her way.

His eyes widened.

Her heart stopped.

What was he doing here? Her stupid heart began to beat again. *Thump, thump, thump.* She stared at him.

He rolled his window down.

After a moment she rolled hers down.

"I was on my way to see you," he said.

Oh, his eyes were so blue! And she was so happy to see him! "I—I was on my way to see you."

"You were?" His eyes lit up, and he grinned.

Allison wanted to cry. She loved his smile so. She loved him so.

A car horn blared, and they both jumped. Kent laughed sheepishly as he realized he was blocking the road. "Turn around," he said. "I'll meet you at your grandmother's house." And with another grin, he took off down the street.

Heart still beating like a tom-tom, Allison backed up and turned her grandmother's Cadillac around. Hardly daring to hope, she pulled into the driveway and around to the back of the house where Kent had already parked his Corvette.

Suddenly afraid, she slowly got out of the car. Kent walked toward her, looking wonderful in baggy white cotton pants and a fire-engine red T-shirt with the University of Houston logo on it.

"Kent—"

"Allison—"

They both spoke at once, then they both fell silent again. Allison knew everything she was feeling must be right there in her eyes for all the world to see. There was so much she wanted to say. But she felt tongue-tied. And afraid.

Finally Kent stirred. He reached for her arm, and his touch sent tingles through her. "Let's go inside," he said, leading her toward the guest house.

As soon as the door closed behind them, Kent turned her to face him. Allison's heart thudded like a mad thing. "Allison, I have so much to tell you, I don't know where to start." Then he laughed. "Oh, hell, I'll start with the most important thing. I love you." He touched her cheek, and she closed her eyes for just a moment, reveling in the warmth of his hand against her skin. When she opened her eyes again, he smiled gently. "Two more things. I'm sorry. And I quit my job."

She could only stare at him. He'd quit his job. What did this mean?

"I was wrong and you were right," he said.

She finally found her voice. "No, no. I wasn't right. I only just realized it today. I was wrong to try to tell you what to do. Did you really quit your job?"

"Yes."

She swallowed hard. Maybe after all things would work out. "Do you really love me?" she whispered.

"I love you with all my heart."

"Oh, Kent. I love you, too."

And then as he opened his arms and she walked into them, he kissed her. And the kiss was like fireworks and bells ringing and love songs playing and all the romantic movies she'd ever seen. She kissed him back, touching her tongue to his, letting him sweep her away into that fairy-tale world where the most wonderful dreams really do come true.

A long time later, as they sat side by side on the sofa, Allison said, "Tell me what happened."

And so he did. And she marveled at his courage, because she knew it had taken a lot of courage to stand up for what he knew was right.

"I finally realized that if I stayed at Keating & Shaw, if I spent years defending clients like Emmett Wilder and working with people like Colin Jamieson, I'd slowly become one of them. And nothing—not money, not financial security, not a partnership with Keating & Shaw—is worth sacrificing my integrity and self-respect," he said.

Allison held his hand tighter.

"And I finally realized," she said, "that the only reason I was so dead set on you going back to the storefront was that I didn't want to feel it was my fault that your dream didn't work out." She looked up at his dear face. "Kent, I don't care what you do for a living. Go to work for another firm, go back to a storefront practice, even go back to Keating & Shaw. It's your decision, and I'm behind you all the way."

He smiled down at her, and then they kissed again.

Later he said, "I'm going to talk to Joel and Michael. Joel's been unhappy with his firm, and Michael would love to go into a partnership with us. How does that sound to you? Berry, Bartlett and Sorensen, attorneys-at-law?"

"Oh, Kent! That sounds wonderful!" Allison's heart

felt too full. She wasn't sure she could handle this much happiness.

"We might not make a lot of money at first," Kent warned.

"That doesn't matter."

"But I might consider a loan from you...."

"Kent! Would you?" Maybe that house was still available. She would call Sunny tonight. She just knew Kent would love the house.

"And just to make you happy," he said, a twinkle in his eyes, "we'll devote part of our business to *pro bono* work. How does that sound?"

She grinned. "Yolanda?"

He gave her a long-suffering look. "You never give up, do you?"

Her grin widened.

"All right. I'll even take on Yolanda's case if she needs me." Then he kissed her ear, and she shivered. "Boy, woman," he whispered, "you certainly drive a hard bargain!"

This time, when Kent pulled the ring out of his pocket and placed it on her finger, Allison knew it would stay there forever.

Because after all, according to all the experts, the third time is a charm.

Epilogue

From the pages of the *Houston Herald*

AROUND HOUSTON
by B. J. Barrette

Once again the Sorensens and Gabriels have been
united. This time the wedding that took place was the
one scheduled for four years ago! Yes, Lee Gabriel's
daughter, Allison Gabriel Fornier, and Diana Sorensen
Gabriel's son, Kent William Sorensen, were finally
united in marriage. The candlelight ceremony at St.
John's was perfect in every way, down to the presence
of the new Mrs. Sorensen's infant daughter, Marianne,
who looked enchanting in a pink-satin-and-lace dress
with matching shoes and hat.

The bride wore her maternal grandmother's—our
own dear Jinx Marlowe's—antique satin wedding dress.

Her two attendants, Marcy Bartlett and Gail Berry, wore wine silk dresses and carried yellow roses. All flowers were provided by Posey's Posies. Both the bride's sumptuous veil and her attendants' dresses were designed by our town's Alaina, who sells her much-sought-after finery through her West University boutique.

The groom, resplendent in black tails, was attended by his two partners in the newly formed law firm of Berry, Bartlett and Sorensen. Both Joel Bartlett, husband to Marcy, and Michael Berry, spouse of Gail, looked handsome and dignified and performed their duties masterfully.

The bride's father and the groom's mother held hands throughout the ceremony, and my spies tell me that the cool Diana actually shed a few tears! You read it here first!

Four hundred guests attended the reception at the country club, and you have it straight from me—the food, wine and music were heavenly. I can't remember when I've had such a good time.

The new Mr. and Mrs. Sorensen, after a wedding trip to Vancouver, will move into their newly purchased home in West University. They will be a welcome addition to the Houston social scene, and you'll probably read their names here in my column on a regular basis.

* * * * *

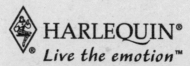

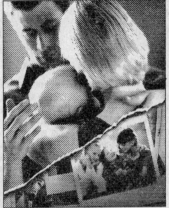
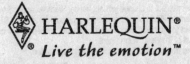

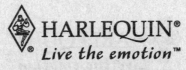

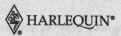

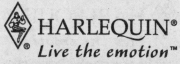

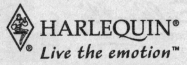